RECIPE FOR LOVE

A FARM-TO-TABLE ROMANCE

Praise for Aurora Rey

Lambda Literary Award Finalist
Crescent City Confidential

"This book blew my socks off...[*Crescent City Confidential*] ticks all the boxes I've started to expect from Aurora Rey. It is written very well and the characters are extremely well developed; I felt like I was getting to know new friends and my excitement grew with every finished chapter."—*Les Rêveur*

"This book will make you want to visit New Orleans if you have never been. I enjoy descriptive writing and Rey does a really wonderful job of creating the setting. You actually feel like you know the place."—*Amanda's Reviews*

"*Crescent City Confidential* pulled me into the wonderful sights, sounds and smells of New Orleans. I was totally captivated by the city and the story of mystery writer Sam and her growing love for the place and for a certain lady...It was slow burning but romantic and sexy too. A mystery thrown into the mix really piqued my interest."—*Kitty Kat's Book Review Blog*

"*Crescent City Confidential* is a sweet romance with a hint of thriller thrown in for good measure."—*The Lesbian Review*

Built to Last

"Rey's frothy contemporary romance brings two women together to restore an ancient farmhouse in Ithaca, NY...[T]he women totally click in bed, as well as when they're poring over paint chips, and readers will enjoy finding out whether love conquers all."
—*Publishers Weekly*

"*Built to Last* by Aurora Rey is a contemporary lesbian romance novel and a very sweet summer read. I love, love, love the way Ms Rey writes bedroom scenes, and I'm not talking about how she describes the furniture."—*The Lesbian Review*

Autumn's Light

"Aurora Rey is by far one of my favourite authors. She writes books that just get me...Her winning formula is butch women who fall for strong femmes. I just love it. Another triumph from the pen of Aurora Rey. 5 stars."—*Les Rêveur*

Spring's Wake

"*Spring's Wake* has shot to number one in my age-gap romance favorites shelf."—*Les Rêveur*

"The Ptown setting was idyllic and the supporting cast of characters from the previous books made it feel welcoming and homey. The love story was slow and perfectly timed, with a fair amount of heat. I loved it and hope that this isn't the last from this particular series."—*Kitty Kat's Book Review Blog*

"The third standalone in Aurora Rey's Cape End series, *Spring's Wake*, features a feel-good romance that would make a perfect beach read. The Provincetown B&B setting is richly painted, feeling both indulgent and cozy."—*RT Book Reviews*

"*Spring's Wake* by Aurora Rey is charming. This is the third story in Aurora Rey's Cape End romance series and every book gets better. Her stories are never the same twice and yet each one has a uniquely her flavour. The character work is strong and I find it exciting to see what she comes up with next."—*The Lesbian Review*

Summer's Cove

"As expected in a small-town romance, *Summer's Cove* evokes a sunny, light-hearted atmosphere that matches its beach setting... Emerson's shy pursuit of Darcy is sure to endear readers to her, though some may be put off during the moments Darcy winds tightly to the point of rigidity. Darcy desires romance yet is unwilling to disrupt her son's life to have it, and you feel for Emerson when she endeavors to show how there's room in her heart for a family."
—*RT Book Reviews*

"From the moment the characters met I was gripped and couldn't wait for the moment that it all made sense to them both and they would finally go for it. Once again, Aurora Rey writes some of the steamiest sex scenes I have read whilst being able to keeping the romance going. I really think this could be one of my favorite series and can't wait to see what comes next. Keep 'em coming, Aurora."—*Les Rêveur*

Winter's Harbor

"This is the story of Lia and Alex and the beautifully romantic and sexy tale of a winter in Provincetown, a seaside holiday haven. A collection of interesting characters, well-fleshed out, as well as a gorgeous setting make for a great read."—*Inked Rainbow Reads*

"*Winter's Harbor* is a charming story. It is a sweet, gentle romance with just enough angst to keep you turning the pages....I adore Rey's characters, and the picture she paints of Provincetown was lovely."—*The Lesbian Review*

"One of my all time favourite Lesbian romance novels and probably the most reread book on my Kindle...Absolutely love this debut novel by Aurora Rey and couldn't put the book down from the moment the main protagonists meet. *Winter's Harbor* was written beautifully and it was full of heart. Unequivocally 5 stars."
—*Les Rêveur*

By the Author

Cape End Romances:

Winter's Harbor

Summer's Cove

Spring's Wake

Autumn's Light

Built to Last

Crescent City Confidential

The Boss of Her: Office Romance Novellas
(with Julie Cannon and M. Ullrich)

Recipe for Love: A Farm-to-Table Romance

Visit us at www.boldstrokesbooks.com

Recipe for Love

A Farm-to-Table Romance

by
Aurora Rey

2019

RECIPE FOR LOVE
© 2019 By Aurora Rey. All Rights Reserved.

ISBN 13: 978-1-63555-367-3

This Trade Paperback Original Is Published By
Bold Strokes Books, Inc.
P.O. Box 249
Valley Falls, NY 12185

First Edition: April 2019

THIS IS A WORK OF FICTION. NAMES, CHARACTERS, PLACES, AND INCIDENTS ARE THE PRODUCT OF THE AUTHOR'S IMAGINATION OR ARE USED FICTITIOUSLY. ANY RESEMBLANCE TO ACTUAL PERSONS, LIVING OR DEAD, BUSINESS ESTABLISHMENTS, EVENTS, OR LOCALES IS ENTIRELY COINCIDENTAL.

THIS BOOK, OR PARTS THEREOF, MAY NOT BE REPRODUCED IN ANY FORM WITHOUT PERMISSION.

Credits
Editor: Ashley Tillman
Production Design: Stacia Seaman
Cover Design by Melody Pond

Acknowledgments

I got the idea for this book while riding my tractor around the front pasture of my little homestead out in the country. While I'm a novice gardener at best, I love digging in the dirt and eating things I managed to grow. I'm thankful to Andie for helping me build and maintain a life in the country I love. I'm also grateful to the small community farmers who do such hard and essential work, especially the folks at Indian Creek Farm, my favorite place to pick all things local and delicious.

I remain so grateful to everyone at Bold Strokes. You are my people and I love you. Particular thanks to Radclyffe and Sandy Lowe, who have such a passion for the art and business of books. Also, to Ruth and Carsen for wrangling all the important details, not to mention the writers. And Ash— I've said this before and I'll say it again—you make me laugh and you make me a better writer. And more importantly, you make me a better person.

Huge thanks to Tracy for being the best beta reader and writing buddy a girl could ask for. Thank you to my friends who listen to me whine, plot, and percolate as much as needed. And, of course, thank you to my readers. You make me feel like the luckiest girl on earth.

For Daniel

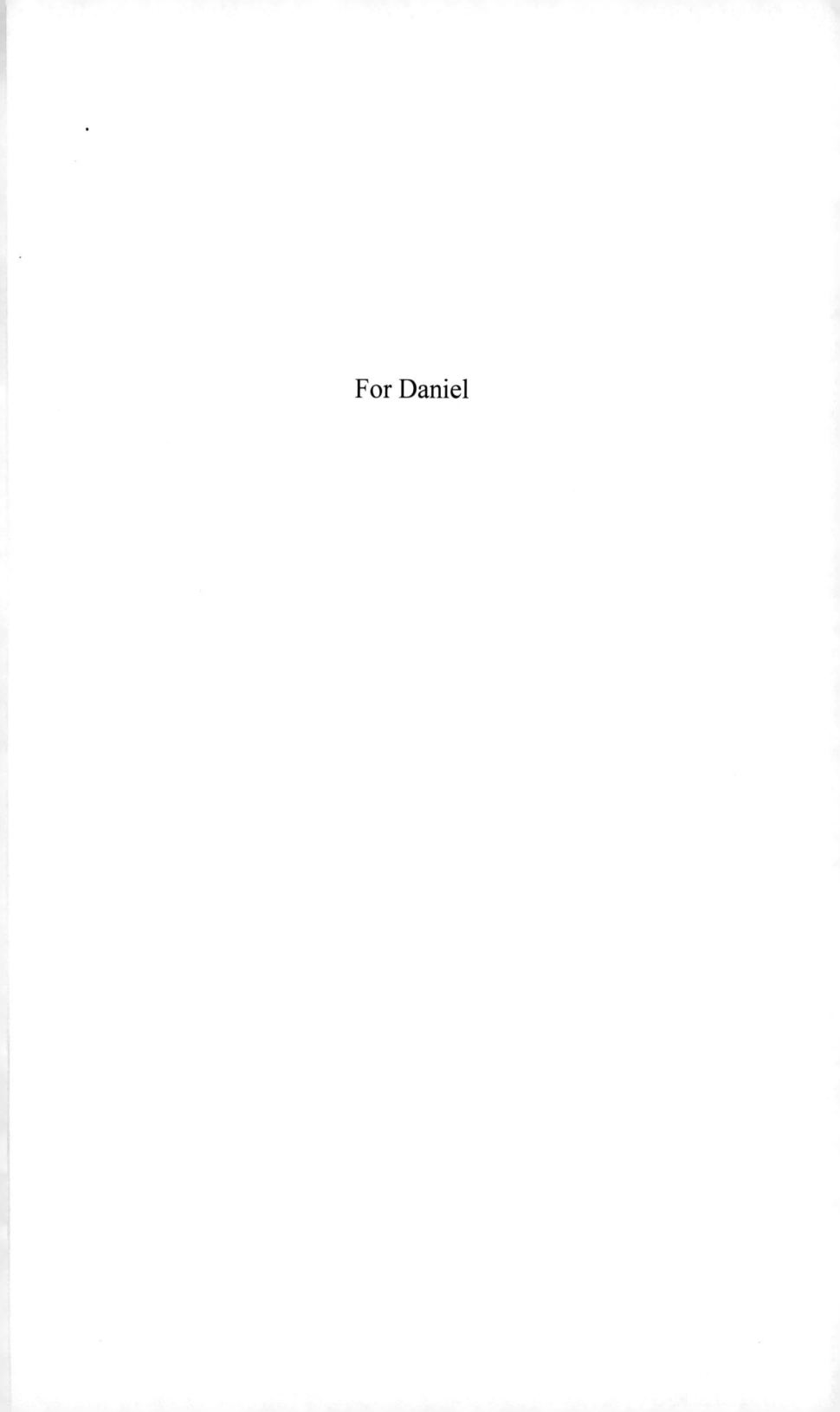

Chapter One

Drew Davis really wanted this job. She surveyed the kitchen. Despite a seating capacity of only eighty, the restaurant, Fig, boasted a kitchen twice the size of any she'd worked in in the city. Between that and parking, upstate might actually have a couple of things going for it. She realized Nick, the owner, was talking again, so she pulled her attention back to him. No point in making plans until he hired her.

"We've got some really great suppliers lined up already for the bar and the kitchen, so you wouldn't have to worry about that at all."

"Sounds great." She had mixed feelings about restaurants who took the farm-to-table concept a bit too literally, but knew better than to say so. Especially when she was angling to be the head chef of said restaurant.

"Your résumé is solid and it helps that you've had some supervisory experience already."

"As sous chef, I ran the day-to-day in the kitchen." As far as she was concerned, she'd already done the work of a head chef, just without the title. Well, title and power to call all the shots. She was ready to rectify that. And if taking a job in some Podunk place in the middle of the Finger Lakes shaved a couple years off the time it would take her to get there in the city, she'd take it. It shouldn't take more than a year or two to make her mark and leverage the experience for a head chef gig back home.

"But you weren't given oversight of the menu." The way Nick said it, she couldn't tell if he'd meant it as a statement or a question.

"That's where I'm most looking forward to flexing my muscles." That had to be a good answer either way.

"I'm glad to hear it. To that end, I'd love to see your skills in action."

Drew nodded. She'd expected a request to prepare a dish on command. She tried not to smirk. "Name your parameters and I'm good to go."

Nick angled his head, narrowed his eyes slightly. "You've got all day, right?"

Did he intend to have her prepare a whole meal by herself? "I do. And I'm prepared to do whatever it takes to prove I'm the chef for you."

"Okay." He dragged the word out. "I'm going to send you on a little field trip."

Her confidence saved her any real worry. "Field trip?"

"I'm going to have you visit two of our suppliers. It'll give you a chance to meet them as well as source your ingredients. Based on what you procure, I'd like one complete entrée, with sides."

He was letting her shop for her own supplies? Could her day get any better? "Excellent. Are there any constraints on time or ingredients?"

"No, I'd like to see you with complete creative oversight. You've seen our previous menu. No need to mimic the style, but I'd like to see something that would fit in the general price point. This isn't your Iron Chef moment."

Drew smiled at the reference. That would have been fun, but she wasn't in it for the extravagance. She wanted to make good food that ordinary people could afford and enjoy. "I've got a rental car, so all I need are addresses."

"Right here." Nick pulled a card out of his pocket and handed it to her. In small, neat handwriting were the addresses for the Piggery and Three Willows Farm. He'd been planning this. Drew appreciated that about him.

"Great."

"There's no service on Mondays, so you'll have the place to yourself."

Even better. "May I poke around to see what you have on hand?"

He made a sweeping gesture. "Help yourself. I'm going to run home to meet my kids when they get off the bus, but I'll be back. Don't worry about locking up when you go."

Fascinating. "Okay. I'll do that and be back in an hour."

He laughed. "Better give yourself two. Things are farther flung up here."

"Right. Well, then, I'll see you soon."

He offered her a casual salute and then he was gone. Drew didn't dawdle. She took a quick inventory of the pantry and cooler, then started a list of things she'd like to pick up. Hopefully, these places Nick had given her would have what she wanted. Deciding to start with the protein, she put the Piggery into her GPS first and off she went.

An hour later, she had two of the most beautiful pork chops she'd ever seen, along with some thick-cut bacon and local maple syrup, sitting on the passenger seat next to her. Next up: Three Willows Farm. This was going to be fun.

She had to admit the drive was lovely, complete with gently rolling hills and the first buds of spring popping from the trees. This farm probably wouldn't have much exciting to show this early in the season, but she hoped they had some root vegetables held over and maybe a couple of greenhouses going. A quaint sign announced her arrival even before the GPS. She turned onto a narrow gravel drive, hitting a massive pothole before realizing she shouldn't be going more than ten miles per hour. She made her way more slowly, avoiding the worst of the divots disguised as puddles. A few of the fields were freshly turned and the fencing looked neat and well-maintained.

Drew crested a small hill. The driveway ended in a parking lot in front of a big red barn. It seriously looked like something out of a movie, or maybe a magazine about country living. She had a soft spot for the produce markets of Manhattan, but even she had to admit it didn't get any fresher than this.

There didn't seem to be designated spots, or other customers, so she pulled her car close to a side door that was propped open. She was so focused on looking around that she missed the giant mud puddle and set her foot right into it. The tip of her Fluevog disappeared with a wet squishing sound. "Shit."

She stepped to the far side of the puddle with her other foot. Not that it was much better. The entire parking lot appeared to be a mixture of gravel and mud. And at the moment, the mud was winning.

Drew gingerly walked the rest of the way to the door. She entered the barn and found herself in a cavernous, mostly empty room. Despite the size, it probably didn't take up more than a quarter of the total floor plan. She imagined it served as a farm store in summer. Now it held empty bins and tables. There was no sign of life.

She wondered if Nick had done this on purpose—a test of her fortitude for the rustic and rural. It made sense, even if she resented the hell out of it in the moment. She closed her eyes for a moment and took a deep breath. This was all part of the master plan. She just needed to keep her eye on the prize. "Hello?"

❖

Hannah covered the seed tray with a plastic dome and moved it to the rack. Few things thrilled her more than starting the first seeds of the season. It carried with it the promise of spring and sprouting things and everything she loved. Not that she didn't appreciate the relatively lazy days of winter, but she didn't become a farmer to be lazy. She moved to the next rack, removing a tray whose dome fogged with condensation. She set it on her worktable and gently removed the lid. Tiny green shoots pushed through the peat moss. Hannah smiled. She'd have enough arugula for a salad in a few short weeks.

At the sound of a voice coming from the market side of the barn, she set the tray, uncovered, under a light. Daisy, who'd been sound asleep on her bed in the corner, perked up. "Coming."

She wiped her hands on her canvas apron. She rounded the wall that separated the two spaces and stopped short. Daisy, who'd followed her, stopped as well. Standing in the middle of the room was a woman she'd never seen before. Dressed in a suit, she looked completely out of place. It didn't help that she was staring at her shoes and muttering. Hannah cleared her throat. "May I help you?"

The woman looked up and Hannah was pretty sure her mouth fell open. She was gorgeous. As in drop dead gorgeous. Flawless sepia skin and short black hair. Really, though, it was the eyes. She had the most exquisite gray eyes, framed by thick lashes.

"Do you have some paper towels or something?"

Hannah raised a brow, glad she'd not been caught staring. "Sure."

She went behind the register and pulled a roll from under the counter. She handed it to the mystery woman, who proceeded to pull off several and wipe her shoes. After what felt like a rather drawn-out process, she seemed to remember she wasn't alone. She looked up and caught Hannah's eye again. "Thanks."

Hannah glanced at the shoes. They looked expensive. As did the pants and shirt. Whoever this woman was, and wherever she came from, one thing was apparent—she was clearly out of her element. "Are you having car trouble? Are you lost?"

"Oh, no." The woman's voice dripped exasperation. "I'm in the right place."

At that exact moment, she remembered the text from Nick earlier. He was doing a head chef interview and planned to send the candidate her way to forage for ingredients. She'd assumed it would be a man, and one dressed more appropriately for a visit to a working farm. "Are you Drew?"

The woman straightened her shoulders and lifted her chin. "I take it you're expecting me."

Hannah fought the urge to laugh. Nick sure knew how to pick them. "I am. Hannah Little."

"Nice to meet you." Drew took the hand she'd offered and seemed to regain some of her composure. "Since you know who I am, I'm guessing you know why I'm here."

Hannah smiled. Drew was clearly in over her head. There was no need to belabor the point. "I do."

Drew looked around. "I take it the pickings are pretty slim."

Although not untrue, Hannah bristled at the assertion. "It's certainly not our peak season. I've got apples and pears in cold storage, along with winter squash and almost any root vegetable you could want."

Drew nodded slowly. Hannah couldn't tell if she was considering her options or her exit strategy. Finally, she narrowed her eyes and tipped her head to one side. "Surprise me."

Given the shoe incident, Hannah hadn't expected that. She gave Drew points for the quick recovery, as well as the answer. Even if she knew better than to take her up on it. "I know what's at stake. Why don't you come with me and you can take your pick?"

Drew's lip curled slightly. "Does it involve tromping through the fields?"

Hannah did laugh then. The idea of a farm-to-table chef balking at the prospect of walking through a field was simply too much. She'd have to tease Nick about it later. "No tromping required. Follow me."

Drew angled her head toward Daisy. "Friendly?"

"She is."

Drew bent down and extended a hand. Daisy lumbered over to investigate. After getting a sniff and a lick, Drew pet the top of her head. "He's sweet. What kind of dog?"

"She's half golden retriever, half Great Pyrenees and her name is Daisy."

"Sorry. She's very sweet." Drew put emphasis on the "she."

Giving Daisy attention earned Drew a few more points. Not enough for her to take Drew seriously, but enough that Hannah didn't wish her ill. She led Drew to the corner of the barn they used for storage, flipping the light on and stepping back so Drew could see what she had to choose from. Drew turned in a slow circle, taking it in. "Wow."

Paired with her dog manners, the respect in her voice almost made up for the slim pickings comment. Almost. "Help yourself."

Drew didn't waste any time. She picked up some turnips, a sweet potato, and a couple of delicata squash. "There was an account at the Piggery when I stopped there, but I have cash if you'd prefer."

Hannah studied Drew for a moment more, convinced this would be the last she saw of her. She waved a hand. "Consider it on the house."

Drew smiled. "Thanks."

It was a good look for her and affected Hannah more than she cared to admit. She decided to be generous. "I've got microgreens started, too, if you'd like some."

"That would be amazing."

If the smile affected her, the look of pure delight on Drew's face held decidedly more dangerous possibilities. It really was a good thing she wouldn't be sticking around. "Follow me."

Hannah led the way to the room where she'd been working. She'd planned to move the plants out to the greenhouse to finish growing, but sacrificing a few now wouldn't be any trouble. She could get them replanted in less than an hour. She grabbed a pulp basket and filled it with tender shoots, then handed it to Drew.

"These are great."

Hannah nodded. "Good luck with the rest of your interview."

She followed Drew back through the market side of the barn and watched her leave. Drew clasped the produce to her and stepped gingerly into the parking lot. Daisy seemed confused by the whole thing. Hannah shook her head and indulged in an eye roll, then ruffled Daisy's ears. "City chefs."

Chapter Two

Back at the restaurant, Drew tried to shake off the jumble of emotions stirred up during her interaction with Hannah. If she had been just prickly, or just beautiful, or just friendly, it would have been fine. But no. She had to be some inexplicable combination of the three. It left Drew unbalanced and infuriatingly off her game. She could not afford to be off her game.

She tried a literal shake off, tipping her head from side to side and rolling her shoulders. Since she was alone in the kitchen, she added, "Get ahold of yourself, Davis," for good measure.

The command helped to calm her. She actually liked working under pressure. That was one of the prerequisites of being a good chef. It helped her focus and made her better.

She spent more time than usual putting together her mise en place. Since she didn't know the stove, it would prevent her from getting distracted and risking an overcooked disaster. She also liked the look of it, the order giving her a sense of precision and control. She checked her watch one more time, nodded to herself. And then she began to cook.

She made a quick brine for the pork chops, then started a dried cranberry and sourdough bread stuffing for them. She settled on a hash for the vegetables, one she could flavor with garlic and thyme. The sauce would be maple with mustard and she'd fry up some lardons to go in the salad on top of the whole thing. It was more of a winter dish than she would have liked for late April, but Nick would know the ingredients were limited. Hopefully. She made a champagne vinaigrette for the salad, figuring that would at least brighten things up.

Nick sauntered back in just as Drew started plating. Had he been keeping an eye on her or did he just have impeccable timing? "Smells good in here," he said.

Okay, so maybe it was more of a nose than an eye. "I hope you find it tastes even better."

Drew presented the plate to him, pleased with the final result. He took a minute to study it, nodding and making sounds of approval. "Looks like you've taken advantage of the local suppliers I sent you to."

Drew's mind flashed to her time at Three Willows Farm—the mud, the massive barn, and the beautiful woman who seemed to dislike her or, at the very least, not take her seriously. "It proved quite educational."

Nick pulled open a drawer and took out a knife and fork. Without ceremony or hesitation, he cut into the pork chop and took a huge bite. Drew barely resisted the urge to laugh. Such a far cry from the almost scientific dissection of her food by previous bosses and head chefs.

"Oh, yeah," he said around a mouthful. She might have preferred something more specific, but she didn't mind the gusto with which Nick attacked the plate. He had a few bites of hash, then another of pork. "What's in the stuffing?"

Drew rattled off the list of ingredients. Nick nodded as he chewed. She took advantage of his full mouth to describe the pan sauce and the dressing on the greens. "I'm glad you like it."

When about half the meal had been devoured, Nick set down his utensils. "Sorry, I haven't eaten all day. That was flawless."

Drew soaked up the praise. People always gave chefs a hard time about their egos, but as far as she was concerned, if it was well-earned, why shouldn't she be confident in her work? "Thank you. I'm not sure where you are in your interview process, but I'm curious to know your next steps and timeline."

Instead of an immediate answer, Nick considered the plate, then took another couple of bites. Finally, he looked her right in the eye. "Our next steps are to discuss salary and start dates."

It took Drew a moment to realize he was offering her the job. Like, on the spot. If there was a tiny voice in the back of her mind, one that questioned any plan that involved leaving the city for a job in the middle of nowhere, she ignored it. She straightened her shoulders and offered him her most winning smile. "Shall we do that right here or in your office?"

❖

Hannah choked on her beer. It took her a good thirty seconds to stop coughing. When she finally did, she looked at Nick with a mixture of confusion and annoyance. "You did what?"

"I hired a new chef. The one I sent your way yesterday for ingredients. She starts in three weeks."

Hannah took a long sip of her IPA, to soothe the irritation in her throat but also to buy time. What the hell was he thinking? There was no way that swaggering city mouse would fit in around here. With her fancy shoes and utter distaste for dirt. Her obvious ego and ridiculously charming smile. "Do you really think she'll be a good fit?"

"Absolutely. She made a great impression at the Piggery and her food was some of the best I've had all year." He narrowed his eyes. "Did you not like her?"

Hannah looked around the room, then at her beer. There was no point in telling Nick what she thought of Drew. The decision had been made. And thanks to the contract she'd signed with Fig, she'd be working with Drew a lot. She couldn't afford to mess with that arrangement. So she looked him in the eye and offered him a bright smile. "I think she'll do great."

Nick didn't seem convinced. "I can tell you're lying. What is it about her you don't like?"

"She's so," Hannah shrugged, searching for the right word, "city."

Nick didn't miss a beat. "She's from New York City. Like, works there now, but grew up there, too."

"And you're okay with that?" Nick was trying to put a newly reimagined Fig on the map, and hiring a big-shot chef from the city was the most obvious way to do that. Still.

"I think, if anything, people from the city can truly appreciate open spaces and fresh food and everything we're trying to do."

Hannah shook her head. Picking an argument wouldn't solve anything. "I just hope her expectations are realistic."

Nick laughed. "About life in the country? You think she'll get bored?"

"Probably." It was more than that, though. "I'm more worried about the arrangement. Farm-to-table seems great until you realize you only have fresh tomatoes two months out of the year."

"Only up here. In the South, you can plant them in waves and have them for more than half the year."

"Yeah, but she's coming up here. I'm worried she's accustomed to getting whatever she wants."

Nick took a long sip of beer, studying her over the rim of his pint glass. He set it down, but his gaze didn't waver. "Are we talking about ingredients or something else?"

"What's that supposed to mean?"

Nick laced his fingers together. "Did she hit on you?"

"What? No." Hannah frowned.

Nick lifted both hands defensively. "Hey, don't shoot the messenger. I just noticed she was kind of your type."

He could be so infuriating sometimes, especially when he was right. "She is most definitely not my type."

"Oh, good. Because it would be awkward if you two started hooking up."

They'd been friends long enough for him to know he could get away with that sort of comment. That didn't stop Hannah from punching him in the arm. She let herself give it a bit more force than usual.

"Ow." He scowled for a moment and rubbed the spot. That quickly gave way to a devilish smile, the kind of smile that said he was on to her.

"Just remember there's more where that came from if you keep harassing me."

"Or decide to play matchmaker?"

Even in the teasing nature of the conversation, it was too far. Hannah set down her glass slowly. "That's not funny."

Nick must have sensed he was on thin ice. "Okay, okay. Too far. Sorry."

She huffed out a breath, ready for this conversation to be over. "Can we change the subject or am I going to have to go home after just one beer?"

"We'll change the subject. And the next round is on me. Deal?"

Free beer could do wonders to smooth things over. And she wasn't really mad. Really. "Deal."

"Tell me about your seedlings."

It was a cheap ploy, getting her to talk about seeds and the first forays into spring planting. But it worked. She'd rather talk about her seedlings than call him out. "I'm almost maxed out. I'm trying to decide whether to splurge on another light rack or put a heater in one of the hoop houses."

That devilish grin returned. "I vote for both."

"I wish."

"I hear you. Hopefully, that won't be the case this time next year."

Hannah indulged in a moment of daydreaming. She'd been supplying Nick's restaurant with odds and ends the last couple of years, but not enough to make a significant contribution to the bottom line. His decision to close Fig and reopen it as a true farm-to-table concept, with Three Willows Farm as one of the primary suppliers, had the potential to change both their lives.

Feeling bad she'd punched him, even good-naturedly, she lifted her glass. "I'll drink to that."

He smiled, clearly not holding a grudge. "And to our new chef."

Hannah was still reserving judgment on that front, but she didn't want to put a damper on the moment. "May she exceed your expectations."

Nick tapped his glass to hers and winked. "And yours."

Chapter Three

Moving turned out to be a less daunting process than Drew had imagined. She'd managed to find a furnished house—a whole house—for almost the same price as her half of the rent for her apartment in Brooklyn. She got a storage unit for her furniture and found someone to sublet online. And since she and her roommate weren't super tight, she'd let her lease run out and be able to start from scratch when she moved back.

"I can't believe you're moving to the sticks."

Drew accepted the box from her best friend, Baker, and wedged it into the back of her car. "It's temporary, dude. Long-term goals. Eye on the prize."

"I get it." Baker shook her head. "This just seems extreme."

"Less extreme than hustling under some asshole who's got less talent than me for five more years."

"Yeah." They'd discussed this enough times that Baker knew the ins and outs of her plan. She made a face. "Did you see a single person who wasn't white?"

She hadn't. It had freaked her out a little, but she'd done some research. With Cornell University close by, the area was more progressive and more diverse than much of upstate. "No, but I only met like four people. It won't be like here, but I won't be the only brown person in town."

Baker looked even less certain than before. "If you say so."

"The kitchen is huge. It won't be all bad." She couldn't tell if she was trying to convince Baker at this point, or herself.

"And you rented a house. Like, a whole house."

"It's a cottage. Eight hundred square feet." Which was still big by her standards, but she didn't say so.

"It has a yard."

"That I have to mow." Drew laughed. She'd been taken aback by that at first, but she'd settled into the idea. It was a waste of money to hire someone to do it. Besides, it made her feel rugged.

Baker shuddered. "That sounds horrifying."

"Yeah, but come July when it's hotter than balls and the whole city smells, you'll be glad to run away for the summer and go upstate."

"I'm trying really hard not to have a *Hamilton* moment right now."

The song where Eliza tries to convince Alexander to take a break played through her mind. She didn't mind *Hamilton*, but Baker's singing left something to be desired. "I think that's my cue."

Baker sighed. "Okay. Drive safe and text me when you get there."

"I will. And I'll send you a picture from my porch."

"There's a porch?" Baker shook her head and laughed, then pulled Drew into a hug. "A porch. I don't even know what to do with you."

For the first time since she accepted the offer, Drew found herself sentimental, and with the tiniest sliver of doubt about her decision. Even the day before, which she'd spent with her mother and grandmother, had felt like a celebration, a step closer to making her dreams come true. "You'll come visit, right?"

"You know it. I can't wait to see you in this exotic new habitat."

"Give me a month to get the restaurant up and running and consider the invitation open." Drew looked at the ground, shrugged slightly. "I'm going to miss you."

Baker dropped her head. "Me, too, dude."

"All right. Glad we established that. I'm going to go before we turn into a couple of weepy girls."

That broke the tension. Baker pulled her into another hug, then Drew climbed into her car. She offered Baker a final wave and hit the road.

It took about an hour to fight her way out of city traffic, but once she hit I-80, the drive went smoothly. The last of the snow had melted and most of the trees boasted little green buds, if not actual leaves. She stopped once for gas, deciding a Slim Jim and a Red Bull made a perfectly suitable lunch.

The final stretch of the drive took her off the highway. She realized for the first time that Trumansburg sat a good thirty miles from the closest interstate. The shock of that eased slightly when she got to Ithaca just after five o'clock. No highways, but at least there was traffic. The flow of cars stayed with her up Route 96, but quickly thinned.

Drew followed Siri's directions, turning onto roads that kept getting smaller and narrower. She had a flash of panic over what it would be like to navigate these roads in winter.

She made it to the house just before six, with plenty of daylight left to unload her things. Since it came furnished and all the rooms were on one floor, it didn't take long to empty her car. She'd seen pictures online of the house itself, as well as the yard, but those pictures hadn't given her a feel for just how isolated she'd be. There was one neighbor across the street, another she could make out to the left of her. The house sat at the edge of the Finger Lakes National Forest, though, and everything else was trees.

Drew stood in the cozy living room and contemplated unpacking. It felt weird to admit, but she was a little intimidated by what the place would be like after it got dark. Given that, and the fact she had no food in the house, she opted to go in search of dinner first.

Her house was situated between Trumansburg, where the restaurant was, and Ithaca, the much larger town home to Ithaca College and Cornell. The latter would have more options, but she wanted to get a feel for T-burg, as it was often called. That would be her neighborhood, not to mention her competition.

She parked right on Main Street and meandered. There wasn't much to it. Well, maybe that wasn't fair. There wasn't much to it by her standards. If she closed one eye, it might pass for a stretch of street in one of the hip neighborhoods of Brooklyn. There were shops and restaurants, a coffee joint and a bar. Oddly, the largest crowd seemed to be at a place called Atlas Bowl, whose facade looked suspiciously like an old supermarket.

Drew wasn't much of a bowler but decided to check it out. The inside, with its shoe rental counter and circular faux-leather benches, had the feel of a vintage bowling alley, but was a little too clean, too new, to have been around that long. Still, people were bowling. Others sat at the bar or in the restaurant. Definitely not a sad, bowling alley snack bar vibe.

Drew sat at the bar and perused the menu. The cocktails were quirky without being pretentious, the list of beers on tap impressive. The bartender, a brunette with short purple hair, a Ramones T-shirt, and really short cut-offs, could have been transplanted from a hipster joint in Park Slope. She was friendly, though, and in under a minute Drew had a cold pint of a local porter.

She took a lazy sip, realizing just how long her day had been, before turning her attention to food. Much like the drink list, the dinner menu was quirky, a mix of bar fare and semi-traditional comfort food. Many items were marked vegetarian or vegan. That was a surprise. If that was a thing in a place like this, she'd definitely need to be mindful of it in her own menu planning. Not that she minded. As far as she was concerned, vegetables could be more interesting than meat.

She settled on fried brussels sprouts and a burger. More food than she needed, perhaps, but it was her only real meal of the day. After putting in her order, she shifted on the stool so she could people watch. Despite being a weeknight, the crowd seemed decent. She wondered if that had more to do with it being the hip place, or being the only place, in town.

When her food came, she devoured it. She really should stop skipping lunch. Both the brussels and the burger were on point, flavorful, and clearly made fresh. She resisted a second beer because falling asleep at the wheel would not be a good start to things.

Drew paid her tab and wandered over to the bowling alley side. More than half the lanes were occupied. A couple had families with little kids, one a group of teenagers. Most, however, were taken by couples and foursomes who appeared to be her age. She chuckled. Maybe this T-burg wasn't such a far cry from Brooklyn after all.

On her way out, she caught a flash of something familiar and did a double take. Hannah, the woman from Three Willows Farm, was one of the bowlers. Her eyes were closed and she was engaged in what Drew figured was a victory dance. Paired with jeans and a flowy peasant top, her modern bowling shoes looked even more ridiculous than the old-fashioned kind. Her hair hung loose in sandy blond waves. A far cry from the day they met. And she'd been beautiful then.

Drew told herself to look away, but before she could, Hannah turned and caught her staring. Terrific. Hannah seemed, not mad, but also not thrilled to see her. Drew smiled and lifted her hand in a casual wave.

She thought Hannah might leave it at that, but she said something to the people she was with and started toward her. Drew met her halfway, near the shoe rental counter. Feeling more confident, Drew smiled. "Hi."

"Hi."

Hannah looked her up and down. Maybe Hannah was checking her out. Maybe. Or maybe it was wishful thinking.

"Nick mentioned you'd be starting this week," Hannah said.

"I got here a few hours ago. Dinner had more appeal than unpacking."

"Can't argue there." Hannah's smile was more of a smirk. Under normal circumstances, Drew might take it for flirting. But for some reason, with Hannah, she couldn't be sure.

"I start in a couple of days, but we don't open until the following week. Which you probably already know." Why was she rambling?

"I do. And I'm sure you want to get a good night's rest so you can unpack and settle in. I won't keep you."

"Uh, yeah." Drew winced mentally. She never had difficulty talking to women. What was it about Hannah that seemed to leave her tongue-tied?

"I'm sure I'll see you sooner rather than later. Congratulations, by the way."

And with that, Hannah turned and left, rejoining her friends. Drew watched her go. What had that been about? Hannah had approached her, right? And instead of flirting, she'd talked about unpacking and her work schedule. Could she have been more awkward? No wonder Hannah escaped as fast as she could. And now here she was, standing in the middle of the bar feeling like an idiot. She shook her head and left, not wanting to be caught looking like an idiot on top of it.

Outside, the sun had set and the air had a real nip to it. Drew hustled back to her car, pulling up the directions to her house. Hopefully, she'd only need to do that a couple more times. At home, she had a moment of regret she hadn't made the bed before going out, then pulled out sheets and the quilt her Grann had made for her. She stripped off her clothes and tumbled into bed naked.

Unpacking could wait. She needed to be ready for the next few days. New staff, new kitchen, hell, new everything. She'd never been brought in new to be anyone's boss before. It would be fine. She was a hardass, but always well-liked in the kitchen. That wouldn't change.

Picturing menus and the line of staff waiting to do her bidding, she burrowed deeper into the pillow, but it was Hannah's smirk she carried with her to sleep.

Chapter Four

Hannah sat back on her heels and surveyed the progress. She'd just completed one row each of the eight tomato varieties she'd selected for the year and the same for a half dozen kinds of peppers. The tiny plants swayed in the breeze, but she could imagine their roots taking hold and the leaves soaking up sunshine.

With temperatures in the mid-seventies for the third day in a row, it was beyond tempting to be more aggressive with the planting. She'd given into that a few years prior, only to have a late frost leave her heartbroken and scrambling to start over. No, this method worked best. In addition to creating waves of vegetables to be harvested, she had a nice insurance policy in the event they got a cold snap.

She caught movement out of the corner of her eye and found Jeremiah loping her way. "How goes it?" she called to him.

He came and stood beside her, looked down the rows. "Peas are weeded and trained. They're coming along nicely."

Hannah grinned. Peas went in as soon as the ground thawed, so they got a head start on everything else. "Perfect."

"Do you need a hand here?"

She gestured to the flat of plants she had left. "I think this is all I want to do for another week or two. How are the beans?"

"Poking through, but not much else. What about squash? Shall I get them going?"

Hannah imagined the first summer squash, sautéed with some toasted pecans and Parmesan cheese. "I think that's a brilliant idea."

Jeremiah headed toward the south field, pushing through the old wooden door she'd installed in the deer fencing. He had such a slow, deliberate way about him, but he worked harder than almost anyone she'd ever met, including herself. He was a rare one these days—

someone who worked on a farm because he loved it, believed in it. She was so grateful for his presence.

Utterly content, Hannah returned her attention to the tomato plants. She poked holes in the heavy black plastic with her trowel, nestling seedlings in the warm soil. She worked her way down the row until her flat was empty, then collected her tools and the empty containers and headed for the barn. Daisy, who'd been napping in the dirt between the rows, followed.

Once there, she found her sister Clare painting on small scraps of wood. "I didn't expect to see you today."

Clare looked up and smiled. "I told Mom you'd moved up my start date."

Hannah narrowed her eyes. "But I didn't."

"I know. You don't have to pay me. I'd just rather hang out here than at home." Clare, twelve years her junior, lived with their parents at the family dairy farm several miles up the lake.

"You're not skipping chores, are you? Or homework?"

Clare sighed dramatically. "No."

"Just checking." Hannah chuckled. Clare was a good kid. It secretly thrilled her that she had little interest in the family farm. She didn't have much interest in Hannah's farm, either, but that was okay. Hannah was pretty sure she had her sights set on art school. Their parents might not appreciate that, but Hannah did.

"I thought I'd make new signs for the store." She held up one. It had a pair of jalapeños with cartoon faces. They appeared to be dancing in tiny yellow and orange flames. The word "jalapeños" was done in a cute script and there was a black square below for the price. "I found a recipe for homemade chalkboard paint, so you can change it anytime you want."

"That's pretty cool. And your artwork is great." It was, and so beyond anything she'd ever come up with.

"So I can make them for all the produce?"

Hannah nodded slowly. "I'd love that. I'll even move up your start date for real and pay you to do it."

Clare beamed. "Really?"

"Yes. That way we won't have to lie to Mom and Dad." She waited a beat, then said, "And I can require you to help me in the greenhouse before you go home for dinner."

Clare's smile faded, but only a little. "Deal. Give me a second to clean my brushes."

It only took her a minute and soon they were walking along the east field toward the greenhouses. "If you're going to be hanging around after school, can you work on the signs and cover the register? It would be nice to officially open, even if there isn't much to sell yet."

"About that." Clare looked at her, but didn't finish the thought.

"What? Too boring? I thought anything that didn't involve tending the cows was your speed."

"No, I didn't mean that. I've been thinking about your website."

"What about it?"

"I was thinking I could redesign it for you." Clare seemed sheepish suddenly, which was so unlike her. "I've been learning how at school."

She was in a web design class as one of her electives. Hannah had been impressed that it was even an offering—far more fun and practical than the choices she'd had in school. "I'd be open to that."

"I'm not a pro or anything, but what you have is pretty bad."

Hannah couldn't take offense at the comment. Three Willows' website was just a hair above terrible, a fill-in-the-blank template she'd found. It contained little more than their address, hours, and a couple of photos. "I'm sure whatever you do with it will be an improvement."

"Cool." Instead of happy, Clare had a hesitant look about her.

"What is it? What aren't you telling me?"

She took a deep breath. "I have the chance to do an independent study next year, like an internship or something. Dad hoped I might do it at the dairy, learning the books if not the cows. But I'd rather do it here."

That didn't surprise Hannah, but she wasn't sure what that had to do with her website. "Okay. Even if he's a little disappointed, I think he'll be okay with that."

"I don't want to learn about farming, though. I want to do your marketing."

"Huh." It wasn't like she'd given no thought to marketing. It was just one of those things that lived perpetually on the back burner. If there were no crops to sell, selling them better or more cleverly didn't accomplish much.

"You think it's a terrible idea."

Only then, looking at Clare's worried expression, did Hannah realize how much this meant to her. She had no idea how it would go, but she committed right then and there to making it happen. "Not at all. I think it's a great idea."

"You do?"

"Absolutely. I'm not sure how much coaching or guidance I can give you, but we'll figure something out."

Clare's entire face lit up. "It's going to be so awesome. We're going to do the website and a newsletter and Instagram and everything."

It occurred to Hannah that she'd probably just signed up for something that would take up time rather than give her an extra pair of hands. Still, she wanted her sister to be happy. And if marketing was what made Clare happy, that's what they'd do. "Sounds good."

"Ms. Grant said I could start the work over the summer even though I won't be in the class until fall. That way, we can implement some strategies this season."

"Implement strategies? Is that marketing speak?"

Clare looked at her like it was the most obvious thing ever. "Uh, yeah."

"Interesting."

They arrived at their destination and Hannah held the small swinging door for her sister. To call the structure a greenhouse might be generous. In reality it was a large hoop house consisting of a curved PVC pipe frame and heavy-duty plastic sheeting. It was large, though—tall enough for her to stand up in—and did a remarkable job of capturing heat and light. She aspired to a real greenhouse, but in the meantime, this wasn't half bad.

"So, what's on the agenda?" Clare asked, surveying the rows of baby spinach and chard.

Hannah handed her a basket. "Harvesting."

Clare gave her a look of suspicion. "Already? Are you really thinking people are going to stop by this early in the season?"

"This isn't for the stand. It's for Fig."

"Oh." Clare dragged the word out, as though there was some juicy story behind the answer.

"They don't open for another week, but the new chef has arrived and will be working on the menu." That didn't qualify as juicy in her book, even if she'd found herself thinking of Drew at odd moments over the last few weeks.

"Kristen says she's from New York City and super queer."

Hannah closed her eyes for a moment. Nick's daughter and Clare were in the same grade at school and best friends. Of course they'd have talked about the person Nick had hired. "You shouldn't assume people are queer based on how they look."

"You only say that because people never assume you are based on how you look."

Clare had a point. It irritated her that she was so often read as straight because she skewed toward the feminine end of the spectrum. Even being a farmer and driving a tractor didn't seem to balance her penchant for dresses and makeup when given the occasion. But that didn't negate her initial comment. Or the fact that her own gaydar lit up the second she was in the same space as Drew. "Chefs have a funky aesthetic. You can't assume anything about them."

"Kristen says her car has an HRC sticker on it."

"Okay, then. Now you can assume she's gay."

"Kristen says she's hot."

Neither Kristen nor Clare had come out at this point, but they both embraced a certain fluidity in how they expressed their own genders and what they found attractive. It annoyed her that Kristen found Drew attractive, but it didn't surprise her. Hannah shrugged. "Maybe, but she's way too city."

"Aren't we Judgy McJudgerpants today?"

She was beyond done with this conversation. "Chard. Basket. Please."

Clare rolled her eyes and huffed, but Hannah could tell she wasn't really mad. She went to the end of a row and started picking. She'd helped out at the farm enough that Hannah didn't need to coach her on technique. She took her own basket to the spinach and began plucking leaves. Once the plants were fully established, she'd be able to go at them with kitchen shears. For now, she plucked leaves off one at a time to make sure the stems and baby leaves remained intact.

Even with the more delicate method, it didn't take long to fill the basket. Of course, she was picking enough for Drew to make some sample dishes, not enough for a dinner service. Hannah shook her head. She wouldn't have signed the contract with Nick if she couldn't keep up with the demand. She simply hadn't had to navigate specific, large-scale demand before. Even the CSA shares they offered were a farmer's choice kind of thing.

She stood up and squared her shoulders. This arrangement was no different. She had a commitment to supply the restaurant, but they'd get what she got. For as much control as she had over that, they'd get the best. Hopefully, Mother Nature wouldn't disagree.

"Are you going to take these over now?"

Clare's question pulled her back to the moment. "I don't think Drew will be there until tomorrow, so Nick's probably home for the day, too. I'll run them over in the morning."

"Drew? Is that the new chef? You've met her?" Clare's voice pitched higher with each question.

Great. Clare would want to make this a thing. "Only briefly, the day of her interview. She stopped by for ingredients." Hannah sighed. "And last night. She was at Atlas for dinner. Just a passing hello."

Clare punched her in the arm as they began the trek back down to the barn. "I can't believe you're holding out on me."

No way was she telling Clare about the way Drew looked at her, or the way her body reacted to that look. "I'm not holding out. There's nothing to tell."

Clare looked at her. Why were teenagers such masters of the withering look? "Do you think she's queer? And hot?"

Drew's face popped into her mind. Even when fussing over her shoes, she'd been attractive. When she saw Hannah's winter vegetable stash, and her eyes lit up and that killer smile came out, hot would have been an understatement. "I'm choosing not to have an opinion on the matter."

"Seriously? That must mean she is hot."

"Don't you need to get home for dinner?" She wasn't usually in a rush to get rid of her sister, but she was done with this conversation.

"Yeah. You want to come? Mom would love to see you, you know."

"I know." But there were still a couple hours of daylight and she hated to waste them. And she wasn't in the mood for her father's lectures on the folly of her business model. "I'll come soon."

"Okay. So, I'll be back tomorrow?"

Hannah thought about the sign Clare had painted. She imagined the store full of summer produce, complete with charming little signs. She could have Clare redo the ones out in the fields for u-pick, too. Maybe this marketing thing wouldn't be so bad after all. "I'll see you then. I can give you money for supplies if you need it."

Clare waved her off. "I've got the paints and the wood is all reclaimed. It's more authentic that way."

Hannah chuckled. "Right. Well, I'm looking forward to seeing them."

Hannah took both baskets and they exchanged a quick hug. Clare headed to the old truck Hannah had driven around when she was that age, and Hannah went back into the barn. She packed up the greens with some garlic, onions, and potatoes. It wasn't quite an inspiring box, but they were getting there. For mid-May, it didn't get much better.

She checked the log and noted that Jeremiah and a couple of the interns were putting in onion plugs. If that got finished today, they could do sweet corn next. Maybe she'd tackle the strawberries. She'd picked up a hundred new plants to supplement the patch she'd started a couple of years prior. Since the beds were already prepped, she might even be able to finish planting them before dark.

Happy with her plan, Hannah headed out to the field that held all her berries. She got to work, imagining strawberry shortcake and strawberry ice cream. In her mind, strawberries were the harbinger of summer. For that reason alone, they were one of her favorites. Before she could stop herself, she wondered what Drew might do with them.

Chapter Five

Drew rolled over and sighed. She'd been awake for the better part of an hour, along with the dozen or so birds that seemed to live right outside her bedroom window. She'd thought the quiet of nighttime would take getting used to, but it had nothing on this. Fatigue would catch up with her later, but for now, she had the anticipation of her first day to get her going. Even if it was still an hour before she needed to be up.

She put on coffee and showered, then used the extra time to make eggs to go with her toast. She sat at the table in the small eating area, which still had to be three times the size of the one in her apartment back home. Sunlight slanted through one of the windows. It was kind of nice, actually. And when the weather warmed just a bit more, she'd be able to drink her coffee on the porch.

Drew shook her head at the idea. So weird.

She finished getting dressed, including one of her brand-new chef coats. She took a second to trace her fingers over the embroidered logo of the restaurant and her name stitched underneath. It wasn't the first personalized chef coat she'd ever owned, but something about seeing it, knowing the respect and the authority it held this time, gave her a thrill.

The drive to the restaurant from her house took all of ten minutes. She pulled into the small lot in back and found two cars already there. Well, a car and an ancient pickup truck. The car was the same one as the day of her interview. She hoped that meant Nick was there. And that he had a key for her so she could come and go as she wished. The truck looked vaguely familiar, but she couldn't quite place it.

The back door was open, so she went inside. She heard voices before she saw who they belonged to. Drew rounded the corner of a large shelving unit and found Nick and Hannah, the woman from the farm, chatting.

Nick noticed her first. "Good morning, Chef. Happy first day."

"Morning. And thanks, I'm happy to be here."

Before Drew could say anything to Hannah, Nick angled his head. "You two know each other, right?"

Hannah narrowed her eyes at Nick for the briefest of moments before turning her attention to Drew. "We've met. Congratulations again on the new position."

There was a coolness in her tone that Drew remembered from their first encounter. "Thank you. I'm excited to get started."

"Hannah was just dropping off some of the first pickings from Three Willows for you to play with."

Drew eyed the contents of the shallow, open box. Nothing earth-shattering, but the greens looked beautifully fresh, so she wasn't going to complain. "I'm looking forward to it."

"Since you're both here, I thought we could talk through some logistics."

Hannah nodded but didn't make eye contact with Drew. Like she was annoyed with her for some reason. "I've got about half an hour. I don't want to waste any more of this gorgeous day than I have to."

Drew bristled at her use of the word "waste." She had half a mind to make a snarky comeback, but that probably wouldn't help the relationship. And since the relationship directly correlated to her supply of ingredients, it was one she intended to preserve. She looked at Nick. "I'm at your disposal, at least until I get my feet wet and my menu approved."

She couldn't be sure, but Drew was pretty sure Hannah rolled her eyes. A very quick, discreet eye roll, but an eye roll. What had she done to get on this woman's bad side? Before she could begin to consider the possibilities, Nick clapped his hands together. "Excellent. I've been doing some research and, as I'm sure you both know, there are no official rules when it comes to farm-to-table. And since it's so in vogue right now, plenty of restaurants are playing fast and loose with it."

That was one of Drew's main problems with the whole fad. It made both chefs and customers feel warm and fuzzy and superior, but often meant practically nothing. She refrained from saying so out loud.

Nick continued. "I don't want to be that kind of restaurant. I know it's not realistic to source every bit of produce locally, but I want it to be a good-faith effort. That means using what's available and making it the centerpiece of the menu as much as possible."

Hannah nodded, all business now. "I was thinking I could scale up what we do with the CSA boxes and do deliveries three days a week."

Drew raised a hand in an effort to get a word in edgewise. "What's a CSA box?"

Hanna sighed like she'd asked the dumbest question on the planet. She might have rolled her eyes again, too. "It stands for community sustained agriculture. People pay up front and get a box each week of whatever is harvested."

"Do I get any say in this or is it a done deal?"

"Is that not suitable for you?" If actual daggers could spring from eyeballs, Drew would be dead and Hannah would be on her way to prison.

"Not the overall arrangement. The delivery. I'm really used to sourcing my own ingredients. I'd rather come and choose from what's available than have a mystery box show up." She tried offering a smile. It was hard to tell if that made things better or worse. "I'd hate to have anything I don't use go to waste."

Nick seemed to sense the hostility. He focused his attention on Hannah. "Will that work for you? It'll save you quite a bit of time in delivery."

If she had to guess, she'd say Hannah saw the logic of that but really didn't want to concede the point. "Of course." Hannah looked right at her. "As long as you understand it's not some kind of farmer's market shopping spree."

In her mind, that's exactly what it was. "What do you mean?"

"I have a responsibility to the people who've purchased farm shares and to the people who come to the stand. I'm not going to pull asparagus from them just because you want it all."

"Ah." Annoying, but not unreasonable. "I assure you, I'm not one of those chefs."

Hannah raised a brow. Nick didn't give her a chance to speak. "I'm sure we'll all get along just fine. Shall we say Tuesday, Thursday, and Saturday?"

Drew nodded. "That would be great."

"And, Hannah, you'll keep a running tab and bill me weekly?"

"That works for me."

"Excellent. Drew, why don't we leave you to settle in and get a lay of the land? I've got the kitchen staff starting tomorrow and the waitstaff will be in training the rest of the week."

Drew's excitement returned. "We'll be ready to open Friday."

Nick smacked his forehead. Drew almost laughed. Did people really do that? "I forgot to tell you. I decided Friday would be a soft launch. One seating, invited guests, fully comped. I figured it would help build buzz and give us a chance to work out any kinks before a full service."

She'd never been at a restaurant when it opened, so that wouldn't have occurred to her. But it was a great idea. It eased some of her anxiety about not knowing any of the staff, including the sous chef. "That's perfect."

"Great." Nick beamed. He probably had some nerves of his own, but he looked excited, too.

"Okay, now we really will get out of your hair. Holler if you need me."

"Will do."

Hannah looked at her for the briefest of moments. "Good luck."

She and Nick disappeared into Nick's office. Drew shook her head. Part of her really wanted to figure Hannah out—what made her tick, what made her seem so reluctant to give Drew the time of day. The other part of her had way too much to do to spend even a minute more than she already had thinking about the prickly green-eyed farmer.

❖

"You'll be there, right?" Nick's expression held excitement, but also a small shadow of worry.

"Of course I'll be there, you idiot. It's your big day. And my food is going to be on your tables." And if the food turned out to be fussy and pretentious, she'd smile and eat it and it wouldn't be the end of the world.

Nick visibly relaxed and grinned from ear to ear. "It's going to be amazing."

"I'm counting on it."

"I'm holding a four top for you. Is that enough? Too much?"

"It's perfect. I'm going to bring Jenn, my mom, and Clare." Maybe not the influencers he was hoping for, but she didn't count a lot of those in her circle.

"Excellent." He continued to smile, as though she'd just offered to bring the *New York Times* restaurant critic.

"Did I tell you Clare has decided Three Willows Farm needs a marketing department?"

"She has?" Nick raised a brow.

"And she wants to be it. She's already set up an Instagram account." Hannah remained equal parts bewildered and proud.

Nick nodded slowly. "Interesting. Is she taking new clients?"

Hannah laughed at the question, then realized Nick was serious. "Uh. I don't know. She's not in business or anything. She wants to learn and I'm going to be her guinea pig."

"Kids these days. They know how to do everything."

"Tell me about it. Speaking of, how are yours?"

"Angling for busboy duty." In addition to Kristen, Nick had two sons, Owen, who was fourteen, and Theo, who was twelve. She'd known them all their whole lives. Babysitting them, along with Clare, had provided her with both spending money and an escape from farm chores during her high school years. They'd been absolute terrors as kids, but had mostly grown out of it. Mostly.

"Impressive."

"Eh." Nick shrugged. "They've got their sights set on the new PlayStation."

Hannah chuckled. "A perfectly reasonable motivator."

"That's what Leda says."

"So, is there anything I can do to help you get ready for Friday night?"

Nick took a deep breath. "I don't think so. Unless you want to come out to the dining room and tell me everything looks good."

"I'd be happy to." Hannah followed him to the front of the restaurant. She'd been by once during renovations but hadn't seen the final product. She didn't really have an eye for design, but the space was beautiful. It had the feel of an old farmhouse but also managed to look crisp and bright. The tables were new and would be covered with cloths, but the chairs were mismatched antiques that Nick had spent months scouting at flea markets and garage sales.

"Well?"

"Nick, it's perfect."

"We decided to display local art that's also for sale. You don't think it's jarring?"

"Not at all. I think as long as you steer clear of anything too funky or modern, you'll be fine. What's up now goes perfectly."

She'd known Nick since she was six and he'd taken a summer job at the dairy. She'd harbored a crush on him for several years, until she realized she was actually attracted to girls, and still had a deep fondness for him. He'd so clearly poured his heart, as well as his life savings, into this place. And she got to be a part of it. A flutter went through her. She vowed to make more of an effort to get along with Drew. It was the least she could do.

"I'm glad you like it. Leda made all the decisions. She's much better at this stuff than I am."

Hannah smiled. "Yeah. Remind me to call her if I ever get around to decorating my house."

"So, when pigs fly."

She swatted at him. "Hey, now."

"Kidding. You've got your priorities and I have nothing but respect for them."

Hannah rolled her eyes. "Speaking of, I should get back."

"I'll see you Friday?"

"And I'll expect Drew Thursday."

"Thank you. I'm so glad that we're sort of in this together."

"Me, too." She was. Even if it meant spending far more time than she cared to think about with one slick, annoyingly good-looking chef.

Chapter Six

Yet another gorgeous day and Hannah was sorry to have to leave the tomato field when her phone chirped that it was four. But by the time she was showered and putting on makeup, she was glad. She didn't have many occasions to get pretty and could almost forget how much she liked it. She added earrings and perfume before slipping on the sheath dress she'd bought herself with the birthday money from her parents. She played with her hair for a minute, then decided to leave it down. It wasn't quite warm enough for sandals, so she decided to go with her favorite heels. It was a party, after all.

By the time she got to the restaurant, all of the street parking was taken. She pulled into the municipal lot a block away, then texted Clare and Jenn. She got immediate replies from both that they were already inside.

Hannah started to climb down from her truck, then leaned back in to check her makeup. She'd never want to have a job where she was expected to do it every day, but she could appreciate why some women did. Her eyes looked brighter and her lips fuller. She smiled. Maybe there'd be someone around tonight she could flirt with.

The second the thought crossed her mind, the image of Drew followed. She frowned. Everything about Drew screamed not her type. Well, except the way she exuded butch confidence when she walked into a room. Or the way her eyes got intense when she talked about ingredients. Or the way her chef coat accentuated her broad shoulders.

Hannah groaned. Was there anyone on the planet she was less suited to than Drew? Why in the world did she keep sneaking into her thoughts?

The chirp of a text pulled her from her self-loathing. It was from Clare. *Are you coming?*

Instead of replying, Hannah hurried to the restaurant. Inside, at least fifty people sat at tables or milled around, sipping drinks and chatting. She found her group standing around a table near the bar and went over. "Sorry. I didn't mean to be running late."

Jenn looked her up and down and offered a low whistle. "No apologies needed, but I can see what kept you."

"Stop it," Hannah said before leaning in to give her mother a hug.

"You look very pretty," she said.

Hannah grinned at her. "Thanks. The dress is from you and Dad."

"I'm glad to see you spent the money on something fun."

"Yeah," Clare said. "And not some tractor attachment."

Hannah poked her sister. "Don't be knocking my tractor attachments."

Jenn hooked a thumb toward the bar. "Can I get you something? Beer, wine, or hard cider."

"Hmm." Hannah glanced at the bar and recognized the guy behind it from before the renovation. "I'll get it."

She caught his eye and offered a hello before ordering a glass of her favorite champagne-style cider. She'd just taken her first sip when Nick clinked a knife on a glass to get the attention of the room. Next to him stood Drew, looking way sexier than she had any right to.

As if sensing Hannah's stare, Drew looked her way. Hannah watched her gaze travel down and back up, then she offered Hannah a slow smile. Hannah's throat went dry. In spite of herself, she licked her lips, then swallowed. With the slightest angle of her head, Drew made it known that she'd caught Hannah's reaction.

Shit.

Nick began to speak and Hannah focused squarely on him. He thanked everyone for coming, then gave shout-outs to those in the room who were involved in the relaunch of Fig, including Hannah and Three Willows Farm. He said some lovely things about his wife and family, thanking them for their support. "And last, but not least, it is my great pleasure to introduce our new head chef. Drew Davis comes to us from Salt in Manhattan, where she worked as sous chef under Michel Berens. Her experience at the cutting edge of New American cuisine is the perfect match for the new and improved Fig."

Nick gestured to Drew and the room filled with applause. Hannah joined in, out of politeness if not enthusiasm. What the hell was New American cuisine anyway? If any of her produce had been turned into a foam, so help her, she'd—

Drew's speech cut her off mid-threat. "I can't thank you enough for coming tonight. And thank you," she bowed to Nick, "for giving me this opportunity. Being here is the culmination of a lifelong dream. If you leave tonight half as happy as I am now, Fig will no doubt be a massive success."

The crowd chuckled. Hannah watched as Drew made eye contact with Nick. He gave her a small nod in return.

"Waitstaff are coming around with the evening's menu. Rather than a set tasting menu, we're test-driving what will be available beginning tomorrow night. This gives you options and gives us a dry run of what to expect during dinner service. The selections include meats, cheeses, and produce from local purveyors, as Nick mentioned. We've also been able to source things like honey and maple syrup from local farms. We hope you enjoy."

Another round of applause and then a flurry of servers worked the room, distributing menus and refilling glasses. Hannah held her breath as she waited to see what Drew had put together. When the cream-colored cardstock finally made it into her hands, she did a quick skim, looking for anything over-the-top strange. "Huh."

"What?" Clare asked the question, but all three of her dining companions looked at her expectantly.

"Nothing."

Jenn gave her a look that indicated no one believed her.

"I guess I expected the menu to be—" What was the word? "Weirder."

Jenn laughed and Clare angled her head. "What do you mean?"

Before Hannah could reply, Jenn jumped in. "Hannah decided that, since the new chef is from the city, she must cook like she's on an episode of *Iron Chef*."

Clare frowned. "What's *Iron Chef*?"

Jenn groaned. "Why does hanging out with you make me feel ancient?"

Her mom laughed. "Imagine how I must feel."

Jenn raised her glass. "You have a point, Cindy. Now, let's get down to business. I think we should all order different things and share so we can try as much of the menu as possible."

Everyone agreed and they settled on which of the appetizers and entrées to order. The server assigned to their table was enthusiastic, commenting on the dishes she'd sampled and decided were her favorites. If Hannah was being honest, there wasn't a single thing on the menu she wouldn't try. Well, except the trout, maybe, but only because she didn't really like fish. She ordered a glass of Chardonnay to go with her dinner and sat back to see if everything tasted as good as it sounded.

A pair of salads came out first. Both had greens from Three Willows Farm—one baby arugula with fennel and lemon and one mixed greens with pomegranate seeds and Brie. They were quickly followed by sweet potato soup and a small baguette with a trio of spreads.

"Oh, my God," Jenn said.

Clare nodded. "So good."

"It really is." Her mom looked at her. "Don't you think?"

It was good. Really good. All of it. Hannah tried to work through the mix of emotions that swirled in her mind—relief, excitement for Nick, and yes, a twinge of disappointment. It was hard not to be at least a little disappointed when proved completely and utterly wrong. "Mmm-hmm."

"Really? That's all you've got?" Jenn's tone was incredulous.

"Wait." Clare threw her arm over the salad plate before Hannah could take another bite.

"What?"

She pulled out her phone. "I want to get a picture."

"Why?"

Clare gave her a look that said, "How dumb are you?" but her actual answer was, "So I can put it on your Instagram account and tag the restaurant."

"Right. Sure."

Clare proceeded to snap photos at a variety of angles, then poked at her phone. Hannah was going to have to download Instagram just so she could keep up. Entrées followed—a pork loin with sweet potato puree, chicken with sun-dried tomatoes and a local goat cheese, and a vegetarian dish that consisted of Romano cheese grits, roasted mushrooms, and sautéed Swiss chard. Each dish included at least one ingredient from the farm and each was more delicious than the last.

By the time desserts appeared, Hannah was stuffed. Despite feeling like she might burst, she tried a bite of each. One bite became two, and by the time they'd finished coffee, all the plates were empty. Nick briefly introduced the pastry chef, a pretty woman named Mariama he'd wooed away from one of the restaurants in Ithaca. Although made by someone different, the desserts seemed to complement Drew's cooking. Hannah wondered how much they'd consulted on the menu.

The pang of irritation caught her off guard. If she didn't know better, she might say it resembled jealousy. But she did know better, and she wasn't jealous.

Before she could analyze the matter any further, Jenn spoke. "Sadly, I've got to work tomorrow."

"Yes," Mom said with a chuckle. "It's awfully close to my bedtime."

Clare sighed dramatically. Hannah took the opportunity to poke her again. "You've got to work, too, punk."

"I know, I know. I'll be there."

Although the pickings were still slim, she'd decided to open the farm stand this weekend. They'd get a few people for sure—her most loyal customers, families looking for a place to have a picnic. Hannah prized being a gathering space as much as a provider of food. "If you come early, I'll pay you to harvest asparagus."

Clare closed one eye and made a face. "Okay."

"You can take pictures and call it marketing research."

Clare smiled. "I like the sound of that."

"I thought you might."

Jenn stood up. "Shall we?"

Hannah waved them off. "You go on. I want to find Nick and congratulate him."

Jenn said, "Thank him again for the invitation and tell him I'm going to recommend Fig to everyone I know."

"Same here," her mom added.

"I will." Hannah hugged them and wished them good night, then went in search of Nick.

❖

Drew slumped against the table for just a moment and took a deep breath. Her first service as head chef had gone off without a hitch. Well, without any major hitches. There was the almost grease fire when one of the interns got some oil too hot before adding onions and two pieces of fish that didn't make the trip from pan to plate in one piece. But, all in all, she was pleased. More than pleased. Ecstatic.

She'd make some time later to gloat, but first they needed to close down the kitchen. She gave some instructions for cleanup, then turned her attention to the menu. Based on timing and one serendipitous error, she had a couple of tweaks for the next night that should streamline getting plates out.

She caught the kitchen door swing open out of the corner of her eye and figured it was Nick coming to check in. "I think that went well. Do you?"

"The food was exceptional."

Drew spun around and found herself face-to-face with Hannah. She'd noticed her from across the dining room, but she looked even more beautiful close up. The outfit was a far cry from what Drew had seen her in to date. Not that she wanted to be a sucker for a beautiful woman in a dress and heels, but she was a total sucker for a beautiful woman in a dress and heels. "Thanks." Drew paused, studied Hannah's face. "You seem surprised."

Hannah shook her head. "Nick wouldn't have hired you if you didn't have talent."

"But?"

She offered a smirk. "But I didn't expect it to be anything I enjoyed."

Drew quirked a brow. "Picky eater?"

Hannah folded her arms across her chest and angled one hip slightly. The posture made her even sexier than when she'd walked in, if that was possible. "No. I expected it to be," she tipped her head back and forth, "precious."

"Precious?" Even without knowing what Hannah meant, she knew it was an insult.

"Things arranged with tweezers. Foams."

The snort escaped before Drew could contain herself. Then she laughed, hard. Never in so few words had she been able to sum up everything wrong with the culinary world. Eventually she stopped, and found Hannah looking increasingly uncomfortable. Drew wiped her eyes. "What made you think I'm that kind of chef?"

Hannah seemed to relax. She shrugged. "New York City, hot shot."

It was Drew's turn to fold her arms. "Who said I was a hot shot?"

"Nick. He wanted someone who'd shake things up, be a little edgy."

"Huh." She'd not gotten that impression from her interview, or from the conversations they'd had since about her approach to the menu. "Maybe edgy is relative."

Hannah smiled at that. "Maybe."

"Does that mean I've won you over?" The second the words were out of her mouth, Drew did a mental face palm. What possessed her to say that?

"I wouldn't go that far."

"Why is that?" And why did it matter so much to her?

"I still think this kind of cooking can be wasteful. It's all about the best cuts and prettiest produce. It's not sustainable or equitable."

Drew nodded slowly. "And what makes you think I'm wasteful?"

Hannah gave her a bland look. "I saw the plates that came out of your kitchen."

There was some waste in her cooking. It was inevitable. But more of what she discarded went into the stockpot than the compost bin. It bothered her that Hannah had such a righteousness about her. It sucked all the fun out of going back and forth with her.

She was saved having to come up with a diplomatic reply when Nick pushed through the swinging door. The enthusiasm radiating from him chased away the weird tension in the air. He carried a bottle and two glasses. "Who's ready to toast an amazing first night?" He stopped when he caught sight of Hannah. "You're still here. Excellent. Let me get another glass."

"No, no. I was just going," she said.

"Nonsense. Stay. Celebrate with us."

Hannah smiled at him, but didn't budge. "I've got an early morning tomorrow, and I've got to drive myself home. I just wanted to say congratulations before I left."

"Thanks." The look on his face told Drew that Hannah was more to him than a supplier. She'd have to remember that.

"No, thank you. Dinner was amazing. Jenn, Clare, and Cindy all said so, too. We're all thrilled for you." Hannah stepped over and gave him a kiss on the cheek. Drew expected her to leave without looking back, but she turned. "Congratulations, again. I'll see you tomorrow?"

In the flurry of activity, Drew forgot that she'd committed to going to the farm three days a week. Refusing to let it spoil her evening, she offered her most charming smile. "Looking forward to it."

Hannah left and Drew tried to ignore the vague disappointment that threatened to creep into her chest. Nick lifted the bottle. "Shall we?"

He poured them each a finger of scotch and raised his glass. "To Fig and many more nights like this."

"Cheers." Drew sipped the amber liquid, enjoying the smooth burn that worked its way to her belly.

Nick set the bottle down. "Are you happy with everything? The staff?"

Drew nodded. "Minor hiccups, nothing I wouldn't expect. A couple of the waiters have a steep learning curve, but I don't have any serious concerns. I think we give it a week or two and reassess."

"Agreed. I'm guessing Vince has already picked up on it. I'll let him know."

Vince was the headwaiter. He had a good twenty years of fine dining experience, some of it in Boston. Drew liked and trusted him. "Sounds good."

"And the kitchen staff?"

"You know, I think they're good." There was a bit of a competitive vibe between her sous chef and the grill chef, but as long as it didn't get out of control, a little competition could be good. It was her job to manage it.

"Good." Nick nodded to the bottle. "Share that with everyone. Let them know how pleased I am with tonight."

"Will do."

Nick left the way he came. Drew slipped out to the bar and returned to the kitchen with a stack of shot glasses. She called everyone together and started to pour. She'd participated in many such rituals through the years, but this was the first one she got to preside over. She looked at the faces of her staff, saw respect and appreciation mixed in with relief and fatigue. Almost more than the service itself, Drew basked in the satisfaction of running her own kitchen.

She might be going home to a weird little house with the crazy-ass birds. She might have to get up at a god-awful hour and trek out to the farm to get her vegetables for the next night. She might be hundreds of miles from home and inexplicably attracted to a woman who seemed to feel nothing for her but disdain. But in that moment, Drew was the head chef, and she was happy.

Chapter Seven

Opening night turned out to be a slightly more hectic version of the soft launch. Sunday included a bustling brunch service but a relatively quiet dinner. Monday rolled around and Drew took full advantage of her first day off by sleeping until noon.

She put on coffee and stared out the kitchen window while it brewed. The sky was a monochromatic pale gray; the steady drizzle made no sound as it fell. She drank her coffee, showered, and wondered what the hell to do with her day. Two hours later, she'd done laundry and cleaned a little, answered her email, and sketched out ideas for the coming week's menu. She spent another hour researching the average harvest dates of things in this area of New York, making notes for when she might expect access to things like green beans, summer squash, and tomatoes. She made a sandwich, cleaned some more, then decided if she didn't get out of the house, she'd lose her mind.

Some web searches confirmed her suspicions. There wasn't much to do at four on a Monday afternoon. She considered another trip to Atlas, just to have a change of scenery. Then inspiration struck. In no time, she had maps of the local wine trails and lists of the craft breweries and distilleries along both Seneca and Cayuga lakes. She could take a ride, try some brews, and it would all count as research.

Although she had dozens to choose from, she decided to stay fairly close to home. She cut across to Seneca Lake and drove south, following the curve of the lake through tiny towns and past vineyards and tasting rooms. The clouds had lifted, leaving the afternoon sunny and mild. Settling on beer instead of wine for this outing, she pulled into the first brewery she passed. The building looked new and the logo featured a mermaid.

Inside, Drew found tables made of old wine barrels and far more people than she would have thought—some at tables and a couple of larger groups at the bar. Eighties music played in the background and the vibe felt downright leisurely. Drew chuckled. Half the population of the city didn't seem to work regular business hours, she wasn't sure why she expected something different upstate.

She snagged a seat at the bar and smiled at the guy behind it. He wore a T-shirt with the brewery logo and sported an impressive beard. "Hi."

He returned her smile. "Welcome to Scale House. Is it your first time with us?"

"It is."

"Excellent." He slid a laminated menu across the bar. "We've got ten brews on tap, all made on-site. You can order a pint of anything or a flight of four."

Drew glanced down. They had everything from lager to stout. "Definitely a flight. What do you recommend?"

"The IPA is my favorite, followed by the oatmeal stout."

It all looked good to her. "You know what? Surprise me."

A minute later, she had four small glasses on a narrow wooden paddle. In addition to the IPA and stout, he'd added a cream ale and their seasonal, called Summer Jam. She thanked him and he nodded before moving away to serve other customers. The summer one was light for her taste, but she could appreciate the appeal of something made to be drunk all day long.

She studied the people. One group talked like they were from out of town, but the rest seemed like locals. She'd considered the tourism angle of the Finger Lakes wine and beer trails, but it also brought more and better options for the people who lived and worked in the area. Like having the pros of gentrification without the cons. She could get behind that.

Drew enjoyed her beers, contemplated dinner. It was still on the early side, though, and she wanted to hit at least one more spot. She paid her tab, offered a nod of thanks to the bartender, and headed out.

The group from earlier was leaving, too. Drew watched them pile onto a small bus, the kind that shuttled people to and from hotels and airports. She chuckled. She could think of worse ways to spend a Monday. Although amused, she was relieved when they turned in the opposite direction as she was headed. She drove south just a couple of miles before seeing the sign for her next stop. She pulled into the lot of Grist Iron and found the parking lot nearly full. Fascinating.

As she approached the building, she noticed that two garage-style doors had been lifted, turning the restaurant and patio into one large, open space. People sat at picnic tables and stood in groups on the grass, others came and went from the bar. Live music spilled out—a decent, if not earth-shattering, cover of a Beatles song. If this was the vibe on a Monday, she might have just stumbled on her new favorite place.

She headed inside and to the bar, going with a pint of unfiltered blonde instead of a flight. Beer in hand, she turned to scope out a spot. And there, sitting at a high-top table just inside the door, were Nick and his wife, someone she didn't know, and Hannah.

Of course, Hannah was the one she noticed first. The one who instantly cranked her heart rate up a few notches. The one who didn't even look her way.

Nick saw her and offered a wave, the kind that was half greeting, half invitation. Not that she would avoid joining them, but now she had no choice. She made her way across the room. "Hey, there."

"Enjoying your day off, I see," Nick said.

"I am. I should have known it was a thing."

"Not always, but we try to get out. And our nephew is the guy on the drums." Nick hooked a thumb in the direction of the band.

"Aha." Drew's gaze followed the gesture. The kid played with enthusiasm and didn't look a day over seventeen. "Is he even old enough to drink?"

Leda laughed. "Not yet. Which is one of the reasons his mom prefers him playing happy hour gigs at breweries instead of late nights at dive bars."

Drew laughed. She was nowhere near even thinking about having kids, but could appreciate the sentiment.

"The two boys dancing around are ours," Nick said.

Drew knew Nick had two sons, but she hadn't met them yet. "Don't you have a daughter, too?"

Leda nodded. "Kristen's at tennis practice."

"And I'm Jenn." The woman Drew didn't know stuck out her hand.

"Drew." Drew shook the hand and smiled. "Were you at the restaurant opening?"

"I was." She tipped her head toward Hannah. "That one let me sit at her VIP table."

"Right. I knew you looked familiar." Drew nodded, then turned her attention toward Hannah, which was what she'd wanted to do the second she saw her. "Hi again."

"Hi." Hannah's smile was friendly, but seemed to hold back a little, like she was still uncertain of Drew as a person, or perhaps of her expanding presence in Hannah's life.

"So, farmers get a day off, too?"

Hannah shrugged, her smile becoming more genuine. "Day might be generous."

Jenn elbowed Hannah. "Be honest, you worked eight hours before coming out."

"Six." Hannah's tone was adamant. Then she tipped her head back and forth a few times. "Ish."

Nick chimed in. "If you think restaurant work is hard, you should try farming. I've helped out a couple of times and, honest to God, I thought I was going to die."

"Stop." Hannah looked exasperated, but in that teasing way friends have. Drew had a flash of hoping Hannah would be playful with her someday. Well, playful and—

Nick interrupted her train of thought. "'We're just going to weed the berries,' she tells me. And then I can't stand up straight for four days."

"That is not what happened," Hannah insisted.

Jenn lifted a finger. "I'm pretty sure it is, because the exact same thing happened to me."

Hannah looked at Drew. "They exaggerate."

Before Drew could respond, the music stopped and the lead singer announced they'd be back in ten. Nick and Leda's nephew came over, along with a couple Drew assumed were his parents. Nick did brief introductions, then the four of them started talking about an upcoming family dinner. Jenn offered good-byes, citing a date. That left her and Hannah.

"Maybe on your next day off, you should come by and try your hand at the growing side of things." Hannah's tone was playful, and held more than a hint of challenge.

The idea of spending the entire day with Hannah, of seeing her in her element, had major appeal. She didn't mind hard work, either, and was used to spending ten hours on her feet. "You don't think I can do it, do you?"

She lifted one shoulder. If Drew didn't know better, she'd be tempted to call the gesture flirtatious. "Not can't. I get the feeling you don't like getting dirty."

Drew laughed. Really laughed. "Are you serious? I'm a chef. I gut fish and defeather chickens. I've done every dirty and disgusting job in a kitchen you can think of."

"Huh." Hannah nodded a few times. "I guess I hadn't thought of it that way."

"Trust me when I say I can handle a little dirt."

Hannah folded her arms and leaned back. She enjoyed watching the emotions play across Drew's face. She'd gone from defensive to confident in a matter of seconds. She might not want to admit it, but the latter suited her. She'd been half teasing with the invitation, but now that Drew seemed to be accepting it, she was curious. "All right. Stop by whenever. I'll show you around and we'll find something you can get your hands in."

Drew leaned back, lifted her chin slightly. "What time do you start?"

Hannah had to tamp down the swell of attraction that caught her by surprise. "At this time of year, six."

To her credit, Drew didn't balk. "I'll be there."

Now Hannah felt bad. "You don't have to do that. I know you work late. I'm probably in bed before you leave the restaurant most nights."

She'd not meant anything by it, but mentioning the word "bed" put a very vivid image in her mind. An image of being in bed and having Drew join her. Hannah cleared her throat and hoped her face hadn't given anything away.

Drew raised an eyebrow, smiled. "If I'm going to do it, I'm going to do it right."

She was talking about farming. She had to be talking about farming. But Hannah's brain, as well as her body, had no trouble interpreting the comment to mean something else entirely. "Okay, then." She needed some air. "I should get going."

Drew continued to smile. "I hope it's not because I showed up and crashed your evening."

This was definitely more than friendly banter, or even the kind of professional sparring of their earlier conversations. It made her panicky, it turned her on, and it gave her the itch to escape. She shook her head a little too fast. "Not at all. I've had my limit and I've got an early morning."

"All right. I'll see you tomorrow, then. Probably around ten."

Why had she agreed to Drew stopping by three times a week again? She stood. "Sure. Sounds good."

"Leaving so soon?" Nick sounded disappointed, but not surprised.

Hannah shrugged. "You know me."

Leda stood up and gave her a hug. "I'm thrilled anytime we get you out between May and September."

Hannah's heart warmed. She loved her family, but these were her people. She said good-bye and headed out. On the drive home, she tried not to think about Drew. It didn't work.

She'd invited Drew to spend the day at the farm. Worse, she was looking forward to it.

She told herself it helped that they'd been able to clear the air a little. Having to see each other three days a week with awkward tension hanging between them would get old quick. But not having an issue with Drew made it easier to think about her in ways that Hannah just as soon wouldn't. A conundrum, one that followed her into the house. She fed Daisy before heading upstairs, where she shed her clothes and brushed her teeth.

Having a thing for Drew would be terribly inconvenient, at best. At worst, she could let her guard down and wind up making an absolute fool of herself. Or making things awkward for Nick. None of that sat well with her. She just needed to distract herself. Fortunately, work was her go-to in that department. And between now and October, she'd have more work than she knew what to do with.

Chapter Eight

Drew stood in front of her closet, debating what to wear. It wasn't like she had farm clothes. Old shorts and a T-shirt? Too casual. She shook her head. She was worried about how she looked to spend the day digging in the dirt. She'd crossed the line into ridiculous. She finally settled on a pair of cargo pants—why she owned cargo pants in the first place remained a mystery—and a gray tee with a whisk on it.

She laced up her boots, contemplating coffee. Should she bring one for Hannah? Would Hannah make fun of her for needing it to be up so early? Well, she did and it was nothing to be ashamed about. She'd bring one for Hannah, too. If Hannah declined it, she'd drink both cups. She could use two cups, too. She'd not gotten home until almost midnight. When her alarm went off at four forty-five, it took more than a few expletives to drag herself from bed. But she was going to be there by six if it killed her.

The sun was up by the time she pulled into the lot by the barn. A lot had changed from the first time she'd come here, the day of her interview. The mud had dried up and everything around her felt green and lush and blooming.

Drew grabbed the coffees and headed into the barn. There was no sign of life, so she walked around back. Fields spread in three directions. A pair of greenhouses sat to the far left and a hill in the distance appeared to be an apple orchard. She didn't know what she'd been expecting, but it was bigger and more vibrant than she'd imagined.

A tractor puttered along to her right, but Drew saw no other signs of life. Could she have beat Hannah here? The thought made her smile and feel just the tiniest bit smug.

"Good morning."

Drew turned. She'd been joined by a handsome guy with longish hair, maybe her age or a little older. "Good morning."

"You must be Drew. I'm Jeremiah." He extended his hand.

Drew tucked one of the coffee cups into the crook of her arm so she could shake it. "I am. I take it you're expecting me."

"Hannah mentioned it." He looked out at the field. "Looks like she beat us both and got an early start."

Drew followed his gaze to the tractor. It was a good size and appeared to be pulling a large tilling implement behind it. The person driving was too far away to see clearly, but they wore a baseball cap and seemed to know what they were doing. "Is that Hannah?"

Jeremiah chuckled and Drew wished she'd been able to keep the surprise from her voice. "It certainly is. She doesn't really like anyone else to drive Bertie if she can help it."

"Bertie?"

"The tractor. Roberta. It's kind of Hannah's baby."

Drew laughed, unsure if she found the whole thing absurd or impressive. Or maybe she was the absurd one. "And here I was, thinking for a second that I beat her here."

Jeremiah's chuckle turned into a full-bellied laugh. "Can I tell her you said that?"

Yep, she was definitely the absurd one. "I'd rather you didn't."

"Yeah, I feel you. Your secret is safe with me."

Drew let out a relieved breath. She looked over at him, dressed similar to her, then down at the cups in her hand. She raised them slightly. "Coffee?"

His face was kind when he returned her gaze. "Did you bring one of those for Hannah?"

She had, of course, but felt like she owed him something. Although the thought of not having any for herself at this ridiculous hour made her beyond sad, she'd suck it up. "Yeah, but I'll share mine."

"No need. She doesn't drink it."

Drew stared at him. Who didn't drink coffee? "Seriously?"

"Well, I shouldn't say doesn't. I don't think she dislikes it. It's not a daily habit, though."

"Wow. Okay." Why she found this so hard to believe, she didn't know. "So, cream and sugar or black?"

"You don't have a preference?" He had this optimistic expression that made Drew like him.

"Nope. I learned a long time ago to appreciate coffee in all its wonderful variations."

"I'll take cream and sugar, then."

Drew handed him a cup. "Enjoy."

"Thank you."

Now that Drew knew it was Hannah, she was surprised she'd ever thought it might be someone else. She wore a tank top, showing off the same gorgeously tanned and toned arms Drew had noticed the night of the restaurant opening. Her hair was braided, but clearly the length and color of Hannah's. It was her, all right, running that tractor like a boss.

Jeremiah coughed, reminding Drew she wasn't alone. How long had she been staring? Probably better not to ask.

She was trying to think of a way to keep the conversation going when Hannah must have caught sight of them. She offered a wave and cut the tractor engine. She hopped down and started their way. Jeremiah began walking toward her, so Drew followed. They skirted a fenced area, then passed through an old door rigged up in a wall of taller fencing.

"I didn't expect you this early," Hannah said.

Drew used a hand to shield her eyes from the sun. Why hadn't she brought a hat? "I said I'd be here."

Hannah smiled. "You did. I should have given you more credit."

It wasn't quite a compliment, but Drew didn't want to split hairs. "I'd have come even earlier if I'd known I could watch you running that tractor around."

The smile turned into a smirk. "You're going to ask for a turn, aren't you?"

Drew shook her head. "I think I'm good. That's some heavy machinery and I'm fond of all my extremities."

That earned her a laugh. Hannah angled her head toward Jeremiah. "I take it you two have met?"

Jeremiah nodded. "I took the liberty of stealing the coffee Drew brought for you."

"I didn't realize you weren't a coffee drinker," Drew said.

Hannah smiled. She took a minute to appreciate the way Drew looked in work clothes. Her chef coat was sexy, but this, this could be dangerous. "Not never. I just don't need it to function."

"Then I find the hours you keep all the more impressive."

She shrugged. "I sleep well so I don't have to sleep late."

"I was going to start with weeding the salad beds." Jeremiah hooked his thumb to the right. "Do you want me to take Drew?"

Part of her wanted to treat Drew like any hired help—another set of hands to chip away at the never-ending work of weeding, watering, and picking. But Drew wasn't a hired hand. She wasn't even really a volunteer, although she'd offered to work. "I'll probably have her join you later, but for now I thought we'd start with a tour."

Drew frowned. "You don't have to treat me like a guest, you know."

"I know." She didn't intend to roll out the red carpet, but a little part of her wanted to show off, to show Drew what really went into the bins and baskets she filled each time she came to the farm. "We'll put you to work. But I'd like to give you the lay of the land, show you what you have to look forward to."

Drew offered that ridiculously sexy smile that always seemed to pack more of a punch than she remembered. "I'm certainly not going to turn that down."

Jeremiah headed to the lettuce patch and Hannah led Drew toward the back field. "Okay. Let's start at the end and work our way—" Hannah stopped in her tracks. "Wait."

"What?" Drew looked alarmed.

"Are you wearing sunscreen?"

She cringed. "I'll be okay."

Hannah shook her head. "No, you won't. Come with me."

Drew didn't protest, which Hannah took to mean she was forgetful, not an idiot. She went in the side door of the barn and to the small break room. She opened her locker and pulled out a tube of SPF 50. "Put that on your face and arms, and don't forget the back of your neck."

Drew took it, looking sheepish. "Thanks."

When she was done, Hannah handed her a hat. "I hope you're not one of those people weirdly obsessed with your hair."

Drew, with a smear of sunscreen on her cheek, went from sheepish to offended in two seconds flat. "Chefs wear hats every day. It's basic kitchen protocol."

Hannah smirked, enjoying herself. "Not if you're Gordon Ramsey."

"I think it's pretty clear I'm not." Drew seemed to be amused, rather than upset by the banter.

"No, you're not." Suddenly the break room felt too small, too close. She needed to get them back to fresh air and broad daylight. "Shall we?"

Drew gestured for her to lead the way. "After you."

Since they'd come back to the barn, Hannah changed up the order of the tour. They walked past the patches overflowing with greens—lettuces, spinach, chard, and kale. "I'm trying collard greens this year, too."

"Collards are great. I hope they do well."

"We put these beds closest to the barn because we harvest from them pretty much daily."

Drew nodded. "Do you rotate the crops at all? That's a thing, right?"

"Some. I'll show you where we plant sweet corn and sunflowers. We divide the field in thirds and always have one third fallow, or with alfalfa." Next were the tomatoes, peppers, and eggplant, followed by cucumbers and squashes, beans and peas. "These all pull the same nutrients, so we just make a point of replenishing the soil each year."

Drew gave her a sideways look and smiled. "Is that layperson for cow manure?"

Hannah chuckled. "Cow and horse, but also compost."

"Do you take the restaurant compost scraps?"

"We do, which is why Nick is fussy about what goes in it. We happily use it, but can't take meat and bones and some of the stuff the industrial composters can."

Drew stopped to study the pepper varieties. "That makes sense. I like the idea of things going full circle."

The comment, combined with a dozen other interactions over the last couple of weeks, tipped the scales. She was starting to like Drew. Combined with the attraction, that might prove problematic. No way could she act on it. They had a business relationship to maintain. She couldn't put Nick in the awkward position of dealing with the fallout if things didn't go well.

She shook her head. She'd not even acted on her attraction and was already thinking about it not ending well. If that didn't temper her impulses, she didn't know what would.

"What's wrong?"

And now she'd been caught daydreaming. Great. "Nothing."

"You look like you might pass out. Or punch something. I can't tell." Drew stood, planted her hands on her hips. Between that and the wide, confident stance, Hannah's mouth went dry. Oh, this was going to be so inconvenient.

"Sorry. I'm fine. I got distracted."

"If you don't have time to do this, it's okay. I came here to help, not take you away from your work."

Hannah shook her head, but intentionally this time. "No, it's not that at all. Come on, I'll show you the rest."

They walked past the berry patch and climbed the hill to the orchard. She pointed out which trees were apple and which were peach. Drew made noises of approval. Then Hannah led her through the greenhouses. She'd started the next round of spinach and lettuce seeds, but the doors were open so things didn't get overheated.

"You have an impressive setup here. You've got more land than I realized, but you also grow more on it than I would have thought possible."

Hannah got a flutter in her chest. The farm wasn't just her livelihood. It was her pride and joy. Like a child, in some ways. Having people say nice things about it meant more than any compliment they could give her personally. "Thanks. We do our best."

Drew narrowed her eyes. "You always say we. I know you have people working for you, but it's really you, isn't it? You're the driving force behind all this."

Great. Now she was blushing. "Sort of. It's definitely my baby."

"I'm sure there's a great story. I hope to hear it one day."

Hannah smiled and tried not to get sentimental. "Maybe."

As if sensing her emotional shift, Drew took a deep breath. "I'll remember you said that. But for now, we work."

Work. Right. That was the point of all this. "Okay. I'll give you some choices. You can go weed with Jeremiah, then pick your own greens for tomorrow. Or you can come with me and train the bean and tomato plants."

"I have no idea what training is, but I'll come with you."

"Excellent." They started with the tomato plants. Hannah showed Drew how to hook the stems onto the twine strung along the rows and how to pinch off the suckers.

"Is it silly that I feel bad pulling off such tender little leaves?" Drew paused and looked across the row at Hannah.

"I promise you'll get used to it. Especially when you realize it can double your production per plant. They're called suckers for a reason. They suck the plant's energy."

"You're right. That does make a difference." Drew resumed pinching. "How long until we get tomatoes?"

"Probably another six weeks or so."

Drew groaned. "That's cruel. If we were in the South, we'd have the first crop already."

"And it would be ninety degrees already. And we wouldn't be able to grow a decent apple."

Drew seemed to mull that over. "But we'd have citrus?"

"But here we can produce wine."

"Ah. Okay. You win."

"Thank you." They worked their way down each row. The plants were just starting to take off, so it was quick work. Beans were next. No pinching needed, but the plants were already bushy, so it took more time to make sure they were properly supported on the makeshift trellises. At the end of a row, Hannah paused, looked up at the sky. "It's probably after eleven. Shall we break for lunch?"

Drew stood and Hannah caught her wince before she smiled. "Lunch sounds fabulous."

They walked back in the direction of the barn. "You can stop anytime, you know. It's hard work."

Drew lifted her chin. "I'm not afraid of hard work."

The edge in her voice softened Hannah even more. "I never said you were. But this uses different muscles than you're used to."

Drew closed one eye, made a face. "Maybe something with less bending?"

Hannah laughed. "I've got just the thing. Let's take a break and grab something to eat first."

"I didn't think to pack a lunch."

"There's lots of stuff in the break room that you're welcome to."

They made peanut butter sandwiches. Drew went on and on about Hannah's blueberry-peach preserves. Jeremiah passed through with his lunch, along with Caroline. The four of them talked about the state of the peach orchard, and the apples. They'd been spared any really hard frosts after April, and it looked like the harvest would be a good one.

Drew didn't utter a word of complaint, but she got up gingerly. It made her feel bad about egging Drew on, setting it up so Drew felt like she had something to prove. She decided they should end the day on a high note. "How do you feel about picking?"

"Picking as in harvesting? As in, things ready to eat?"

Hannah chuckled at the incredulous tone. "That is the point of all this work, you know."

"Yes, but you broke my heart once today with a six-week wait for tomatoes. I'm feeling very skittish."

She bit her lip to keep from smiling, wishing Drew wasn't quite so charming, and led them back past the green beans to where the pea fences stood. "Okay, there's a little bending involved here, but I think you'll find it manageable. And you can take whatever you pick with you."

Drew's face lit up. "What do I get to harvest?"

"Sugar snap peas."

Drew rubbed her hands together, clearly delighted. "That's the best thing I've heard all day."

"I thought you'd think so. The question is whether you can handle it on your own."

Drew gave her a look of utter exasperation. "I think I can manage."

"Just checking. I abandoned the tractor in the back pasture this morning and I hate leaving it out overnight."

"Don't you mean her?" Drew smirked. It was a disarmingly good look on her. "I was told her name is Roberta."

Hannah snickered, not really embarrassed. "If men can name their sports cars, I can name my tractor."

"I'm not disagreeing. I think Bertie is a great name for a tractor."

"Thank you." Hannah walked Drew to the pea fence, pointed out the sugar snaps. She did a quick demo of the easiest way to pick, handed her a basket, and then left her to her own devices. "I'll be back in less than an hour."

Drew had already started picking. "I'll be here."

Hannah went to finish her tilling, almost sad to be ending her time with Drew. Which was ridiculous. One of her favorite things about farming was the solitary time. Drew was an entertaining diversion, nothing more. But as she fired up the diesel engine and got to work, Drew never completely left her thoughts. There was no "starting to" about it. She liked Drew, full on. She found Drew interesting. She enjoyed her company. And she couldn't stop thinking about what it might be like to kiss her. Ugh.

Hannah finished the remaining rows, then pulled the tractor into its shed. It was close to four, but the sun remained high. She found Drew where she'd left her, only at the end of the row instead of the beginning. Her basket was full and she'd turned the bottom half of her shirt into a makeshift one. Hannah tried to ignore the swath of exposed skin. She grabbed a spare basket from the snow pea fence and walked down to meet her. "You're making quick work, I see."

Drew transferred the contents of her shirt to the basket and gave Hannah an apologetic look. "I hope that's okay. There are so many of them. I couldn't stop myself."

"Perfectly fine. On one condition."

"What's that?" The look of apology vanished and Drew seemed on the verge of flirting with her.

"I was going to say tell me what you're going to make with them, but maybe I should ask for a sample instead."

Drew grinned and any question Hannah had about whether they were flirting vanished. "I was thinking of a flash roast. Get a hint of char but make sure they keep their crunch."

Hannah closed her eyes for a second and imagined the flavor. "Yum."

"If you want to stop by on your way home tomorrow, I'll save some for you."

Hannah looked down at her dirt-streaked clothes. "I couldn't inflict this on Nick's customers."

"That's why you come around back." The wink that accompanied Drew's statement was laced with suggestion.

Hannah swallowed, reminded herself to stay focused on the task at hand. "I guess I could do that."

"You most definitely should. I'll pack you up a full dinner to make it worthwhile."

At this time of year, the promise of a dinner she didn't have to think about or cook would be sufficient enticement. The extra layer, friendliness or flirtation or whatever it was, maybe should have dissuaded her. But it didn't. "That would be really nice."

"Cool. Text me when you're on your way and I'll have it ready for you."

"Thanks. Really." Hannah felt a ripple of awkwardness. "On that note, I should probably let you go. You've more than earned your keep today."

"I'm not going to argue with you. There's a shower and a cold beer with my name on it at home."

"Both well earned." The awkwardness factor doubled when Hannah's brain pictured Drew wet and naked. She coughed to cover up the involuntary sound that escaped her lips. "Oh, do you want to take tomorrow's produce with you now?"

"That would be perfect."

They walked back to the barn and Drew made her selections. They loaded the boxes into her car and Hannah offered a wave as she pulled away. She stood in the parking lot for a moment, exchanging greetings with folks who'd come to pick veggies or snag a few things from the farm stand. She technically could do a few more chores before calling it a day, but a cool shower of her own had major appeal.

She popped inside the store to make sure everything was under control. Clare was chatting with a customer while Caroline restocked chard. Hannah wished them both a good night, then headed for her truck. She drove home with the windows down, telling herself repeatedly, if unconvincingly, she was not going to spend her evening thinking about Drew.

Chapter Nine

*I**had a great time playing farmer. Can I return the favor?*
Drew's text came only a couple hours after they parted ways. Hannah obsessed more than she cared to admit over her reply. She settled for the obvious. *Aren't you making me dinner tomorrow?*

Her phrasing made it sound like a date, but whatever.

That's for the peas. I want to thank you for letting me tag along. The dots told Hannah more was coming. *I'm pretty sure I slowed you down.*

She laughed at the assertion, and the awkward toothy emoji that accompanied it. *You didn't slow me down. And you're the one who did free labor. I should be thanking you.*

She kind of wanted to be flirty but couldn't come up with anything that didn't sound obvious and cheesy. She stared at her phone. She set it aside, annoyed that she was staring. But when it chirped with an incoming message, she couldn't pick it up fast enough.

I suggest a gesture of mutual gratitude. I'll pack the picnic. You show me the best place around here to have one.

Hannah took a screen shot and sent it to Jenn. *Is this a date?*

Jenn's reply was instant. *100% yes. Who's asking you on a date?*

She'd cut the name off the top of the photo. Her answer was rewarded with a string of emojis, including a shocked face, a laughing one, and the one blowing a kiss. Next came the dancing lady, bread, cheese, wine, and two pairs of lips. *Seriously? Tell me everything.*

She started an answer. Crap, she'd abandoned the conversation with Drew. She switched back. Definitely didn't want to give the wrong impression there. Despite Jenn's assessment, it might not actually be a date. Or it might. *Deal. When's your next day off?*

Next Monday. (Always Monday.) That okay?

She didn't have a set day off, but once the farm stand opened, she rarely took a day off on the weekend. She smiled. Dating a chef might turn out to be convenient on that score. She stopped smiling and looked around, as though someone might be nearby and catch her. Had she really just used the word "dating" to refer to Drew? That was bad. Wasn't it?

Without answering any of the questions her brain had posed, she typed out a reply. *Great. Text me your address and I'll pick you up.*

The place she had in mind didn't really have an address. And it was easier to get to with a truck. That's why she offered to pick Drew up. Should she explain that? Or would it make it seem like she was thinking too much?

Ooh, a ride in the pickup truck. Yes, please. You probably want to work in the morning. 4:00?

Of course Drew had to go and be considerate of her work on top of everything else. And make a cute comment about her truck. She shook her head and stared at the ceiling. This had such a high chance of becoming dangerous. *Perfect.*

A text with Drew's address followed, then one wishing her sweet dreams. She said good night, set her phone aside, and then rubbed her hands over her face. What was she getting herself into? She'd just started to slide down the rabbit hole of possibilities when her phone rang. Jenn. Crap, Hannah had forgotten all about her.

"Hi."

Jenn didn't bother returning the greeting. "You can't put that out there and then leave me hanging."

Hannah laughed. "Sorry."

"Don't apologize. Spill."

She did a quick overview of her day with Drew, the text that started the whole thing, and the plans that came out of it. "Do you still think it's a date?"

"Hell yes. And a romantic one at that. Where are you going to take her?"

There were plenty of good spots right on the farm, but she might as well pull out all the stops. "Probably that spot at the edge of Pete's property. It's got a view of the vineyard and the lake."

"Excellent choice. Are you going to bring her back to your place after?"

"Jenn." She made her voice stern, even though the thought had already crossed her mind. "It's a first date."

"Yeah, but be honest. You two have been dancing around each other since you met."

Even if that was true. "I am not inviting her back to my place."

"You could go to hers. I mean, you're going to be dropping her off, right?"

In spite of herself, Hannah's imagination ran with it. What would it be like? Would Drew make the first move? How would she respond if Hannah did? She shook her head, even though Jenn wasn't there to see it. "I do not have sex on the first date."

"Fine, fine. The date is plenty exciting. And the first date is the prerequisite for the second date. And I know for a fact you'll have sex on the second date."

Before Hannah and Jenn were best friends, they'd gone on exactly two dates. The second had ended in the most awkward sexual encounter of Hannah's life. She was pretty sure that was true for Jenn, too. "Maybe not the thing to say if you think I should be having second-date sex."

Jenn laughed. "You have a point. Still. How long has it been exactly?"

Hannah did the math and frowned. "Not quite a year."

Jenn snorted. "Way too long. I'd tell you to relax your standards, but Drew's pretty hot, so maybe you won't have to."

"Could we wait until I've gone on a date with her to decide about the sex?"

"I bet she's good."

"What makes you say that?" Hannah almost didn't want to know. But then, she did.

"Chefs are passionate by nature, creative. Good with their hands."

At the description, heat gathered in Hannah's center. She pressed her thighs together. She'd noticed Drew's hands while they were training the tomato plants. Her long fingers moved deftly over the leaves and stems.

"Hannah? You still there."

"Uh. Yeah. I'm here."

"You were thinking about her hands, weren't you?"

No point in lying. "Maybe."

"Good. You can be so serious sometimes. A little daydreaming is good for you."

"I daydream plenty."

Jenn sighed. "Let me clarify. Daydreaming about sex is good for you. It'll heighten the anticipation. Make you want it more."

Wanting Drew more than she already did seemed like a terrible idea. But she didn't need to pick apart the reasons for that with Jenn.

"Well, it's a week away, so I'll have plenty of time to think about it."

"I wish I had someone to fantasize about. My life is so boring."

"What about the woman from Rochester? The professor?"

Jenn sighed. "She was a little uptight. And I don't think she liked that I work with money. Like it's not a reputable profession or something."

Hannah hadn't met her, but she'd not been terribly impressed with what Jenn had shared. "Good riddance, then. You're completely reputable. Well, professionally at least."

Jenn laughed. "I love you, Hannah Little."

"I love you back."

"Dinner Friday still, yeah?" Jenn asked.

"Yep. You bring the beer and I'll make dinner."

"And we can plot your date and pick your outfit."

Hannah couldn't help but snicker. "You make us sound about sixteen."

"I like to think my taste in beer has improved since then. And women, for that matter."

Since she'd still thought herself straight at that age, she couldn't disagree. "I'll see you then."

Jenn ended the call and Hannah pulled up her texts to reread her conversation with Drew. It really did seem like a date. So, if she went on that premise, it meant she might have to decide whether or not to have sex with Drew. Again, her imagination had no problem taking that idea and running with it. Of course, if they had sex, some version of a relationship might follow. That still seemed more complicated and weird than she was ready for. If Jenn were there, she'd tell Hannah she was getting ahead of herself. Hannah chuckled. She'd be absolutely right.

❖

Since it was a week away, Drew tried not to spend too much time thinking about going on a picnic with Hannah. Especially since she'd see Hannah at least a couple of times before then. Including tonight.

Dinner service was bumping for a Tuesday. There was some kind of concert in the park and it seemed like people decided to kick off the evening with a nice dinner. And nice dinner meant Fig.

She preferred things busy. The frenetic pace gave her energy. It also made Nick happy and helped her reputation. People weren't just coming to the restaurant. They were coming to eat her food. And that made Drew very happy.

Also making her happy was the prospect of Hannah dropping by any minute.

She was not one to obsessively check her phone, certainly not during dinner service. But she'd pulled it out of her back pocket at least a dozen times already. She told herself because, even with the volume up and vibrate setting on, she might miss a text. That wasn't why, but she told herself anyway.

It wouldn't be the first time Hannah had eaten her cooking, but she was excited to share what she'd come up with. She had gone with a quick roast, pairing the peas with baby radishes. She served them with a honey-brined chicken breast and creamy polenta. Summery without being delicate. She pulled out her phone again and, in the five minutes since the last time, Hannah had texted. Not hearing it made her feel better about the obsessive checking.

Heading your way.

Hannah probably hadn't meant it that way, but something in the phrasing struck Drew as intimate. She liked it. *Just come right in the back door. I'll have it waiting for you.*

Rather than bothering with a to-go ticket, she grabbed a foil container and assembled the meal herself, including a drizzle of velouté over the chicken and a sprinkling of fresh parsley. She'd just lidded it up when Hannah appeared, looking stunning despite the day of manual labor. Drew offered her an enthusiastic smile. "Hi."

"Hi." Hannah returned the smile. "I can't tell you how much I'm looking forward to dinner."

"Good. I didn't take the liberty of packing it up, but we're doing a riff on strawberry shortcake tonight. Would you like one?"

Her eyes widened. "Where did you get strawberries? Mine won't be ripe for another week at least."

"Ithaca Organics, on the other side of the lake."

Hannah shook her head. "Of course. They've been doing berries way longer than I have. They've got established plants and probably some tricks up their sleeves."

"So, is that a no?"

"Oh, no. Not at all. I want some. I want two, but I won't be greedy."

She liked the idea of Hannah being greedy about dessert, or maybe indulgences more generally. "If I put two in one container, we can all pretend it's just one."

Hannah pointed at her. "I like the way you think."

"Good. Give me two minutes." Drew grabbed another container, putting two cornmeal shortcakes in it. Then she filled one paper soup cup with macerated strawberries and another with whipped cream. She returned to where Hannah stood watching Poppy plate salmon. "Let me grab a bag for you."

"I thought you said one container."

Drew quirked a brow. "I decided to keep things separate. You don't want soggy shortcake and melted cream."

Hannah laughed. "No, no I don't."

Drew loaded the containers into a paper bag. "No one saw what I put in. Your secret is safe with me."

"Oh, I'm not ashamed of eating two desserts. Just requesting two."

"I respect that distinction." She handed Hannah the bag.

"Are you sure I can't pay you?"

"Completely." Drew turned at the sound of the printer spitting out a new round of tickets. "I need to take care of that."

"Go, go. Thank you again."

"My pleasure." Drew leaned in to kiss her, then caught herself. She had to shake off just how natural it felt. "I'd love to know what you think when you're done."

"I'll be sure to text you in the very brief period between my finishing and falling into a food coma."

Drew grinned. "Deal."

Drew returned to her work and Hannah stood for a moment, watching. It was the first time she'd really had the chance to see Drew in action. She moved around the kitchen with such confidence. She barked out orders, but there was no aggression in it. The staff worked seamlessly at the various stations, calling out a "yes, Chef" in response to Drew's commands.

Drew had joked about slowing Hannah down, but farming had nothing on this. It probably came in waves, but the hustle was enough to make her head spin. She wouldn't choose it for herself in a million years, but she had a newfound respect for Drew's mastery.

Realizing she'd lost track of how long she'd stayed there, staring, Hannah hurried out. By the time she got home, the aromas of the food had crept into her senses. As much as she liked the idea of a nice shower and a cozy dinner on the sofa, she didn't think she could wait that long.

She put the berries and cream in the fridge to stay cold and, spying a bottle of Chardonnay, decided to pour a glass. She took it and her dinner out to the back deck, joined by an ever-optimistic Daisy. After carefully removing the lid, Hannah sighed. It looked so good.

She plucked a pea pod out with her fingers and popped it into her mouth. As promised, it still had the crunch she wanted in a sugar snap. But it had a hint of char and a kiss of garlic that was unexpected. Heaven. The chicken might have been the most delicious chicken she'd ever had and the polenta was both luxurious and comforting, even after the twenty-minute ride home. Probably for the best no one was there to see her, because she ate it all way too fast. Except for one bite.

"I don't really want to share, but I love you." Daisy took the chicken gently from her fingers, but then swallowed it whole. "You're supposed to savor."

She scraped the last of the polenta from the bottom of the container with her fork, satisfied but a little sad. Oh, but there was still the strawberry shortcake. That could wait until she was clean and in comfy clothes. She showered, her thoughts swirling between the dessert waiting for her and the image of Drew's face—a mixture of amusement and approval—when she joked about wanting two servings. The whole thing left her aroused and confused. Not confused about being aroused, she just couldn't remember the last time she'd been so drawn to someone.

She dried off and slipped into cotton pajama pants and a tank top. She padded back to the kitchen barefoot, grabbing the containers from the fridge. She opened the shortcake and contemplated having only one. With a shrug, she dumped the entire cup of strawberries over them and scraped a giant mound of whipped cream on top.

Hannah took the whole thing to the couch and flipped on the television. Her phone chirped just as she took the first bite. She took a second to enjoy it—the slight crunch the cornmeal imparted on the shortcake and the sweet-tart juiciness of the berries went together perfectly, complemented by the sweet cream. God, it was good.

She picked up her phone. Drew. Just seeing the name on her screen made her smile. *How was your dinner?*

Hannah looked from her phone to the strawberry shortcake. She snapped a photo of the inelegant mound of it and attached it to her reply. *Amazing, but it's got nothing on dessert.*

She took another bite while she waited for Drew's response. She

hadn't told Drew, but strawberry shortcake was one of her favorite desserts of all time. And this was, hands down, the best she'd ever eaten.
Good. You deserve a great meal after the days you put in.

There was something sweet about the comment. It gave Hannah a warm, fuzzy feeling until she realized warm and fuzzy was not what she wanted from Drew. Right? She shook her head. Right. *Well, I can certainly put away my share. I'm eating all this shortcake, BTW.*

Drew didn't respond right away. She had a flash of disappointment, then shook her head. Drew would still be in the middle of dinner service. She took another bite of dessert and started flipping through the handful of channels she grudgingly paid for. She settled on a Mets game, flipping between that and a yard makeover show on HGTV.

It might be fun to give her yard a little sprucing up. Not like the crazy, over-the-top things on the show, but a small water feature shouldn't be too much work. And it would attract birds. Maybe she could ask Jeremiah to help her put one in.

A text interrupted her musings. This one was from Jenn. *Are you in bed yet?*

She chuckled at the question. It wasn't unheard of for her to go to bed by 8:30 at this time of year. She sent the picture she'd taken for Drew. *Better than sleep.*

That led to a litany of questions about whether her berries were ripe yet, why Jenn hadn't been invited over, and why it was in a takeout container. Hannah filled her in, got another slew of questions about why she hadn't mentioned Drew making her dinner and what it all meant. Hannah offered what she thought were perfectly reasonable explanations and endured some teasing about Drew having a thing for her. It was fun, as long as she didn't think too hard about the meaning or implications.

She finished every last morsel of dessert and bid Jenn a good night. Still nothing from Drew. Which was fine. She was working. And it wasn't like they were dating. Or flirting. Or anything, really.

Hannah brought her dishes to the kitchen, rinsing the containers and tossing them in the recycle bin, then pouring a glass of water to take to bed. The moon was nearly full, so she made her way upstairs without turning on any lights, switched on her fan, and crawled under the covers. Daisy curled up on her bed with a contented sigh. She'd just started to doze when her phone went off.

I so enjoy a woman with a healthy appetite. Looking forward to next week when we can finally share a meal. Have a good night.

There was nothing overly suggestive in the comment. It made no sense that her body would respond the way it did. But telling herself that didn't seem to make a lick of difference. She returned the wishes for a good night and set her phone on the nightstand. Then she rolled onto her back and stared at the ceiling. She was looking forward to next week, too.

Chapter Ten

The days of late June clocked in as some of the longest, but that didn't stop them from flying by. Hannah worked twelve-hour days, breaking up physical labor with time at the farm stand. Summer was shaping up to be sunny and warmer than average. Most of the crops loved it, even if the spinach and arugula kept bolting and needing to be replanted. They'd have tomatoes by mid-July if her irrigation didn't put too much pressure on the wells.

Clare was in the final days of the school year, so she spent almost every afternoon at the farm, managing the stand and working on the website. Her energy was such a welcome addition. Not that the rest of the staff lagged, but something about teenage zeal proved infectious.

And, of course, she had that date to look forward to.

Well, maybe a date. Drew hadn't called it a date. And despite her back and forth with Jenn, if they were in any sort of gray area, Hannah needed to keep them firmly out of date territory. Because dates might lead to kissing and kissing might lead to sex and having sex with a cocky city-dweller went against every ounce of sense she had.

Even though thinking about spending time alone with Drew made her insides fluttery. Even if, the week before, she'd given way too much thought to what she'd wear. Even if, the night of, she consciously dabbed perfume behind each ear and between her breasts.

She told herself for the hundredth time it didn't mean anything as she climbed into her truck and headed to the address Drew had given her. She pulled in and found Drew sitting on her porch, looking easy and relaxed and every bit the part of the casual country butch. Her throat went dry and she had to remind herself Drew wasn't that at all. She might look like Hannah's fantasy come to life, but that whole thing about looks being deceiving? It was a saying for a reason.

Snap out of it. She rolled down the window and waved a greeting.

Drew returned the wave and stood. She'd imagined what Hannah would look like behind the wheel, but it was even better in reality. Whatever she had on showed off her arms, and her hair hung loose around her shoulders.

She walked over to the passenger side, set her things on the wide bench seat, and climbed in. It was probably good to have so much space between them. It made it less likely she'd lean over and kiss Hannah's freckled shoulder. "Hi there."

Hannah smiled. "Hi. I hope you haven't been waiting long."

"Just enjoying the afternoon. I've never had a porch before."

"I bought my house for the deck more than the inside."

Drew chuckled. "I'm beginning to understand the appeal."

"All set?"

She buckled her seat belt, one of those old metal ones with the release button in the middle. "All set."

Hannah backed out of the driveway. With Hannah's attention on the road, Drew gave herself permission to study her. The juxtaposition of the old truck and Hannah in a bright fuchsia sundress made her smile. It should have been jarring, but somehow it suited Hannah perfectly.

Not wanting to be caught staring, she turned her gaze to the scenery. Sunlight dappled the road, shifting as the breeze ruffled the trees. Flashes of the lake appeared as the road curved and dipped. Winter was probably an absolute bitch, but Drew was ready to concede that summer upstate had a lot going for it.

Hannah turned off Route 89 onto an unmarked road that ran between row after row of grapevines. They'd been just starting to bud when she arrived but now boasted lush green leaves. A pair of workers in straw hats worked in one of the rows, stripping some of the leaves away. At the sight of the truck, both waved, which Hannah returned.

"Do you know them?" Drew asked.

"Pete and Bill. They own the Thirsty Owl. We're crashing one of their lookout spots."

Drew chuckled. "Is there anyone in a twenty-mile radius you don't know?"

"Plenty of people. But they're old friends from my farmer's market days. Our stalls were right next to each other."

Drew tried to think of something comparable in the city. She had other chef friends, considered herself friendly with some of the suppliers she'd met along the way. But even within the restaurants where she'd worked, she'd lacked that casual sense of community. Did it have to do with her line of work or geography? Or was it her?

"Why do you look sad all of a sudden?" Hannah looked at her with concern.

"Huh?" She shook her head. "Oh, nothing. I'm fine. Not sad, just reminiscing I guess."

"Okay." Hannah didn't seem convinced, but she didn't press it. She turned again, this time onto either a driveway or a dirt road. She slowed, but the truck still jostled with ruts and potholes. "Not much farther."

They pulled into a clearing, surrounded by vineyard to the back, trees and undergrowth to the left. In front of them, a wide vista of Cayuga Lake and the rolling hills on the opposite shore. "Wow."

"You asked for the best spot."

The view chased away any melancholy thoughts. "And you definitely delivered. This is gorgeous."

Hannah cut the engine and unlatched her seatbelt. "It's not technically public, but I could put in a good word for you. As long as they recognize your car, you'll be fine."

Drew studied her, decided to take a chance. "Or I could just always come here with you."

Hannah smiled and, if Drew wasn't mistaken, blushed. "I guess we'll have to see how good your picnic is."

She liked where this was going. "Shall we?"

Drew grabbed the picnic basket and cooler. Hannah pulled a blanket from behind the bench seat. She spread it out and took the basket. They sat down, Hannah slipping off her sandals and tucking her feet beneath her. The view of the lake had nothing on that.

"I hope you're hungry."

Hannah quirked a brow. "I'm a farmer. I'm always hungry."

Drew laughed, both at the sentiment and the phrase. She opened the cooler first, taking out the Riesling she'd chilled the night before. "I hope you're thirsty, too. Although I feel bad drinking the competition's product on winery grounds."

"Your secret is safe with me."

She handed over the bottle and corkscrew. "If you open this, I'll get glasses."

Hannah opened the wine and watched as Drew pulled out not only wineglasses but plates and silverware from the basket. "I hope you know I'd be just as happy with plastic utensils and paper towels."

Drew winked. "Now where's the charm in that?"

She poured two glasses, then handed the bottle back to Drew, who tucked it into the now empty cooler. Between the cooler and the picnic basket, Drew had set out no fewer than ten takeout containers and plastic tubs. "Do you always go overboard?"

"I believe if something is worth doing, it's worth doing right." Her tone was playful but held the promise of double meaning.

Hannah swallowed. "I can't disagree with you there."

Drew opened containers. Cheese and salami, sliced baguette, a farro salad, fruit, pickled vegetables, and more. They took turns filling their plates and Hannah dove in. "This is really good."

"I tried to keep it simple." Drew grinned. "I know how you feel about fussy food."

Hannah laughed. "I'm pretty sure simple picnic fare is sandwiches and a bag of chips, but I'm not complaining."

"Well, you have to grant me artistic license at least."

"I suppose." She helped herself to more of the farro. It had radishes and pistachios and what tasted like mint. She'd never have dreamed of putting those things together, but it worked. More, it tapped into all the things that were fresh and available at the moment. "I'm sorry I ever questioned your talent."

"Did you?" Drew's tone was more curious than offended.

"Not your talent, exactly. More whether you'd fit in here, be good for Nick's restaurant."

"And the verdict?"

"You're good."

Drew laughed, a low, rich sound that drove Hannah nuts, in a good way. "You're kind of stingy with the compliments."

Hannah straightened her shoulders. Probably not a good idea to do the flirty banter thing with Drew, but she couldn't seem to help it. "You're talented. But even more importantly, you're good in the kitchen. The staff seems to really like you, the customers love you. Nick is so pleased. That's what matters."

"I don't think I realized how close you two are."

"He was super tight with my older brothers when I was growing up. You'd think that would be enough to make us mortal enemies."

Drew tipped her head. "I guess that would depend on how much he tortured you."

"Very little." Hannah smiled at the memory. "If anything, he was a calming presence. I had such a crush on him but never wanted to kiss him. It's part of what helped me realize I was a lesbian."

That got her the laugh again. Drew reached into the cooler, topped off their wine. "I'm sure that was very confusing."

"I wish I still had my diary from that time. What about you? How did you realize you were attracted to women?"

Drew let out a sigh, the kind that came with a good memory. "I had it bad for my third-grade teacher."

"Seriously? You knew that young?"

She shrugged. "Not what it meant. More in retrospect. I was kind of in awe of her, but not in the way other girls in my class wanted to grow up and be her."

"That makes sense." Hannah tried to think of a similar feeling. It definitely hadn't come that early, but she could remember having strong attachments to her girlfriends growing up, especially the tomboy types.

Drew looked out over the water. "I was terrified to come out. My family is pretty Catholic and I was scared of disappointing them, especially after my father died."

The comment jarred Hannah, a stark reminder of how little she knew about Drew. "I didn't realize you'd lost your father. I'm sorry."

Drew smiled, offered a casual shrug. "I hardly remember him. He was in the Marines and was killed in a helicopter crash when I was six."

"Oh, wow. Still, I'm sure it was hard." She didn't get along with her father, but she also couldn't imagine him not being around.

"It was harder for my mom, I think. She had a lot of help from her mother, but she raised me on her own."

"You're close to her, aren't you?"

"Very. She sacrificed so much so that I could have opportunities, everything I could possibly need. I owe her and my Grann everything."

Hannah thought about her relationship with her family. Fraught might be an overstatement, but she had nothing like the closeness Drew seemed to share with hers. Might it be different if her father weren't such an overwhelming force in the equation? As soon as the thought crossed her mind, she banished it. She might not see eye to eye with him on everything, but she'd never wish him ill. And just like Drew alluded to, the financial strain on top of the loss would be devastating. No, she didn't want to think about that at all.

"Are you okay? You looked a million miles away just then."

"Sorry. My mind wandered." Hannah took a sip of her wine and grabbed a slice of baguette. "I'm good. Tell me about culinary school, assuming you went to culinary school, of course."

Drew grinned and launched into the story of her first day. She joked about the incessant competition, especially with her male counterparts. It was no wonder she had that chip on her shoulder. Hannah might not get the appeal, but she could appreciate it was part of the culture. And she could definitely relate to the desire to do something well, proving the naysayers wrong in the process. Especially something seen as men's work.

They polished off the wine and put a dent in the massive amount of food. Drew packed up containers and they sat on the blanket, side by side, gazing out at the lake. They were on the wrong side to see the sunset, too, but it cast a soft, warm glow over everything.

Hannah felt her body relax. Like, really relax. The work of the day, the work waiting for her tomorrow, melted away. The sexual tension that seemed ever-present didn't vanish, but it settled into a gentle simmer, the kind of delicious anticipation that came with looking forward to something really good. Hannah didn't try to chase it away or figure it out. She simply sat and enjoyed it.

When Drew took her hand, it felt like the most natural thing in the world. She felt Drew's gaze shift from the lake to her. Hannah turned to meet it. Drew's stare managed to be both intense and playful. It flicked down to her mouth, then back to her eyes.

Hannah knew the kiss was coming. She could have stopped it. But she really, really didn't want to.

Drew's mouth grazed hers. Hannah's lips parted unconsciously, asking for more. Drew obliged with a teasing play of tongue. So much better than she'd imagined, fantasized about. So much more dangerous. She broke the kiss. "This probably isn't a good idea."

Drew pulled back, tried to process Hannah's words. It wasn't easy, over the roaring in her ears and other parts of her body. "What? Why?" She hated the needy edge that had crept into her voice.

"We work together."

"Not really." Surely, that wasn't the real reason.

"We do. And it's through Nick. I care about him way too much to mess with his head chef."

Drew frowned. "Who said anything about messing with anyone? We're adults. And unless I'm mistaken, the attraction is mutual."

"Until it isn't. Then there's a mess."

She didn't know which bothered her more—the implication her attraction was ephemeral or the idea that Hannah's was. "I don't think that needs to be the case. I'm not planning to turn into an asshole. So unless you are..."

Hannah closed her eyes and shook her head slowly. "It's more complicated than that."

"Look, I'm not trying to be contrary, but I happen to think two mature people can explore being attracted to each other without it turning into a high-stakes negotiation." She meant it, too. Sure, she'd had her fair share of misfires and the awkwardness of one-way feelings, but it didn't have to be that way. Hell, she'd go out of her way to make sure it didn't. She decided to try a different tactic. "I like you."

Hannah angled her head, looking suspicious. "I like you, too."

Realization struck. Drew tapped her index finger to her lips, then pointed at Hannah. "But you didn't want to. Don't want to, still."

Hannah folded her arms. "That's not true."

Drew raised a brow.

"Mostly not true."

"And you do now and you don't like it. I get it. I've been there. I'm not going to pressure you. It's gross and not how I operate. But I hope you'll reconsider. Eventually."

Hannah dropped her hands into her lap and smiled. "Thanks."

"And I'm not just saying that because I want to get in your pants." She did want to get in Hannah's pants, but it wasn't her only, or even primary, motivation.

Hannah laughed, breaking the tension of the moment. "Good to know."

"I'll let you take me home now. Not because I don't want to keep spending time with you, but because I know you get up at an ungodly hour. And I probably took you away from your work today." And because she wanted to keep things from getting awkward.

"We probably should head back." Hannah's voice had a slight wistful quality to it, which Drew took as a good sign.

They packed everything back into the truck and climbed in. Hannah was quiet, but it seemed to be reflective more than uncomfortable. Drew hoped it meant Hannah was considering what she said.

When Hannah pulled into her driveway, she opened the passenger door, but paused. "Thanks for sharing such a special spot with me."

Hannah smiled. "I could come up with a few more I could show you if you're bringing the picnic."

"You name the day and the place and I'll be there." She cringed. "Name the Monday, or odd Tuesday, actually."

"You got it."

Drew gathered her things and headed inside, a strange mix of pent-up energy and contentment settling inside her. It seemed like she and Hannah were closer, but that closeness brought into focus the things that kept them apart. She wanted to respect Hannah's wishes, her boundaries. But with the taste of Hannah's mouth lingering on hers, the warmth of Hannah's body burned into her brain, all Drew could think about was wanting to kiss her again.

Chapter Eleven

I've got something that's going to make you smile.
Drew read the text and smiled. *Really hard not to make a suggestive comment right now.*
Hannah answered with the eye roll emoji. Followed by, *I'm talking about tomatoes.*
She might have been interested in something more salacious, but Hannah was right. The prospect of tomatoes did make her happy. *Can't wait.*
If you want to swing by this evening instead of tomorrow, I'll show you my favorite way to have them.
Drew sighed. She couldn't stop herself from thinking about what might be her favorite ways to have Hannah. Saying so might be pushing her luck. *What time?*
We'll knock off by 7. Or you can come early and pick your own.
She hadn't picked anything since the day she spent learning the workings of the farm. She wasn't in a rush to have another full day of farm labor, but picking tomatoes seemed easy enough. And it felt like she'd been waiting on them for fucking ever. *Be there by 5.*
It was only three now. She'd planned to finish laundry and head to the brewery for a beer, but the prospect of spending some time with Hannah had far more appeal. Did the invitation mean sharing a meal together? Hannah had been hesitant to do that in the two weeks since their picnic, or perhaps more accurately, how that picnic ended.
If she closed her eyes, she could still summon the incredible softness of Hannah's mouth, the way she tasted like summer laced with wine and strawberries. The skin of her thigh, the lines of her neck. The abrupt end to what she'd hoped was just the beginning.

The sound of her phone jarred her back to the moment. She swiped a finger across the screen. "Hey, Grann."

"How's my country girl today?"

Drew chuckled. "Fixin' to go pick some tomatoes."

Grann let out a contented hum. "I can't remember the last time I had a tomato right from the vine."

"Aw, come on. We get fresh stuff in the city."

"Child, until you've eaten a tomato still warm from the sun, don't talk to me about fresh."

"You and Manman should come up for a visit." The words were out of her mouth before she'd thought it through, but Drew warmed to the idea immediately. Why hadn't she thought of that before?

Grann laughed. "Not two months ago, you insisted you wouldn't live there long enough to make it worth the trouble. Are you changing your tune?"

She shook her head, remembering the conversation. "Not changing my tune. I've just decided upstate in the summer is rather charming. You should come enjoy it while I've got a place we can all stay."

"Your Manman will be done with summer school in a couple of weeks. Let me see if I can talk her into it."

"I'll do some research. I think there's a bus that goes direct to the town just south of here. You wouldn't even have to drive." Her mother drove, but only to work and when absolutely necessary. Not having to navigate out of the city and drive for four hours would up the appeal considerably.

Grann hummed again, then asked about Drew's work, her house. Drew got caught up on the neighborhood, including two babies, one divorce, and one quick and dirty elopement. She'd not lived at home for a good ten years, but the news and gossip made her homesick—for the place, but also for life before the complexities of adulthood.

Drew ended the call and took a moment to laugh at herself. She couldn't remember the last time she'd felt so nostalgic. Living in the country was making her soft. She shook off the idea and got ready to head to the farm, including sunscreen. She probably didn't need it for only a couple of hours, but she didn't want to risk Hannah making fun of her again.

On the way there, she put down the windows and cranked the music loud. The temperature had crept close to ninety earlier in the afternoon, but it was already inching downward, making the air pleasantly warm rather than oppressively hot. She'd never put a lot of stock in the idea of urban heat islands, but living here made her accept they existed.

She turned into the parking lot, having to take a spot along the driveway to the back fields. Word must be out that tomatoes were picking. She decided to stop in at the barn first. If Hannah wasn't there, whoever was would know where to find her. The farm stand was hopping—kids running around, people clutching baskets and canvas bags full of produce, and several people carrying large plastic totes. She'd forgotten that Monday was farm share day.

"Hey, Drew."

She turned toward the voice and found Hannah's sister smiling at her from behind the register. "Hey, Clare. Do you know where Hannah is?"

"Far field, by the picnic area."

"Thanks."

She escaped the bustle of the retail space and headed toward the back vegetable patch. Fewer people were picking produce than buying it, but the rows were dotted with people hunched over plants or surveying their options. She spotted Hannah right away, wearing a floppy straw hat and chatting with a couple who looked overdressed for picking vegetables.

As if sensing Drew's gaze, Hannah looked her way. Her body instantly responded and she did her best to ignore it. She made her way toward Hannah, exchanging hellos and nods with the people she passed. By the time she got there, the couple had moved down the row and were eagerly filling a small basket with jalapeños.

"I thought I might be getting first dibs, but it looks like the word is out."

Hannah laughed. "You can thank Clare for that. Her fresh crop alerts seem to be working."

"That's too bad." She shook her head in mock disapproval. "I'll have to see if I can get some kind of advance notice."

"I can't be caught playing favorites, you know."

Hannah saying such a thing implied Drew might fall into the category of favorites. That made her happy. "I wouldn't tell. It could be our little secret."

Hannah shook her head, but it was accompanied by a playful smile and her eyes sparkled. "Well, you are usually the first person to show up at the market in the mornings."

"That should earn me some special consideration, don't you think?"

"Maybe."

Drew got the feeling they were talking about more than first pick of the day's produce. But she wanted to tread lightly. She'd already scared Hannah off once. "It looks like there are plenty still to pick today."

Hannah grinned. "Plenty. Well, plenty cherries. You'll be able to snag a few heirlooms, but probably not enough for the restaurant for a few more days."

"I'll take it."

Hannah handed her a basket and pointed down a row. "There are several varieties. Sweet 100, Sun Golds, Chocolate Cherry."

Drew nodded and surveyed the plants. There had to be at least fifty in this row alone. She could see bite-size fruits poking out between the leaves, just waiting to be picked. She envisioned them in a simple caprese salad, or maybe a panzanella. Or roasted, their juices caramelizing to sweet and tangy perfection. "Do I get to sample as I go?"

Hannah moved the basket she'd been holding to her hip and studied Drew with sudden intensity. "Have you ever had a tomato right off the vine?"

Drew smirked. "I take it you mean a vine still attached to the plant."

"I do." Hannah leaned down. When she stood, two perfectly tiny tomatoes were in her hand, one red and one orange. "Here. Try these."

"You know, I was just on the phone with my grandmother and she was carrying on about the same thing." Drew popped one of the tomatoes in her mouth. The flavor exploded on her tongue, the quintessential taste of summer. And just like Grann had described, still warm from the sun. "Wow."

"I know it's hard to wait until July, but it's worth it, right?" Hannah took one from her basket and put it in her mouth. She closed her eyes and Drew watched the pleasure play across her face.

Although Hannah's enjoyment had nothing to do with her, Drew's body reacted. It reminded her of the moment after the kiss, before Hannah's defenses went up. It was the same kind of unguarded pleasure, sensuous and pure. "So worth it."

Hannah opened her eyes. Her smile remained, but the moment was gone. "I've got a flat already in the barn for the restaurant, so whatever you pick now is for your own enjoyment."

Her stomach dropped like the comment was foreplay. Relax, dude, she's talking about tomatoes. "So, was that it?"

"Was what it?"

"Right off the vine. Is that your favorite way to eat them?"

"No." The playful exasperation was a good look on her. "I've got a couple of heirlooms stashed in the barn for us."

Drew liked her use of the word "us," the intimacy it sort of implied. She'd take what she could get. "I'm intrigued."

"It does require going to my house when we're done here. Is that okay with you?"

She resisted the urge to chuckle. Not exactly how she'd hoped to score an invite to Hannah's place. Then again, nothing about Hannah was what she expected. And whether she wanted to admit it or not, it turned out she kind of liked it that way. "Absolutely."

They picked for an hour, then stopped by the barn to make sure everything was settled for the night. Clare had already counted money and stacked the credit card receipts. Hannah took an envelope for depositing at the bank, then secured the rest in the office safe. She locked up and then gestured to her truck. "Do you want to follow me? It's not far."

Drew nodded. "Sounds good."

❖

Hannah pulled into her driveway, Drew right behind. It occurred to her as she was sending the text that it carried with it an invitation to her house. But she hadn't changed her mind, or the wording. And now here they were. Her insides felt like a bundle of nerves, anticipating—what, exactly?

She hadn't implied anything more than a shared meal. But even as she made that argument to herself, it fell flat. There was an unspoken intimacy in what they were doing, whether it led to anything physical or not. An intimacy of her own making.

She climbed out of her truck, willing herself to offer a casual smile. Drew did not need to know the nature of her thoughts. Nor did she need to know just how attracted to her Hannah remained.

"This is a great place," Drew said.

"Thanks." It was the polite thing to say, but she got the feeling Drew really meant it. She reached back into her truck to grab the tomatoes.

Drew peered into the basket. "What do we have?"

"A Big Rainbow, a Brandywine, and a Cherokee Purple."

Drew grinned. "Be still my beating heart."

She led Drew to the side door and into her kitchen. She watched Drew take it all in. Hannah wouldn't call her style country, but she wondered if that was how Drew would categorize it.

"You've got a nice setup here."

"It was a disaster when I moved in. I like to cook enough that I had to do something."

"Yeah. Definitely a perk of buying. I mean, my place here is decent, but the kitchen in my apartment back home was seriously cramped." Drew smiled. "So, what are you making me for dinner?"

"You have to promise to embrace the simplicity, okay?" Hannah cringed at the sudden self-consciousness in her voice.

"The best ingredients are always better when allowed to shine. I thought you knew that about me already."

Hannah sighed. Right. Nothing to be self-conscious about. "I do."

"So, what are you making me?"

She lifted her chin. "A BLT."

Drew's eyes narrowed and, for a second, Hannah read the gesture as disappointment. Then Drew grinned from ear to ear. "I love BLTs. I cannot think of a better application."

The response felt so genuine, she didn't feel the need to equivocate further. "Oh, good. I didn't make the bread myself, but I got a fresh loaf from Ithaca Bakery. It's probably better than I could manage anyway."

"Sounds perfect. Utterly perfect."

She went to the fridge, pulled out thick-cut bacon and the jar of mayo. "Let me get the bacon in the oven and then we can relax, open a beer." She turned to look at Drew and found her making a face. "What is it? What's wrong?"

Drew shook her head. "Nothing. Nothing's wrong."

"You're lying."

Drew smiled. "How would you feel about me contributing something to the meal?"

She set down the jar and resisted crossing her arms. "What do you mean?"

"Do you keep eggs and olive oil on hand?"

Hannah slumped. "You're judging my mayo."

"Not judging. I have nothing against the jarred stuff. But if these tomatoes are half as good as the ones I tried earlier, they deserve the best."

Hannah chuckled. "It's hard to argue with that."

"And we get to be in the kitchen together, which is always more fun."

Drew seemed to mean it. But was she talking about cooking, or the company? "I'd have thought you were the type who loathed sharing a kitchen."

Drew folded her arms and looked offended. "I've shared the tiniest kitchens with half a dozen people. And I grew up cooking at my Grann's knee."

"Okay, okay. I stand corrected." Hannah lifted both hands defensively, but smiled. This was fine. Relaxed. Nothing sexual or romantic about it.

"Does that mean you'll let me make mayo?"

Drew's eyes sparkled and Hannah's reaction was nothing but sexual and romantic. Great. "Yes. Tell me what you need."

Drew's smile completed the whole dangerously attractive look. "A bowl and a whisk."

She got out the tools and ingredients Drew requested. While Drew worked, she rinsed some baby lettuce and put it through the salad spinner, then sliced the tomatoes.

Drew glanced over. "I'll happily eat whatever doesn't fit on the sandwiches."

"I like the way you think." She set some aside for the sandwiches and dressed what was left with olive oil, salt, and pepper.

Half an hour later, they sat on Hannah's back deck, each with a large sandwich, a tomato salad, and a local IPA. Drew took a huge bite, closed her eyes, and groaned. "Oh, my God."

Hannah took a bite of her own sandwich. She didn't audibly groan, but her sentiments were the same. "I don't know what it is about this combination, but it gets me every time."

Drew finished chewing her second bite, licked tomato juice from her thumb. "It's everything in one package. Crunchy and soft, salty and tangy and sweet. Oh, and fat. Fat makes everything taste better."

"High praise from a fancy chef."

"You've got me wondering if I can find a way to put BLTs on the menu at the restaurant."

Hannah smirked. "If anyone can, it would be you."

They finished the sandwiches, then decided to split a third. Hannah pulled two more beers from the fridge. The sun was setting, so she lit citronella candles to ward off mosquitoes.

After polishing off the second round, Drew slumped back in her chair and put a hand on her stomach. "Have I gorged myself enough for you to know, without hesitation, that I approve of BLTs?"

"I'd say so. And I'm completely converted to homemade mayo. Which is a rather dangerous development, actually." Among other things.

Drew waved a hand. "All things are okay in moderation."

"Is that a rule for food or more of a life philosophy?" She was skirting the boundaries of flirtation now.

"I think you can apply it to most things, don't you?" Her playful smile sent Hannah's pulse skittering.

"I suppose." She tipped her head to the side. "It's just that some things are more addictive than others."

"You have a point there. But I guess it's a risk I'm willing to take. I'm so over the notion of self-denial as a virtue." The playfulness vanished. In its place, a piercing intensity that skirted nothing. This was flirtation, pure and simple.

"Ah." Hannah wanted to say more, but words eluded her.

"You don't agree?"

"No." Hannah shook her head. Her throat had gone inexplicably dry. "I do. Mostly."

Drew pushed her plate to the side and leaned forward, resting her elbows on the table. "Do you like to indulge yourself, Hannah?"

The way Drew said her name was almost too much. She imagined what it would feel like against her ear. Drew's breath warm against her skin, her hand—

"Too personal?"

"Huh?" Hannah blinked.

"I asked if you were one for indulging yourself. You didn't answer, so I wondered if it was too personal a question."

"Oh." Hannah tried to collect herself. "No."

"No to indulgence?" Drew sat back. "That's too bad."

She might be playing with fire, but she wasn't going to be dishonest. She leaned forward, mirroring Drew's earlier posture. "No, it wasn't too personal. I'm quite fond of indulging, actually."

Desire flicked through Drew's eyes. "I see."

"It's just that some things are hard to enjoy in moderation. Ice cream, for example." Or you, she almost added.

Drew chuckled. "So, what do you do?"

"When the opportunity presents itself, I don't say no." Hannah shrugged casually, as though she meant nothing beyond her penchant for sweets. "But I also don't keep it in the house to tempt me at all hours."

Drew laughed. The sound, low and seductive, had no hint of teasing in it. "I'll have to keep that in mind."

The conversation lulled and they fell into a comfortable silence. Well, not uncomfortable, at least. Sexual tension remained in the air, but more of a gentle hum than a crackle. Dusk set in and fireflies dotted the perimeter of the yard.

"I don't think I ever saw a firefly before this summer," Drew said.

"Really?" The idea gave Hannah a pang of sadness.

"I'd never even thought about them, really, to even know what I was missing."

Hannah sighed. She couldn't imagine living anywhere so awash in streetlights that it was never fully dark. Why anyone would choose to live in a city baffled her. "Sounds like you might be saying life in the country has at least a few things going for it."

Drew turned. Even in the dim light of dusk, her eyes were full of meaning. "It certainly does."

Chapter Twelve

Hannah stepped into the shower, bone tired. She loved the hot days of summer when everything seemed to grow heavy and ripe at once, but it was killer on the back. And the legs and arms and feet and pretty much everything else. And the rush to get in a day's worth of work before a late-afternoon thunderstorm only intensified that fact.

She kept the temperature lukewarm but let the water pelt her skin. After washing her hair, she squirted a generous blob of honeysuckle shower gel onto a loofah and scrubbed away the dirt and sweat of the day. By the time she emerged, she wanted nothing more than a cold beer and a nap in her hammock. Unfortunately, it was pouring down rain and she had plans.

At least the plans were good.

She slipped on a pair of shorts and light V-neck tee, then decided on sneakers instead of flip-flops. The dash to her truck didn't quite soak her through. She plopped the bottle of rosé on the seat next to her and started the short drive to Jenn's.

Despite the intensity of the storm, the worst of it seemed to pass before she arrived. As steam rolled off the pavement, she said a prayer of thanks they'd managed to get so many tomatoes picked before it blew through. After months of weeding and watering and care, split skins and bruised fruit drove her absolutely nuts.

She went to Jenn's side door, knocking but not waiting for a reply. Jenn stood in her kitchen, chopping garlic. She smiled at Hannah over her shoulder. "You made it."

"Did you think I wouldn't?"

Jenn set down her knife. "No, but it was really nasty here for a bit. I thought you might wait it out."

"I was afraid if I sat down, I might fall asleep."

Jenn laughed. "Rough day?"

"Great day. We're having a killer season."

"But it's killer on you."

Hannah shrugged. "You'll never catch me complaining about a bountiful harvest."

"I know. So put up your feet and take a load off. Wine?"

Hannah handed her the bottle. "Yes, please."

When they were seated on Jenn's sofa, underneath the blissful breeze of the ceiling fan and with their feet on the coffee table, Jenn turned to her. "So, tell me everything."

"I'm not sure there's much to tell."

"Liar. You had her to your house for dinner. There is most definitely something to tell."

"I think we're friends. It was flirty, but she didn't try to kiss me again, if that's what you're asking."

Jenn gave her an exasperated look. "She probably isn't going to. You put the brakes on, you have to be the one to restart the sexy train."

"The sexy train?" Hannah raised a brow. Who said that?

"Yes, you got on it. And you never actually got off. You just signaled a stop."

"That might be the cheesiest analogy I've ever heard." Annoying in its accuracy, but cheesy.

Jenn ran her finger through the condensation on her glass and pointed at Hannah. "Maybe, but you're deflecting. And stringing that poor woman along."

Hannah sat up straight, almost sloshing her wine all over. "I'm not doing that." She looked at Jenn. "Am I?"

"More like holding the door but not inviting her in."

Even teasing, she didn't like the sound of that. But she let the words sink in. It was exactly what she was doing. Because she was interested in Drew. Even if she thought it a bad idea, she couldn't bring herself to close the door on the possibility of something happening between them. Being a tease did not sit well. "Ugh."

"You know I'm not trying to make you feel bad, right?"

"I know." She didn't need Jenn to make her, she could manage all on her own.

"It's just so unlike you. You're always decisive."

"Yeah." She was decisive. Not a trait she came by naturally, either. She'd had to work at it and come to terms with knowing what she wanted out of life wasn't going to fall in her lap. Being able to articulate it, taking action to make it happen, were her biggest assets. A mild disgust settled in the pit of her stomach.

"I can see your wheels turning. This isn't a value judgment thing. Relationships aren't like work or other things."

"Relationships." At what point did talking about Drew turn into talking about relationships?

"Relax. I'm not implying you're in one, or should be."

She couldn't decide which was worse—Jenn using the word "relationships" or how instantly it freaked her out. "But I've crossed a line with Drew. We're definitely more than two people with a professional connection."

Jenn shrugged. "Whatever it is, and whatever you want to call it, is up to you. I'm just saying you should maybe worry a little less."

"Oh, well, as long as you're just saying." It kind of felt like she wasn't worrying enough. Like, if she let her guard down, she might get so caught up in Drew she might lose sight of herself completely.

Jenn laughed. "Shall we eat? I promise not to torture you with any more talk of relationships."

"Yes." Hannah nodded. "And yes."

They went back to the kitchen. Jenn waved off her offer of help and assembled the bruschetta. If BLTs were her favorite use of tomatoes, this came in a close second. She'd gone so far as to adopt Jenn's version—with garlic, balsamic, and basil, topped with fresh mozzarella—as her own. They filled plates and returned to the sofa, eating with their fingers and moaning about how good it was.

"What about you? Anything shaking in your dating world?"

Jenn rolled her eyes. "I've gone back to the app."

Hannah chuckled at the euphemism for Tinder, as well as Jenn's sullen delivery. "You don't seem happy about it."

"I've decided for the time being that proximity is more important than perfection."

"I hear you." Hannah sighed. They'd spent a good deal of time hashing through the relative pros and cons of the various online dating platforms. None, of course, were perfect. Nor were the people who used them. Hannah had not dipped her toe in those waters, but she'd learned a lot. She told herself she didn't really have time for meeting a bunch of new people, but even without that excuse, it seemed like an ungodly amount of work. And she had more than enough of that.

"I had dinner with a woman last night." Jenn paused. "And went home with her after."

"You did what?" Hannah cringed at the high-pitched shock in her voice. She cleared her throat. "How did you not lead with that?"

Jenn shrugged. "I wanted to know about you and Drew."

Hannah gave her an exasperated look. "Spill. Now."

"Her name is Suri and she's a yoga instructor."

"Seriously? Wow. Okay. Give me the details."

She lived up the lake near Seneca Falls. Not only was she a yoga instructor, she ran her own studio. As far as Hannah was concerned, it was an important distinction. Jenn had dated a number of people who seemed to have absolutely no ambition in life. Money wasn't the be-all and end-all, but it helped if someone had a professional life and goals and stuff.

Hannah was happy for her. Truly. Even if she envied Jenn's uncomplicated approach to dating. Proximity over perfection. Was that what Drew was? The attraction was certainly there, and based on the kiss, there was chemistry to back it up. And as Drew had argued, neither of them technically worked for the other. Hannah shook her head. She'd need to think on that some more. Or, maybe, figure out a way not to think about it. For the moment, that entailed bringing her thoughts, and questions, back to Jenn. "So, you're going to see her again?"

"She's coming to my place tomorrow."

"You're already taking turns. That seems like a good sign." Hannah tamped down the flash of envy. "Is the conversation as good as the sex?"

Jenn reached over and put her hand on Hannah's arm, her I'm being serious right now gesture. "No. But only because the sex is that good."

Hannah laughed. There was no one in her life she could talk about sex with the way she did with Jenn. "Yeah?"

"She's a switch. Not an 'I'll try that if you're really into it.' Like an honest to God loves to top and bottom equally."

"Huh." Hannah hadn't given much thought to the idea. She was mostly drawn to women who identified as masculine of center, and while she liked being assertive, they were the ones doing the fucking. Since she liked it, she'd never pushed for anything else. That could prove interesting. "You got all that from one night?"

Jenn's eyes sparkled with mischief. "Well, night, morning. We made good use of our time."

Jenn's words intensified the envy to a sharper pang of longing.

Hannah's last few times hadn't been bad per se. They'd been nice. Not exactly the word she wanted to describe sex. "I'm happy for you."

"Then why do you look so deflated?" Jenn's tone was more concerned than accusing.

"Just thinking about how my own exploits have been kind of flat lately."

"I hear you." Jenn nodded slowly. "I have an idea what might fix that."

"Oh, you do?"

"Yeah. Her name is Drew. She's about yea high." Jen lifted her hand to approximate height.

Hannah rolled her eyes. "Seriously?"

Jenn shrugged. "If the shoe fits."

"Maybe you're right." The idea made her nervous, but it came with a lick of anticipation, too. The good kind of anticipation.

Jenn grinned. "I usually am."

They finished eating and brought the dishes to the kitchen. She'd given Jenn a quart of strawberries, so they sliced some up for dessert. Jenn hadn't bothered with shortcakes, which was fine by Hannah, but she'd whipped some heavy cream with a splash of Grand Marnier.

"Fancy," Hannah said.

"I do what I can." Jenn shoveled a big bite into her mouth and Hannah followed suit.

After, Hannah hugged her and wished her a good night. "Get some rest. Sounds like you're going to need it."

Jenn laughed. "I already do."

She drove home with the windows down. The rain had ended and a breeze had blown in, leaving the evening cool instead of muggy. The first stars sprinkled the dusky sky. She considered driving over to Drew's.

How would Drew respond to Hannah showing up on her doorstep? If the kiss was anything to go on, she probably wouldn't mind. Hannah imagined giving her a sultry smile. She'd step inside, close the door behind her. Then she'd press Drew against it and kiss her senseless. Drew would kiss her back, pulling her to bed. Drew would slip her shirt over her head, push her onto the mattress.

Hannah's breath caught at just how vivid the images were, the way her body responded to them. She wouldn't do it tonight. It was too forward, even for her. But the images remained achingly clear. And as she pulled into her own driveway and cut the engine, she realized not acting on them was becoming a less and less appealing option.

❖

Drew looked at her phone and smiled. Just seeing Hannah's name pop up would have done the trick, but the message made it even better. *Had some great berries tonight, but left me craving your shortcake.*

Drew tucked her tongue in her cheek as she crafted her response. *I don't want to confess those were Mariama's creation.*

As much as she wanted to wait for a reply, she had work to do. She returned her attention to the duck breast resting on the board in front of her. She sliced it on an angle and fanned the pieces over the pile of garlic mashed potatoes. She added baby carrots and leeks, then spooned the cherry and port demi-glace around the plate. She slid the plate onto the warming shelf with the pasta dish already waiting. "Table twelve."

A server appeared and whisked the plates away. She had two more tickets waiting, so she pulled more meat from the cooler under the table, heated her skillets, and started the process again. While the skin of the duck seared, she sneaked a quick peek at her phone.

Oh, right. Well, that's too bad.

She'd added a winky face, though, so Drew didn't hesitate to tease back. *Now, now. I can make shortcakes.*

Again, she tucked her phone away and tended the meat browning in front of her. She chuckled. If she caught a sous chef doing that, she'd have their head. Eh. One of the perks of being in charge. And it wasn't like she'd overcook anything.

She plated the next order just as before, then took a quick turn around the kitchen to check on her staff. They'd opened the patio, and even with the increased number of tables, things ran smoothly. It helped that Nick didn't scrimp on staff. He'd let her hire an intern as temporary prep cook, a student at the Culinary Institute home for the summer.

Satisfied she wasn't shirking, she returned to her station. And smiled to find a message from Hannah waiting for her. *I don't know. You might have to prove it.*

A trio of tickets popped out of the printer. She typed quickly. *Is that an invitation?*

A surge of tickets followed and the phone went away for

good. She had four sauté pans going, enjoying the rush of a kitchen operating on all cylinders, when the intern sliced his finger open. As injuries involving blood usually did, someone screamed and someone announced they were about to pass out. Drew made her way over to bring order to the chaos. To his credit, the intern wasn't freaking out. Someone had handed him a towel and he had his hand elevated. "Kyle, you okay?"

He looked more embarrassed than anything. "I think so."

"Let's go take a look and make sure you don't need stitches."

He flinched at the mention of stitches. "Okay."

"Carrie, clean and sanitize the station. Landon, can you handle prep while we sort this out?"

"Yes, Chef," they said in unison.

"Poppy, can you cover my station and grill?"

"Yes, Chef."

"Excellent. Everyone else, back to work. We've got customers to serve."

The command snapped everyone back to action. Her staff scattered back to their stations. A dozen tickets came in during the incident, but she wasn't worried. No one in the dining room would even sense anything was off.

She led Kyle to the hand wash station, carefully unwinding the towel from his left index finger. She had him run it under cool water for a good thirty seconds. It was long and bleeding pretty good, but it didn't seem deep. "I don't think it's too serious, but it's completely your call. If you want to get it looked at, you should."

Kyle examined the cut, poking at it lightly. "Nah. It's not that bad. Sorry I disrupted service."

He was afraid she'd be mad, or maybe more, disappointed. That was one of those things about being head chef she'd not really thought about before. Maybe it was because Kyle was African American and reminded Drew of herself a decade ago. Whatever the reason, her opinion mattered to him, and she didn't want to take that lightly. She clapped a hand on his shoulder and offered an encouraging smile. "It happens to the best of us. I've seen your knife skills. They're on point. Don't start second-guessing yourself."

The slightly lopsided grin he offered in return went all the way to his eyes. "Thanks."

"Let's get you bandaged up. My guess is that's going to start throbbing like a mother if it hasn't already. Even if you don't want to go see a doctor, you might want to call it a night."

"Do I have to?"

Drew admired his spunk. "You do not. Tight bandage and double gloves will do the trick. Just don't feel like you have something to prove."

"Nah. I'm in it for the money."

She laughed. Gritty and smart. "You're going to do well in this business, Kyle. I can feel it."

"Thanks, Chef."

She pulled out the first aid kit and wrapped up his finger. In less than ten minutes, they were back at their stations. Poppy was moving between stations with ease and everything looked under control. Drew walked up behind her and peered over her shoulder. "Should I worry about being superfluous?"

"No, Chef." Poppy moved back to her station. "Those need two more minutes apiece."

"Thanks." Drew hoped she would have loosened up by now. Then again, it hadn't even been two months. She'd done the same, keeping her guard up in a new position—hustling until it was clear she could run the kitchen if called upon. "Good work."

"Thanks, Chef."

Drew finished and plated the food. A look around told her everyone's attention appeared focused on the tasks at hand. In fact, they'd entered a lull. She checked the clock. Just after nine. It would be all downhill from here.

She checked her phone and found a pair of messages waiting for her. The first had come immediately after Drew's last comment and read, *If you're cooking, you're invited. Or I'm inviting myself. Either way.* The second came several minutes later. *But not tonight. It's my bedtime. #notaninvitation*

Drew laughed out loud. If Hannah was joking about a bedtime invitation, it meant they were legit flirting. But since it had come almost half an hour before, she resisted texting back. Jarring someone out of a sound sleep did not count as flirting.

The rest of dinner service passed without incident. Drew left the kitchen in the hands of the cleanup crew. She drove home, enjoying the summer night and the very real prospect of sharing a meal, and maybe more, with Hannah in the not-too-distant future.

Chapter Thirteen

Despite the singular nature of Hannah's thoughts about Drew, July had other ideas. She worked crazy hours and only saw Drew in passing when she stopped by to pick up the day's produce. The ripening of peppers and tomatoes brought waves of u-pickers to the farm. Between them and the people stopping by the farm stand, it felt like supply could barely keep up with demand. Hannah carefully set aside enough of everything to fill the CSA bins, knowing the people who got them were some of her most loyal customers. She even agreed to do some setting aside for Drew, especially since Drew had crafted an entire tasting menu around local tomatoes.

Drew seemed plenty busy herself. Nick had furnished the small patio off the back of the restaurant, adding two dozen more seats to the capacity of the restaurant. Things seemed to be thriving. It probably helped that they were in the peak of local produce season, but Hannah hoped it would last long after the first frost.

Drew continued to stop by the farm three mornings a week, even after Hannah offered to revisit the idea of delivery. "It's on my way," she said.

They chatted back and forth over text—flirty, but nothing more. Hannah couldn't decide how she felt about that. No, that wasn't true. She felt, when not completely exhausted from work, aroused and frustrated. That made mornings especially challenging. She'd get to the farm fresh from a good night's sleep, with the anticipation of seeing Drew at the forefront of her mind.

It was uncharted territory for her, wanting someone so badly.

As she'd taken to doing the last week or two, she busied herself in the barn instead of heading right out to the fields. Drew still had her pick of things, but what she wanted had become pretty predictable and Hannah liked to save her the trouble. She filled boxes and bins, humming to herself, until she went looking for the tomatoes and came up empty. "Where are the flats of tomatoes I set aside?"

"Um." Clare looked around. "I don't know. Were they in the cellar room?"

Hannah's stomach dropped uncomfortably. "I had them tucked behind the CSA bins."

"I haven't seen them. Ask Jeremiah, maybe?"

Hannah headed to do just that, even though she already knew the answer.

"Shit." He winced and rubbed a hand over the back of his neck. "I had Guy fill the bins yesterday and he must have seen them and thought that's what they were for."

Half the bins had been picked up the evening before. She flipped open one of the ones remaining and, sure enough, it held a generous pint of cherry tomatoes and a half dozen heirlooms. Hannah groaned. A lot of the people who got farm shares knew each other, so she couldn't go rifling and reclaiming at least part of what she owed Drew. "What are the chances we could pick three flats' worth this morning?" Hannah asked.

"Slim. Maybe one, if we were generous in our definition of ripe. The u-pickers were out in force yesterday."

He was right. The weather had been gorgeous and the flow of people constant. The farm stand receipts were higher than average by almost a third. She'd been thrilled. Now, unfortunately, she was screwed. She pulled out her phone to text Drew, trying to tamp down the dread creeping up her spine.

There's been a mix-up. Your tomatoes got sold.

No. The reply was instant and included the angry, red-faced emoji.

Hannah pinched the bridge of her nose. *Let me make some calls. I can't promise exactly what you want, but I'll try to come close.*

Okay.

Hannah groaned. It was hard to gauge the level of Drew's irritation. Was her answer terse because she was in the car? Because texts were almost always terse? Or was she truly angry? Not knowing was as bad as her being really pissed. Worse, Hannah couldn't blame anyone for the mix-up but herself. She should have labeled the boxes or put them in a much more out-of-the-way spot. Stupid.

Before she could beat up on herself more, Drew walked in, holding her phone. "What happened?"

She took a deep breath and steeled herself. "Demand has been outpacing ripening. I had some set aside for you, but I didn't label them. It's my fault."

"It's fine." Despite her words, Drew's face told Hannah it was absolutely not fine.

"If you want to take everything else, I'm going to see what kind of strings I can pull."

Drew raised a brow.

"What do you need for today?"

"If I don't change the menu?" Drew's tone was frigid.

She winced. "Yeah."

"Four flats."

"Okay. I can't promise you that, but let me see what I can do."

"You don't have to—"

Hannah cut her off. "I want to. I screwed up and I want to make it right. Barring a trip to the grocery store, I'll get you what I can."

Drew nodded. "Okay. I appreciate that."

Again, the tone of Drew's voice didn't quite match her words. Hannah squared her shoulders. "Let me help you load the rest of your order and I'll swing by the restaurant this afternoon."

They carried boxes and bins out in silence, then Drew left. Hannah returned to the barn and went to her office. She took out her phone and began pulling up contacts, starting with her old neighbors at the farmer's market. Half an hour later, she'd arranged to procure more than half of what she owed Drew. Not bad, all things considered. But not what she'd promised. And not what Drew was counting on.

She grabbed her keys and left her office. Clare was behind the register, chatting with a couple buying peppers and eggplant. She glanced at Hannah. "Did you find what you were looking for?"

Hannah shook her head. "I'm going out. I'll be back later."

Clare gave her a funny look, but she didn't stick around to explain. Raging out in front of customers would not improve her day or her mood. She made a giant loop, stopping at three different farms around her. Most didn't do retail sales, so the owners were doing her a huge favor.

She arrived back at the farm early afternoon. The farm stand had several customers and Clare said they'd had a steady stream all day.

Only a few complained about them being out of tomatoes. Her regular customers, at least, were used to things coming in waves.

Hannah went through the barn and out the back. She tracked down Jeremiah planting a new row of spinach. He stood and offered her a wave. "I managed to scrounge half a flat before the u-pickers showed up. They're in the office."

Hannah sighed. She was lucky to have found a manager who understood the business side of farming, even if he didn't like it. "Thank you. I got close to three from our generous neighbors, so it's less of a disaster than it could be."

"I'm glad." He chuckled. "It's funny how, in some parts of the country at this time of year, you can barely give them away."

Hannah laughed, appreciating for a moment the absurdity of her day. "Yeah. Don't tell me that."

Jeremiah shrugged in his easygoing way. "I'll still take my chances here."

"Agreed." Hannah looked around. She could see a few u-pickers wandering the fields, but not too many. "Do you feel like things are under control here? I want to run what I've got down to the restaurant."

"Absolutely. Go. I'm going to get these in, check on irrigation, and call it a day."

"Thank you. You're the best." She left him to his work and went back to the barn.

❖

When she'd finished stewing, Drew turned her attention to a backup menu. Or backup specials at least. If Hannah pulled together even a quarter of what she'd been expecting, she'd have enough for the salads and the cold farro.

She didn't want to admit it, but she'd gotten a little lazy. Hannah's tomatoes needed so little to shine, she'd been riding that train for close to three weeks. So even though she was annoyed, it was sort of a blessing in disguise. She considered staying mad on principle. Problems like this were the main reason she preferred a more traditional supplier. But even as she made that rationalization in her head, it fell flat.

The fact of the matter was that she had come to appreciate being so close to the source. Sure, the quality couldn't be beat, but it was more than that. She liked the anticipation of things ripening on the vine, the authenticity of getting whatever was ready to pick. And, if she was being completely honest, she liked being kept on her toes.

Tonight's specials now included a bruschetta with pepperonata—sautéed sweet peppers with garlic, capers, golden raisins, and a splash of vinegar at the end. She also pulled together a zucchini involtini, serving it on a bed of kale pesto instead of tomato sauce. If the staff response was anything to go on, she had two winners.

She had just finished instructing the prep cooks when the back door to the restaurant swung open. Hannah swept in, hair disheveled and an almost wild look in her eyes. She held a long, flat box full of tomatoes. "I've got three flats."

Even if Drew had wanted to stay mad, any hard feelings would have melted in that moment. Hannah had clearly worked herself into a frenzy to make things right. She probably would have done it for anyone, but today, she'd done it for her. "You really didn't have to."

Hannah lifted her chin. The show of pride did wicked things to Drew's libido. "I said I would come through."

She smiled, hoping to convey that her appreciation went beyond the tomatoes. "I'm more than grateful."

Hannah handed her the box. "I'll go grab the other two."

"I'll help."

Hannah narrowed her eyes but didn't argue. "I'm parked right outside."

She followed Hannah to her truck, taking the second box while Hannah grabbed the third. "This took you all day, didn't it?"

Hannah blew a piece of hair from her eyes and cracked a smile. "Not all day."

She didn't believe her even a little. "I really do appreciate it. I'm also sorry if my behavior this morning made you feel like you had to do this."

"It didn't."

She led the way back into the kitchen. They set the tomatoes on one of the prep counters. "I think maybe it did. I don't like surprises, at least not when it comes to ingredients."

"Yes, you made that clear from the day we started working together. It was one of the reasons I was hesitant to contract with the restaurant in the first place," Hannah said.

The truth of Hannah's words hit home and made her feel small. "I did feel that way in the beginning."

She raised a brow. "And you don't now?"

"I'm not saying I love having my plans thrown out the window. But a curveball every now and then is good for me."

Hannah scowled. "I don't think I want to be your curveball."

She was such a damn perfectionist. Drew hadn't picked up on that aspect of her personality at first. "I get that." She paused. "Do you have a minute or are you running off to avert another crisis?"

Hannah chuckled. "Oh, no. I'm done for the day."

"Great. I want to show you what came out of all this."

"Okay." Hannah's tone seemed mildly suspicious.

"Actually, I have an even better idea. We don't open for another hour. Go out front and let Carlton pour you a glass of wine. I'll join you shortly."

"Uh."

"Just do it." She offered her most charming smile. "Please?"

Whether it was the charm or merely giving in to the offer to relax for a minute, she didn't know. But Hannah relented. "I haven't seen Nick all week. I guess I could stay for a bit."

"Perfect."

Hannah headed to the front of the house and Drew got to work. A few minutes later, she carried a pair of plates out to the bar. There was no sign of Nick, but Hannah was perched on one of the stools, a glass of wine in front of her. The juxtaposition of her—faded jeans, work boots, plaid shirt with the sleeves rolled up—with the gleaming bar and white linen tablecloths stirred something in Drew.

She opened her mouth, but no words came out. She cleared her throat and tried again. "I hope you're hungry."

Hannah turned and smiled. "I'm always hungry."

Drew set the plates on the bar and took the stool next to her. She explained what each of them was. "These are the specials tonight."

Hannah took a bite of the bruschetta first, then the zucchini. "Wow."

"Thanks." Seeing the pleasure on Hannah's face sent a surge of warmth through her. "And if I'd had my tomatoes, I wouldn't be serving either of them."

Hannah took a sip of wine. "I'm not sure I can bring myself to be glad I screwed up, but I am glad it turned out so well."

She tipped her head. "I'll take that, I suppose."

It felt like they might be on the verge of a moment. Drew angled her body toward Hannah. Not that they would kiss in the middle of the restaurant, but she wanted to see how Hannah would respond. Hannah looked at her and, for a second, their eyes caught and held.

But then Hannah's attention shifted to something behind Drew. "I was looking for you," she said.

Nick. Drew turned and, sure enough, he stood behind her. "I had soccer practice with the boys this afternoon."

"Of course you did," Hannah said.

"If I'd known we were sampling things, I would have shown up sooner."

Drew laughed. "You realize, as the owner, you can sample whatever you want anytime you want."

"I keep forgetting." He winked at her. "What do we have here?"

Drew explained the dishes and, even though she didn't have to, Hannah added the back story. Nick seemed to find the entire thing amusing. Then he tasted the dishes and told Hannah she should mess up orders more often, to which Hannah groaned. It was all so much easier and more relaxed compared to her first few interactions with Hannah. Before she could decide whether or not to say so, Chris, the hostess, walked by. Drew glanced at her watch and realized the doors would be open in a matter of minutes. "I better get back to the kitchen."

"Yeah." Nick lifted his chin in challenge. "What am I paying you for?"

"That." Drew pointed at the now-empty plates. She turned to Hannah. "Thank you for bringing the tomatoes. I promise they will still go to excellent use."

"I'm sure they will." Hannah smiled, but she looked exhausted.

It struck Drew as funny that a day of chasing down some tomatoes seemed to take more out of her than a full day of manual labor. "Go home and take a load off. I'll see you in a couple of days."

"Sounds good."

Drew returned to the kitchen. If anything, she and Hannah had just made up. Not that they were technically fighting. So why did she have this weird unsettled feeling in her chest? Even as she told herself it didn't make sense, she knew exactly what had caused it. The problem was she had no idea if Hannah felt the same way or if she'd ever get the chance to act on it. She shook her head, as if that might chase away the desire to spend more time with Hannah, to kiss her senseless, to see if those kisses might lead to more.

She wasn't one to pine and she had no intention to start now. Especially with a full slate of reservations and dinner service ahead.

Chapter Fourteen

Hannah's invitation to dinner took Drew by surprise. She called it a peace offering for the tomato fiasco, as she had taken to calling it. Drew insisted it wasn't necessary, that it hadn't been a fiasco at all, but accepted the invitation anyway. She wasn't about to pass up the chance to have dinner with Hannah, especially if that dinner was taking place at Hannah's house.

She pulled into the driveway. It might only be her second time there, but it felt familiar somehow. The first time had felt like an agreement to be friends. This time, Drew was less sure. Yes, Hannah insisted on doing something by way of apology for the tomato mix-up. But she could have done that with a gift of produce or a bottle of wine. Making dinner felt much more personal. Since she was more interested in the latter—getting to know Hannah more personally—she hadn't argued.

And now here she was, a bottle of wine in hand and no idea what to expect.

Hannah's front door was open, so she walked up the porch steps and opened the screen door. She paused for a moment in the doorway to announce her presence. "Hello?"

"In the kitchen," Hannah called.

It felt for a second like they'd done this a million times before. It struck her just how appealing that notion was. She made her way through the living room to the kitchen at the back of the house. "It smells great in here."

"Thanks." Hannah, in a floral print sundress with an apron over it, turned to her and smiled. Her feet were bare and the whole package proved to be a manifestation of a fantasy Drew didn't know she had.

"I…" She swallowed. "I brought a red, but if it doesn't go with what we're having, you can save it for some other time." Why was she stuttering like an idiot all of a sudden?

"Red is perfect, actually. Since I'm sure I'm no match for you in the kitchen, I thought I'd grill a steak."

The comment helped her relax. "I'm sure you're more than competent in the kitchen, but I'd never say no to steak."

"Oh, good." Hannah opened a drawer, pulled out a corkscrew, and handed it over. She pointed to a cabinet. "Glasses are there."

Drew busied herself opening the wine and pouring two glasses. She stole glances at Hannah, who seemed to be prepping a myriad of vegetables for the grill—zucchini and summer squash, wedges of sweet potato, thick slices of red onion. "Looks delicious."

"Anytime I don't need to turn on the stove or oven in the summer feels like a win."

"When I'm at home, I completely agree."

Hannah smiled again. If Drew didn't know better, she'd say it had a shy quality to it. "Thank you for coming, for letting me do something nice for you."

Oh. Of course that's why she would be sheepish. Not a simmering attraction or any of the other reasons Drew might like to imagine. "I accepted your apology. I'm very glad to be here, but I hope you know it wasn't necessary."

Hannah took a deep breath but didn't argue. "I'm glad you're here either way."

"Good." That felt a bit more promising.

"Do you mind bringing out the wine? I'll grab the food."

Drew tucked the bottle in her arm, picked up the glasses, and followed Hannah out the back door, which was also opened to the screen. The table on the back deck had been set. The paisley linen napkins felt homey, the citronella candle already burning off to the side practical more than romantic. Not formal by any means, but much more intentional than the night they'd shared BLTs and beers. "This is really nice."

Hannah smiled the same shy smile again, then went over to the grill and turned it on. Drew enjoyed watching her adjust the burners, adeptly position and move food around over the flames. A sexy mix of handy and domestic, although she knew better than to say as much out loud.

They chatted about the weather, which felt more like legitimate conversation than small talk. Drew mentioned that her friend Baker was planning a visit. Hannah talked about her family, mostly her mother and sister, the social media maven. Everything about the meal was perfect, from the food to the view of the hills to the conversation. And even if it wasn't technically a date, it was far superior to many of the dates Drew had been on. She liked to think it was a sign of how well they clicked, of things to come. All the same, she worried it indicated they'd landed in friend territory, never to kiss—or more than kiss—again.

When they'd polished off the wine and finished eating, they settled into an easy silence. Just like the picnic. If it weren't for the hum of arousal coursing through her veins, she might be tempted to call it relaxing. But there was that pesky hum. And having Hannah across from her, looking gorgeous and content, turned the volume distractingly high.

Drew gave in to the urge to touch her, if only with a gentle nudge of her foot under the table. "If this is how you're going to make things up to me, you have my permission to mess up anytime you'd like."

Hannah chuckled and rolled her eyes. She was never going to live that down. "Can't we just agree to have dinner together again? I'm not fond of screwing up."

"That sounds even better."

Hannah took a deep breath. "Good."

"Does that mean you want to keep having dinner with me?" Drew's teasing tone remained, but her eyes cooled.

She winced slightly. "I do."

"Your mouth says yes, but the rest of you is screaming something else." Drew frowned. "Like torture."

"It's not that." She never wanted to be one of those women who wanted to process everything to death, but she owed Drew the truth. "I do want to have dinner with you, spend time with you."

"I can feel the 'but' on the tip of your tongue."

"No but. I feel like I owe you an explanation, though."

"You really don't."

Hannah shook her head. "That's nice of you to say, but I want you to know that this hot and cold thing isn't my style. I'm not trying to play games with you."

Drew's eyebrows went up slightly. "Not trying to?"

Hannah sat up straight. "I'm not playing games, but I admit my behavior might feel otherwise. I've been waffling."

Instead of laughing or asking her what she meant, Drew looked at her intently. "Why do you think that is?"

Since she was telling the truth, she might as well go all in. "Obviously, I'm attracted to you."

Drew angled her head. "Obviously?"

It helped that she was taking a lighthearted approach to all this. Hannah smiled. "Yes, but as we've discussed, I was pretty intent on not liking you."

"Right, right." Drew nodded affably. "You did show up in my barn, mud all over your fancy shoes. You seemed so out of place and full of disdain. I couldn't believe Nick hired you."

Hannah was afraid she might have been too blunt, but Drew laughed. "Those shoes will never be the same. For the record, I was dressed for a job interview. Fetching ingredients from the source was a complete surprise."

She'd been so quick to judge. She hated when people did that to her and here she was no better. "In retrospect, that makes perfect sense. I shouldn't have given you such a hard time."

"And you called me a tweezer chef."

She cringed. It was a wonder Drew was even interested in her. "I said I thought you might be."

Drew's eyes gleamed. Hopefully, that meant this was playful banter and not a dissection of all the ways Hannah was a jerk. Drew shrugged. "Oh, well, then."

"Is this your way of saying I owe you another dinner?"

Drew shook her head, her expression suddenly serious. "I want to have dinner with you again, but not because you owe me."

"Oh." Although unspoken, the underlying meaning of Drew's words came across loud and clear. Needing something to do with her hands, Hannah stood to clear the dishes. "That's good to know."

Drew joined her carrying things inside. "I'll even offer to cook next time, at my place."

Next time. A frisson of anticipation ran through her. They'd not even followed through with the first time and Hannah was already looking forward to the next. Jenn would be so proud. "I'll take care of these later."

Drew gestured to the sink. "I don't mind doing dishes, you know. Didn't we just establish I'm not that kind of chef?"

It would have been so easy to laugh, to cede the point and stand chummily at the sink together. But she was afraid if she didn't act now, she might lose her nerve. "Yes, but they'll keep until later."

"If—"

She didn't let Drew finish. She turned toward her, taking only a second to appreciate the way the evening sunlight pouring in bathed Drew in an almost movielike glow. And then she did what she'd been wanting to do from the moment Drew kissed her the first time. She leaned in, took Drew's face in her hands, and kissed her.

Drew held herself in check, but barely. "I thought you said this was a terrible idea."

Hannah pulled back. Her eyes were dark with passion, pupils dilated. "I changed my mind."

If part of Drew thought she should step back, investigate the specifics of Hannah's declaration, it was a small part. Small and quickly overwhelmed by the need that had been building in her for the last two months. She hauled Hannah back to her, let herself take what she'd been wanting for so long.

She pushed her tongue into Hannah's mouth. Hannah welcomed her in. There was nothing sweet or romantic about the scrape of Hannah's teeth, the way her tongue slid and played over Drew's. She filled her hands with Hannah's hair. All that thick, beautiful hair. The smell of it had been haunting her dreams, the image of it spread over a pillow as Hannah looked up at her with longing.

The image made her realize how close she was to taking Hannah right there in the kitchen. There was something to be said for sex on kitchen counters and dining room tables, but this wasn't one of those moments. Knowing full well Hannah might change her mind again tomorrow made Drew want to do it right, make the most of it. She wrenched her mouth away. "Bed?"

Hannah was already breathing hard. "Right. Yes. Follow me."

She took Drew's hand and led them through the front of the house to the stairs. Without pausing, she ascended, pulling Drew behind. Having Hannah a few steps ahead gave her a lovely view of Hannah's ass. She gave in, placing her free hand on it. Between her ass and her hip, actually, right where she could feel the sway of Hannah's body as she climbed.

Hannah pulled her into the first room, flipped a switch. A lamp by the bed came on, casting a soft glow. Drew tried to absorb a few details despite the singular focus in her brain. Sea green walls, paisley curtains, a quilt of pinks and greens and yellows on the bed—definitely a feminine space. The significance of being allowed into it wasn't lost on her. She stopped walking but kept her grasp on Hannah's hand.

At the tug on her arm, Hannah stopped and turned. "What is it?"

"I just need to make sure this is what you want. I don't want to be something you regret in the morning."

Hannah smiled, slow and sensual. "I want this. You. No regrets."

Hannah's consent, the articulation of her desire, was as much of a turn-on as the kiss. "Anything I should know? Likes, dislikes, things that will make you come unglued?"

There was barely a foot between them, but Hannah took her time closing the distance. When no more than a couple of inches remained, she stopped. She looked into Drew's eyes, then down at her mouth. She waited a beat, then looked back into Drew's eyes. "I'm not delicate and I don't need you to be gentle."

More than a demand, more than an elaborate description of what Hannah wanted her to do, the simple declaration sent Drew into overdrive. She grabbed the fabric of Hannah's dress at her hips and yanked it over her head. Underneath, Hannah wore nothing.

"Underwear is so overrated in the summer, don't you think?"

Aware that her mouth was hanging open, Drew consciously closed it. She nodded. "I do now."

Hannah's smile told her she'd done that on purpose. Without waiting for further instruction, Hannah went to work on Drew's clothing. Although she was wearing considerably more than Hannah—a shirt, shorts, a sports bra, and boxers—Hannah dispensed with them in no time. "There, that's so much better."

She enjoyed watching Hannah's gaze rake over her. It helped to know the pure lust coursing through her veins was reciprocated. But even if part of her thought she could simply stare at Hannah's body for hours, they weren't there to look at each other all night. She stepped forward, running her hands up Hannah's sides to her breasts.

Hannah's body leaned into the touch. Her eyes closed and a tiny sound escaped her lips. It took all of Drew's willpower not to toss her on the bed and do all the things she'd been thinking about doing. Instead, she brushed her thumbs over Hannah's nipples. They hardened instantly. She dipped her head, swiped her tongue over one of the peaks.

"Mmm."

Hannah's hum of pleasure made Drew smile. She went back and forth for a moment—nipping, sucking, and teasing. Hannah skimmed her fingers over the back of Drew's neck, driving her just the right amount of crazy.

Hannah shifted her hands to Drew's face, placing one on each cheek and guiding Drew's mouth to hers. The kiss had even more heat than the one downstairs and Drew responded with abandon. It made her think of her younger days, eagerness bordering on desperation.

She walked them slowly back toward the bed. When they reached it, Hannah fell back, a smile of invitation on her lips. Drew didn't need to be asked twice. She braced one knee next to Hannah, the other between her thighs. She held herself up on one elbow but allowed her body to press into Hannah's. Hannah arched against her, intensifying the contact. Her arms snaked around Drew. She danced her fingers down Drew's spine, then scraped her nails back up. It did wicked things to Drew's already overloaded system. "Fuck."

"Yes. Now. I want you inside me." Hannah's demand was breathless but confident.

Drew eased far enough away to slide a hand between them. Normally, she would have taken a moment to caress, to tease, to allow the woman she was with to acclimate to the intimacy. But Hannah's eyes locked on hers. The need reflected in them was urgent, both a challenge and a command.

Drew slid her fingers into Hannah's wetness. The silky heat of her threatened to snap the thread of Drew's self-control. She circled her clit once, twice, before moving down. She pressed one finger into Hannah, felt Hannah clench around her.

"More." Hannah's voice was ragged, but no less demanding.

Drew swallowed the wave of arousal that swelled up and threatened to pull her under. She obliged, adding her index finger to the one already inside. She turned her hand, curling her fingers slightly each time she pulled out. She shifted, bringing herself to more of a kneeling position. She needed to see Hannah's face. She wanted to watch Hannah's body pull her in over and over again.

She used her new vantage point to graze her free hand over Hannah's breasts. She moved the hand down Hannah's torso and into the patch of light brown curls. She pressed her thumb to Hannah's clit, gently at first.

Hannah arched into her and groaned. "Harder."

Drew smiled. Clearly, she should have taken Hannah's assertion about not being gentle to heart. She increased the pressure of her thumb, but also the force behind each thrust. The undulations of Hannah's body became less fluid. She rose to meet Drew's hand, swallowing Drew's fingers each time. She was fine letting Hannah call the shots, especially since it was their first time, but a little voice in Drew's mind told her not to. "Can you handle one more?"

Hannah's movements stilled for a moment, her eyes opened. Drew could literally get lost in those eyes. Hannah didn't speak. She merely nodded.

Drew shifted her hand again to accommodate the addition. Hannah's body took her in, expanding and then contracting around her fingers. She could feel Hannah's pulse, feel each curve and contour. Drew swallowed and closed her eyes for a second, not wanting to show just how in awe she was.

Hannah began to move again, breaking the weird spell that threatened to overwhelm Drew's emotions. She started to moan with each thrust of Drew's hand. Drew focused her attention on Hannah's body, her pleasure. She returned her thumb to Hannah's clit, circling it in time with the movement of her fingers. Hannah's hands fisted in the sheet, her noises became louder and more urgent. Drew continued to push her, wanting her to come, but not wanting the moment to end.

When Hannah's whole body arched, Drew pushed into her one final time and held her there. The way Hannah contracted around her, the flood of liquid heat that poured from her, sent an arrow straight through Drew's body, lodging between her legs. It was exquisite and left Drew in an almost painful state of arousal.

Drew slowly eased her hand away, sending a tingling rush of blood and sensation back to her fingers. She let her gaze linger on Hannah's body—long, lean, and with the tan lines of someone who worked outdoors. "Damn, that was hot."

Hannah's eyes fluttered open. She smiled in a way that reminded Drew of a contented cat, basking in the sun. "It really was."

Drew dropped onto the bed next to her, aching with need but content to lie together for a moment. She expected Hannah to take a while to recover, but she almost immediately rolled over, draping herself across Drew's body. Drew tucked a piece of hair behind her ear. "Hi."

"Hi, yourself." Hannah leaned in and kissed her, slower than before, but with plenty of heat to it. "I'm going to do my best to reciprocate that, but I just want to state for the record it's a tall order."

She laughed, enjoying the compliment implied in the assertion. "It's not a competition."

"Says the chef who I'm pretty sure is competitive about everything."

Before she could respond, Hannah propped herself up and wrapped her mouth around one of Drew's nipples. Given her already turned-on state, her response was immediate and intense. "Fuck."

Hannah gave her a devilish grin. "And this time, it's my turn."

Without further discussion or warning, Hannah slid her hand down Drew's body and between her legs. Drew couldn't remember the last time she'd been so aroused. Her whole body bucked.

Hannah's mouth was at her ear. "Don't worry, I'll go easy on you." She nipped Drew's lobe. "At least at first."

Drew let her head fall back. She laughed again. And then she let Hannah take charge.

That's exactly what she did. Hannah straddled one of Drew's thighs, reminding her just how hot and wet she was. And then she played Drew's body like an instrument, winding her tighter and higher than Drew thought possible. Not aggressive, but confident. More force than Drew was accustomed to, but in a good way. Hannah managed to make her feel strong without giving up an ounce of control.

Drew came with a force she felt all the way to the tips of her fingernails. The orgasm exploded from her and left her quaking. But instead of easing her down, Hannah started again. She was gentler this time, but there was no mistaking her intention.

Drew was about to tell her she rarely came twice in such a short span. Her body, it seemed, had other ideas. It was as though Hannah knew her better than she knew herself.

Lazy strokes that avoided her hypersensitive center, teasing around her opening without pressing inside. Before she knew it, Drew was moving with her, wanting more. Hannah shifted, touching her more directly, easing fingers into Drew. Her pace quickened. Drew followed her lead, letting her body trust where they were going.

The second orgasm rocked her more slowly, deeply. It emanated from her core in a pulsing wave, more bass notes than treble. It left her sweaty, breathless, and exposed.

Hannah crawled up the bed, kissed her lightly. "That was even better than I imagined, and I've been imagining it a lot."

Drew chuckled weakly. "I think you've melted my bones. I can't move."

"Perfect." Hannah grabbed the sheet and draped it over them both.

"I…" Drew trailed off. She wanted to say something but wasn't sure what.

"Same." Hannah settled herself into the curve of Drew's arm.

Drew glanced out the window. Venus and a few stars dotted the sky, but the last bit of daylight still clung to the horizon. "It's not even dark yet."

Hannah lifted her head. "Close enough. Especially since we have to get up at five."

Five. Right. Because she was dating a farmer and it was the middle of summer and farmers got up at five. "You're right. Close enough."

Despite the early hour and the dusky sky, despite the tickle of worry over just how powerful a hold Hannah seemed to have over her, she slid quickly toward sleep.

Chapter Fifteen

Not only did Hannah bound out of bed at five in the morning, she seemed completely happy about it. Despite the early bedtime, Drew wasn't able to muster anything close to her level of enthusiasm. It rubbed off a little, though, and she couldn't remember the last time she'd seen such a beautiful sunrise. Hannah headed off to the farm and Drew went home. Although tempted to crawl back into bed for a couple of hours, she decided to start her day. She might regret it come the eight o'clock dinner rush, but she'd powered through worse before.

Instead of taking a shower, she mixed up an iced coffee and changed into work clothes. Once outside, she tackled the weeds in the small garden where she'd planted herbs. After that, she fired up the little push mower that came with her place and gave the lawn some attention. She showered, dressed, and was still on her way to the farm an hour earlier than usual. Maybe getting up early wasn't all bad.

No sign of Hannah in the barn, but her sister was there, at the register and tapping away on her computer. "Hi, Clare."

Clare looked up and offered her a wide smile. "Hey, Drew."

"How's summer treating you?"

"Really good." Clare blushed, but Drew wasn't sure why. "Hannah said to tell you there are some boxes ready for you in the back, but to take whatever else you want and just have me write it down."

"Cool. Thanks." She tried to ignore the stab of disappointment that Hannah might be avoiding her.

"She also told me to tell you she's sorry she missed you, but she's at a farm equipment auction in Hector."

Drew chuckled. She'd had women avoid her in the past, but that particular reason might be a first. And in truth, it didn't even count as avoiding since Hannah probably had no control over the timing of it.

That made her feel considerably better. "I wonder what she's hoping to buy."

"She said something about a post digger for the three point hitch."

"Sure, sure." Drew nodded, then shrugged. "I have no idea what that means."

Clare laughed. "It's an attachment for the tractor."

"Right. Of course." Like a whole new language. "Okay, I'm going to go see what she's got for me."

She headed to the back and found two flats of tomatoes, one of peppers and summer squash, and a bin filled with spinach and other greens. She carried them out to her car and loaded them, then returned to the barn. She perused the other offerings and decided on green beans and some cucumbers. She brought them to Clare to have them weighed and recorded.

"So, how are things?" Clare asked.

If Drew didn't know better, she'd have thought Clare knew what she and Hannah had been up to the night before. Technically, she supposed that was possible, but for some reason, it didn't seem like Hannah's style to kiss and tell. At least with her little sister. "Great. Hard not to love summer, right?"

Clare beamed. "Totally. So, what are you making today?"

She ran down a few of the dishes she'd made regulars on the menu, a couple of things she had in mind for specials. Clare made noises of approval and Drew got the distinct feeling she was fishing for something. "Do you like to cook?"

Clare shrugged, but her face was anything but disinterested. "Yeah, but I don't know how to do anything fancy."

Drew chuckled. "Who are you trying to impress?"

As soon as the question was out of Drew's mouth, Clare blushed furiously. "Uh, no one."

Drew didn't know her well enough to tease, so she lifted both hands in apology. "Just kidding. Wanting to learn is a good enough reason. You don't need to impress anyone."

To her credit, Clare recovered quickly. "Maybe if I offer to do some advertising for you, you'll agree to give me a lesson."

She would have agreed even without the offer of a trade, because she was Hannah's sister, but also because she had a soft spot for teenagers who thought cooking was cool. "Deal."

Clare nodded and went back to totaling the order. "Let me know when you have time. I'm pretty flexible."

"How about Wednesday afternoon?" It was one of the slower days at the restaurant and probably one of the less busy days at the farm stand, too.

"That would be awesome."

"Can you come around two? We'll just be starting dinner prep and I can show you a few basic techniques, then we can make a dish. Any requests?"

Clare shook her head. "Everything you make is great."

She couldn't wait to tell Hannah about this development, not because it would earn her points. No, she had a feeling Hannah would know the why—or perhaps the who—of what made Clare blush. "I'll surprise you then. Tell Hannah I said hi, okay?"

"I will."

The knowing look was back. Maybe Clare did know about Hannah and her. Or maybe she simply knew that Hannah liked Drew, that they'd had a date or two. For some reason, that made her happy. "I'll see you Wednesday. Are you good to drive yourself?"

"I am. Thanks. I'm going to post stuff on our channels, but if you want to get the info from Nick, I can put them on Fig's, too."

It took Drew a second to process what she meant. She wasn't clueless when it came to social media, but she probably didn't give it the attention she should. "Sounds good."

A couple of women with kids came in and Drew took that as her cue to leave. She picked up the rest of her produce and offered Clare a wave. She headed to the restaurant, disappointed still that she hadn't seen Hannah but glad to have had the chance to chat with Clare. She didn't put a lot of stock in scoring points or palling it up with the family of women she dated, but in this case, it felt natural. Nice, even. Maybe this was just one more way life was different upstate.

❖

Hannah got back from the auction, equal parts relieved and disappointed to have missed Drew. She was also the proud owner of an auger, which would make building and maintaining fences a hell of a lot easier. Clare was full of stories about her morning, including a group of tourists who didn't speak English but bought one of everything and her planned cooking lesson with Drew.

"Since when are you interested in cooking?" She was pretty sure it had something to do with Kristen, but she wanted Clare to own it.

"I've always been interested."

She looked at Clare blandly, but didn't say anything.

It didn't take long for Clare to get squirmy. "Kristen said something about learning from her dad. I love mom's cooking and all, and I've learned plenty from her, but it's just not the same."

Hannah nodded slowly. "And are you hoping to have the chance to show off your new skills? Maybe the next time you and Kristen hang out?"

Clare winced. "That's dumb, isn't it? Her dad owns a restaurant. Why would she be impressed by something I made?"

"I think it's the fact that you went to the trouble that will impress her."

"Yeah." Clare looked relieved for a second, then horrified. She must have realized the reassurance meant Hannah was on to her.

"Don't worry, your secret is safe with me."

"It's not like there's anything to tell," Clare said quickly.

"Maybe there will be and maybe there won't be. It's cool either way."

Clare nodded sheepishly. "Thanks."

"Do you have things under control here? I've got morning chores to make up and then I need to get things together for the CSA bins."

"I'm good. I updated all the signs with the price list you gave me and restocked from the back. I also did a fresh crop alert for the last wave of strawberries."

Hannah grinned at her. "You keep this up and I'm going to have to give you a raise."

"I'm going to remember you said that."

She left Clare to run the stand and headed out to the fields. They'd had a ton of rain in the last week, leaving her crops happy but everything else a muddy mess. She mucked through pruning tomato plants, then went to check on the orchard. After a late freeze had decimated her peaches the year before, it gave her an extra thrill to see the branches laden with fruit. They needed a couple more weeks, but the harvest would be a good one.

She checked on Jeremiah, who'd managed to do most of the harvesting she had planned. That meant she could get an early start on the CSA bins. She set up twenty plastic totes on the table in her storeroom, pausing to make a list of what she wanted to include before she began filling them. She'd just finished gathering things when Jenn poked her head in. Hannah smiled. "Hey, you."

"I left work early so I'd be sure I caught you. Tell me everything."

"I made her dinner and then I took her to bed."

Jenn shook her head slowly. "I can't believe it."

Hannah made a face. "What do you mean you can't believe it? You've been telling me to go for it for weeks."

"Yeah, but I didn't think you were going to listen to me. You're very stubborn."

Hannah crossed her arms. "I am not."

Jenn raised a brow.

"Okay, maybe a little."

Still, Jenn said nothing.

"Maybe more than a little. But I'm not unreasonable. Drew and I have chemistry. It was silly to pretend that didn't exist."

"Even if you disliked her on principle."

"Dislike is a strong word." Why was she being so contrary? She'd had an amazing time with Drew, wanted to repeat it sooner rather than later. If anything, she should be gloating. "But you're right. I was hesitant at first. Thank you for giving me a nudge. It was beyond worth it."

It was Jenn's turn to fold her arms. "That's more like it. So, it was good, huh?"

Just thinking about Drew sent a ripple of arousal through her. "Yeah. Really, really good."

"So, are you dating? Like, officially?" Jenn looked incredulous.

Hannah shrugged. "I'm not sure why you find that surprising."

"I know." Jenn's brows furrowed. "I don't know why either."

"You're the one who told me to be decisive," she said as she packed up the bins. She circled the large table, adding a pulp basket of green beans to each one.

Jenn lifted a finger. "Hey, now. I did not tell you what to do. I would never tell you what to do."

Hannah smiled. Jenn was right, which was one of the reasons they got along so well. "You didn't. But you did point out that I was being indecisive, which is out of character for me."

"That, I'll take."

Hannah pointed to a large bin of bell peppers. "Would you put two of those in each bin?"

"Sure." Jenn hefted the bin and followed behind her. "You still didn't answer my question."

"What question was that?" Hannah finished with the green beans and started on eggplant.

"If you two are dating. Like girlfriends."

"God, no." Hannah frowned. Then, seeing Jenn had finished the peppers, she pointed at bags of salad greens that had been assembled earlier. "Those next."

Jenn followed the directions but kept her gaze on Hannah. "Why do you sound so offended by the idea?"

She stopped what she was doing and let her shoulders drop. "I'm not offended. I—" What was she? "I just don't think it's that kind of arrangement."

Jenn caught up to her. She nudged Hannah in the rear with her bin, snapping her attention back to the task at hand. "What kind of arrangement is it?"

Hannah sighed. That was exactly the problem. She didn't know. She placed an eggplant in the bin and started moving again. "I'm not sure."

"That's your problem."

That gave her exactly zero clarity. "What is?"

"You don't know, you don't like that you don't know, and you're acting like a wallflower too timid to just find out already."

Great. "That sounds like three problems."

Jenn gave her a look that held absolutely no sympathy. "I have a proposition for you."

Hannah closed her eyes. "That sounds dangerous."

"Let's do a wine tour. You and Drew and me and Suri."

"Oh, God." The thought of a double date with Jenn and her new girlfriend sent a panicky feeling through her.

Jenn finished with the lettuce and put her hands on her hips. "You don't have to act so offended by the idea."

"I'm not offended."

"You're terrified."

"I am not." She wasn't. Was she?

"Not terrified, but nervous. You want answers, you probably even want to see what girlfriend territory might look like, but you're totally freaked out by what you might learn."

"Aren't finance people supposed to be good with numbers and bad with feelings?"

"That's stockbrokers. Wealth managers are all about relationships. I am great at feelings." Jenn pointed her thumb back at her chest.

Yeah. She was. And she was right. "This could go very badly, you know."

"It could also be a ton of fun. Either way, you'll know where you stand."

"True. Okay." She nodded, slightly more confident with the idea. "I think Drew is only off Mondays and some Tuesdays, though."

"Not a problem. I make my own schedule, remember?"

"And there's not a lot of demand for yoga on Monday afternoons?"

"Suri does some private classes, so let me double-check. Want to try for next week?"

She got a twinge of guilt. She rarely took this many days off in the summer. Then again, things seemed to be running just fine. In truth, it was probably a good idea for Jeremiah to flex his manager muscles a bit more. "I'll text Drew and let you know."

"Excellent. I'm looking forward to getting to know her." Jenn pointed at the bins. "Are these done? May I take mine?"

"One more thing." Hannah grabbed a pint of cherry tomatoes and tucked it into one of the bins. Ever since the tomato fiasco, they'd been coming in good and heavy, much to her relief. "Now it's done."

"I know what I'm having for dinner." Jenn grinned and picked up the bin. "I'll see you, hopefully soon."

"Hopefully." Hannah sent her an air-kiss. Jenn left and she placed tomatoes in the remaining bins. When they were done, she closed them up and stacked them for pickup.

She walked to the front of the barn and let Clare know they were ready. Official pickup didn't start until six, but early birds weren't uncommon. Then she headed out to the shed where Roberta sat. Peaches would be ready for picking any day and she wanted to mow between the trees once more before people started coming through.

She slid open the door, topped off the tank with diesel, and climbed on. Before starting the engine, she pulled out her phone and texted Drew an invite. It made her feel better, like she was taking control of the situation. It didn't hurt that she'd not be able to check for a reply for the next two hours.

Chapter Sixteen

Drew had been plotting what to propose for her next date with Hannah when she got the invite to do a wine tour double date. A perfect suggestion, really. She hadn't wanted it to seem like she was only interested in a second round of sex, but she wanted something more interesting than dinner out. Not that there was anything wrong with a nice dinner at a great restaurant. Obviously.

She found herself oddly excited by the prospect of spending time with Hannah's best friend. It would give her the chance to see another side of Hannah, learn more about her. In her experience, best friend dynamics were just as telling as family ones.

Rain had been in the forecast, but the storm shifted overnight, leaving a warm and sunny day. Drew slipped on a pair of navy shorts and a short-sleeved white button-down with little navy anchors on it. It was officially the preppiest thing she owned.

Ready a good half hour before she expected to be picked up, she took up residence on the porch and called her own best friend. It rang and rang, but just as she resigned herself to leaving a voice mail, Baker picked up. "Hey, hey, Chef. What's shaking?"

The sound of Baker's voice never failed to make her smile. "Just hanging in my favorite rocking chair. Thought I'd see what was up."

"Dude. A rocking chair? Really? Are you eighty?"

"It's about ambience, man, not age."

"Uh-huh. And you've settled right into that, haven't you?"

Drew looked out at her front yard. She'd mowed that morning, so everything looked neat and fresh and perfect. And the herbs she'd planted in the flower bed were thriving. "You know, it's not half bad."

"Sellout." Baker laughed, taking any sting out of the insult.

"Well, I'm spending the afternoon touring wineries with a beautiful woman and her friends and I'm hoping to get laid tonight. If this is selling out, I should have done it ages ago."

That earned her a hoot of laughter. "I can't disagree with you there."

"What about you? What are you up to?"

"Same old, same old, man. Another day, another dollar. I'm taking over the Long Island accounts."

Baker was a regional account manager for an office supply company. She joked that it was a bougie bullshit job, but Drew worked with enough suppliers to know it was legit. "Are you switching? I thought you loved handling Brooklyn and Queens."

"Adding. Twice the work and I'm going to have to deal with all the five-one-sixers."

Five-one-six, one of the area codes for Long Island, served as shorthand for a specific type of Long Island resident. "Are they giving you twice the pay to do it?"

"Eh. Not quite, but close."

Only Baker would downplay a promotion this hard. "Dude, that's awesome. Congratulations."

"I'm going to have to wear a suit when I go out there. A suit."

Drew laughed. She was pretty sure Baker secretly loved her suits. And wining and dining big clients. And closing deals. "Your life is so hard."

"I start next month, so if I'm going to come up and play, it'll have to be soon."

The idea of having Baker visit made her even happier. "How's next week?"

"Perfect, actually. You sure you can swing it?"

"Of course. My family decided not to come until August, right before my mom goes back to school, so it's perfect."

"Do I get to sit on the porch with you?"

She imagined them side by side, drinking beers and talking about life and women. "There's a rocking chair with your name on it."

"Cool. I'll text you later with dates. I got to run. I'm taking a client to lunch."

Of course she was. "Go get 'em, tiger."

Drew ended the call. She got up and went inside, wanting to start a list of things she needed to do to get ready for Baker's visit. They were going to have such a great time. At the sound of a vehicle in the driveway, Drew nodded approval at what she'd come up with so far, grabbed her keys, and headed out. A sleek black SUV sat with its engine running. Drew locked her front door and headed toward it. The driver's side window went down and a familiar face leaned out. "Are you okay in the back?"

"Sure."

As she got closer, a hand came out. "Jenn. We met briefly at the brewery."

"Right, right." Drew shook the hand. "Great to see you again."

"Likewise."

Drew opened the back door and found Hannah sitting at the opposite end of the bench seat. She looked gorgeous, as usual, in a vibrant pink and purple paisley dress. She loved that Hannah's style seemed to be full-on farmer or full-on feminine. It made her wonder if there was anything in the middle. "Hi."

Hannah smiled, sliding her sunglasses off and looking her right in the eyes. "Hi."

Jenn turned around in her seat. "Drew, this is Suri. Suri, Drew."

Drew turned her attention to the other woman in the front seat. She looked Indian, maybe, with a deep complexion and wavy black hair. Very pretty. "Nice to meet you."

Suri offered her a bright smile. "Same. And thanks for coming drinking with us today."

Drew glanced between Suri and Hannah. "Thanks for the invite."

With everyone introduced and buckled in, Jenn backed out of the driveway and headed to their first stop. It was the Thirsty Owl, the place Hannah had taken her for their picnic. Drew indulged in a few pleasant memories of that afternoon while Jenn parked. Inside, the tasting room featured a huge wooden bar and rack after rack of wine. Only one other group was there and they were already sampling things. Hannah led them up to the counter. "Hey, Lisa. Is Pete in today?"

The woman behind the bar smiled at them. "He's at some kind of vintner's convention up in Canada."

"Vintner's convention?" Jenn said what Drew was thinking.

Lisa waved a hand back and forth. "New techniques, cool gadgets. Winemakers nerding out with each other and drinking lots of wine."

Suri shrugged. "I could think of worse conventions."

Everyone laughed. Jenn slid a hand around Suri's waist and squeezed. "True story."

"Four tastings?" Lisa asked.

"Yep." Jenn slid money across the bar before anyone else had a chance. She glanced at Hannah, then Drew. "We can take turns."

That seemed more reasonable than fighting over it. She nodded at Jenn. "Thanks."

Lisa slid four laminated menus across the bar. "I'll let you peruse for a minute."

There were a good twenty wines on the list. Different varietals, but also different vintages. Drew's experience with Finger Lakes wine was still somewhat limited, coming mostly from working with Nick and the bartender at Fig. She'd been pleasantly surprised thus far.

Hannah leaned over. She pointed to a couple. "Those are your party bus wines. Everything else here is pretty good."

"Party bus wines?"

"Sweet table wines. Popular with the party bus crowds. The ones here are better than others, but still on the sweet side."

"Ah. Thanks for the warning."

Hannah pointed to two others. "The dry Riesling here is one of my favorites, as well as Sauvignon Blanc."

"Perfect. What about reds?"

Suri chimed in. "The Finger Lakes are still sorting out how to do a great red. I think they've had the most success with Cab Francs."

Hannah nodded. "Agreed. The one here is quite good."

Drew grabbed one of the dry erase markers and made her selections. Lisa worked her way through, pouring about an ounce of each in their glasses and offering commentary on the vintage or the specific process used for each. Drew had done wine tastings before, but always as part of her job. Doing it socially proved a lot more fun.

They did a second stop at a place called Lamoreaux Landing, then headed to Red Newt. Like the others, some of their selections were on the wine list at Fig. At Red Newt, instead of a tasting, they each settled on a single glass and ordered a cheese board to share. In addition to great wine, Red Newt boasted a large deck overlooking the lake. Drew got a little of Hannah and Jenn's history and learned about Suri's yoga studio. Conversation was easy and relaxed, like they'd all known each other for years. It didn't take her long to think about what it might be like to do this sort of thing again and again.

When the food was gone, Jenn and Suri went inside so Suri could find a birthday present for her aunt. With the two of them poking around the shop, Drew was left on the deck alone with Hannah. They left the table and went over to the railing. Sunlight glinted off the lake, and the vineyard boasted row after row of lush green leaves and craggy old vines sprawled over the gentle slope down toward the water. She took a deep breath—honeysuckle mixed with Hannah's perfume. "This is nice."

"It's one of my favorite whites."

Drew shot Hannah a sideways glance. "It's an exceptional Chardonnay, but I wasn't talking about the wine."

"Oh." Hannah turned toward her, making Drew wish she could see her eyes behind the dark glasses. After what felt like an eternity, Hannah smiled. "Yeah. This is nice, too."

They'd not discussed PDAs, but in that moment, she didn't think she could help herself. She closed the distance between them, brushed her lips against Hannah's. Her mouth was soft and warm, and she tasted faintly of wine. By rights, she should be used to it by now. But each time she kissed Hannah felt new—exciting and better than she'd imagined. This time was no exception. Drew thought she might simply melt into Hannah. It felt that good.

"Hey, lovebirds. You two ready to go?"

Hannah broke the kiss first, but she lingered for a second. It felt like a promise of to-be-continued more than annoyance at being caught. She looked Jenn's way. "Almost."

Drew tipped back the last of her wine. "Yes, an exceptional Chardonnay."

Hannah laughed in that way that sent a jolt of electricity right to Drew's gut. For the briefest of moments, she wished they were alone. She'd bury her fingers in Hannah's hair, bring Hannah's mouth to hers. She had to shake off the stab of desire the fantasy caused. But as they walked back to Jenn's car, she gave in to wanting to touch Hannah, have her close. She took Hannah's hand, giving it a squeeze before they split to climb into the back seat.

On the ride back to Trumansburg, Hannah weighed her options. She could have Jenn drop Drew off first, then bring her home. Since Jenn had picked them both up, that probably made the most sense. But she wasn't in the mood to make sense. She was in the mood to spend more time with Drew. And she felt pretty confident Drew felt the same. "If I get out at your place, would you give me a ride home later?"

She'd kept her tone light, but Drew shot her a glance that said she knew exactly what Hannah had in mind. Instead of embarrassing her, it turned her on. "Sure."

Jenn probably knew what she was about, too, but her only response was, "Works for me."

When they pulled into Drew's driveway, Hannah gave Jenn a half hug from the back seat. "Suri, it was so great getting to know you. Let's get together again soon."

"Same." Suri turned to face Drew. "You, too."

"Ditto," Drew said.

Hannah and Drew got out and she offered a wave as Jenn pulled away. No sooner was the car out of the driveway than Drew turned to her. "I'm glad you stayed."

"Me too."

"Hungry?"

Part of Hannah wanted to say no, to drag Drew to her bedroom and rip all of her clothes off. But the other part of her was starved. Other than the nibble of cheese, she hadn't eaten since breakfast. "I kind of am."

Drew grinned. "Well, lucky for you, I've got food in the house and I know what to do with it."

Hannah winced. "I hope you don't think I invited myself over just so you'd feed me."

"Of course not. I'm hoping you invited yourself over for sex."

She laughed at the deadpan delivery. "I did. Dinner is a total bonus."

"I like the way you think, Hannah Little."

And just like that, the negotiation was done. Drew took her hand and led her inside.

Chapter Seventeen

Once in the house, Hannah had a moment of almost changing her mind, of forgetting about dinner after all. But then her stomach growled, loud enough for both of them to hear. Drew smiled. "Okay, dinner. Any requests?"

Hannah shook her head. "I invited myself over without notice. I'm not about to be picky."

Drew angled her head toward the kitchen area. "Let's see what we've got."

Drew went to the fridge and Hannah took a moment to study the space. The kitchen, dining, and living areas were all one open room. Paired with the Adirondack décor, it felt more like a cabin than a house. It didn't seem like Drew's style. She'd made a comment about renting it furnished, but Hannah was a little surprised she'd not done more to personalize it.

The one exception was photos. There had to be at least a dozen framed photos scattered around the room. She made out Drew in one, wearing a cap and gown and flanked by two older women. She wanted to look closer, to investigate the others, but didn't want to come across as too nosy. She pointed to the one. "Is this you with your mom?"

Drew glanced at the photo. "My mom and Grann. That was the day I graduated culinary school."

She took that as permission to study the image. It couldn't have been that long ago, but Drew looked so much younger. And the women beamed. "They seem very proud."

"They were. Are." Drew smiled. "They sacrificed a lot to get me there. It felt like an accomplishment for all of us."

"That's really nice." So different from her family. They weren't unhappy for her, but her dreams had been hers alone.

"I'm plenty ambitious on my own, but I think a lot about making them proud, of finding a way to pay them back." Drew closed the refrigerator door. "So, we can do pasta, which will be quick, or I can do a risotto, which will be less quick. I also have the stuff for BLTs since you've got me completely hooked on them."

Hannah chuckled. "I can't bring myself to feel bad about that. How about pasta, though, if it's not too much trouble?"

"Not at all. Pesto good for you?"

"Perfect. Can I help?"

Drew handed her a pair of kitchen shears. "You can go out and get me about a cup of basil. It's right in front of the porch."

"Happily." Hannah gathered the basil. Drew had her open wine. In less than half an hour, they sat at Drew's small table with plates of linguine.

"Cheers." Drew lifted her glass.

"Cheers." Hannah sipped her wine, sampled the food. "Oh, this is so good."

"Thank you."

They ate, talking about the restaurant and the farm and what things would be ready to harvest next. When they were done, Hannah offered to wash dishes while Drew put away the leftovers. The mundane tasks didn't make her forget why she invited herself over in the first place. She wiped her hands on a towel and turned to Drew. "That really was delicious. Who knew you could do Italian as well as everything else?"

Drew shrugged. "I like to think I'm versatile."

What a perfect opening to switch gears. Hannah asked, "Are you as versatile out of the kitchen as you are in it?"

Drew quirked a brow. "I like to think so."

"Do you strap?"

Drew's expression changed from playful to serious like the flip of a switch, but she took her time answering. "I've been known to, when the moment is right."

Hannah nodded slowly, not breaking eye contact. She could already imagine herself beneath Drew, legs wrapped around her waist. "And how do you know when the moment is right?"

Again, Drew didn't answer immediately, leaving her on the precipice of anticipation, arousal already thrumming through her veins like a drug. Eventually, she smiled. It was slow, knowing. "When a beautiful woman asks me to."

"I see." Hannah resisted the urge to lunge at Drew right there in the kitchen. She didn't want a frantic tumble that was over almost as quickly as it began.

"Are you asking me to?"

Hannah licked her lip. There were a thousand ways she could answer the question, from coy to playful to aggressive. But all that felt like a performance and she didn't want to do that with Drew. She decided on the simple answer, the truth. "Yes."

Drew's eyes focused on her like a laser and her body went still. "Now? Tonight?"

She waited a beat. Some people found the negotiation cumbersome or awkward. To her, it was foreplay. "Yes."

Drew extended her hand. "Let's go to bed."

The command turned Hannah's churned-up insides into a bundle of raw need. She could already imagine what it would be like to have Drew inside her. Wetness pooled between her thighs, and her breath caught in her throat. And they weren't even touching yet. "Yes, let's."

She took Drew's hand and Drew led her to the bedroom.

"Make yourself comfortable. I'll be right back." Drew went to the closet, pulled out a black case the size of a shoe box, then left the room.

Hannah sat on the edge of the bed. She let out a shaky breath and looked around. The simple furnishings and generic décor didn't make being there any less intimate. She wasn't shy about asking for what she wanted, but being alone in the room, waiting, made her restless. The pulse between her thighs didn't help. Knowing exactly what that box contained, what Drew planned to do with it, had her on edge.

Suddenly, her clothes felt hot and restrictive. Hannah slipped her dress over her head and draped it over the chair in the corner. She considered stripping all the way. No, too eager. Just like crawling into bed solo. Not the vibe she was going for.

She tried to arrange herself on the bed again in a way that looked sexy but not like she was trying to be sexy. Was it her imagination or was Drew taking forever? Was she having second thoughts? What if she came back in to say she'd changed her mind and found Hannah sprawled on her bed, practically begging to be taken?

Unable to sit still, she went to the window that overlooked the small yard and adjacent woods. Sparrows pecked at the ground and a chipmunk scurried along the edge of the grass. Hannah had never made love when it was still light out. She should have felt insecure standing in her underwear by the window, but the soft light and promise of Drew's body over hers made her brazen instead.

Drew didn't speak, but Hannah knew the second she reentered the room. The air crackled with energy. Hannah chuckled. She'd always thought it was so stupid when people said that sort of thing. Until now, until Drew.

"I'm afraid to ask what's funny."

Hannah turned to face Drew. She'd ditched her clothes and was wearing a pair of tight black boxer briefs. Hannah could make out the straps of the harness underneath, the bulge in front. She bit her lip, wanting to touch it, test its weight in her hand. "That's a good look for you."

"So, you weren't laughing at me? That's a relief."

"Not at all. Myself, I think. But good-naturedly."

Drew slid a hand along the curve of Hannah's side. "As long as it's good-natured."

Hannah thought of a clever comeback, but swallowed it. With Drew's hand on her bare skin she was feeling a lot of things—raw, hungry, horny as hell—but funny wasn't one of them. She stroked along Drew's rib cage, right under her breast, then grazed over Drew's stomach.

She paused for just a second at the waistband of Drew's shorts. Once she slipped her hand inside, Drew would be ready against her palm and there would be no going back for either of them, not that she wanted to. But something about the way Drew's abs contracted under her touch had her savoring the moment. Anticipation skittered down her spine. Was she crazy for drawing this out when all she had to say was "now" and Drew would be inside her? Maybe. She'd had fast and reckless before; there was a lot to recommend it. But not this time. Not now. Not with Drew.

When Hannah cupped the cock through the thin, stretchy material, Drew groaned. The sound went straight to Hannah's clit. It was almost as if Drew was touching her and not the other way around.

Drew's eyes were dark with arousal and her gaze intense. She smirked. "I have one that's a bit smaller, but I had a feeling you'd prefer this."

Hannah eased her hand in. The silicone was hard and already warm from Drew's body. Every muscle below her belly button tightened. She couldn't remember the last time she'd been so turned on. "This will do just fine. I'm really looking forward to taking a turn."

Drew's hands came to cup her face, pulling her into a searing kiss. The kind of kiss that made Hannah's toes curl. The kind of kiss that said Drew was about to fuck her senseless.

They kissed until she was on the verge of asking Drew to take her right there against the windowsill. The hunger Drew stirred in her bordered on desperation, clouding her mind. Hannah pulled her mouth away. "Bed. Now. Please."

Drew's answer was to tighten her arms around Hannah's waist and lift her off the ground. She wrapped her legs around Drew for the short journey. The cock pressed against her, making her crave a hard and fast release. But Drew set her on the bed with something close to reverence. Hannah swallowed, at a loss for words.

Drew reached around and flicked open Hannah's bra, slipping it from her shoulders and down her arms slowly. She did the same with Hannah's panties, taking an eternity to slide them down her legs. Drew seemed to have all the time in the world, while Hannah felt like she might spontaneously combust at any second.

Drew moved to rejoin her, but Hannah grasped at her hips. "These, too, if you don't mind. I want to feel all of you."

Drew stood, worked the underwear off. The dildo stood at attention, held in place by a black leather harness. It was the color of caramel, not quite the same as Drew's sepia-toned skin, but close. "Better?"

Hannah let her gaze travel the length of Drew's body. "Much."

Drew crawled onto the bed, settling herself into Hannah's open thighs. She propped herself on one elbow. God, she'd spent so many nights fantasizing about this exact moment, it was hard to believe it was finally real. "Do you want to tell me how you like it?"

Hannah smiled. "Hard and fast."

"I see." With her free hand, Drew traced a finger along Hannah's jaw. Tempting, but not what she had in mind. "And what if I said I wanted to take my time?"

She could see Hannah swallow. "I'd probably try to convince you otherwise."

Drew nipped her jaw. "Let's just see, shall we?"

Hannah arched her back, causing her nipples to graze Drew's. "That sounds like a challenge."

"Challenge accepted." Drew loved a challenge. She eased just far enough away to be out of Hannah's reach. She angled her head to plant a row of kisses along Hannah's neck, from her shoulder up to her head and back down, ending at her collarbone. The pale skin of her torso stood in stark contrast to her tanned arms. She worked her way down to Hannah's breasts, kissing and sucking but stopping short of her nipples. They stood erect, practically begging for attention. But as Hannah had said, now it was a challenge.

Hannah moved beneath her, not quite writhing, but close. Under normal circumstances, it would be all the invitation she needed to take the nipple into her mouth or to let her fingers roam to where she knew Hannah would be hot and wet and ready. Instead, she skimmed her tongue across Hannah's sternum and repeated the teasing kisses on the other breast.

Ribs came next, then Hannah's belly button. It gave her immense satisfaction to see Hannah's abs contract, her breath hitch. She continued to inch down, working her way closer and closer to Hannah's core. Along the crease of her thighs, through the triangle of hair. Drew barely skimmed her mouth over Hannah's clit and was rewarded with a sharp intake of breath.

"Please," Hannah said.

"Please what?" Drew kept her voice light.

"Please fuck me."

The request did as much to turn Drew on as being nestled between Hannah's thighs. "Oh, I will. I promise. I just want to make you really want it first."

"I do. I do want it." The slight edge in Hannah's voice was sexy as hell. It almost made her relent. Almost.

"I know you do, baby. I want you to want it more."

Without waiting for a response, she slid her tongue into Hannah. Her salty sweet taste tested Drew's resolve. It would be so easy to make her come like this, so satisfying. Hannah squirmed and made incredibly sexy little sounds. Drew kept her movements varied, trying to ensure Hannah couldn't settle into a rhythm that would allow her to come.

She teased until she thought neither of them could take much more. She got herself into a kneeling position, moved the head of the cock up and down, lubing it with Hannah's wetness. It was intoxicating to watch. She tore her gaze away so she could look at Hannah's face.

Hannah stared at her with hunger in her eyes. "You win. Please, I need you inside me."

Drew pushed the tip in, felt Hannah clamp around her, pull her in. She slid in and out a few times, then locked eyes with Hannah again. "Oh, I think we both win."

Drew thrust into her completely. Hannah's eyes closed. "Oh, yes."

The last of Drew's restraint evaporated. She gave Hannah what Hannah had insisted she wanted all along—hard and fast. It made Drew feel dominant, invincible. She curved her fingers around Hannah's ankles. She lifted Hannah's legs, resting her feet on her shoulders. "I've got you."

Hannah relaxed into the new position, and the change in angle allowed Drew to go even deeper. The pressure on her clit started to build. The look of complete abandon on Hannah's face, the noises she made, just about did Drew in. She held herself back until Hannah's body convulsed around her. She finally let go, coming with the sound of Hannah's orgasm echoing in her ears.

They collapsed on the bed, sweaty and spent. Hannah couldn't remember the last time she'd been fucked so well. Maybe she never had been. Not that she made a habit of comparing sexual experiences, or partners, but this definitely stood out. Should she say that to Drew or would it be weird?

She was so busy contemplating, she missed something Drew said. "Huh?"

"Do you remember when you made that comment earlier about taking your turn?"

Hannah smiled and planted a small kiss on the side of Drew's breast. "Yeah."

"I thought you meant with the cock."

Hannah lifted her head, looked right into Drew's eyes. She swallowed the strange mix of arousal and unease. "You did? Is that something you want?"

Drew quirked a brow, more playful than judgmental. "Not always, but it can be fun to mix things up every now and then."

Hannah nodded slowly, turning the idea over in her mind. The unease, she realized, came from lack of experience, not desire. "I haven't, but I would."

Drew offered a casual shrug. "You don't have to. I just thought I'd float the idea, since you inadvertently put it in my head in the first place."

"No, no." The more she sat with it, the more intrigued she became. "I'd like to. As long as you're okay with the fact I may have no idea what I'm doing."

Drew raised a hand, ran it through Hannah's hair. "Something tells me you'll be a complete natural."

"Well, despite my reputation for being stubborn, I like to learn new things. And I don't mind taking direction from experts." She trailed a finger between Drew's breasts. "You, for example, seem to know exactly what you're doing."

"I'd be happy to be your guide."

"Excellent. So, when might I be able to schedule this lesson?"

Drew slid her hand down Hannah's back, gave her ass a playful squeeze. "How's every night next week?"

Hannah let the images of what might unfold dance through her mind. "Sounds perfect."

Something in Drew's face shifted. "Only we can't."

She didn't immediately elaborate, so Hannah ventured a "Why?"

"My friend, Baker, she's coming from the city for a visit."

Ah. Despite her disappointment, Hannah couldn't begrudge her that. "That's fun."

"It is. Or, at least, I thought it was. Now all I want to do is tell her not to come and have sex with you instead."

Even though Drew was teasing, Hannah appreciated the sentiment. "We can wait. We're not animals."

Drew rolled over so that she was half on top of Hannah. The feeling of Drew's body on her was enough to stir her desire yet again. "Speak for yourself. I have serious animal tendencies. And you definitely bring them out."

Hannah squirmed against Drew, had the pleasure of watching her eyes lose focus for a second before looking intensely at her. "Yeah? What do those animal tendencies look like?"

"Oh, I'll show you." Drew nipped her jaw and then proceeded to do exactly that.

Chapter Eighteen

Baker stood in the middle of the room, hands on hips. She looked around, nodding slowly. "Interesting."

"Dude, I didn't decorate it myself. Don't hate."

"I'm not hating. It's charming." She pressed her lips together and continued to nod.

"I think the style is called Adirondack. It's better than country."

Baker snickered. "You realize the hilarity of you even knowing the difference."

Drew scowled, but without malice. Giving each other a hard time was part of their dynamic. It had been ever since high school. "You get your own bedroom. It's got a real bed, too, not a futon."

"Movin' on up." Baker turned and looked at Drew. "It's totally nice, dude. And you get it all to yourself. That's a ten in my book."

Drew narrowed her eyes. The positivity made her suspicious. "You're developing a thing for Long Island, aren't you?"

"What? No. Of course not." She answered a little too quickly.

"You are. You're going to go all suburban on me. I can feel it." Suburban was way worse than country, especially without any mitigating factors.

"It's not that."

The tone made Drew worry that something might be wrong. "What is it? Tell me. I won't give you a hard time, I swear."

Baker offered a half shrug. "I've just been seeing this girl is all."

Oh. "And she lives out on Long Island."

"Northport."

The location registered. She let out a low whistle. "Dude, that's swanky."

"She's a teacher there, not some princess. It's just," Baker shrugged again, "I'm driving all over for work anyway. She's always going to the same place."

Drew tried to keep the surprise from her voice. "You're already talking about moving in together?"

"Just hypothetical. What might make sense, what we could afford."

Drew had no idea Baker was even dating someone. She had a pang of regret over being so far away. It was homesickness, not envy. "That's awesome. I'm happy for you."

"Well, I mean, it's not like we're talking exposed wood and plaid sofas." Baker gestured around her. Clearly, they'd maxed out her tolerance for the sentimental.

Drew chuckled. "Well, as long as it's not that."

"So, when do I get to meet your farmer?"

She didn't call Baker out on the abrupt change of subject. "I thought we'd take a ride out to the farm together in the morning. I need to pick up my ingredients for the weekend anyway. I took the liberty of inviting her to dinner on Monday."

Baker's eyes brightened. "Do I get to pick stuff?"

Baker fixated on that instead of the dinner invite? Interesting. "We'll leave early so there's time for that."

"I don't think I've ever picked stuff before. How weird is that?"

"Not weird at all. We're city folk." Drew sighed. "It's kind of nice."

Baker raised a brow.

"Not, like, as something I want to do with my life, but having the option is cool. There's something to be said for eating food you harvested yourself." Grown by a beautiful farmer she couldn't seem to get enough of.

"That totally makes sense." Baker nodded. "Speaking of food, do I get to come to the restaurant with you tonight?"

"Absolutely. I thought we'd go in early. You can see the kitchen, then hang at the bar for a bit. I'll feed you, then you can take my car to come back here. I'll get a ride home from Poppy." She'd planned it all out so they could maximize their time together even though she didn't have a ton of time off.

"Are you sure that's cool? I brought some work with me, so I'd love some time tonight to plow through it."

"It'll work great. Then we'll hit the farm tomorrow and have a fun lunch somewhere before I have to go in."

Baker nodded, seemingly happy with the plan. "And Sunday I'll putter around on my own."

"I'm sorry I couldn't take more time off."

Baker bumped her shoulder. "No worries, dude. You're a big shot now."

"When I'm really a big shot, I'll have a bigger staff who'll do my bidding when I want to take a night off."

Baker's arm came around her shoulders now, gave her a squeeze. "You'll get there, my friend. You'll get there."

She would. She was closer now than she'd ever been before. They got into Drew's car, complete with Baker's fancy laptop bag, and headed into town. They had a few minutes, so Drew pointed out a few places she thought Baker might like.

Baker nodded, soaking it all in. "It's a little Boerum Hill, isn't it?"

Drew laughed. The Brooklyn vibe hadn't been her imagination. "A little. But this is all of it. Five minutes in any direction and you're in cornfields, forest, or the lake."

Baker offered a shrug. "There are worse things, I suppose."

"True story." More so than she'd believed when she arrived only a couple of months ago.

When they got to the restaurant, Drew introduced her around and showed her the kitchen. Baker grinned, clearly impressed. "This is nice, dude. Way nicer than most of the kitchens you've worked in."

"Yeah, and about twice the size." It would be hard to go back to the cramped spaces of city kitchens. Well, not hard, just an adjustment.

"I know I made fun of you, but I'm happy for you."

Drew dropped her head to the side. As much as she craved accolades from critics and customers, getting praise from someone who was like family made her weirdly uncomfortable. "Let's get you set up at the bar."

She introduced Baker to Carlton, garnered a promise that he'd look out for her, then retreated to the kitchen. She'd come in later than usual and wanted to make sure everything was prepped for dinner service. It was. Clearly, her tirade the week before about the importance of it had left a lasting impression. She gathered the staff to run through the menu, then did a preparation of each of the specials. It probably wasn't necessary at this point, but she liked knowing there could be no misunderstanding her vision. And letting the waitstaff sample them made it much more likely they'd promote them to customers.

By the time she finished, the first customers of the night were settled in the dining room. The kitchen sprang into action and Drew found her groove. She knew enough about what Baker liked that she didn't bother offering a menu. She created small plate versions of things between orders and walked them out herself. She also made a few turns around the dining room. Drew didn't need to be the literal face of the restaurant, but she'd discovered the attention made customers feel special and, as a result, more likely to return.

Baker took off a little before eight and the rest of the night passed uneventfully. Almost as much as her family, Baker's approval meant a lot to her. She hoped she'd be able to say the same after the visit to the farm the next day, and after introducing Baker to Hannah.

❖

Hannah was happy to get an invite to join Drew and her best friend for dinner. She wasn't expecting them to visit the farm on top of it. But as she saw Drew headed her way, accompanied by someone she didn't recognize, she realized she'd get to meet Baker sooner rather than later.

She used their approach to study the two of them. They weren't siblings, but they could have been. Baker had the same complexion as Drew, the same confident stride. It was fascinating to watch and made her wonder what Drew's life in the city had looked like, what she'd been like as a child.

Drew caught her staring and offered a wave. Hannah returned it and went to meet them at the corner of the pepper patch. "Welcome to Three Willows Farm." She pulled off a work glove and stuck out her hand. "I'm Hannah."

"Baker." The woman took her hand, offered her a smile. "This place is spectacular."

Hannah beamed, unable to resist the compliment. "Thank you." She glanced at Drew. "I'm sorry I wasn't expecting you or I wouldn't have made you come out to the farthest field."

Drew waved a hand in dismissal. "We didn't want to interrupt your work, especially since you're coming for dinner Monday. But Baker's never been to a real farm before."

"Ever?" It shouldn't surprise her at this point, but she couldn't help it.

"I'm even more of a city rat than this one." Baker angled her head toward Drew.

Drew chuckled. "I may have told her she could pick some stuff."

Hannah smiled at Baker's enthusiastic nod. "All right. What's your pleasure?"

"Anything you'll let me get my hands on."

Hannah glanced at Drew, who shrugged. "I've already boxed up what I need for the restaurant."

"Do you cook? Do you want things you can take home with you?"

Baker's eyes lit up. "My girlfriend loves to cook."

"Perfect." She leaned down and picked up a basket. "Sweet and hot peppers will transport well. And as long as you pick some just shy of ripe, tomatoes will, too."

Since Hannah was harvesting as well, she stayed with them, asking questions about how long they'd been friends, what they did for fun in the city. Baker proved utterly charming. A bit smoother than Drew, but still sincere. Hannah liked her, and liked seeing Drew interact with someone she so clearly felt comfortable with.

When Baker had filled her basket to the brim, Hannah tipped her head toward the orchard. "How do you feel about peaches?"

Drew lifted both arms and looked at Hannah like she'd been betrayed. "Peaches are ready? I thought you promised me first dibs."

"Ooh, farm drama," Baker said, dropping her voice low.

Hannah folded her arms, enjoying the back and forth. "This is first dibs. I checked them this morning and the first wave is ready."

She had the pleasure of watching Drew's expression change. "Okay, I take it back. I humbly offer my eternal gratitude."

"As you should. The second Clare posts a crop alert, we'll be cleaned out." Hannah pointed to the far hill, then began leading the way to the orchard.

"Peaches grow on trees, right?" Baker asked.

Hannah laughed and Drew let out an exasperated, "Dude."

Baker lifted both hands in defense. "Kidding, kidding." She shrugged. "Mostly."

They walked along the side of the cornfield and up past the first few rows of apples. Drew pointed at them. "When will those be ready?"

"Not until early October." Drew frowned, so Hannah added, "But we have a couple of varieties that we'll be picking by mid-September."

Drew curled a lip. "Are they any good?"

Baker elbowed Drew in the ribs. "Don't imply she grows anything that isn't good." She glanced at Hannah and rolled her eyes. "Jeez."

"I didn't bring you here so you two could gang up on me," Drew said with mock annoyance.

Baker shrugged. "It's not my fault you make it so easy."

Hannah snickered. She liked Baker on her own but had a special appreciation for her dynamic with Drew. The unbridled ribbing reminded her of Jenn and told her a lot about Drew as a person. They got to the row of peaches Hannah had scoped out that morning. She went up to the first tree, felt a few of the peaches whose color had turned, and finally settled on one. She gave it a twist, then repeated the process with a second. She handed one to each of them. "As long as you don't mind the fuzz, have a taste."

Both Drew and Baker took a bite, but Hannah's gaze was on Drew. The way her eyes closed with pleasure. The way a drop of juice ran down her chin. The whole thing was way more sensual than it should be. Had Baker not been standing right there, she would have been tempted to catch the drip with her tongue, kiss Drew right there in the middle of the orchard.

"Okay, that's officially the best peach I've ever had in my life." Baker's voice snapped Hannah from her fantasy.

"Agreed." Drew nodded. "When do I get some for the restaurant?"

"My plan was next week, but only because I didn't have hands to pick any for you for today's order."

"So, we could pick some now and take them with us?" Drew angled her head at Baker. "She'll work for free."

Baker shrugged. "I will. For her, at least. Not in general."

Hannah chuckled. She grabbed three bushel baskets, handing one to each of them. "You want to make sure you're picking ripe ones. Give it the gentlest squeeze. It needs to give just a little. If it's hard, it'll take a week to ripen and still won't be quite as good."

Drew and Baker nodded like attentive students. "One of these will be enough for me, but I know Mariama would be ecstatic if I brought her some, too."

"That shouldn't be a problem."

They worked their way down a row, working each side of it. Hannah used a ladder for her picking, since most of the u-pickers would keep to the ground. It didn't take more than fifteen minutes or so to fill the baskets.

"I can't believe how much fun this is," Baker said.

Before Hannah could say anything, Drew chimed in. "Well, it's not all fun and games. You should be here on weeding day. Or when the things needing to be picked are on the ground."

The adamant tone made Hannah laugh. "I knew I worked you too hard."

"Oh, no. You're not going to take it back now. I kept up."

"You did. You definitely did."

Baker seemed to find the whole exchange beyond humorous. "I think I like this version of you," she said to Drew.

For some reason, the comment sent a flutter through Hannah's chest. She'd told herself it didn't matter if Drew remained a city person at heart. She'd done it convincingly, even. The last thing she needed to think about right now was Drew's heart.

They carried the peaches down to the barn. Both Drew and Baker worked in a comment about how freaking heavy they were. Hannah didn't, but only because she'd known they would be.

Drew popped the back hatch of her car. They loaded the peaches, then the rest of Drew's produce for the weekend. Hannah wished them a good day and was about to head back to the field when Drew snagged her hand. "Thanks for giving me first dibs on peaches."

It felt like she might be talking about more than peaches. Hannah swallowed the flutter that hadn't really gone away. "Of course. I'm sure you'll make something delicious."

"You should stop by for dinner. You can keep Baker company."

"I—"

"No pressure," Baker offered her a charming smile, "but I'd love company."

"Let me see what I can get done here in the next few hours. Can I text you one way or the other?"

"If you can't swing it, you can always sneak in the back door again." Drew offered a playful smirk that was way sexier than it had any right to be.

"No, no." Had it been just the two of them, Hannah might have ventured a racy comeback. But with Baker right there, she had a hard enough time not blushing. "If I can make it, I'll take a quick shower and put on clean clothes."

"I hope to see you," Baker said. "But if you're beat, don't worry about it."

Hannah nodded. "Thanks."

She realized Drew was still holding her hand. Such a casually intimate gesture. It reminded her of that night on her deck when they shared beers and BLTs, before they'd even kissed. It hadn't been that long ago, but so much had changed.

She was prevented from getting too lost in her thoughts when Drew gave her hand a squeeze. "I'll hope to see you, too."

Drew leaned in and kissed her. Nothing intense or lingering, but it sent little shivers of pleasure up and down her spine. She tried to keep her face casual, not give away just how much Drew affected her. "You two have a great day."

Another squeeze, then Drew let her hand go. "You too. Don't work too hard."

They got into Drew's car and left. Hannah headed into the barn to do a quick check of things, then back out to her peppers. She did the math of when she'd need to call it a day if she wanted to get home and change and make it to the restaurant at a decent hour. It was unlike her to blow off hours of daylight, but the invitation, she admitted to herself, was one she didn't want to pass up.

Chapter Nineteen

Hannah found Baker at the bar, nursing a beer and chatting with Carlton. Baker smiled and stood when Hannah caught her eye. "Hey. I wasn't sure you'd make it."

"I'm technically shirking, but my boss will understand."

Baker narrowed her eyes. "Aren't you the boss?"

"Indeed I am."

Baker pulled out the stool next to hers. "Well, in that case, let me get the boss something to drink. Beer? Wine?"

Hannah sat and glanced at Carlton. "The dry Riesling, please."

"You got it." Carlton poured a glass and set it in front of her. Hannah thanked him, then turned her attention to Baker.

Baker took her seat again but angled herself toward Hannah. "That's a really impressive operation you have."

Hannah smiled. "Thanks. It's small, but I'm proud of it."

"The fact that it's small but that you grow as much as you do is what makes it so impressive."

She tapped her finger on the bar. "You know just the right thing to say to a girl."

"I do." Baker winked. "But in your case, it's the truth."

Hannah had a flash of Drew and Baker out together, trying to chat up women. Was that Drew's usual modus operandi? "So, how long have you and Drew been friends?"

Baker looked up at the ceiling. "Oh, man, since fifth grade. So, like, twenty years. That makes me feel so old."

Hannah chuckled. She knew the feeling. "My friend Jenn and I are the same. Which makes me wonder if you two had an ill-fated attempt to date or hook up like she and I did."

Baker choked on her beer and coughed. The cough morphed into laughter, the kind that had her bent over, with tears running down her face. "We didn't, thank God. We went right to being bros."

Hannah chuckled. Drew had probably been the cutest baby dyke ever. "It must be easier in a big school in the city. I think we were the only queer people we knew. Well, except for a really sweet drama club kid named Tyler, but you know what I mean."

"Yeah, you're probably right." Baker wiped her eyes and her expression grew serious. "Was it hard for you to come out?"

"More awkward than hard. My family is religious, but not in the extreme. I never worried about being disowned or anything. It was more the weirdness of talking to my parents about anything that had to do with sex." She shuddered at the memory.

"Sure. Do you have siblings? Were you the oldest?"

"Two older brothers, actually. Between that and growing up on a dairy farm, you'd think I would have gotten over any shyness about sex at an early age." Talking with her mother hadn't been all that bad. She'd just never been close with her father. Even before she decided to go off on her own and grow vegetables, he'd never seemed to know what to do with her. And vice versa.

Baker smiled. "It's always harder when it's about you. I had three older sisters, one of whom was married with a baby by the time I started high school. I think it took the pressure off me."

She'd never thought of it that way. "You're so right. My brothers gave my mother grandbabies and my father the promise of taking over the farm and the family name. Saved me from being the big disappointment."

"Are you close to them now?"

Hannah ran a finger up and down the stem of her wineglass. "Yes and no. They're only fifteen minutes or so up the road, so I spend a good amount of time with them. I'm close to my mom and my little sister. My dad and I don't see eye to eye on most things."

"Politics?"

If only it was that simple. "Yes, but also business. He thinks running a farm the way I do is impractical and self-indulgent."

Baker took a swig of beer and raised a brow. "Self-indulgent?"

"Yeah." Hannah searched for the right words, words that would explain the rift without vilifying him. "Like, it's a nice idea for a perfect world, but it's no way to earn a living."

"Ah. He's a quantity over quality kind of guy."

"He wouldn't appreciate any digs on the quality of the milk he produces, but yeah. He grows his own corn, but he keeps the cows cooped up in the barn and feeds them corn instead of letting them pasture graze. That kind of thing." God, the number of arguments they'd had over pesticides.

"That sounds really hard. I'm sorry." Baker gave her a look of such understanding, Hannah couldn't help but wonder if she had a similar experience with her own parents.

"Oh, it's not as bad as all that. We're all still on speaking terms and I'm at the house at least a couple times a month for family dinner."

Baker's gaze remained kind. "Still. Good for you for blazing your own path."

"Thanks." Hannah rolled her eyes. "Now, let's talk about something more fun. Like what Drew was like in high school."

Baker laughed in a way that told Hannah there was no shortage of stories. "Where do I even begin?"

❖

Drew emerged from the kitchen and glanced toward the bar. Baker was still there, but she appeared to be deep in conversation with the woman next to her. It only took a second to register the woman was Hannah. Hannah was laughing and had her hand on Baker's leg. Drew's instant delight at seeing her clashed with something else, something not at all pleasant.

Knowing the stab of jealousy was irrational did little to squelch it. Drew considered returning to the kitchen until she could pull it together, but Baker looked up and their eyes met. Drew growled under her breath. She was stuck now.

She headed to the bar. Hannah turned. She wouldn't say Baker vanished, but it was like she faded into the background. Hannah's eyes fixed on hers and Drew felt like the only person in the room. It probably wasn't good that Hannah had such an effect on her, or that she liked it so much, but she didn't care. Hannah's gaze—happy, easy, intimate—was all that mattered. She couldn't help but smile. "Hey. I didn't think I'd see you again."

Hannah shrugged. "You did promise free dinner."

Baker tutted. "And here I thought she showed up for the company."

Hannah glanced at Baker, offered a wink. "That, too."

"Likely story."

The banter was more friendly than flirtatious, but it didn't help the weird jealous vibe coursing through her. "So, did Carlton give you menus? Do you know what you want?"

Baker snagged the menu card from the bar. "I want the chicken with sundried tomatoes and goat cheese. And the summer squash with pecans to start."

"Excellent choices." Drew looked at Hannah. "And for you?"

Hannah didn't look to the menu. In fact, she didn't break eye contact at all. She bit her bottom lip just long enough to make Drew's insides churn. "Surprise me."

It didn't matter that she was talking about dinner or that Baker was right there. It didn't matter that they were in the middle of the crowded restaurant or that order tickets were popping out of the printer at full speed. In that moment, Drew wanted nothing more than to push Hannah up against the bar and fill her hands with Hannah's hair and put her mouth—

"Drew?" Hannah asked.

She blinked. Even with Hannah pulling her back, it took a minute for the intensity of her reaction to subside. When her vision cleared, both Hannah and Baker were staring at her—Baker with a look of amusement and Hannah with one that bordered on smug. She focused on Hannah. "My pleasure."

As much as she hated to leave them, she needed to get back to work. Drew returned to the kitchen and put in the order for Baker's first course. For Hannah, she settled on the eggplant puree with roasted peppers. She carried the plates out herself but did a loop of the dining room instead of lingering. Between the two of them, it would be too easy to lose track of time and leave the kitchen scrambling.

She checked the tickets, jumped in on the sauté station to help Poppy get a half dozen plates of fish out at once, then turned her attention to making Hannah and Baker's entrées. She settled on the lamb for Hannah, thinking she'd like the toasted orzo laced with lemon and mint she'd created to pair with it.

When she returned to the dining room, Baker and Hannah had their heads together, like they were sharing secrets. She was torn between wanting to know what they were discussing, since it likely had to do with her, and not. Not was probably better. On her way back to the kitchen, Baker gave her a knowing smile but didn't tease her about anything—unusual to say the least. And when things slowed down enough for her to join them while they devoured a pair of lavender honey crème brûlées, conversation had lulled into the kind of quiet comfort that came from being friends.

Hannah kissed Drew's cheek and thanked her for dinner, then headed home. Baker decided to linger at the now-empty bar with her computer and get some work done. Drew returned to the kitchen to finish service, only to find Poppy trying to mediate a screaming match between two of the prep cooks over the whereabouts of several bunches of basil.

"Have you two lost your mind?" Drew stepped between them and sullen silence ensued. "I can hear you in the dining room." That part wasn't true, but it would help shame them into acting like grownups.

"Sorry, Chef," they both mumbled.

"Back to work. Now."

The entire kitchen staff, who'd paused whatever task they were doing to watch the fray, launched into a flurry of movement and attention directed anywhere but at her. Drew rolled her eyes and shook her head. She'd not had any drama in weeks, so it was overdue, but that didn't make her any more tolerant of it. Satisfied things were back on track, she pulled Poppy aside. "Was that really about basil?"

Poppy chuckled. "Word on the street is they hooked up last weekend, but now Carrie isn't returning Kyle's texts."

"Seriously?" It was easier to date other people in the restaurant business, if for no other reason than scheduling. But Drew had learned very early in her career to steer clear of anyone who worked in the same kitchen. Too much potential for things to head south, and the prospect of working in such close quarters with an ex of any kind was, well, never a good thing.

"It's handled. Don't worry about it."

Her instinct was to wade in anyway. She had absolutely no patience for petty bickering, especially if it threatened to derail the flow that kept service running smoothly. But she trusted Poppy and wanted the rest of the staff to see her as a leader. It was good for business and would also make it a hell of a lot easier for her to take a day off every now and then. "All right. If you say it's handled, it's handled."

She focused her attention on the handful of tickets that came in during the scene, getting the plates done and out the door. The last couple hours of her shift dragged by. It was the first time since opening she'd had that feeling, and she didn't like it. By the time she and Baker were in the car back to her place, Drew had a gross mix of exhaustion and crankiness simmering.

"So, you and Hannah looked pretty chummy tonight."

Baker shifted, angling her body toward Drew. "She's really great. And not that she wasn't cute in her farmer clothes, but, damn, she cleans up fine."

The stab of jealousy from earlier in the evening returned, multiplied by about ten. Drew bit back a snarky comeback. "What did you two talk about, anyway?"

"Everything, really. The farm, my job, books, movies, family. I guess I expected her to be, I don't know, kind of country. But she's smart and sophisticated. I totally get why you have the hots for her."

Drew scowled, her irritation bubbling over. "Don't you have a girlfriend?"

"Dude." Baker looked at her like she'd grown a pair of horns. "I'm not moving in on her. She's your girlfriend. And as I made clear, I'm pretty much in love with Lucy."

"Sorry." It came out more accusation than apology.

"Don't apologize, just tell me why you're so pissed." Before Drew could formulate an answer, Baker leaned over and smacked her arm. "Oh, my God. You're jealous."

"I'm not jealous." That's exactly what she was, she just didn't want to admit it. Or why.

"You are. That means you've gotten all weird and possessive or you're way more gone over her than you've let on. Please tell me it's the latter."

Drew didn't answer. It was definitely the latter. She'd been dancing around that reality, content to let it hover around the edges of her consciousness. Now, with someone who knew her better than almost anyone, she could no longer do that. "Yeah."

Baker studied her, seeming more satisfied than surprised. "Good for you."

They pulled into the driveway and Drew cut the engine. "Is it, though?"

"I don't see why not. Hannah's awesome."

Drew drummed her fingers on the steering wheel. "She is. She's also really rooted here. I'm not."

"I feel you." Baker sighed. "But maybe don't borrow trouble. You're here for at least a year or two, right? Anything could happen, good or bad."

"Is that supposed to make me feel better?" Because it didn't.

"It's just the truth, dude. I'm saying you shouldn't fight it based on what might play out in the distant future. She could get sick of your ass by then."

It was the kind of advice Drew would give. As much as she knew what she wanted in life, she also believed in living in the moment, especially when it came to relationships. "Maybe you're right."

"I usually am." Baker tipped her head toward the house. "Now let's go in. It's way past my bedtime."

Drew wished Baker a good night and went to take a shower. She did a quick towel dry and pulled on a pair of loose cotton boxers. Alone in the quiet, she gave herself a minute to mull over her feelings for Hannah. Being invested in a relationship didn't make a whole lot of sense right now, for her career or otherwise. But maybe Baker was right. She really liked spending time with Hannah and it seemed to be mutual. Maybe, for the moment, that's all that mattered.

Chapter Twenty

Hannah worked her way down the row, filling a crate with bell peppers. Baker had left for the city less than a week ago and now Drew's family was coming up for a visit. And she found herself with yet another invitation to dinner. It shouldn't have mattered to her one way or the other, but it weighed on her, almost like dealing with her own family.

"Dealing with" probably wasn't the right phrase, or a fair one. She had no reason to be nervous about meeting them. It wasn't like they were coming to meet the girlfriend. But something in Drew's demeanor the last couple of days gave Hannah that impression. What was she supposed to do with that? Nothing. She wasn't supposed to do anything. Even if she'd started to think about Drew as more than a casual thing, they'd not talked about it. And she had a hard time imagining Drew talking about her the way Baker talked about her girlfriend, or the way Jenn had taken to talking about Suri.

Daisy loped across the field from the orchard and settled herself in the dirt between the rows. "It's a hot one, isn't it? Don't worry. We'll get rain before the day is done."

They were supposed to get torrential rain, the edge of a slow-moving front forecast to soak the region for several days. She was grateful for the rain but worried about the intensity of the storm. She hustled through picking peppers so she could get started on peaches before the worst of it blew in. She pulled her cart to the barn and did a quick check on Clare. Jeremiah had Guy out harvesting tomatoes, so she left the wagon for them and grabbed a stack of bushel baskets. She took them out to her truck and started up the dirt road to the orchard.

Hannah found a few people picking. Seeing people on her land, appreciating the fruits of her labor, never failed to make her heart swell. She pulled around to the far end of the rows and got to work. The u-pick crowd had been big over the weekend, so there were few fully ripe peaches to be had. She focused on those that were close, the ones that would be likely to fall with high winds. They could finish ripening off the tree and keep the farm stand stocked if it was too soggy for folks to want to pick themselves.

She moved one of the tripod ladders around, snagging big beautiful fruit just starting to blush. She'd filled close to a dozen baskets when the wind really started to pick up. Dark clouds gathered from the west. She picked up her pace. There was the financial implication of losing part of a crop to weather, but she had an emotional reaction that went beyond the money. Seeing fruit bruised and ruined on the ground broke her heart.

The rumbles of thunder started, paired with flashes of lighting in the distance. The last of the u-pickers called it a day, leaving Hannah alone among the trees. She refocused her efforts closer to the ground, knowing better than to take chances on becoming a human lightning rod.

As so often happened with summer storms, the sky opened up all at once. She went from perfectly dry to completely soaked in about ten seconds. The rain was the hard, pelting kind, but it cooled her skin and made her feel alive. She filled her final basket, climbed into her truck, and headed back to the barn. She pulled around back and started unloading.

"Are you out of your mind?"

The sharpness of Drew's voice startled her and she almost dropped a whole basket of peaches. She tightened her grip on the handles and turned. "What are you talking about?"

"You were out in this? Are you trying to get yourself killed?"

Nothing in Drew's tone indicated she was joking, but Hannah couldn't stop the laugh that escaped. "Don't worry, I've been at this awhile. I know what I'm doing."

Drew's brooding expression didn't change. "I saw a tree get hit by lightning on my way over here."

"And as soon as the lightning got close, I headed in." Was Drew really going to scold her like she was some willful child?

"But you're soaked, which means you were out in it. I don't see why you'd take that risk. To save a few peaches?"

Normally, she'd find that kind of comment condescending, leading her to fight back or shut down entirely. But something in Drew's tone held her in check. She seemed genuinely worried. Hannah set down the basket, then went over to her. "Hey, it's okay. I'm okay. I was just getting into my truck when the rain started."

Drew closed her eyes. "I'm sorry. I'm being an ass."

"Not an ass." Hannah gave her arm a squeeze. "Overprotective maybe, but not an ass."

"Okay, sure. Still, I'm sorry."

Hannah narrowed her eyes. "Are you okay? Is something else bothering you?"

"Totally fine."

Hannah didn't believe her for a second. But it wasn't really her place to pry and she didn't know what she'd do with the answer even if Drew did open up. "If you say so."

"I do." Drew nodded and offered a smile, the kind of gesture that said they were done discussing it.

"So, what brings you by? Did you run out of tomatoes?" She made sure her tone was playful. She didn't want Drew to think she was picking a fight on top of it.

"I'm having my mom and grandmother come to the restaurant for dinner Saturday and I wanted to see if you wanted to join them."

She'd already agreed to dinner at Drew's place Monday. Sharing a meal with just the two of them and Drew stopping by the table from time to time did not sound like a good time. She was relieved she already had plans. "It's my dad's birthday. I'm already locked into dinner with the fam."

"Ah. No worries, then." Drew didn't sound disappointed or relieved.

"But we're still on for Monday, right?"

"Absolutely. It'll be great. I thought they'd enjoy company at the restaurant and I know how you feel about free dinner."

Drew's teasing dispelled any awkwardness over her declining the invitation. "This is true."

"I might still bring them by the farm. My Grann in particular said she wanted to see it."

Hannah smiled. "I like her already."

"I'll get out of your hair. I'm sure you have plenty to do." Drew started to leave, but stopped. She turned back to Hannah. "Sorry I flipped out earlier. It's not my style."

"It's all good, city mouse."

That got her a laugh. Drew offered a wave and then she was gone. Hannah resumed spreading the peaches out so they could dry. Jeremiah came in to help. He'd been caught in the rain as well and was soaked. They finished the chore and Hannah sent him home early. They'd have to do some work in the rain, but she'd meant what she said to Drew. She didn't take chances when it came to lightning.

❖

Just as she had the day Baker arrived, Drew drove into town and over to the Cornell campus. She had the same excitement, tinged with nerves. The source of the nerves, though, felt different. Drew wasn't worried about her family having a good time, or even meeting Hannah. No, this time Drew worried they would see just how much she'd settled into her life upstate. She wasn't ready for the questions that revelation might stir up. And she certainly didn't have any answers.

She tried to put it out of her mind while she waited for the bus. Manman and Grann would pick up even a hint of stress or weirdness in her.

When the bus pulled in, she got out of her car. The downpour had slowed to a drizzle at least. She stood, shifting her weight from one foot to the other. People began to disembark—college students and professor types and older couples. Like at the airport, a few people had loved ones waiting for them. Some shared hugs and smiles, others an enthusiastic kiss.

Grann appeared first. She held a newspaper over her head with one hand, grasped her cane in the other. Despite the cane, she looked as formidable as ever. Drew waved. "Grann."

She turned toward Drew, nodded her recognition. By then, Manman was right behind her. Drew hurried over and took turns hugging them. She lingered for a moment in her mother's embrace, absorbing the smell of orange blossom and clove. "I'm so glad you're here."

"About damn time you invited us," Grann said. "We were contemplating showing up on your doorstep unannounced."

"She exaggerates." Manman patted Drew's cheek. "But we were glad to get an invitation."

Drew lifted a shoulder, feeling like she was ten and had been caught hiding something. "It's not that I didn't want you to come."

Grann swung her cane with surprising dexterity, bumping Drew on the behind. "We know, child. We know."

Drew collected their bags from where they'd been stored under the bus and carried them to her car. After securing them in the trunk, she opened the passenger side doors. "I'm only about fifteen minutes up the lake."

Grann laughed. "Did you hear that, Angelique? Up the lake."

She took Route 89 instead of 96 to give them a glimpse of said lake. Even in the rain, the view was beautiful. It surprised her to feel a little surge of pride pointing it out between the trees. When they passed Taughannock Park, she gestured to the picnic tables set up right on the water. "Assuming the rain lets up at some point, we can come spend the day if you want. I've been told it gets really busy on the weekends, but weekdays aren't bad."

She turned off the main road, winding her way home. When she pulled into the driveway, her Grann reached over and patted her knee. "It's adorable."

"It's amazing what you can get for the money up here," she said, suddenly self-conscious of having the whole house to herself.

"No doubt," Manman said from the back seat. "Let's see the inside."

Drew grabbed their bags and ushered them up the front steps. She unlocked the door, then motioned for them to go in ahead of her. "After you."

"It's like a cabin in the mountains," Grann said with what sounded more like amusement than surprise.

Manman laughed. "When have you ever been to a cabin in the mountains?"

She planted her hands on her hips. "I watch television, don't I?"

"You are right." Drew nudged the door closed with her butt. "It's called Adirondack style. It's a thing, I'm told."

"See?" She nodded, a look of vindication on her face.

"I'll have you two share my room, if you're okay with that. The bed's a queen."

Manman came up and kissed her cheek. "That'll do just fine."

Drew carried the bags to her room and set them on the chest at the foot of the bed. She gave them the tour, which consisted of the second bedroom, the bathroom, and then the kitchen and living room area where they'd come in. Even with the rustic decor, it was nicer than pretty much any of the apartments she'd had to date. Hopefully, by the time she moved back, she'd be able to afford something even nicer that she didn't need to share with a roommate.

She glanced at the clock on the stove. "Cocktails?"

Both women heartily agreed. Drew set them up at the small table and made a batch of Manhattans before starting dinner. She got caught up on the neighborhood gossip and heard all about the new principal at her mother's school. She put the chicken she'd been brining in to roast and assembled the roasted vegetable salad she'd planned as a first course.

Drew joined them at the table and soaked up the compliments. Neither her mother nor grandmother had been stingy with praise during her childhood or when she was in training to be a chef, but they'd been judicious. When they said something of hers was good, she knew they meant it.

"So, what would the two of you most like to do while you're here? I know wineries are on the list, but what else?"

"We want to see your restaurant," Manman said.

"Of course. I reserved a table for you for dinner Saturday."

"You don't have to treat us to dinner. We know what a good cook you are."

"Nick, my boss, insisted. It'll be on the house."

Grann raised a brow. "On the house, huh?"

Drew smiled. Her prior bosses had rarely been so generous or invested in their chefs' personal lives. "He's a great guy, super focused on family. He's excited to meet you."

Manman sipped her Manhattan. "Then we're excited to meet him."

Drew tapped her foot a few times, trying to ignore the sudden wave of nervous energy. "I want to take you to one of the farms, too. I've gotten to know the owner pretty well."

Despite the innocuous nature of her words, the underlying meaning came through. The women gave her identical looks—curious and clearly expecting an explanation. Manman spoke first. "Tell us more."

"It's the place I went the day of my interview. The owner, Hannah, is friends with the owner of the restaurant. Her farm is one of our primary local suppliers."

"She's the one with the tomatoes." Grann nodded knowingly.

"Tomatoes?"

Drew ran a hand up the back of her neck. "I've spent some time at the farm, sourcing ingredients, but also learning about things. Including tomatoes."

"Ah." With that single syllable, Manman conveyed plenty.

"Are you doing more than picking tomatoes with her?" Grann had never been one to mince words.

Drew was saved from answering by the oven timer. She'd never been so grateful for the shrill beep. She took her time plating the chicken, arranging it just so on the rice and making perfect piles of sautéed green beans. She carried the plates to the table, opened a bottle of Chardonnay, and poured glasses. She took her seat again and found two expectant faces, patient but unfazed, watching her. She took a sip of wine. "Yes."

"Why do you seem so unhappy about it?" Her mother's face had taken on a shadow of worry.

"Oh, I'm not unhappy." How could she explain it in a way that didn't make her seem like a total player? "I'm just not sure about where it's going in the long term. I mean, I don't plan on living here forever."

"Ah." Again with the one syllable that said so much more.

"I invited her to dinner here on Monday." She'd done so casually, thinking her grandmother especially would get a kick out of meeting the female farmer who supplied much of the restaurant. Now, of course, it felt like a much bigger deal. And canceling would draw more attention rather than less.

"That sounds lovely. We certainly want to meet the people who are part of your life up here." Grann's tone was encouraging, almost too encouraging.

"Agreed." Manman was much more matter-of-fact. It effectively closed any discussion on the matter, a skill she carried over from her classroom that Drew both admired and envied.

With dinner finished, both women opted to call it an early night. Drew got them settled into her room, then found herself in the spare one, book on her chest and staring out the window. She still had moments of awe over the night sky and all its variations. Tonight, the moon was full, leaving only Venus and the brightest stars visible. It cast a silvery light that seemed more like something out of a movie than real life.

She could use the same analogy to talk about her life here. It wasn't shimmery or perfect by any means, but it felt at times like she was more a character in a movie than herself. Maybe that's what made it all feel so strange. Rather than freak her out, the idea made Drew feel better. It was her current situation that made everything seem so different, not any intrinsic change in her.

Chapter Twenty-one

Birthday dinners at the Little household were serious business. Regardless of whose birthday it was, the celebrations were some of Hannah's favorite memories. A huge meal, chosen by the birthday girl or boy, complete with one of her mother's homemade cakes. Presents were always practical, but with one indulgent one thrown in. Best of all, though, was that everyone was on their best behavior. What had been a sternly enforced edict as a child had become an unspoken rule. At birthday dinners, there was no bickering and no judgment, at least none spoken out loud.

She sat next to Clare at the dining room table. Even with her nieces and nephews at a kids' table, there were eight of them. She wondered idly what would happen if she or Clare ever brought someone home. They'd have to squeeze in extra chairs from the kitchen. She shook off the idea and turned her attention to the meal—fried chicken, mashed potatoes, green beans, and biscuits—100 percent her father's favorites.

"How's your little deal with the restaurant going?"

Hannah's jaw tightened. He could be dismissive without even trying. She wondered if it came naturally or was a skill he'd worked to hone. "Really well, actually. It's probably accounting for close to twenty percent of our sales right now."

He sniffed, but nodded. "Well, I think it's one of the smartest things you've done. A contract with consistent income is worth it, even if the profit margins are lower."

Hannah let out a small chuckle. "Look at us, agreeing on something."

"You say that like we disagree about everything." His scowl exaggerated the crease between his eyes.

"Don't we?" She'd kept her tone light enough to be teasing, but it still garnered a warning look from her mother.

"Of course not. We both respect the land, believe in the value of an honest day's work."

It didn't seem like he was baiting her, but Hannah remained leery. She'd been sucked into too many fights with him to be anything else. And she'd promised her mother, as well as herself, that she wouldn't cause a scene on his birthday. "Traits I'm proud to have gotten from you."

At the compliment, he sat a little taller in his chair. "I thank God for that every day."

She wasn't sure what to make of his sentimentality. She glanced at her mother, who lifted her shoulder an inch and smiled. As if sensing her discomfort, Clare announced they should do presents before cake. Hannah chuckled to herself. She thanked God for Clare every day.

Everyone filed out to the living room, her father settling into his easy chair like a monarch presiding over court. The grandkids went first, offering homemade cards and a mug with a collage of photos of them printed on it. He made his way through the pile. It was clear he enjoyed the attention and was embarrassed by it at the same time. Yet another trait she'd inherited from him.

She felt silly giving him yet another pair of Columbia pants, but he loved them, wearing them for work as much as on his fly fishing trips. And since they cost just enough that he refused to buy them for himself, it seemed to work out well for everyone.

Over cake, she heard about the newest calves, the effects of the recent storm on the corn crop, and the ever-fluctuating price of milk. For the first time in as long as she could remember, she felt relaxed as she and her brothers and parents hashed out the ups and downs of farm life. She was so used to anticipating traps or potential arguments, she'd forgotten just how nice it was to talk shop with people in the business. Even if they weren't technically in the same business.

Clare dragged Hannah to her room and pulled out her computer to show off the analytics on her web traffic and social media sites. Hannah didn't know what half the words meant, but Clare's enthusiasm came through loud and clear. And the numbers—hits and click-throughs and other things Hannah had never heard of—were higher than she'd even hoped for. "I've been thinking the increase in customers had to do with the weather, but it's you, isn't it? This stuff is working."

Clare beamed. "I think so. I mean, I don't want to take all the credit, but—"

Hannah cut her off. "Let me give credit where credit is due."

"I'm glad you're happy because I need to talk to you about something."

Hannah made a face. "Are you bored? You don't want to do it anymore?"

"No, no, no." Clare waved her hands back and forth. "It's not that at all. I'm considering taking on a new client and I wanted to make sure you're okay with it."

She'd never tell Clare she couldn't work for someone else, but she was curious. "What kind of client?"

Clare's expression was so serious. "I'd never take on another farm. That would be a conflict of interest. But I think this would be an excellent addition to my portfolio and has some real potential for audience overlap."

When did her little sister start sounding like an advertising executive instead of a teenager? "Audience overlap?"

"It's Fig. Nick follows Three Willows and asked if I'd be willing to do some work for him, too. It wouldn't interfere with my hours at the farm. I'd just need to stop by a few times a week to take pictures."

She was proud of Clare's talent, not to mention her ambition. She intended to tell her as much, too, but it didn't mean she couldn't do a little reconnaissance first. "So, is this about expanding your portfolio or expanding the amount of time you spend with Kristen?"

Clare turned bright pink. "I mean, Kristen and I are best friends. We see each other all the time."

"And?"

"And I like her a lot and always want to hang out with her."

Hannah didn't relish making her squirm, but she was pretty sure her gut was spot-on with this and it would probably be less painful for everyone to just get it out in the open. "As a friend?"

"As a friend." Clare took a deep breath. She made eye contact with Hannah for a second, then stared at her hands. "And maybe more."

"Do you know if the maybe more is mutual?"

Clare looked up, clearly startled. Like it was the last question in the world she expected Hannah to ask. She bit her lip, looked over Hannah's shoulder. Eventually she nodded. "Yeah."

Hannah couldn't quell her enthusiasm. "Clare, that's great."

"You can't tell Mom and Dad."

Hannah tried not to laugh. "You know they're okay with the gay thing, right? I kind of blazed that trail for you." Clare still looked mortified, so Hannah added, "You're welcome, by the way."

"Kristen's parents don't know."

"Nick and Leda?" Hannah didn't think she could come up with a more progressive couple if she tried. "They're cool. Way cooler than Mom and Dad, actually."

"I know!" Clare practically shouted her reply. "I keep telling her that, but she's nervous. She keeps talking about what happened when Alyn came out."

Hannah didn't know Alyn aside from meeting her in passing at Clare's basketball games, but her father was a real piece of work. Carl Wilson made Rudolph Little seem like Santa Claus. "I imagine that didn't go well. But she has to know her parents are nothing like the Wilsons."

Clare shrugged. "She just needs time, I think. I mean, that's what she says."

Poor Clare. "We all have to get there in our own time. I'm sorry for you, though. I'm sure it's hard."

"It's not so bad." Clare blushed.

"You make out when it's just the two of you in the farm stand, don't you?"

She looked at Hannah then, right in the eyes, and winced. "Are you mad?"

"Of course not." Hannah thought back to some of the more creative places on the farm she and her first girlfriend had used for making out. To this day, the hayloft of her parents' barn made her think of hot summer afternoons and stolen kisses. "As long as it's only kissing."

"Jeez, Hannah. God. I wouldn't do that."

"No, but you are teenagers. I was up to all sorts of trouble by the time I was your age. And don't get me started on your brothers."

Clare's eyes got huge. "Really?"

"I'm pretty sure sneaking around is an essential part of growing up and of figuring out who you are."

That seemed to make her feel better. "Yeah."

"But just because you don't have to worry about getting pregnant, it doesn't mean you don't need to talk about things like safety and consent."

"Hannah." Clare dragged out the word, embarrassment back in full force.

"Hey, you can have this conversation with me or you can have it with Mom."

The prospect of talking about sex with their mother proved a persuasive motivator. They spent the next half hour talking about safe sex practices and ways to make talking about them less daunting. By the time they were done, Hannah had learned a few things herself. Sex ed had clearly come a long way in the last decade.

The party broke up and Hannah hugged her good-byes. She drove home with the windows down and the radio up. Often, she did so to cool off, to clear her mind after yet another verbal sparring match with her father. Tonight, she simply basked in the wind blowing through her hair, cool and damp from another day of rain. She wondered what Drew was doing, how her family had enjoyed their dinner at Fig.

At home, she changed into pajamas and curled up on the sofa with a book and her phone. She texted Jenn to share the oddity of her day, then gave in and sent a message to Drew. Neither of them answered immediately, though, and Hannah's eyes started to feel heavy. Tomorrow was supposed to be another soggy one, but there were chores she couldn't put off any longer, so she hauled herself upstairs and crawled into bed. Thoughts of Drew and her family swirled in her mind, but instead of keeping her awake, they carried her to sleep.

❖

Hannah pulled into Drew's driveway and cut the engine. She sat for a moment and closed her eyes. She'd spent a full eight hours at the farm, more than half of it harvesting things in the unyielding rain, her boots heavy with mud. She'd almost fallen asleep in the shower. She took a deep breath. At least she was too tired to be nervous.

She dashed to Drew's porch, trying to dodge the drops that continued to fall. Before she could knock, the front door swung open. On the other side, a woman with snow white hair and skin much darker than Drew's smiled at her. "Hello, you must be Hannah. I'm Rose."

In spite of her fatigue, Hannah found herself smiling. This must be Drew's grandmother. She extended her hand. "It's nice to meet you, Rose."

Rose took the hand with a grip much stronger than she expected and pulled her into a hug. It could have been awkward, but it wasn't. Rose let go, then patted her arm. "We're so glad you could join us."

Hannah stepped the rest of the way into the house, looking for Drew. She stood at the stove, tending a pot of something. Next to her, a tall and elegant woman looked on. Process of elimination would have told her it was Drew's mother, but the family resemblance was keen. Like Rose, her skin was darker, almost the color of umber. But the shape of her eyes, the line of her jaw—Drew had definitely inherited them from her.

"Hey." Drew looked over her shoulder. "I was afraid you might get washed out."

"Almost." Hannah chuckled.

Drew remained at the stove, but her mother crossed the room to where Hannah was. She offered a hand. "It was nice of you to come. I'm sure you had a long day already. I'm Angelique."

Her demeanor might have been more reserved than Rose's, but Hannah instinctively liked her. She took the hand. "Hannah. And thank you for having me. I'm happy to meet you." She paused, then decided complimenting Drew couldn't hurt. "I'm also happy to go anywhere that gets me dinner made by Drew."

The comment earned her a laugh. Drew offered her a warm smile but didn't move to kiss her. She wondered if it had to do with her family being there or tending whatever she had on the stove. Which smelled absolutely amazing, actually. As if following the trail of her thoughts, Drew gestured to the pot. "I took the liberty of getting started. You tend to arrive hungry."

Hannah winced. "If that wasn't true, I'd be offended."

Rose gave Hannah's arm another pat. "A woman after my own heart. Can I get you a cocktail, dear? We're having Manhattans."

Of course Drew's beautiful, poised mother and ninety-pound grandmother were drinking Manhattans. "I'd love to say yes, but I'm afraid I'd nod off into my plate."

"Wine, then." Angelique pointed to the fridge. "We have a couple bottles of white chilling."

"That would be lovely." Angelique started opening the wine, leaving Hannah with nothing to do. She walked over to the stove and peered around Drew. "So, what are we having?"

Drew leaned in and kissed her cheek. It caught Hannah off guard, both in its casual intimacy and because she'd just talked herself out of being disappointed that Drew hadn't kissed her when she arrived. "Bouillon with yams and beef patties."

"Oh, that sounds delicious." Hannah glanced at Drew's grandmother, who sat at the small kitchen table with a cocktail glass in her hand. "Did she learn it from you?"

"She did." Rose flipped her hand back and forth. "She's taken some liberties, but they work."

Hannah accepted a glass of white wine from Angelique. She thanked her, then raised a brow at Drew. "Liberties?"

"I knew better than to think I could ever make the original better than either of them, so I had to come up with my own version," Drew said.

Hannah took a sip. "A very diplomatic answer."

"My mother didn't raise a fool." Drew winked at Angelique and was met with a look that managed to be at once bland and deeply affectionate. It reminded Hannah of her relationship with her mother and added to her own affection for Drew.

She asked Rose and Angelique about their visit and the things they'd done. Dishes were passed family-style. Not unlike the picnic, really, or the meals they'd shared together at Drew's house or hers. But those times were dates in a way, even if she'd not acknowledged it at the time, and this felt like a family meal. The food was beyond good, but there was an easiness to it that still surprised her. Such a departure from what she'd expected when she first met Drew.

When she didn't think she could manage another bite, she insisted on doing the dishes as a token of her gratitude for being fed so well. Angelique offered to join her, and the next thing she knew, she washed while Angelique dried. It was at once surreal and completely natural to be at the sink next to Drew's mom.

"You must be so proud, seeing Drew as an executive chef at such a young age."

Angelique nodded. "When she puts her mind to something, there's no stopping her. She's always been that way."

Something she and Drew had in common. "It's obvious having your support means the world to her. Seeing how close you are, I'm sure it was hard when she took a job that required such a move."

"Harder on her than us, I think." Angelique shook her head. "I don't think she ever thought she'd have to leave the city."

Hannah chuckled. "The first time we met, she was so obviously out of her element. I didn't think I'd ever see her again. I'm glad to have been wrong."

"Drew will rise to any occasion if it's part of her master plan." She imagined a young Drew, slogging through some inane task with fierce determination. "How long has this been her plan?"

Angelique stopped drying and looked up at the ceiling. "I think since she was about nine. She discovered the original Japanese *Iron Chef* series on the Food Channel and never looked back. She'd beg me to buy some random ingredient at the store and surprise her. And when I'd bring it home and present her with it, I had to say, '*Allez cuisine!*'"

Hannah laughed and her heart swelled. "That might be the most adorable thing I've ever heard. And now here she is."

Angelique smiled and took another plate from Hannah. "Yes, one step closer."

Closer? As far as Hannah knew, a head chef gig was the plan. "What's next, world domination?"

"I'm sure she wants to open her own restaurant someday. In the meantime, with this position, she can skip a few rungs on the ladder to a Michelin-starred restaurant back home."

Home. Of course. For as much as Drew had acclimated to life upstate, it wasn't where the real opportunities were. It wasn't where her family was. It wasn't home. She made sure to keep her tone one of mild curiosity. "How long will that take, do you think?"

Angelique waved a hand. "Oh, I'm no expert on these things. But she thought it would be a few years until she had any sort of head chef position, so probably less time than is the norm."

Hannah kept her eyes on the pot she was scrubbing. Nick considered it quite the coup to lure an up-and-coming city chef to Fig. She'd been suspicious at first, convinced someone like Drew would never fit in. But Drew did fit in. She'd put Fig on the map and become sort of a fixture in town. Not to mention in Hannah's life. She'd been so foolish. Just because Drew had grown comfortable, it didn't mean she'd be satisfied with life here. Of course she would want to return to the city. Her time at the quirky restaurant in the Finger Lakes would be a nice feather in her cap, a bullet on her résumé. Their relationship would be little more than a pleasant diversion.

"I think it's clean."

Angelique's comment yanked her back to the present—to the pot and the sink and doing dishes in Drew's kitchen with Drew's mother. "Oh." She chuckled feebly. "Sorry. My mind must have wandered."

"It's fine. I'm the same when I'm doing dishes." Something in Angelique's expression said she knew it was more than that, but she didn't press.

"Yeah." Hannah rinsed the pot and handed it over to be dried. She tried to shake off the weird sinking feeling in her stomach. Nothing Angelique said should bother her. Even more, it shouldn't come as any surprise.

Drew, who'd been packing away leftovers, came over to take the pot from her mother. "Why do I get the feeling you two are talking about me?"

Angelique didn't miss a beat. "What makes you think you're the only thing of interest?"

Hannah bit her lip, but a laugh escaped anyway. The teasing broke the tension. Did it count as tension if she was the only one who felt it?

"So, what were you talking about?" Drew put the pot away, then crossed her arms and stared at them both.

Hannah looked to Angelique, who shrugged and said, "You, but not because you're the only thing of interest."

Hannah thought Drew might come back with a quick dig, but she didn't. "I have no doubt."

She lingered long enough to eat a piece of the most ridiculously intense chocolate tart, then begged off for the night, citing an early morning at the farm. The reason was legitimate. The forecast promised a few precious hours of sunshine before more rain and she really wanted to pick the wave of ripe peaches while they were dry. It made for so much less work after the fact. On top of that, she was beat. It was past her bedtime and she'd indulged in a huge dinner and a glass and a half of wine.

Still, as she drove the winding roads between Drew's house and hers, it wasn't fatigue tugging unpleasantly at the corners of her mind. Angelique's words stayed with her. She didn't begrudge Drew her ambition or wanting to be where her friends, her family, her life were. And nothing about the relationship, if she could even call it that, had warranted big discussions about the future. That was exactly how she wanted it. Wasn't it?

Chapter Twenty-two

In spite of the rain that never really let up, Drew was pleased with Manman and Grann's visit. She'd brought them to the farm. Grann seemed genuinely disappointed not to be traipsing through the fields, but they had a little shopping spree at the farm stand. The wine tour was great, even if the view of the lake was a bit misty, and dinner at the restaurant perfect. Nick had been gracious and charming, treating her family like his own.

And the dinner at her place with Hannah? It had gone well, better than well, actually. Her mother and grandmother had not only liked Hannah, they'd been easy with her. Drew had expected Hannah to be friendly and gracious, but it went beyond that. It was as though they'd all known one another for years, like Hannah was one of them. Like family.

Instead of relief, it left her uneasy and out of sorts. It reminded her of going to Niagara Falls as a child and watching the water rush over the craggy edge—hypnotizing, but with inherent danger. She tried to hide behind fatigue, but Grann saw through it. But instead of taking Drew to task, her usual approach, she kept looking at Drew with what felt an awful lot like pity.

Just like that morning, when they were due to leave. Manman was getting dressed, and Grann sat at the table with her coffee. But she couldn't just sit there and drink it, she had to give Drew that look. Drew couldn't take it anymore. "What?"

"You're in love with her, yes?" Her tone was gentle, but it felt like an accusation.

Drew didn't make eye contact as she replied. "What makes you say that?"

"I have eyes, don't I? I'm not blind."

"I'm not sure I know what being in love looks like."

"Child, that might be the saddest thing I ever heard."

Drew chuckled. "I don't mean it in some tragic way. I just mean I've never really been in love. Infatuation, sure. Puppy love. But I mean the kind you and Pépé had. Or Manman and Papa. The forever kind."

"The thing about that kind of love is that you have to be willing to see it, feel it, in order to find it."

That made it all sound far more intentional than Drew believed. The idea of having some modicum of control over the heart should have been a solace. But it meant she'd have to work for it, pay attention to make it happen if she decided she wanted it one day. That was a huge responsibility. "Manman always said it hit her like a lightning bolt. The day she met Papa, the earth tipped on its axis and she was never the same."

Grann smiled as though she was reliving the memory of that day. "For her, yes, it was like that. For me, not so much."

"I thought Pépé courted you the old-fashioned way."

"He did." Grann laughed. "That didn't mean I wanted what he was peddling. At least not at first."

Drew had never heard this version of the story. She set down her coffee and gave her grandmother her full attention. "No?"

Grann offered a playful shrug. "I'd known him since we were babies. We grew up in the same village, our mothers were friends."

"You used to run around the yard naked together." Drew offered a shrug of her own. "Or so I hear."

"Yes. And not a soul was surprised when we became sweethearts. But I wanted to move to the U.S., go to college, become a teacher. And your Pépé was a homebody. He was perfectly content in the life we'd grown up with."

That resonated with Drew, like familiar church bells marking time or calling people to pray. "You weren't willing to give up your dreams to be with him."

Grann shifted her gaze to the window and suddenly seemed a thousand miles away. "I was very stubborn. I convinced myself what we had was the love of children, that it wasn't meant to be."

"You broke it off and he came to New York anyway."

"I thought he'd done it out of male pigheadedness. But he was determined to build a life that I would consider good enough, that I would want. He was always one for big gestures."

Drew's memories of her grandfather were almost as foggy as

those of her dad. His larger-than-life personality—booming voice, big laugh, with stories to match—was one of the few things that remained vivid. "How did he convince you to marry him?"

"He showed up at my apartment every morning before I went to class. He gave me a coffee and told me to study hard so I could be the best teacher there ever was."

"How long did it take for him to win you over?"

Grann smiled. "One school year. He never missed a day and I'm pretty sure he intended to keep it up until I finished my degree. I agreed to have dinner with him after I finished my exams. He took me to his apartment, and even though he shared it with four other young men, I realized he was more settled into life in New York than I was. That's what convinced me it wasn't some romantic thing to get my attention. He was committed, completely and without hesitation."

"That is a very special kind of love."

"Yes, it was. He was a special kind of man. Yet I missed almost a year with him because I was stubborn and refused to see what was right in front of me."

Drew sighed. She certainly aspired to the kind of love that her grandparents had. Her parents, too, for that matter. But it was some mythical thing in the distant future. She always figured that when it happened, she'd know. "It's a wonderful story, Grann. I'm not sure how much it applies to my situation, but I'm glad you told me."

"The life you think you want isn't always the one you're meant to lead. That is a lesson you can take with you now. And the person you fall in love with is sometimes the last person you'd expect."

"But that's just it. I know the life I'm meant to lead. It's back home, in the city. It's the one thing I'm sure of." Well, that and the fact that Hannah wouldn't move to the city if her life depended on it.

Grann patted her hand. "We're always sure, child, until we aren't."

That might be the least reassuring thing she'd ever heard. She was spared having to respond by her mother coming into the room. "You're looking especially beautiful today, Manman."

She waved a hand. "This country air, it's nice. Good for the skin."

"Good for the soul, too." Grann had the faraway look again. Drew had thought of her as a city dweller inside and out. The same way Pépé had felt tied to Haiti. That hadn't changed, necessarily, but there was perhaps more nuance to it than she'd previously considered.

Drew loaded their bags and drove them into town. As they

exchanged good-byes, she lingered in each embrace. She missed her life in the city, sure, but it was not seeing her family a couple times every week that was the hardest.

"We'll see you in a few weeks, yes?" Manman asked.

"Oh, yes. No way I'm going to miss Grann turning eighty."

"You should invite Hannah." Grann's tone was casual, like she'd just suggested they have fish instead of chicken.

"Uh," Drew grasped for a reply. She didn't want to say yes, but she didn't want to say no either. "I'm not sure—"

"I liked her very much. And she probably never gets to visit the city." As they so often did, Grann's eyes sparkled with mischief. "You tell her the invitation came from me."

Drew shook her head. "Well played, Grann."

"I just think it would be nice to see her again."

"Okay, okay. I'll ask her." She might not even say yes.

Having gotten her way, she smiled and patted Drew's cheek. "I love you, child. I'll see you soon."

Drew hugged them both again and they boarded the bus. She waited for the bus to pull away, waving as it did. She was suddenly in no rush to get back to her empty house. Fortunately, she didn't have much time before work. It wouldn't hurt to go in early, really. Between taking a day off and shaving her hours here and there over the past few days, the kitchen could use some extra attention.

Since she kept a change of clothes at the restaurant, she headed straight there. She arrived even before Nick, letting herself in the back and flipping on lights as she went. She made her way through the pantry and cooler, taking inventory and starting to think about specials for the rest of the week. The task demanded most of her attention, but Grann's invitation turned over in the back of her mind.

Whether or not it implied anything about their relationship, she wanted to show Hannah the city. Her version of the city, not Times Square and the Empire State Building. Would Hannah accept the invitation? She was even more loath to take time off than Drew. But she and Rose had hit it off. If anything would sway her, that would probably be it. Drew chuckled at the absurdity of it. She'd do it and, hopefully, Hannah would say yes.

Buoyed by her decision, she finished the inventory and started sketching out menu ideas for the next wave of produce that would come from the farm. The official start of fall was a few weeks away still, but she'd swear the air had already changed. The nights bordered on downright cold and the mornings had a chill different from the cool and dewy starts of the summer.

She thought back to the very first meal she'd prepared for Nick, the one that landed her the job. It would be a great fall dish, and the hash could be reworked as a vegetarian entrée. Maybe a coq au vin as the poultry, with lots of garlic and thyme. She was lost in that train of thought when the back door opened. Standing there, as if conjured from her earlier thoughts, stood Hannah. She smiled brightly. "Hi."

"Hey." Drew let herself enjoy the ripple of pleasure that passed through her. Don't overthink it. "I wasn't expecting to see you today."

"I picked the first of the beets and I thought you might like some." She offered a box to Drew.

"You're spoiling me, you know, with all this first dibs business."

Hannah shrugged. "Well, I held some back for the farm shares. I want all my customers to be happy."

"Oh, I see. I'm nothing special."

Hannah smirked, more suggestive that snarky. "I never said that."

"That's a relief. I was worried there for a second. Especially since I was about to invite you to go away with me for a few days."

"Oh?" She quirked a brow.

"Grann is turning eighty in a couple of weeks and I'm going down to the city for her party. She explicitly asked me to invite you."

"I see. So it wasn't your doing."

Hannah's tone was playful, but Drew felt compelled to clarify. "I mean, I want you to come, too. I thought we could spend one day in the city, then one with my family for the party."

Hannah laughed. "I'd hate to disappoint both of you."

It was Drew's turn to smirk. "Then don't."

"When is it? Weekends are tough, but I might be able to get Jeremiah to cover for me. And if it's before school starts, I'll still have Clare helping at the farm stand—"

"They actually scheduled it for mid-week since it's easier for me to get away then."

"Of course. How nice. Convenient, too."

For as much as she'd started out on the fence, Drew hoped the answer would be yes. "So, you'll come?"

Hannah nodded slowly, as if deciding with each up and down motion of her head. "Yes. That sounds fun."

"Have you been to the city before?" She had so many ideas. Including a night in a hotel overlooking the skyline.

"Twice, but once was when I was a kid and the last time was for my twenty-first birthday. It's been ages."

Drew lifted a hand. "I promise to indulge any touristy things you'd like to do as long as I get to show you a few of my favorite spots."

Hannah chuckled. "I don't think I need to do anything particularly touristy. I'd love to see it through your eyes."

Should it freak her out Hannah used almost the same language as she had? "It's going to be great."

Hannah nodded. "You'll let me know the specifics? I don't have time now."

"I'll text you and we can talk details later." Drew smiled. "I'm glad you're coming."

"Me, too. I'll talk to you." Hannah took a step back, not ready to leave but needing to get back. She stepped forward and gave Drew a quick kiss before letting herself out the way she came in. On the ride back to the farm, she stuck her Bluetooth in her ear and called Jenn.

"Hey, lady."

"Hey. I feel bad calling you in the middle of the day. Do you have a few minutes?"

"Your timing is perfect. I'm just out for my 'I promise to leave my desk at least once a day' stroll."

Hannah laughed. "Oh, good. I need you to tell me if going away with Drew for a couple of days is significant."

"Ooh. Where are you thinking about going?"

"New York City. It's her grandmother's birthday." Of course it was significant. She knew this. Why was she asking? "I may have already said yes."

"In that case, it's exactly as significant as you want it to be."

For as much as she and Jenn gave each other a hard time, Jenn never failed to say the right thing when it mattered. "I appreciate the sentiment, but really. Did I just make a terrible mistake?"

"Absolutely not. One, you never take time off and you should. Two, you've not gone to the city in a billion years. Three, if Drew invited you, she clearly wants you there."

"Number three is the problem." Hannah explained that the invitation came from Drew's grandmother first. "I'm not sure if that makes it better or worse. Like, is it less of a big deal because Drew didn't cook up the idea on her own or more of a big deal because it involves a family thing?"

"Which do you want it to be?"

"I'm not sure." Hannah crossed out of the town limits and increased her speed.

"Well, if anything is stressing you out, it's probably that."

The blessing and the curse of having a best friend who knew her inside and out. She hated uncertainty. She had enough of it at the farm. "Yeah."

"And that's okay. You've not connected with anyone in a while. Plus, you weren't looking to." That was true. "And even if you were, Drew's not what you would have had in mind."

"Why do you have to be so smart? It's kind of annoying." Helpful, but also annoying.

"Is this the point in the conversation where I remind you that you're the one who called me?"

Right. "Sorry. You're right, as always. It's just inconvenient."

"Love usually is."

Hannah's heart leapt in her chest and she gripped the steering wheel. "Whoa, whoa, whoa. We're talking about going away together, not using the L-word."

"Hey, settle down. I didn't mean capital *L* love. Relationships, lowercase *R*."

Relationships didn't freak Hannah out. Really, they didn't. Even with Drew, she'd sort of settled into the fact that they had more than physical chemistry. And she'd already met Rose and Angelique, so that shouldn't feel like a big deal either. "So, I'm overreacting."

"Well, I'd say your gut is trying to tell you something. You shouldn't ignore it, but you probably shouldn't insta-panic either."

"You're right. Again."

"When're you going?"

"In a couple of weeks. Just for two nights."

"I say go, have fun, and see how you get along in a different setting."

The advice made perfect sense. And it would be interesting to see Drew on her home turf. "Yeah, okay."

"Good."

Hannah took that as her chance to change the subject. "Thanks. How are you? I feel like I haven't seen you in forever."

Jenn sighed. "I've been better. Suri and I broke up."

Hannah banged her fist on the steering wheel. "Why didn't you tell me? I've been prattling on about my non-problems."

"It's okay, really. She got a job offer in London, working with her yogi mentor. There was no way she could pass it up and I'm not looking to cross the pond, at least not permanently."

"I hear you. Still, that sucks."

"Eh." Hannah could imagine her shrugging on the other end of the line. "It is what it is. We had a great time while it lasted. And she's thinking pretty hardcore about babies and I'm so not."

She and Jenn had talked babies plenty of times through the years. Jenn had no interest whatsoever, while Hannah remained open—wanting them, but only if she ended up with the right person. "Maybe it's for the best, then."

Jenn sighed. "Agreed. So, do we get to commiserate before you jet off?"

"Absolutely. Name the night. I'll cook."

They made plans and Hannah ended the call just as she pulled up behind the barn. She went in to check on Clare before heading out to fire up Roberta. She puttered up and down the rows of the orchard, cutting the grass short in anticipation of the crowds who'd be coming through in search of the first wave of September apples. Jenn was right. Going to New York with Drew didn't need to be a big deal. It would be fun, and even if she wasn't in any hurry to figure out where she and Drew stood, it would be good to see what Drew was like in her hometown. Not to mention being a mini vacation. How long had it been since she'd done that? Too long.

Chapter Twenty-three

Hannah angsted more than she should have over what to pack. When Drew picked her up, though, their bags were almost identical in size. Drew nodded her approval. That made the twenty texts with Jenn about the whole business worth it.

They boarded the bus and settled in. She made Drew pull up a map of the city on her phone so she could get her bearings. Drew pointed out where the bus would drop them, the location of their hotel for the night in Manhattan, and where in Brooklyn Drew's mother lived. Drew ran through their agenda, ambitious but not frantic, then they settled into comfortable quiet. Hannah read and Drew pored over a crossword.

The time flew by. Before she knew it, Drew nudged her and pointed out the window. "You can see the skyline from here."

Sure enough, Hannah could make out the iconic skyline on the horizon. "Wow."

"The bus will take the Lincoln Tunnel and drop us right in midtown, then we can grab a subway to our hotel and leave our bags. Unless the subway freaks you out. If it does, we can get a cab."

Hannah shook her head. "I don't mind the subway. I'm not a complete bumpkin."

Drew laughed, squeezed her hand. "I never thought you were. There are people who've lived their whole lives in the city and never taken a subway. I mean, a lot of them are billionaires, but still."

The comment lightened the mood, wiping away any apprehension Hannah had about being in the city. It wasn't like she'd never been. It just had been a while. "I'm cool."

"And here I thought you were smoking hot."

"Oh, God. You didn't just say that."

Drew shrugged. "Are you reconsidering this whole trip now?"

Hannah made a face before laughing. "No. I mean, a little, but no."

She let Drew take the lead in getting them to the hotel. It was too early to check in, but they stored their bags and then headed out. Her two picks for their time in Manhattan were Central Park and the Metropolitan Museum of Art. They did the park first, buying falafel from a guy with a cart and meandering the wide paths. It was the middle of the week, but they passed dozens of joggers and dog walkers and people with strollers.

She glanced over at Drew, who was eying her with curiosity. "What? Do I have tzatziki on my face?"

"Not at all. I'm just trying to figure out why a woman who spends most of her time surrounded by nature would find anything about Central Park interesting."

Hannah chuckled. She'd not thought of it that way. "It's so different, so much more controlled than a state park. Each element was chosen, you know, intentionally."

Drew nodded. That made sense. It was fun to see the city, parts of it she took for granted, through Hannah's eyes. "Almost like a museum."

"Yes." Hannah's eyes lit up. "It feels curated. It's kind of fascinating."

"You are fascinating." She took Hannah's empty foil and napkin and tossed the trash in a bin. "And speaking of curated, shall we head to the museum? I want you to feel like you have time to see what you want."

"Sure. I know we won't get to half of it, but I've got a list."

Drew took her hand, unable to remember the last time she'd enjoyed a day in Manhattan. "I'm sure you do."

At the Met, Hannah insisted on paying their admission and grabbed a map. Even though they'd gotten to know each other, Drew had no idea what exhibits Hannah would find appealing. When Drew insisted she had no preference or agenda, Hannah didn't hesitate to take the lead. She led them through Egyptian antiquities, early American paintings, and the sculpture garden. Hannah didn't seem to have much use for the impressionists but was obsessed with Degas, especially his dancers.

"Did you want to be a ballerina?" Drew asked, imagining Hannah as a child in a leotard and tutu.

Hannah laughed. Not quite rueful, but it gave Drew the impression a less-than-pleasant memory simmered under the surface. "No. It's not really something you think about growing up on a dairy farm."

Again, she didn't seem sad or angry about it, but Drew had an urge to sweep her into a hug and tell her she could do anything she wanted. Instead, she offered an empathetic smile. "What did you think about growing up on a dairy farm?"

"How to avoid chores." She delivered the line without a moment of hesitation and a completely straight face. It broke the tension that perhaps Drew had been imagining.

"Did it work?"

"You can't grow up on a farm and avoid chores completely. I learned that getting up early and doing the ones I didn't mind without being asked got me out of the ones I hated. At least some of them."

"That's kind of genius."

Hannah shrugged. "My brothers always had to be nagged. I'm not saying that's the reason they ended up mucking more stalls than I did, but I think it didn't help their cause."

"So, why the love for Degas's dancers?"

Hannah's face softened and her smile went all the way to her eyes. "My aunt gave me this calendar for Christmas. Each day featured a piece of art. One of them was *Dancer Looking at the Sole of Her Left Foot.* I thought the title was hilarious, but I also loved that she was a little lumpy, doing something not entirely graceful. I decided Degas was my favorite artist and never looked back."

It wasn't an especially intimate story, but Drew felt like it gave her insight to Hannah's past, how she got to be who she was now. "How old were you?"

"Twelve, I think. I was still all limbs at that age. So awkward."

"Some might argue you had the body of a dancer."

"Only I couldn't—can't—dance to save my life. I literally used to trip over my own feet."

Drew had a hard time imagining Hannah as anything but graceful. At the farm, in bed—she was lithe and elegant and moved with confidence. "Surely you dance at least a little. I've seen the way you carry yourself."

"Oh. No. You're sweet, but no."

Drew laughed at the adamant tone and the look of horror on Hannah's face. "Maybe you just need the right person to lead."

Hannah turned away from the statue and focused her full attention on Drew. "Are you offering?"

Drew raised a brow. "Yes."

"I won't tell you no, but I might tell you I told you so."

A moment ago, she'd wanted to sweep Hannah up and offer words of encouragement and reassurance. Now Drew had to fight the desire to yank Hannah against her and kiss her senseless. The juxtaposition proved unsettling, especially in a crowded gallery. She pictured the room she'd reserved, thought about what she had in mind. "I can't wait to have you in my arms."

"Why does it feel like we're not talking about dancing anymore?"

"Because we aren't."

❖

Drew let Hannah into the room first. Hannah went right to the window. "Wow."

The view was pretty spectacular. Although Drew hadn't grown up with a view of the skyline, it was one of the things she loved about the city. Nighttime, with the buildings and a view of the bridge lit up, was her favorite. And the floor-to-ceiling windows were absolutely perfect. "I thought you'd enjoy that."

"Almost as much as I'm going to enjoy fucking you," Hannah said almost casually over her shoulder.

The comment sent a stab of heat right to Drew's core. They'd discussed using the night in the city to switch things up, but still. The arousal she'd carried all evening, stirred by wine and candlelight and the way Hannah looked at her across the table, exploded into a fire that seemed to scorch from the inside out. She cleared her throat, not wanting Hannah to know just how much power she held. "Oh, we'll get there."

Hannah's smirk held just the right mix of challenge and promise. "Are we going somewhere else first?"

"No, but we do have all night." And she intended to use it.

"Do you mind if I shower first? Between traveling and the city, I feel as gross as I do after a day in the fields."

"Only if I get to join you."

Without another word, Hannah took her dress off and angled her head toward the bathroom. She kicked off her shoes and disappeared through the door. A second later, Drew heard water running. She hastily stripped and went to join her. The water was cool and the rain-style showerhead created a soothing flow of water. As tempting as it was to have her way with Hannah right there in the shower, she had other things in mind. And the idea of cleaning up just to get dirty was a major turn-on.

Hannah stepped out first, handed Drew a towel. "Thanks. I'll meet you out there."

Drew used the minute alone to get ready, sliding the harness on and tightening it around her thighs, but also to center herself. They'd not discussed tonight being any different from their previous times together, aside from switching up the play, but something about it felt different, significant. She shook it off.

Hannah had adjusted the lights, leaving on a single lamp near the bed. She stood at the window in a plush robe, looking as comfortable in a fancy hotel as she did atop her tractor. The sight of her did wicked things to Drew's libido. Drew stepped up behind her, tugged at the belt. "I don't think we need this."

Hannah let her untie it and ease it from her shoulders. She glanced out the window.

Drew kissed her. "Someone would need binoculars to get much of a show. Are you worried about being seen?"

Hannah smiled and shook her head without breaking eye contact. "No."

"Good." Drew turned her toward the window. She covered Hannah's hands with her own and placed them against the glass. She leaned in close to Hannah's ear, bit it gently. "Don't move."

She took a step back to appreciate the visual of Hannah—arms and legs spread, the curve of her body a creamy silhouette against the dark outside. Even with arousal jangling through her like too much caffeine, she could have stayed there for hours. Just looking.

No, looking was nice, but it had nothing on touch. She traced a finger down Hannah's spine, lingering at the top of her perfect ass. Hannah shifted, the movement so subtle she might have missed it had she not been staring. "I said don't move."

Hannah made a noise that sounded like pleasure laced with frustration. Drew smiled. Being in control was such a turn-on, especially knowing the tables would be turned before the night ended. She splayed her fingers, filling her hands with Hannah's rear end. She gave each cheek a playful squeeze before sliding her hands around, over the slight swell of Hannah's hips. Hannah's position gave her perfect access and she couldn't resist sliding two fingers between her legs.

She'd expected Hannah to be turned on, but she was so hot, so wet, Drew almost lost it. She clenched her jaw, bit back a groan. "You're ready for me, aren't you?"

Hannah nodded.

"Okay, then. Tell me what you want."

"Fuck me. Please."

"It would be my pleasure."

Before shifting her hand, she gave Hannah's clit a few teasing strokes. Hannah's hips pressed forward. Drew smiled and pulled her fingers away. Hannah moaned. Drew brought her mouth to Hannah's ear a second time. "Patience."

She wasn't going to make Hannah wait, not really. But she relished calling the shots, leaving Hannah guessing.

Drew brought her fingers to her lips, tasted Hannah's arousal. "Fuck, you taste good."

Hannah made that noise again and thrust her hips back, pressing herself against the cock that bobbed between Drew's thighs. It hardly made for any pressure at all against Drew's throbbing clit, but it was all she needed to move things along.

She eased her hand between Hannah's legs, this time from behind. Drew didn't hesitate to slide two fingers into her, all the way. Hannah moaned and bucked against her. "Please."

"I will. Don't you worry." Drew slid in and out a few times. The way Hannah clamped around her, seemed to pull her in even deeper, drove her absolutely crazy.

She pulled out and positioned the cock where her fingers had just been. Since the condom came lubed, she didn't bother with more. Hannah wouldn't need it.

She eased the tip in. The way it disappeared, while creating just the right pressure against her clit, drove her nuts. She pushed the rest of the way in, as deep as she could go. "Oh, yes. That feels so good."

Hannah ground against her. "Mmm-hmm."

The front of Hannah's body reflected in the glass. Her eyes were closed, her lips pressed together. Her nipples stood erect.

Drew reached around and cupped a hand over each breast. They swayed slightly with each thrust, filling Drew's palms. She fought the urge to hurry, to drive them both over the edge, but it didn't take long for Hannah to completely overwhelm her senses. Hannah came with an uninhibited scream that sent Drew tumbling into her own orgasm.

She clasped an arm around Hannah's waist, doing her best to hold them both up. Eventually, Hannah laughed and righted herself. "God, you're sexy."

Drew let her go and took a step back. "I was just thinking the same thing about you."

Hannah turned to face Drew. She looked from Drew's face to the cock, then back to her face. Her desire bounced back instantaneously, reignited by the idea of being with Drew in a way that was completely new to her. To both of them. "Does that mean I get that turn now?"

Drew peeled off the condom and tossed it in the trash. She loosened the buckles of the harness and slid it down her legs. "Do you want a hand getting it on?"

"I got it." Hannah took it from her and headed toward the bathroom. "I'll be right back."

She closed the door and took a minute to get it situated, tightening the straps until they were nice and snug. She shifted back and forth in front of the mirror. The dildo bounced up and down lightly. Such a strange sensation, but sexy, too. It made her feel powerful. She strode into the bedroom, clad in nothing but Drew's black harness.

"Fuck, that's hot." Drew sat on the bed. Her eyes went right to the cock, making Hannah smile.

Hannah joined her on the bed. She took her time kissing Drew and sliding up and down her body. She was never passive in bed, but wearing the strap-on made her extra assertive. After making Drew squirm, she pushed herself up and knelt between Drew's thighs. The look on Drew's face was one of hunger and it gave Hannah confidence. Any lingering shadows of awkwardness disappeared. Still, she didn't want things to go sideways. "You'll talk to me, right? Be honest if I'm not doing it right?"

"I will. I'm not worried, but I will."

She grabbed another condom from the nightstand, glad Drew had thought to bring them, and rolled it on. "Okay. We're doing this. Are you ready?"

Drew placed a hand on each of her hips. "I'm ready. And I'm so glad I'm doing this with you."

The sentiment echoed what had been playing through Hannah's mind. "Same."

She traced her fingers over Drew, then positioned the cock. She eased it in, not wanting to rush. The pressure against her own clit made her gasp.

"It's pretty incredible, right?"

Hannah nodded, at a loss for words.

She started slowly, soaking up the newness of the experience as much as the pleasure. The way Drew moved against her, communicating things without any words at all. It was so intimate. Did that have to do with what she was doing or with Drew?

She continued to thrust, enjoying the way Drew arched beneath her. She hoped she looked half that sexy when being fucked. Drew's eyes never left hers, although she looked down now and again to where their bodies were joined. It was mesmerizing, knowing she was the one controlling it.

Her pace quickened, more instinct than intention. She could tell she was pushing Drew harder, higher, closer to the edge. It fueled her. She wanted Drew undone, completely at her mercy.

She watched the pleasure play across Drew's face, felt her tremble. It was the tremble that did her in, the surrender. Drew's fingers dug into her hips, nudging her the last little bit into oblivion. She let it take her, rock her, until she and Drew were collapsed in a sweaty heap on the bed.

When she was finally able to move, and to feel her limbs, Hannah lifted her head. "Was it just me or was that extra incredible?"

Drew smiled. "It wasn't just you."

Hannah nodded and eased just far enough away to shed the harness. She flipped off the light but left the shades open, letting the light of the city cast a faint glow across the bed. "Do we have to go tomorrow?"

"Nope." Drew's answer was immediate, her tone playful.

"I want to go. Just tell me we can do that again before we have to check out."

Drew nodded seriously. "Oh, at least once more."

"Good."

Hannah tucked herself into the crook of Drew's arm. She couldn't think of a time she felt more satisfied, or more spent. But it was more than that. She felt so connected to Drew. Not just that they'd shared something new. No, it was like they'd moved into some new plane of being together. Not love, surely, but something more than hookups and hanging out. Maybe that should freak her out, but in the moment, the only thing she felt was content.

Chapter Twenty-four

The next morning, they headed to Brooklyn and walked hand in hand, window-shopping and popping in and out of quirky shops. Hannah realized what a singular idea of the city she'd held. Which was unfair, considering how much she hated it when people did that with the whole of New York state. She picked up a set of funky linen napkins for her mother and a shirt emblazoned with "The Future Is Female" for Clare. They had lunch at a funky bar that reminded her a lot of Atlas, minus the bowling.

They were just heading back to Drew's mother's house for the party when someone called Drew's name. Drew stopped and turned, let go of her hand.

"Javier." Drew extended a hand and seemed truly happy to see him.

"Where have you been hiding? I haven't seen you in months." Javier's smile was huge and Hannah thought his accent might be Spanish. She got a gay vibe, too, but that was just conjecture.

"Upstate. I took a head chef job at a little farm-to-table place in the Finger Lakes."

Javier tutted and shook his head. "Upstate. I never would have thought it of you."

Hannah would have taken offense had she not thought the exact same thing at first. She was so glad to have been proved wrong on that front.

Drew shrugged. "A step on the ladder, my friend. A means to an end."

It shouldn't surprise her that Drew would say such a thing, especially in the long run of her career. Something about the tone, though, struck her. Detached, almost dismissive. She was grateful they seemed to have forgotten her presence.

"I'll gladly hire you whenever you've had your fill and want to come back. You just let me know."

"I have to say, life in the country has its perks." She turned to Hannah. "Like this beautiful woman. She runs one of the farms that supplies the restaurant. Hannah, Javier."

"Pleasure to meet you." He took Hannah's extended hand and brought it to his lips.

The gesture would have irritated her had he not been European. Well, that and the fact she was already irritated over Drew referring to her as a perk. She plastered a fake smile on her face and said, "Likewise."

Javier gave Drew his latest phone number and he went on his way. Hannah turned the conversation over in her mind, trying to figure out exactly why it bothered her so much. She wanted it to be Drew's offhand comment, but really, it was the bigger picture. The one where Drew would pick up and leave the second a better offer came along. Maybe she shouldn't be bothered by that, but she was.

Drew, on the other hand, seemed unfazed by the interaction. She grabbed Hannah's hand again and they continued walking.

Maybe she was putting too much stock in a passing conversation. The knee-jerk reaction was unlike her, and not in line with the seriousness of their relationship. She gave herself a little shake, a physical gesture to match her resolution not to let it get under her skin.

"You okay?" Drew gave her a look more quizzical than concerned.

"Of course. Looking forward to the party." Which wasn't a lie, even if she had a whole new slate of reservations about spending time with Drew's family.

They boarded a subway bound for Drew's neighborhood, then made the short walk to Angelique's house. They arrived early so Drew could help with food preparations. Hannah assigned herself to helping with setup, situating the table and arranging chairs in the small backyard. She liked feeling useful. Having a few minutes away from Drew to regroup didn't hurt either. The last thing she wanted was to be snippy or sullen.

Rose joined her outside. Despite being eighty and dressed to the nines, she carried chairs around and helped Hannah move a patio table.

When they were done, Hannah put her hands on her hips and surveyed the space. "I think that looks very nice."

"It certainly does. Thank you for your help." Rose put a hand on Hannah's arm. "And thank you for coming all this way to help me celebrate."

"I should be thanking you for including me." Even if it muddied the waters with Drew.

"Family is who you choose, dear, as much as who you're born with."

"I couldn't agree more." She embraced that sentiment. Really, she did. But she'd never been in a position to extend the philosophy to girlfriends and their families. She'd never considered whether it was a conscious choice or something that just sort of happened. Either way, she and Drew weren't there. Even if Drew had invited her. And even if Drew's family felt, in some ways, more welcoming than her own.

With the yard set, she and Rose went inside. Rose went off to greet the guests who'd started to arrive. Hannah steeled herself and headed to the kitchen to see if Drew needed help with any of the food. Angelique happily assigned her to fruit salad, so she peeled and sliced mangoes, papaya, and pineapple in a quiet corner of the kitchen. The task made her feel at home and spared her having to be introduced to literally everyone who set foot through the front door.

By the time she stood next to Drew with a plate heaped full of food, at least a dozen conversations swirled around her. A few were in English, a couple in Creole, and one, she was pretty sure, was in Spanish. Way more diverse than an average party at home, in a good way. She'd not given a lot of thought to just how homogeneous her upbringing had been.

Still feeling weird about Drew, she turned her attention to the woman next to her, who didn't look a day over sixty but who'd apparently started teaching the same year as Rose. Growing up on a dairy farm proved quite the novelty. It didn't take long for her to become the center of attention, fielding questions about corn and cows and other upstate oddities.

At one point, Drew got pulled away. Hannah answered her apologetic look with a reassuring smile. She never minded being the ambassador for small farms. Not to mention conversations squarely in her comfort zone.

❖

After kissing a second cousin and making sure the buffet was full, Drew wound her way back to Hannah. The unease of leaving her on her own evaporated when she found her chatting up three of her grandmother's church friends, practically holding court. The women laughed, Hannah's story clearly the source of their amusement. She had a flash of the first day she and Hannah met at the farm. She'd been not rude exactly, but aloof. It made Drew chuckle to realize that had little to do with Hannah's personality and everything to do with Hannah's initial assessment of her. Not her best moment, trying to save her best shoes from the mud pit that had been the farm parking lot.

So much had changed since that day. Getting the job and moving, sure, but more than that. She'd never expected to be happy in the tiny town, but that's exactly what she was. She loved her restaurant and her weird little cottage. She loved the friendships she'd built with the staff and her relationship with Nick. She loved Hannah and all the time they'd been able to spend together.

Drew froze, beer bottle suspended halfway to her lips. She looked around, as though someone nearby might have heard her thoughts. The conversations around her continued. The jolting realization had been hers alone.

She loved Hannah.

The statement surprised her, but it didn't set off all the alarm bells she would have expected. If anything, she had this almost eerie sense of calm. Like when a recipe she'd been fighting for weeks finally clicked—textures and flavors and colors aligned in perfect balance. She'd never been in love before, not as an adult at least. She didn't expect it to feel like this.

"Drew, do you think we should bring out the cake now?"

"Huh?" Her mother's face came into focus and the words slowly coalesced. "Oh, cake. Yes, we should."

Manman's eyes narrowed. Little escaped her. When it came to Drew, it was like she had a sixth sense. "What's wrong?"

"Nothing at all."

She nodded. "We'll talk later."

Drew didn't need to fake the smile. "I'm sure we will. It's all good, I promise."

"All right, then. If you say so."

She took a deep breath. It was all good. Well, the feelings part of it. The logistics were another matter. But worrying about that was like worrying about the name she'd give the first restaurant she opened on her own. She could spend hours coming up with something, but whether it worked would all depend on how things played out—location and feel, what the restaurant scene looked like when it came together. Thinking too much in advance wasted time and promised nothing.

She'd sort things out with Hannah when she needed to. In the meantime, she'd enjoy the ride. She'd need to decide when and what to tell Hannah, but there was no rush. Neither of them were going anywhere anytime soon.

She mirrored her mother's nod. It would all be fine. "I do say so. You gather the masses and I'll light the candles."

Chapter Twenty-five

In exchange for holding down the fort while she was gone, Hannah had offered Jeremiah a week off. She didn't begrudge him kayaking in the Adirondacks with his boyfriend, especially after doing her such a huge favor, but Christ she was exhausted. She wiped the sweat from her forehead with an old bandanna and surveyed the field in front of her. September was usually lovely, but sometimes, it could be a real bitch.

Even in her overheated, overworked state, she couldn't really be angry. Hot days and cool nights made just about all her crops happy. Even with the irrigation working to keep up with the lack of rain, she had more produce than she could harvest on any given day. She worked crazy hours, fell into bed face first every night, and hardly saw Drew at all. She was completely happy and utterly miserable at the same time.

She loaded the last crate of squash on the wagon and climbed onto Roberta. The old diesel engine roared to life. The ride to the barn wasn't quick, but it managed to create a hint of breeze, cooling her face and stirring the damp strands of hair from the back of her neck.

She pulled up to the washing station and, instead of handing things off to Caroline, unloaded the crates herself. She dunked a dozen or so at a time, rinsing off the dirt and setting each one on an open rack to dry. She'd fill the CSA boxes and still have plenty for Drew. Assuming Drew wanted them. She'd made a comment about zucchini coming out of her ears the day before and Hannah hadn't been able to tell if she was joking.

She finished washing and went in to check on things at the farm stand. Clare had gone back to school and was only coming to the farm for a couple of hours each afternoon. For this week, she'd rotated through her seasonal staff. No one complained about getting the break from weeding or harvesting. Today, Guy stood behind the register, chatting up the bartender from Atlas. It might have been flirting, but she couldn't be sure. "All right out here?"

Guy glanced her way. "Easy-peasy. Hannah, do you know Leah?"

"You know, I don't think we've ever formally met." Hannah extended a hand that, thanks to the washing tub, wasn't entirely caked in dirt. "How's it going?"

Leah shook it. "Good. And good to meet you."

Guy said, "Do you want to take a turn in here? You look beat."

"Thanks." Hannah laced the comment with sarcasm, but she smiled. "I'm good, actually, and Clare will be here any minute."

"I'll weed the greens when she does, unless there's something else you want."

She must look even more exhausted than she felt. Guy hated weeding. "That would be great. I'm going to check on the orchard."

"Are the apples ready yet?" Leah looked at her eagerly.

"We've got Ginger Golds, but Macs and such won't be ready for another couple of weeks at least. It's not getting cool enough at night yet."

Leah's smile didn't waver. "Can't wait, even if it does mean winter's around the corner."

"I couldn't agree more." Having seen Leah at least a dozen times before, she was glad they'd been officially introduced. "If you follow us on Instagram, you'll know when they're ready."

"Oh, I already do. Your stuff is so clever. Do you do it yourself?"

Hannah smiled with pride. "My sister. She's all of seventeen."

"Well, if she decides to make a business of it, let me know. Our marketing could use some help."

Hannah said, "You'll have to get in line behind Nick. I think he's called dibs."

"And if he hasn't, I have." Drew's voice came from behind her.

Hannah turned, unable to temper the quick swell of pleasure at hearing Drew's voice. The feelings stirred up during their trip had mellowed and she'd settled back into enjoying the bits of time they managed to spend together. "Hey, you. Shouldn't you be at the restaurant by now?"

Drew shrugged. She had gone back and forth about stopping by, but now that she had Hannah in her sights, she was glad she did. She offered hellos to Guy and Leah, then let her attention settle on Hannah. God, she missed her. "On my way there now. Just thought I'd pop by to see if there's anything new."

"Not since yesterday, I'm afraid. You're getting sick of squash, aren't you?"

Drew winced. "No, no. I didn't mean it like that."

"No?"

Great. She'd stopped in with the sole purpose of seeing Hannah and now she was coming off like an ass. "I wanted to say hi, since I haven't seen you much this week."

She dared a glance at Leah, whose lips were pressed together in what Drew assumed was an attempt not to laugh.

"Oh."

Was it better to look like an idiot than an ass? Probably. "Do you have a few minutes?"

Now Hannah seemed worried, or at the very least suspicious. "Sure. I was just heading out to the orchard."

Escape. Thank God. "I'll walk you."

"Okay." Hannah still seemed convinced something was up. "Guy, if I don't see you before you clock out, have a good night. Leah, glad we finally met. I'll be sure to say hi next time I'm at Atlas."

Drew said her good-byes as well and followed Hannah through the storeroom. Before Hannah could step out the back barn door, Drew grabbed her hand.

"What—"

Drew silenced her with a kiss. A long, wet, slow kiss that wound her up more than it quieted the desire that had been raging through her veins, but she didn't even care. "I've missed you. I can't stop thinking about you. I had to get my hands on you."

The surprise in Hannah's eyes evaporated. In its place, something that seemed to mirror Drew's feelings. A satisfied smile crept over her lips. "Well, why didn't you say so?"

Drew quirked a brow. "I thought you might not appreciate being kissed in front of your employees and customers."

Hannah angled her head. "I suppose you have a point."

"Now that I'm here, I'm finding it really hard not to hoist you onto that work table and have my way with you."

Hannah's gaze went to the table, then returned to Drew.

"Is that your way of saying yes?"

"No." Hannah sighed. "I mean, I want to say yes, but no."

"I understand." It didn't lessen her desire. "If I pulled that at the restaurant, my staff would inevitably catch us and I'd never live it down."

"I'm also sweaty and filthy and disgusting."

Drew shrugged. "I don't mind that so much, but I get not feeling sexy. Can I convince you to come to my place tonight? Or invite myself to yours? It'll be late, but I'm not sure how much longer I can go without having you."

Hannah trailed a finger down the front of Drew's shirt, right between her breasts. "Come to my place. I might crash before you get there, but I'll leave the door unlocked and you can wake me when you climb in."

Her feelings for Hannah, the ones she'd yet to own out loud, superseded her horniness, at least for a moment. "I'd hate to wake you. I know you're working extra hours this week."

The smug smile returned. "If you crawl into my bed naked and don't wake me up, I'm not sure I could forgive you."

Drew imagined slipping into Hannah's bed, her warm body a stark contrast to the cool night air. She'd kiss the back of Hannah's neck, her shoulders. Hannah would stir and roll toward her, pliant from sleep but wanting. "I'll be there."

Hannah looked her up and down. "Good. I've missed you, too."

"I should go to work now."

Hannah smiled. "Go, go. I'm glad you stopped by."

"Me, too."

Drew smiled the entire drive to the restaurant. Only when she caught her goofy grin in the rearview mirror did she stop. Goofy looks would lead to serious shit from Poppy and at least half the kitchen staff. It was the price of giving as good as she got. She strolled into the kitchen whistling. She'd schooled her expression, but not the underlying thoughts about Hannah and her body and all the things she wanted to do with it.

Prep cooks bustled around under the watchful eye of Poppy. Drew donned her chef coat and took a look at the specials they'd slated for the evening. She caught Poppy's eye and they had a quick chat about coverage and inventory. For probably the hundredth time since hiring her, Drew congratulated herself on trusting her gut. Despite being a bit green, Poppy had grown into her position and already exceeded Drew's expectations.

Feeling good about her night, she got to work, losing track of time until her phone buzzed in her pocket. She stepped away from the bustle to a relatively quiet corner and swiped her finger across the screen. "Javier. To what do I owe this pleasure?"

"How far back do you want me to go? I'm thinking it all started with a broken condom."

Even allowing for his eccentric tendencies, she had no idea what he was talking about. "Huh?"

"Priscilla. She's gotten herself in a family way and she's leaving me."

"Oh." Priscilla was the head chef at Javier's flagship restaurant, George. Located between the theater district and Hell's Kitchen, it was one of the it places for locals and tourists alike. Drew had done a six-month stint there, alternating between poissonier and saucier as needed. It sat squarely in the top ten list of kitchens she'd love to run one day.

"She seems happy about it, so it's my bad luck more than hers. But I'm hoping it doesn't have to be."

Drew gripped the edge of the prep table, her mind racing ahead. "Are you offering me a job?"

"I said I would call you, no?"

"You did." A thousand thoughts jockeyed for position in her mind.

"She's adamant she's good for at least three more months, so you don't have to decide today. Or tomorrow, for that matter."

Thank God. "Okay. That helps. I can't tell you how much it means to me that I'm the first person you called."

"I've been reading reviews of your little farm-to-table experiment. You've come into your own, Drew. I'd rather that talent end up in one of my kitchens than some Bobby Flay circus."

Drew laughed at the slight. Javier still wasn't over Bobby's celebrity. "I would never."

"I'd rather not leave it to chance. Come work for me."

"I'm not sure I could think of a more appealing offer."

"Good. She may or may not decide to return, but if she does, I promise I will find a position suitable to your talent and experience. I might even have a new project up my sleeve."

"Wow. Okay. Thank you." Drew's mind raced. Working for Javier would be a dream come true. Possibly helping him launch a new restaurant? Hell, that came in a close second to opening a place of her own. But instead of elated, she thought she might be on the verge of a panic attack. Not that she'd ever had a panic attack. But her face flushed while the rest of her broke into a cold sweat. Her heart thundered like she'd run a mile and she couldn't seem to get enough oxygen into her lungs.

"I'm sure you're at work. Let's talk soon. Ciao."

She blinked at the screen. Did that really just happen? She pulled up her recent calls and, sure enough, Javier's name sat at the top of the list. Holy fuck.

"Doors are open." Poppy clapped a few times. "Let's get this show on the road."

Drew shook her head and rolled her shoulders a few times. She didn't know whether to celebrate or freak out. What she did know was she didn't have time for either. She looked around the kitchen, catching the eye of each member of her staff. "Have a great service, everyone. Let's do this."

The night went by in a blur. The restaurant wasn't especially busy, but Drew threw herself into every minute detail of cooking and plating. She managed to keep Javier and his offer from the forefront of her mind, but it lurked around the edges, never really leaving. She should walk into Nick's office and give notice. But the idea of doing it filled her with dread. Of course, the prospect of letting the opportunity of a lifetime slip through her fingers felt just as awful.

When the restaurant closed, she helped herself to a fortifying glass of whiskey. It didn't get her any closer to a decision, but it settled her some. She drove to Hannah's, convincing herself there was no rush. Obviously, she'd have to talk to Hannah about it. But doing that before she'd even wrapped her head around what was on the table wouldn't do either of them any good.

The house was dark, but Hannah had left the porch light on. Drew let herself in, locking the door behind her. A light burned at the top of the stairs like a beacon, beckoning her to Hannah's bed. She climbed the stairs slowly, trying to avoid the ones she remembered being creaky. She needn't have bothered. A peek into Hannah's room revealed her sound asleep, sprawled on her stomach with her cheek pressed into the pillow.

Drew tiptoed into the bathroom. She peeled off her clothes and cranked the shower. She helped herself to Hannah's shampoo and soap, smiling over the fragrance of mango and some flower she couldn't quite place. So freaking girly.

The sound of the shower hadn't woken Hannah. Hopefully, her subconscious remembered Drew was coming. She had a feeling Hannah would land some pretty solid punches if she thought an intruder had invaded her home.

Drew slid in beside her. Hannah was completely naked, her skin soft and warm, just like she'd fantasized about earlier in the day. She pressed her body against Hannah's side, planted kisses along her shoulder. Hannah moaned in that half-asleep, half-aroused way that drove her absolutely crazy. Better than work and way better than whiskey, having Hannah against her quieted her mind.

She trailed her hands over Hannah's body, keeping her touch light, but letting her fingers go everywhere—the length of Hannah's spine, the swell of her ass, the line of her thigh where the toned muscles met. Just as she'd imagined would happen, Hannah rolled toward her, her body seeking Drew's instinctively. In some ways, it was even better that Hannah wanted her on such a basic level.

Hannah's breasts grazed Drew's, sending her into overdrive. She groaned, hesitation over waking Hannah from such a sound sleep gone. "God, I missed you."

"I missed you, too." Hannah's words came out as more of a mumble than a fully formed sentence, but it was all the invitation Drew needed.

"I really need to touch you, to be inside you."

"Mmm." Hannah hooked her leg over Drew's and pressed her pelvis forward. "Yes."

Drew slipped her hand between Hannah's legs, finding her already hot and wet. "Fuck."

Hannah smiled, but didn't open her eyes. "I've been waiting for you."

She stroked Hannah, mesmerized by how soft and slick she was. Drew circled her clit a few times, then dipped her first two fingers inside. Hannah arched and moaned again. Drew forced herself to go easy, keep her movements slow.

She let Hannah set the pace, letting her body rock forward and back. Hannah bit her lip, gripped Drew's shoulder. Her eyes opened. "God, you feel good."

Drew kissed her. "I was just thinking the same thing."

Hannah shifted onto her back, opening her legs wider and giving Drew even better access. She took advantage, adding a third finger. But she kept the pressure and the pace gentle so she could revel in the way Hannah's body molded to her, as though they were made to go together.

Hannah became more demanding, pumping her hips and thrusting against Drew's hand. Drew succumbed, fucking her in earnest now. Hannah made the sweetest sounds. Drew closed her eyes and tried to commit them to memory. In that moment, there was no job offer, no question about whether she and Hannah had a future. There was only Hannah and the exquisite pleasure of making her come.

Hannah did come, coating Drew's fingers with liquid heat and saying her name the way no one else had. Before she could recover, could demand her turn, Drew pulled Hannah against her, Hannah's back to her front. She kissed Hannah's hair and whispered soothing words about sleep and plenty of time tomorrow.

Despite her otherwise stubborn disposition, Hannah acquiesced. Her breathing evened out and Drew could tell she'd fallen back asleep. Drew gave her an extra squeeze. Tomorrow. There'd be time to figure out what to do tomorrow.

Chapter Twenty-six

Jeremiah was back from his week off. The heat wave had broken. Drew had spent every night of the last week at her house and the sex kept getting better, if that was even possible. To top things off, Clare, marketing genius that she'd quickly become, suggested a garlic harvesting party. So instead of digging up a thousand or so heads of the stuff, she found herself working a makeshift checkout station in the field, giving away one head for every twenty unearthed. People loved it. It was a welcome reprieve from the backbreaking work she'd been up to most of the week. And at the rate things were going, the entire crop would be ready for drying by the end of the weekend.

"It's not just free labor," Clare said, laying the newly harvested bulbs in a crate. "People feel invested. And since they're spending the day here, you know they're posting and tagging us the whole time."

Social media was a language Hannah was just starting to understand, but she got the gist of Clare's declaration. She offered a dirt-streaked thumbs-up. "Hashtag awesome."

Clare laughed, although Hannah couldn't tell if she'd been funny or ridiculous. She was fine either way, truth be told. "So, you'll let me come up with some other promotions?"

Hannah nodded. "Absolutely."

Clare nodded back, all business. "You probably don't need it with apples or pears, though."

"True. But I'm sure you'll think of something."

"Yeah, I'm pretty good at finding hidden potential."

Hannah folded her arms. "Speaking of, how are things with Kristen?"

"Oh, my God. That was about as smooth as Dad. You're losing your touch."

Hannah laughed. She'd resisted the urge to be nosy, but she was pretty sure Clare wasn't confiding in their parents and she wanted to make sure things were okay. "Don't try to distract me with insults."

Clare shrugged. "They're cool."

Apparently acting like the parent qualified her for non-answers. "So, either they're terrible or they're so good it would be decidedly uncool to talk about it. Which is it?"

Clare blushed. "The second."

"That's really great, Clare. There's nothing like your first love." Her own had been right around Clare's age. Maybe not love, but it sure had felt that way at the time.

"I haven't told Mom and Dad yet. I know it's supposed to be easy since you did it first, but—"

She lifted a hand. "I hope it makes it easier for you, but you still get to do it in your own way, in your own time."

Clare's shoulders dropped several inches, relief evident on her face. "Thanks."

"And if you want me there or want me to help pave the way, I can do that, too." Her heart swelled. She hadn't hoped specifically for Clare to turn out queer, but now that it seemed to be the case, she could be happy about it.

"That would be chicken shit of me, wouldn't it? Have you help me after you did it all on your own?"

She slung an arm around Clare's shoulders. "It's not a contest. It's about you being happy and feeling good about who you are."

"Yeah." Clare perked up. "Thanks."

"What about Kristen? Is she still nervous about talking to her parents?"

"Yes, but it's getting better. She's been asking them about you. Kind of laying the groundwork, I'd say."

Hannah laughed. "I'm the tester lesbian. Like the canary you put in the coal mine."

Clare winced. "Is that bad?"

"Not at all. It's my right and privilege as a lesbian who has gone before."

"Cool." Clare's affable nod told Hannah she meant it. "So, what about you and Drew? You two seem pretty cozy."

Cozy. That was one word for it. "Pretty good, I guess."

"Uh, you went away together. That's a big deal."

They had. But if the time with Drew's family made her feel like more than Drew's girlfriend, other parts of the trip had thrown it all up in the air. She was saved from having to put that into words by a group of college students with armfuls of garlic stalks. She tipped the brim of her ball cap. "I'm going to leave you to it."

Clare shot her a this-is-not-over look and then turned her attention to the customers. It reminded Hannah so much of their mother, which made her laugh. She headed to the barn to check stock and get a report on the flow of other u-pickers. Based on the number of cars making their way around the loop road, she guessed it would be high.

Things at the barn were bumping. She'd already missed Drew, but close to a dozen families milled around the farm stand and parking lot. She ate a quick sandwich and reapplied sunscreen, then headed back to work. She called it a day just after seven. Tired, but not the bone tired that came with the peak of summer. A perfect end to a pretty perfect day.

❖

For the first time since meeting him, Drew hesitated to take the call from Javier. A week had passed since his initial phone call and she'd specifically not reached out to him. Or told Hannah. Or her family. Instead of gaining any clarity, each day made the decision feel all the more impossible. One thing was certain—being indecisive would not go over well with Javier.

It was cowardly as shit and she didn't even care. She was going to play dumb. "Hello?"

"How are you, my little country bumpkin?"

At least he didn't seem annoyed with her. "I'm good. What's up?"

"I can't give you those three months after all."

Drew's first thought was that something had happened and he was rescinding the offer. An unexpected wave of relief washed over her. "Let me guess. Bobby Flay came begging."

"What? No. Of course not." She'd been kidding, but his tone told her he wasn't amused.

"Okay. What, then?" It would sting if he filled the slot with some bigger name, but she'd refused to make a decision. She'd have no one to blame but herself.

"Priscilla. The doctor has put her on bed rest."

Her stomach lurched. She told herself it was concern for the woman she'd met a handful of times. "Oh, no. Is she okay?"

Javier sighed. She could imagine him swishing a hand back and forth while he spoke. "She's fine. The kitchen work, it's very hard on the body. They don't want to chance the baby coming too early."

That made sense. Something similar had happened with Baker's sister. She'd been bored out of her mind and miserable by the end of it, but two months off her feet did the trick and she had a healthy baby boy. "So, she's—"

"Out. Immediately."

The meaning of his earlier statement hit her. He wasn't rescinding his offer and she didn't have three months to decide. "You need an answer from me."

"By the end of this week. I know you have to give notice, but if your answer is no, I need to look elsewhere. I cannot go any longer than I must without a head chef."

"I understand completely." Fuck. He probably expected her to answer on the spot. At any other moment in her life, she'd have answered already.

He waited a beat. "Does this mean your answer is no?"

"No. But it's not yes, either."

"I see."

What the hell was wrong with her? "It's not that I don't want to say yes, it's just—"

"Is it this restaurant you've fallen for? Or is it the girl?"

And when had she become so transparent? "It's complicated."

"In my experience, it's complicated means it's the girl. Or in my case, the boy. You know what I mean."

She did, and her feelings for Hannah were definitely at the forefront of her mind. Hannah wasn't the only factor, though. She liked running the kitchen at Fig. She had full creative license without the cutthroat atmosphere of the New York City scene. She loved her staff and working for Nick. She'd even grown fond of her house. Drew shook her head. It was the exact circle her mind had been stuck on since the first time they talked. Since she'd realized at her grandmother's birthday party just how much she'd become attached to her life.

"Was it something I said?"

Shit. How long had she left him hanging? "No. I mean yes, but no. Sorry."

"I've seen you in some pretty crazy situations, Drew, and I think this is the first time I've seen you flustered. I'm sorry I've given you a Sadie's choice."

Drew chuckled. "Sophie. It's Sophie's choice."

Javier tutted. "They're all the same to me, kid."

"I'll let you know in a couple of days, I promise."

"You will. I can wait only so long, even for you." He paused, like maybe he was weighing whether or not to continue. "If I can give you one piece of advice, it's this."

Drew looked out the window and braced herself for a treatise on ambition and opportunities that don't roll around every day.

"Follow your heart. Work isn't all it's cracked up to be."

Wow. "I wouldn't have expected that from you."

"I'm lucky. My husband, he loves the business and this crazy life. But if he didn't? Well, let's just say I love him more than I love running restaurants. I know this and he knows it, too."

One of the top restaurateurs in North America had offered her a job and now he was giving her love advice. What kind of bizarro world had she stepped into? "Thanks, Javier. That's really good advice."

"You figure out your heart and you give me a call."

"I will. Talk soon." Drew ended the call but didn't get up. She stared at the screen, as though some other life-altering thing might spring from it and turn her world even more upside down. Nothing did, which was good since Drew didn't think she could handle another bomb dropping. Of course, thinking of being offered her dream job as a bomb dropping didn't help. She needed to make a decision in four days. What the fuck was she going to do?

She got up and spent some time pacing the span of the kitchen and living room. That succeeded in making her feel like a caged animal. Not helpful. Drew stopped and looked out the window. She practically lived in a state forest. There had to be a dozen trails at her disposal. It was as good a time as any to finally use them.

She changed into athletic shorts and a long-sleeved T-shirt, then pulled on the sneakers she rarely wore. She contemplated bringing water or a snack or something but decided against it. She wasn't hiking a fucking mountain.

Although tempted to walk out her back door and right into the woods, she wasn't an idiot. Instead, she jogged down the street to the large sign announcing the state forest. Next to it, a map showed various trails, each marked with a different colored line. She chose one labeled flat that would loop her back to her starting point.

She moved purposefully at first, her gaze shooting back and forth between her feet and the patches of paint on trees that told her which way to go. She expected it to work like the gym, where the combination of monotony and feeling like her lungs were on fire made thinking difficult if not impossible. The woods, it seemed, didn't work that way.

She had to move slower because of the uneven ground, so she hardly broke a sweat. Still, the deeper into the forest she got, the more she found herself pulled in by the texture of the trees and plants, the sounds of leaves rustling and birds singing. It soothed rather than distracted. Like all those things people said about spending time in nature were true. By the time she got home, she felt calmer, if no closer to the answer.

Chapter Twenty-seven

With the days getting shorter, Hannah cut back her hours at the farm. She'd been looking forward to the more relaxed pace of fall. Even with plenty still to harvest, very little planting needed to be done and the weeds were finally tamed. But even as she had more time, she suddenly seemed to be spending less of it with Drew. The last week especially, Drew seemed distracted and on edge. Hannah asked her about it a couple of times, but Drew brushed her off. She wasn't about to beg.

And then, almost out of the blue, Drew asked to come over. Not for dinner, not for the night. It was the middle of the day and she'd asked simply to come over. Maybe finally she'd open up about whatever was bugging her.

Sure enough, she showed up and said she needed to talk about something. They sat on the sofa, Drew's leg bouncing like it was on a spring. Seconds ticked by. Finally, Hannah put her hand on Drew's knee. "Clearly, something's bothering you. Just spit it out already."

"Do you remember that guy we ran into when we were in New York City? Javier?"

Oh, she remembered. She also remembered the indignant feeling that pressed against her rib cage at their condescending banter about the quaint little place upstate. That feeling returned, although she couldn't figure out why. "I do."

Drew took a deep breath. She looked miserable, like she'd been charged with delivering terrible news. "He's offered me a job."

Maybe she should have been grateful Drew had the courtesy to at least pretend to be torn. She consciously formed her lips into a smile. "That's great."

"It's an honor, that's for sure. He's launched some of the biggest chefs in the last decade."

She wasn't oblivious to the world of celebrity chefs. Feature stories in her monthly *Food and Wine* sometimes felt like they belonged in *People* instead. She didn't get the appeal, with actors or athletes or any other kind of celebrity. But Drew would aspire to that. The pressure in her ribs gave way to a sinking in her stomach. "When do you start?"

Drew looked at her like the question made no sense. "I haven't accepted it yet. Javier initially gave me a couple of months to decide, but he needs someone sooner. I have to let him know this week."

What did she mean she hadn't accepted it yet? "So, like, do you want my blessing or something?"

"I—" Drew closed her mouth, opened it again. "I wanted to talk to you about it."

A dozen different moments, comments, replayed in Hannah's mind. Phrases like "step on the ladder" and "means to an end." What Angelique said about Drew's aspirations. The look on Drew's face when she talked about opening a restaurant on her own. Of course, it wasn't that simple. She also remembered Drew picking peaches and sitting on her back deck. In her kitchen, making dinner. In her bed, making—

"Hannah?"

How long had she'd zoned out? "I don't see how there's much to talk about. You're not going to turn it down."

Drew took a deep breath and studied Hannah's face, searching for meaning. She didn't know what she expected, but it sure as hell wasn't this. Hannah didn't seem angry or even all that upset. "I thought I at least owed you, us, the chance to have a conversation. We're involved, probably more than either of us expected going in."

Hannah's face was expressionless. "Your life is in the city. You've been clear about that from the beginning. Let's not pretend we're going to juggle some kind of long-distance arrangement that will leave us both disappointed and exhausted."

A few months ago, Drew might have said those exact words. It made no sense for them to feel utterly devastating now. "I didn't realize you felt that way."

Hannah took a deep breath. Drew couldn't tell if she was trying to steel her resolve or find a nice way to tell Drew to get lost. "I'm not minimizing what we had. I'm being realistic, and honest."

Hannah's use of the past tense wasn't lost on Drew. Nor was the almost bored look on her face. As much as it felt like her heart was being wrung out from the inside, it made her decision a whole hell of a lot easier. "I appreciate your honesty."

Hannah smiled. It looked plastic and turned Drew's stomach. "I am happy for you." She put emphasis on the "am" like it might make Drew believe her. "It's quite an accomplishment."

Drew squared her shoulders. "It is. It's what I've worked for my entire life."

"Then you deserve it." Something passed through Hannah's eyes. It might have been sadness, or maybe disappointment. But it disappeared almost immediately, leaving Drew to wonder if she'd imagined it.

"I haven't told Nick yet. I'm going to do that today, but I'd appreciate if you didn't say anything to anyone. At least until tomorrow."

"Of course."

Hannah's living room suddenly felt claustrophobic, the air thick and stifling. "Okay, I think I'm going to go."

Again, that look passed through Hannah's eyes. "I hope you don't feel like I'm kicking you to the curb."

Oh, no. It felt much worse than that. Like a kick to the chest that stole her breath and made her feel like she might never get it back. "Not at all. But it feels awkward to stay."

"Yeah. You're right. No hard feelings, though, right?"

"No hard feelings." The lie clung to her like stale smoke, permeating her skin and clothes.

Hannah stepped forward. She had the audacity to kiss Drew on the cheek. "Congratulations."

Drew fled, unable to stand being in the same room any longer. She climbed into her car and left, not having a destination but needing to be as far away from Hannah as possible.

She drove south toward town. She knew where Nick lived, but it felt weird to show up at his house unannounced. But now that she'd told Hannah, now that her decision had been made, she wanted to let him know as soon as possible. She owed him that. And even if she still trusted Hannah not to break confidence, the less time that elapsed, the better. She pulled to the side of the road and texted him, asking if he might be free to meet. She didn't expect an immediate reply, but one came, offering a beer and a promise not to rope her into the yard work he was doing.

The message had such an easiness to it. They'd become friends. It made her feel like shit to be quitting on him not six months into her position. It didn't help to think he might be more upset by her leaving than Hannah had been.

She shook her head. Her complete misread of things with Hannah wasn't Nick's problem. His problem was losing his head chef, nothing more. And on that front, at least, she might be able to help. Poppy had progressed so much, both in her cooking style and her leadership in the kitchen, Drew feared she might not be long for Fig. She had no hesitation recommending her for the promotion. If Nick agreed, the transition would be seamless.

Almost like she'd never been there.

❖

When Drew had gone, Hannah gave into the urge to drop her head into her hands. She didn't cry, so that counted for something. But she did feel like she might throw up any second. She took a deep breath and tried to settle the churning in her stomach.

She'd done the right thing. She knew in her heart she'd done the right thing. Why did the right thing have to feel so shitty? And why did it feel like her heart was broken into pieces? Hannah had ended relationships before, but never had it felt like this. She stood. She didn't know what would make it go away, but sitting by herself and moping would only make it worse.

It was her day off, but there were a few hours of daylight left. She could distract herself in the fields, then find something in the barn to keep her busy. She'd just have to figure out a way to avoid talking to anyone. If she had any hope of keeping it together, not talking was a must.

During the time she'd been inside, a swath of dark clouds had moved in from the west. It looked like the cold front would be arriving a few hours ahead of schedule. Just like her mood. All the more reason to get in as much work as possible.

She got to the farm and spent a minute debating between picking the greens for the week's CSA boxes and picking apples. Since the storm would probably take down apples more than it would damage the kale, she settled on apples. She grabbed her rain jacket from her locker and pulled on boots. On her way out, she snagged a few over-the-shoulder canvas bags. A minute later, she stalked up the path to the orchard, grateful the weather and day of the week saved her from having to cross paths with any u-pickers.

After Red Delicious, McIntosh might be her least favorite apple. Their soft flesh and mild flavor bored her to tears, but they remained a perennial crowd favorite, so she had planted several rows beyond the older trees that had been on the property when she bought it. They'd filled out nicely in the last five years and were consistently good producers. Maybe they weren't so terrible after all.

She surveyed the rows. The lower branches had been pretty well picked. She'd leave what remained for the next wave of u-pickers. That still left plenty of apples out of reach for the average person on the ground. Although she'd placed a few modest stepladders here and there, most folks didn't brave the climb, especially when beautiful fruit sat at eye level. She didn't mind, as she'd yet to have a single injured customer. As soon as she had the thought, she went up to one of the trees and rapped her knuckles against it.

She and Jeremiah had parked a huge wooden crate just off the road. They'd filled one of Macs already and tractored it to the farm stand. This one sat empty and waiting. Perfect.

Hannah grabbed one of the ladders and positioned it under a tree. Even just a few feet off the ground, the wind was stronger. It whipped through her jacket and sent a chill rippling down her spine. She shook it off and started to pick, filling the bags she'd hung on either side of her.

Fill the bags, empty the bags. Move the ladder, fill the bags. On a good day, picking apples was one of her favorite chores. Today she went at it with a vengeance, stomping up and down the ladder each time. She mumbled to herself, mostly expletives. When the rain started, she didn't even pause. The wind picked up, whipping cold drops into her face. When tears started to fall, they mixed with the rain, making them slightly less humiliating. How could she have been such a fool?

She lost track of time, lost track of how many trips she made up and down, how many apples she added to the crate. When she heard a vehicle on the loop road, she paused to see who it was. Jeremiah.

He stopped his truck and cut the engine. He got out, pulling the hood of his rain jacket over his head. "If you were worried about the apples, you should have told me. I'd have come up to help."

Hannah wiped her face instinctively. "I wasn't really. Just needed to burn off some energy."

He eyed her, as though weighing whether or not to say anything about how bedraggled she must look or what a bad liar she was. Eventually, he asked, "Are you okay?"

There were few people in her life she could count on more than Jeremiah. He'd been at the farm almost since it opened. Hannah always appreciated his work ethic and the sixth sense he seemed to have when it came to plants and the land. She didn't always appreciate what a calm, consistent force he was in her life. He was one of the few men that got her—more than Nick, and certainly more than her brothers or her father.

She started to cry in earnest, the ugly sort of crying that sent most guys running for the hills. Jeremiah came closer, pulling her into a hug. He rubbed her back as she sobbed. "It's okay. I don't know what it is, but it's going to be okay."

It took a few minutes for her to calm down. The tears stopped and embarrassment set in. She sniffed and pulled away. "Sorry."

He looked at her with nothing but kindness. "Don't apologize. I'd like to think we could fall apart in front of each other at this point."

Hannah chuckled. "I'd rather not fall apart in the first place."

"Well, sure." He nodded affably. "Do you want to talk about it?"

"Not really." A shadow of something resembling hurt passed through his eyes, making her reconsider. "Drew is leaving."

"Oh."

"She got some big, fancy job offer in the city."

Jeremiah frowned. "Did you ask her to stay?"

"God, no. This is her dream. I told her she should take it."

"Ah." He might get her, but he remained a man of few words.

"I guess I was more upset than I cared to admit. I'm fine." She squared her shoulders. "Let's not stand out here in the rain. Can I ride back to the barn with you?"

"Of course. But I don't mind the rain if you want to get more picking done."

Hannah looked at the bin. It was close to half full. "No, I think we're fine. I'm ready to call it a day."

They rode the short distance in silence. When they pulled up behind the barn, she took a deep breath. "I won't apologize again, but I'll say thank you. And ask if we could keep that between us."

"Absolutely. And, hey, anytime. That's what friends are for."

Hannah nodded. "Right. Thanks. And same goes. If you need to fall apart, I'm your girl."

And that was that. Jeremiah went to finish his tasks and Hannah went to the locker room to leave her jacket and change her shoes. She sat there for a minute, hunched over the laces and staring at the floor, and let the truth settle around her.

She had feelings for Drew. Way more feelings than she wanted to have or admit, but there was no point in telling herself otherwise. Even if she couldn't change the way things ended or change what Drew wanted and make her come back. There was something cathartic in admitting it. Admitting it meant she could move on. That was the saying, right?

Hannah avoided the farm stand. No way could she deal with Clare's questions, no matter how well intentioned. She went home and took a shower, letting the heat sink into her cold and cramping muscles. It was barely dark out, but she crawled into bed anyway. She didn't expect to sleep, but there was something to be said for burrowing under the covers and pretending the rest of the world didn't exist.

Chapter Twenty-eight

Nick took the news of her leaving hard, but he was such a nice guy, he was offering her congratulations and well wishes by the end of the conversation. He took her advice about Poppy to heart and Drew spent a week training her to take over the kitchen. Boxes of produce appeared at the restaurant every morning. She took that as a sign Hannah didn't want to see her. So much for no hard feelings.

She slept terribly, had a hard time staying focused. She told herself it was nerves over the new position. The prestige was one thing, but the visibility of being head chef at one of Javier's restaurants was another. The job at Fig might have helped her get to this point, but it would be working for Javier that would make or break her career.

She reminded herself of that each time her thoughts drifted to Hannah. Each time she caught herself staring into space, thinking about Hannah's voice or smile or body. Each time she started kicking herself for thinking there'd been something real between them.

Drew packed up most of her clothes and personal things, but she left enough behind that she'd need to make another trip. She told herself it was easier than having to Tetris it all into her car, unloading it at a storage unit while she figured out a place of her own. The truth of the matter, though, was that she wasn't quite ready to close the door. Not on her little house or the restaurant or Hannah. Even if all evidence pointed to the door already being firmly shut.

She'd give herself to the end of the month. That's when she'd need to give her landlord notice anyway. It would be easier once she had the reality of her new job to focus on, once the weird emptiness in her chest went away. Not seeing Hannah for a few weeks would help. It had to help.

But as she drove south, through Ithaca and down to Owego,

over the river toward Binghamton and onto I-81, she felt less and less convinced that would be the case. After stopping for gas, she cued up the *Hamilton* soundtrack extra loud to drown out her own thoughts with the political machinations and exploits of Hamilton and Burr. On top of that, it made her think of Baker and the fact they'd go back to seeing each other every few days instead of every few months.

She'd just finished vowing not to throw away her shot when it hit her that she wouldn't see Baker every few days. Even if her new place on Long Island wasn't that far away, she would be sharing it with her girlfriend. Hell, it probably wouldn't be long before Lucy became Baker's fiancée. As happy as she was for them, the reality of Baker's domestic bliss hit her like a bucket of cold water. Drew turned the music off altogether and drove in silence.

She got to her mother's just before six and found Grann puttering around the kitchen. "Your mother is at some union meeting. She won't be home for a while yet."

"That's okay. What can I do to help?"

Grann waved her off. "You get yourself settled. I'm sure you're exhausted."

Drew couldn't argue there. She unloaded her car, making several trips down to the basement where she'd lived all four years of culinary school. It felt equal parts comforting and stifling. She unpacked the essentials. Hopefully, she wouldn't be there more than a few weeks.

She heard movement upstairs and abandoned her suitcases to greet her mother. When she entered the kitchen, Manman and Grann were waiting. Grann held a bottle of champagne and Manman had a large bouquet of flowers and a big Mylar balloon. Grann beamed. "Congratulations, child."

"We're so proud of you." Manman handed her the flowers and gave her a hug.

For the first time since accepting Javier's offer, the warmth of genuine happiness spread through her. It might be more complicated than she'd planned or hoped, but she'd made it. Even more importantly, she'd not made it alone. She shoved aside her hesitation and her self-pity and did what she was supposed to do. She celebrated.

❖

A small part of Hannah regretted not seeing Drew before she left. But as much as she would have liked to be the bigger person, she wasn't sure she had it in her. Self-preservation beat moral high ground any day of the week.

Even knowing she'd made the right call, she'd been moody and short-tempered. Without saying a word, Jeremiah acted as a buffer, assigning tasks and beginning the preparations for putting parts of the farm to sleep for winter. Daisy stuck by her side, as if sensing she needed a friend who wouldn't ask questions or care if she smiled. She hated herself for being so affected by Drew's departure. She hated herself even more for oscillating between being angry with Drew for leaving and angry with herself for getting invested when she should have known better.

She shook her head. Berating herself was even more a waste of time than pining. And she needed to finish paying bills if she hoped to make it out to the orchard before sunset.

She worked her way through the usual suspects—utilities, mortgage, insurance. Then she picked up the pile of other mail and began to sort. Most of it was junk, but she opened everything to make sure. When she got to a letter from an attorney's office based in Ithaca, she hesitated. Letters from lawyers rarely brought good news. She took a deep breath and opened it. Not like her mood could get much worse.

Hannah read the letter. What started as a general sinking feeling became a lead weight, dragging her down and sucking all the air from her lungs. Just when she thought she knew what it was like to feel low. Ha.

Her farm was being sold out from under her.

She read the letter a second time, hoping perhaps the words or their meaning might magically change. They didn't.

This had always been a possibility. She'd known it going in. But with each passing year, the farm felt more solid, more permanent. She'd succeeded in pushing it from her mind almost completely. Which, clearly, had been a mistake.

She owned about a third of her land outright. Well, owned with a mortgage, but close enough. The rest she leased from her next-door neighbor. The family had stopped farming decades ago but hadn't wanted to break up the property. As Hannah's operations and her need for land grew, it had felt like the perfect solution. She went from leasing ten acres to twenty, from twenty to fifty.

But now they were selling.

The good news, she supposed, was that they no longer cared about keeping the eighty acres intact. Hannah was welcome to buy the land she currently used at a very reasonable price. They were even giving her the right of first refusal, which hadn't been one of the conditions of her lease. It was quite generous, really.

There was only one problem. She didn't have the money.

Three Willows Farm was profitable, perhaps even more so than she'd dared to hope more than a couple of years ago. But she did not have three hundred grand in reserves. She didn't even have a tenth of that. And while she could probably swing a bigger mortgage, she didn't have the equity or collateral that would be required for a bigger loan. Not that she wouldn't try. But if her initial efforts at getting financed were anything to go on, things didn't look good.

She sat down at her desk and, since no one was there to see, rested her head on it. She wasn't ready to curl up and admit defeat. She just wasn't ready to tackle it quite yet. Or put on a brave face for her staff. Or listen to her father's disapproval.

"What's wrong?"

She'd not heard Jeremiah approach. She sat up, folded the letter quickly, and stuffed it in a drawer. "Nothing. I just dropped something."

"Okay." He didn't look convinced, but he wasn't the kind of person who'd press. She liked that about him. Respected it. Or maybe he was afraid she'd start crying on him again. "I'm going to take Guy to start picking delicatas. Is that cool with you?"

It was hard to believe they were already harvesting winter squash. But her wishing it not to be so didn't mean they weren't ready for harvest. She nodded. "That sounds great. Thanks."

He left and she pulled the letter out, read it again. The words hadn't changed.

Was there a way for her to scrape together a down payment? And even if she did, would she qualify for another mortgage?

The obvious solution would be to ask her parents to cosign for her. Three Willows was established enough that it would be virtually no risk to them. And the payment would probably be on par with the rent she paid. She shook her head. Just as obvious as the solution was, she knew she'd never take it. Even if her father agreed, it would be admitting to him that she couldn't make it on her own.

There had to be another way. She was pretty good at finding other ways. No chance of that happening right now, though. Right now, what she needed was someone who'd listen and then pour her a stiff drink. She called Jenn.

Chapter Twenty-nine

The kitchen at George was bright, modern, and well equipped. A little smaller than her kitchen at Fig, but not by much. It felt impersonal, but it had to be because it was still new to her. She'd yet to make it hers.

The same could be said of the staff. Well-trained, respectful, efficient. But not hers.

Drew shook her head. She needed to snap out of it. She'd made it through a dozen dinner services without incident. But if she wasn't careful, people would start to pick up on the fact that her head wasn't in the game. She thought yet again about Javier's advice when he offered her the job. Maybe her head wasn't the problem.

"Delivery, Chef."

Drew turned in the direction of the voice. It was one of the dishwashers. Mike? Matt. "Thanks, Matt."

She headed to the back door and found a short, dark-skinned man she'd never seen before. "Hi."

"Eastside Produce. I got your order." His smile was friendly and his accent reminded her of her grandmother.

"Thanks." She signed his clipboard and followed him to the truck. She took the flats he handed her, led the way back into the kitchen. He followed with the rest, then was gone as quickly as he'd come. She didn't want to make small talk, necessarily, but she hated not even having the option.

She opened the first box and found exactly what she'd ordered—greens, butternut squash, eggplant, and peppers. By pretty much any standard, it was superior produce. Drew couldn't help but find it ordinary, uninspired.

Before she could mope about it, Bente, her sous chef, appeared. "Shall I have the prep cooks start on this as we discussed?"

They'd set the weekend's menu the day before, so there were no new instructions to worry about. "That would be great. Thanks."

Bente took a box and moved over to the prep station. Drew appreciated her ability to give directions and keep an eye on things. In a lot of ways, she was exactly the kind of sous chef Drew had been—one who was perfectly capable of running the kitchen herself. She might have found it presumptuous, but it turned out to be a relief. She only hoped Bente didn't start resenting her a month into their time together.

With preparations under way, Drew turned her attention to sauces. She'd just added the milk and nutmeg to her béchamel when her phone vibrated in her pocket. The text was from Clare. Worried something might be wrong with Hannah, Drew unlocked her phone so she could read it. *I'm glad you got your dream job, but not having you around sux. Just saying.*

Drew smiled. Leave it to a teenager to sum up the entirety of her emotions on the matter in a single text. *Thanks, Clare. I miss you, too. All of you.*

That wasn't too much, was it?

You heard about the farm, right?

Drew frowned at her phone. *No. What about the farm?*

Before Clare's reply came through, Javier swept into the kitchen for his pre-service visit. She grudgingly tucked her phone away so she could run down the specials and listen to his nightly pep talk. She listened, then wrapped up the impromptu gathering with her own words of encouragement for the staff. And then they were off.

Between searing a porterhouse and plating it, she grabbed her phone. There were a trio of messages waiting for her. The first simply said, *Shit. I'm probably not supposed to tell you.* The second added, *Or say shit.* The third finally got to the heart of the matter. *Half the land the farm is on is up for sale and Hannah doesn't know what'll happen.*

Drew returned her phone to her pocket and plated the steak resting in front of her. She did two more, then left her grill chef in charge while she made a loop around the kitchen. Satisfied things were under control, she ducked into the walk-in cooler and fired off a text to Nick. Her instinct was to reach out to Hannah, but she needed more information before she could even pretend to know what to say.

The rest of dinner passed in a blur. Despite having a rock star sous chef, she had to hustle nonstop to keep up with everything. That was one thing about New York. If the restaurant was hot, there was no such thing as a slow night.

She'd promised to go out drinking with the staff, so it was close to two before Drew made it onto a Brooklyn-bound 9 train. Nick had sent a slew of texts confirming what Clare had said. He elaborated, though, adding Hannah's desire to buy the land, her uncertainty of being able to make it happen, and the general damper the whole matter had put on things both at the farm and at the restaurant. He closed with a comment about the funk at the restaurant having more to do with missing her.

Drew sat slumped in the mostly empty subway car. Her reflection in the opposite window looked gray and tired. The ghastly fluorescent light didn't help, but she couldn't blame it entirely.

She shook her head in defeat. Not too old to be a chef, maybe, but too old to go out drinking like a twenty-three-year-old. Add to that the fact she was miserable. Not the miserable of having to settle into a new job and new people and new surroundings but the kind that comes with realizing she'd made a terrible mistake.

And now it was compounded by the knowledge that Hannah was in trouble. Not only was she not there to help, but she'd screwed things up so royally, she had no idea if her help would even be welcome. Even as she sat with that knowledge, Drew started to formulate a plan.

She got so caught up in formulating, she almost missed her stop. She just cleared the doors as they started to close. Like the train, the platform was almost empty. She dragged herself up the stairs and toward home. Drew let herself in quietly and headed to the finished basement where she still was crashing. She took a shower, pulled on boxers and an undershirt, and fell into bed.

She lay on one side, then the other. Then her back. The mixture of physical exhaustion and a restless mind aggravated her. Her aggravation made her even more awake. It was after five when she finally fell asleep, only to find herself jarred awake by her phone ringing and vibrating on the nightstand.

Drew knocked it to the ground, swore, then picked it up. Why was her alarm going off at eight in the morning? She realized it was Saturday, the day she'd promised to help her grandmother bring things to church for the rummage sale, and groaned.

On the heels of that realization came remembering her text conversations from the night before. She'd abandoned them, not wanting to risk waking anyone at the obscene hour she finished work. She pulled them up, starting with an apology to Clare for not getting back to her. She then turned her attention to Nick. A minute later, her phone was ringing. It was Nick.

"Isn't there something we can do to help?" she asked.

"I've offered, but what I can tap into wouldn't do much good. And unless you've got a trust fund you hide remarkably well—"

"What about a fundraiser?" She'd half-baked the idea the night before and probably should have finished sorting it out in her mind first, but she couldn't stop herself.

"Like at the restaurant?" He sounded incredulous.

"Yes. Big fancy dinner, all proceeds going to keep Three Willows Farm alive and well in the community."

"She's pretty beloved. The farm is, too."

"Exactly. We probably won't raise enough to buy the land, but a healthy down payment might help her secure financing."

Nick didn't say anything and she thought he might be looking for a way to gently nix the whole idea. "I can't believe I didn't think of that."

She smiled. He was such a good guy. "I don't have a trust fund, but I'd volunteer time and could even cover some of the costs."

"If we did one night's receipts, just with regular dinner service, that would be huge."

It didn't surprise her that he agreed, but she was taken aback by the level of generosity he was immediately prepared to throw out there. She started to get excited. "We could do something special, a one-night-only menu. Prix fixe will keep costs down. Even if you held some back to cover labor, it could be huge."

"I think it's a great idea. Big city chef, back for one night only."

Oh, she hadn't thought of that angle. "What if I could convince a couple of big names to join me? Turn it into a celebrity event."

"Could you do that?"

"I'd have to ask around. But my boss is crazy connected." Javier would probably find the whole thing charming. And in a way, it would be free publicity.

Nick sighed. "There's only one problem."

She really couldn't see any. "What's that?"

"Convincing Hannah to let us do it."

Drew chuckled ruefully. "Right."

"I mean, I probably can. Especially if I play the card of wanting to make sure she doesn't have to lay off staff."

"Good call." Drew hesitated. She didn't want to, but she needed to put it out there if this was going to fly. "You probably shouldn't mention my involvement."

"What do you mean?" He seemed genuinely confused. "If you're hoping she gives you a second chance, wouldn't you want her to know?"

"I'm afraid she might think I'm doing it to try to get her back. She'd hate that. And I'm afraid it might make her say no on principle."

Nick made a tutting noise that sounded like sympathy. "I don't want to admit you're right, but you might be."

"Let's not take a chance, at least before she agrees to it. This matters too much."

"You're a good person, Drew, in addition to being a good chef."

Drew smiled. "Save the compliments for when we pull it off."

Nick laughed. "Fair enough. I'll talk to Hannah and hopefully get back to you with some dates."

"Sounds good. I'll talk to you soon." She was about to hang up, but hesitated. "Hey, Nick?"

"Yeah?"

"Thanks for letting me in on this after I quit on you."

"No hard feelings, Drew. I promise."

She ended the call and sat on the edge of the bed for a moment. Part of her ached for the stress Hannah must be under. The other part of her was giddy at the prospect of being able to help and of having a reason to see Hannah again. She shook her head. A lot of things had to fall into place for that to happen. And even if it did, it still didn't mean Hannah would want anything to do with her.

Chapter Thirty

Hannah pinched the bridge of her nose, guilt and hope swirling in her chest like a tornado. "I don't know how I could ever repay you."

Nick reached across the desk in her little office and covered her hand with his. "You repay me by staying in business and continuing to supply my restaurant. Do you not see how much my success depends on yours?"

"You're being generous. There are at least a dozen farms who could provide you with fresh produce."

Nick shook his head. "It wouldn't be the same. One, our system works. You don't mess with something that works. Two, people love making the connection to a place they can go themselves. It's not some random purveyor whose name they see on the chalkboard by the door. And three, you aren't some random purveyor. You're family."

That single comment, about family, tipped the scales. With the exception of her initial conversation with Jenn, she'd held it together and not cried once. But now the tears fell. Like dams giving way or floodgates or all those other stupid analogies, they kept coming, a deluge of all her pent up stress and anxiety. In between sniffles, she managed to say, "You're the best family."

"So, is that a yes?"

She wiped her eyes and took a steadying breath. "It is. On one condition."

He regarded her with suspicion. "What's that?"

"You let me pay back the costs of putting it on with produce."

"You really don't need—"

She lifted a hand. "I insist. It's literally the least I can do and agree to this much generosity."

"Okay. We'll work something out."

Maybe this would work. She allowed hope to swell. "Thank you."

"Lord knows the only person more stubborn than Leda is you." He shook his head but was smiling.

Some of the pressure in her chest eased. "You like strong women, admit it."

"I do. I love them." He leaned in and kissed her on the cheek.

"So, what do you need from me?" Hannah asked. They were really doing this, and it might actually save her farm.

"For you to help me pick a date, then stand back and trust me. Oh, and provide some of the ingredients, obviously."

His choice of words gave her the slightest hitch of hesitation, but she pushed it aside. It was her own desire for independence that made it so hard to give up control, nothing more. He knew what he was doing and, even more importantly, she did trust him. "Okay."

"Excellent." He beamed at her as though she'd just given him the best possible news. It was humbling to realize just how invested he was in her success.

Nick pulled out his phone and ran through a couple of options for day and time. In the end, she left even that decision up to him. It wasn't like she had any burning plans on the horizon.

He left and she stayed in her office for a moment. She'd been racking her brain for over a week and hadn't come up with a viable plan. Selling farm shares in advance, renting out space for parties or rustic weddings—none of it would pull in the capital she needed fast enough to make a difference. She'd never considered asking the community to chip in. They already supported her so much. Nick's idea was charity, but not. People would be getting something for their money, something good. And as much as it pained her to need help, Nick might be the one person on the planet she could accept it from and still feel good. Plus, she had a built-in way of paying him back, at least some.

Maybe she could do gift certificates or something for the people who came. It would help justify the ticket price and it would make her feel like she was contributing. She'd need to ask Clare for help designing it. Since Clare was working for Nick now, too, she could also help with marketing.

Hannah took a deep breath and stood. Having a plan was great. Having tasks related to it was even better. She could do this. They could do this.

She left her office and went in search of Jeremiah. It felt easier telling him what was happening now that she had a plan. Well, that and knowing once Nick started planning in earnest, word would get out. She wanted to tell all of her staff personally about the situation, but especially Jeremiah. She owed him that.

He took the news in stride, perhaps because he was an optimist at heart and her plan sounded reasonable. Whatever the cause, his confidence that everything would work out buoyed her. She went back to work with a renewed sense of purpose.

When she got home a few hours later, she was exhausted from work as much as from the emotional roller coaster of the last few days. But for the first time since she'd opened that damn letter, she didn't worry about being able to fall asleep. Maybe a small part of her pined for Drew—her warmth or her solid presence or her innate ability to distract Hannah from whatever filled her mind—but she set it aside. She had much bigger things to think about than a smooth-talking chef who couldn't get out of town fast enough.

❖

"Child, are you going to tell me why you're so sad?"

Drew smiled at the term of endearment. It was one she'd never outgrown and, at this point, she didn't want to. Hearing it now put a lump in Drew's throat. "I'm not sad, Grann. I'm blessed. I have the job of my dreams and I'm here with you."

"Those things might be true, but your eyes are sad. When the eyes are sad, the heart is, too." She had such a talent for cutting to the heart of something.

"I'm just missing upstate. I didn't think I'd get so attached in such a short amount of time." And the more time she spent planning the gala with Nick, the worse it seemed to get.

"Tell me what you miss. It lessens the load to talk." Drew must have looked incredulous because Grann gave her a stern look. "I've lived a lot longer than you. Trust me."

Drew took a deep breath. "I miss the restaurant. My staff, Nick—they were a great group of people. Different from restaurant people in the city."

Grann nodded. "And what else?"

"My little house. I never in a million years thought I'd get used to the quiet, the stillness of it." She chuckled. "All the nature."

"But you did. There is a streak of country folk in your heart. You got that from your father."

For reasons she couldn't explain, the mention of her father brought Drew to the verge of tears. Her memories of him were so fuzzy at this point, more the work of the stories she heard about him than her own experiences, including the fact that he'd grown up in the Catskills. But in that moment, the loss of him from her life hit her, a visceral ache deep in her chest. She shook her head, as though she might deny entry to the grief she usually held at bay. "I've always loved the city."

"You can love one thing but realize your heart belongs to something else, to someone else."

From Grann's lips, it sounded like a simple truth, an obvious condition of life. But it didn't feel simple. "What if those things are in direct opposition to each other?"

"Then you must stretch your heart so that you may hold them both."

Drew turned the idea over in her mind. It sounded like a nice sentiment. Even if she didn't have much use for the more outlandish bits of philosophy and religion her grandmother espoused, this felt sound in principle. Personal growth and expanded worldviews and all that. Too bad the logistics seemed impossible.

"You feel disloyal, don't you?"

The question ground Drew's thoughts to a halt. Loyalty was a point of pride for her. She joked about her ego, but fealty drove her above all else. It was why she was back in the city—to fulfill a promise she'd made to herself and to her family. "Disloyal?"

Grann moved her hand back and forth. "Perhaps this is not the right word. You are driven by loyalty. You are letting it lead you when it should be the other way around."

"I don't understand."

She looked to Manman, who stood at the sink. A look Drew didn't understand passed between them, then she placed a hand on Drew's knee. "When your father died, your mother and I discussed returning to the island. It felt safe, familiar. And the cost of living would have been a fraction of what it took to stay in the city."

"You never told me that."

Manman joined them at the table. "You were young. We didn't

want you worrying about your life being turned upside down even more than it already had."

"What made you decide to stay?" Drew had a sinking feeling she didn't want the answer.

Grann shrugged, as though it was the most obvious thing in the world. "Our lives would have been easier there, but your life was here. Your opportunities were here."

The ache in Drew's chest became a knot. "You both have sacrificed so much for me. All I ever wanted was to repay you for that, to make you proud."

Manman pointed at her, looking every part the stern teacher. "You make us proud by living your life, being happy. Nothing more."

Could she believe that? Did she want to? Even if she did, it might not matter. Hannah had broken things off without even a hint of hesitation.

"It's the girl, isn't it? Hannah?" Grann may have phrased it as a question, but her face made it clear she already knew the answer.

"She didn't want me to stay. If anything, she made it clear I should go and not look back."

Manman looked down at her hands. "I fear I may have had something to do with that."

"What do you mean?"

"When your grandmother and I were visiting, when we all had dinner together, I said something about you coming back to the city as a head chef. I said it would be the thing that made all the work and sacrifice worthwhile. I think she may have taken that to heart."

Drew's stomach twisted. Could that really be why Hannah brushed her off so quickly? Not because she didn't care but because it felt like the right thing to do? That changed everything.

Manman and Grann went to bed, leaving Drew at the table with her whiskey and her thoughts. She'd always considered herself a risk-taker, willing to push the boundaries of what was acceptable or expected. For as much as that might be true in the kitchen, she'd done a pretty shit job of it in the rest of her life.

Manman's words echoed in her mind. Living her life and being happy. She'd thought she knew what those things looked like, what it would take to achieve them. Whether she'd been completely wrong or they'd somehow shifted on her hardly mattered. What mattered now was knowing what she needed to do, feeling more certain than she had about pretty much anything in her life to date, including becoming a chef in the first place.

She looked at the clock on the stove. Just after ten. Javier would probably just be finishing dinner. She pulled him up in her contacts and initiated the call, prepared to do what just a month ago would have been unfathomable. He answered after only one ring.

"Calling me on your day off? It's either wonderful news or terrible."

She smiled at his signature lack of a hello and seeming ability to read her thoughts. "Maybe a little of both."

"You're not pregnant, are you?"

The question was absurd, but the underlying meaning cut close. She let out an uneasy laugh. "Not exactly. I'd like to talk in person. Are you free?"

"You're quitting."

She flinched at the statement, both for its accuracy and what it said about her that she was looking to quit a second job in as many months. "What makes you think that?"

"Because you hesitated to take the job in the first place and because your heart has been elsewhere since you got here."

Okay, so apparently they were having the conversation right now. "I'm sorry I haven't been giving you my all."

"Your cooking is fine. I'm not taking issue. But your heart, it's not in your work. Tell me you're in love and that I was right all along."

She winced, embarrassed but relieved. "I'm in love and you were right all along."

"I knew it." His voice held more triumph than displeasure. "Love is the only good reason for abandoning me, and the very best reason of all."

Drew scratched her temple. "I had no idea you were such a hopeless romantic, Javier."

"It's because if my chefs knew, they'd walk all over me."

"Are you enough of a romantic to help the chef who just walked all over you?" Maybe she should have asked for his help before quitting on him.

"Is it about getting the girl?"

It so was. "Yes."

"Then I'm in."

Drew smiled. "Hannah's farm is in trouble."

An hour later, she hung up the phone with Javier's promise to attend the gala and bring two of his better-known chefs with him. She had no job, but she'd worry about that part later. She had a plan and a sliver of hope. For now, it was enough.

Chapter Thirty-one

Drew's Trumansburg landlord probably thought she was insane. She'd given notice, paid her last month's rent, then called him about renting the house she'd just vacated, all in less than a month's time. Given the many and varied ways she was acting like a crazy person these days, it didn't really bother her. She was just glad he'd not found a new tenant yet.

Being in the house again was at once familiar and strange. She didn't linger or bother unpacking. She needed to get to her meeting with Nick to talk about the guest chefs and the final details for the gala. Oh, and the minor matter of begging for her job back.

They met at Atlas, which should have felt like neutral territory but reminded her of her first day in town. It was noon on a weekday, though, and the bowling lanes sat empty. Not that it stopped her from imagining Hannah, beautiful and triumphant in her tight jeans and those ridiculous shoes. She'd felt the spark that day, even if she'd had no idea what it would become.

She and Nick ordered beers from the bar but took them to a hi-top table in the corner.

"How did she take the news?" Drew asked. It was cowardly on her part, but she'd let Nick tell Hannah about her involvement in the gala. It seemed better, though, than reaching out via text. Or showing up completely unannounced.

"You know Hannah. She's proud and doesn't like accepting help, much less having people know she needs it."

"So, really bad?"

Nick offered her a sheepish smile. "I wouldn't say really bad."

She tried not to let it sting too much. Had the tables been turned, she probably wouldn't have taken it well, either. "It's okay. You don't need to protect my feelings."

"She was mad that I kept it from her, but I think she's come around."

Drew sighed. She could tell he was being kind. Still, the show would go on. They talked about the schedule for the night, the staffing, and the menu before falling into a comfortable silence. It reminded her of all the reasons she loved working for Nick, why she hoped to again. She'd just steeled herself for broaching the subject when Nick set down his beer.

"I already know the answer, but I'll ask you anyway. Any chance you want to come back?"

She studied his face, looking for signs he might be joking. He didn't know about her conversation with Javier. He couldn't. "Are you not happy with Poppy?"

He shook his head. "It's the other way around. She's not happy in her new role. She's not going anywhere, but she's made it clear she doesn't want the position permanently. Too much people, not enough cooking. I believe those were her exact words."

She could appreciate the sentiment. She didn't share it, but she could appreciate it. "Well—"

"Drew, I was kidding. Please don't feel bad or like I'm trying to pressure you."

He was such a fucking good guy. Just like Javier. How had she managed to hit the jackpot of nice bosses in an industry known for the opposite? "It's not that. I'm," she paused, "actually, I am interested in coming back."

He blinked a few times, narrowed his eyes. "Seriously?"

"Yeah."

"Wow."

Discomfort, laced with guilt, made her press on. "I get that you might not believe a word I'm saying, but I mean it. I made a mistake leaving and I want to come back."

"Is it Hannah?"

Wasn't that the million-dollar question? He might not believe her on that front either, but she decided to go with the truth. "I'd be lying if I said she wasn't part of it, but it's more than that. I love Fig—the kitchen, the people, you. I even love the little town and my weird little house. I didn't realize how much until I left."

She was pretty sure that was the cheesiest speech ever given, but it was true, all of it.

"I felt that way once, sort of in reverse. I couldn't wait to get out of here when I turned eighteen. It was only after I left that I realized this was where I wanted to be."

Just like Grann's story, Nick's made her realize how little she knew about many of the people she cared about. Hell, how little she knew about anything. "You really want to hire me back?"

He shrugged. "We could consider it more of a leave of absence if it would make you feel better."

Drew chuckled. "It might."

"I assume you'll need some time to tie things up at your other job?"

"A couple of weeks. I want to stay on Javier's good side, especially since he's doing me such a huge favor this weekend."

"Of course. I'm looking forward to meeting him. I'd like to be on his good side, too. And Poppy isn't running for the hills. I'm sure she'll be happy just knowing you're coming back."

"Thanks, man. I don't think I could have imagined a better outcome if I'd tried."

"And Hannah?" He raised a brow.

On that front, she'd not even allowed herself to imagine an outcome. "I'm going to see her now."

Nick stood, clapped a hand on her shoulder. "I hope she comes around."

Drew thought about the ache that had taken up residence in her chest. Not as acute as the day Hannah basically told her to go to hell, but it never went away completely. She really hoped she wouldn't have to learn if it was one of those things that faded with time. But she couldn't worry about that now. "Thanks."

"You're really in love with her, aren't you?"

Everyone seemed to know it. Except, of course, Hannah. "Totally gone. Trying not to be pathetic about it."

"You're not pathetic."

"I'm not heroic, either."

Nick pointed at her, looked her right in the eye. "Hannah doesn't need a hero. She needs a partner, someone by her side she can count on no matter what."

Drew sighed. She'd fucked that up pretty good, too. "Yeah."

"If it counts for anything, I think you're perfect for each other."

It might not count in her chances of winning Hannah back, but it sure as hell was nice to hear. "It does."

"Good luck."

"Thanks." She got up, rolled her shoulders. "I think I'm going to need it."

❖

Hannah finished arranging jugs of apple cider and stepped back to admire the neat rows. She put her hands on her hips and looked around, pleased to see so many people in the farm stand on a weekday. It felt normal, the kind of normal she'd been missing ever since Drew left and the land went up for sale and everything turned chaotic.

And then the people and the apples and everything faded into a blurry background and nothing felt normal at all. Drew stood just inside the entrance, looking right at her, like she had so many times before, like nothing had changed. Hannah's heart thudded and her knees threatened to buckle. She should have expected it, really, but she hadn't. She swallowed, willed her legs to support her. Drew closed the distance between them, a hesitant smile on her lips. Those gorgeous, full lips that Hannah immediately imagined on her neck, on her breast, on her—

"Hi." Drew was now right in front of her, so close Hannah could smell her cologne.

"What are you doing here?" She swallowed the emotion that swelled in her throat, refusing to let Drew's presence unnerve her. But even with the advance warning from Nick, it did. She clutched at indignation like a life preserver. "Why did you come back?"

"I—" Just as Drew started to speak, she stopped. As though she'd thought better of whatever she was going to say. She glanced at the ground for a moment, then looked right into Hannah's eyes. "I wanted to be here. I wanted to help."

It was horrifying enough to need help in the first place, but to have Drew here like some celebrity on a charity mission, it was almost too much. Pride made her straighten her shoulders, lift her chin. "I don't need your help."

Drew narrowed her eyes. "You agreed to let Nick host the event. If I can help him pull it off, maybe up the ticket price, why would you have a problem with that?"

"Nick is invested in the farm. He has a stake in it succeeding. Even more than that, he's like family."

Drew's jaw clenched, the muscles in her cheeks moving back and forth. "And in your mind, I'm neither of those things."

"I think you made it clear you're not." It came out as more of an accusation than a simple statement, but it was too late to take it back now.

Drew's eyes flashed with anger and something else, something Hannah couldn't put her finger on. "Only after you made it clear you couldn't get rid of me fast enough."

"That's not what happened at all."

"'Let's not pretend,' you said. I'm pretty sure that's an exact quote."

She wasn't about to take responsibility for Drew's leaving. Yes, she'd tried to make it as drama-free as possible, but surely she hadn't affected the outcome. "Your mind was made up from the day you moved here." That fact, and the knowledge she'd let herself fall for Drew in the first place, still haunted her. "Don't apologize for it. You were clear about your intentions from the beginning."

Drew's expression shifted. The anger seemed to dissolve. In its place, something that looked an awful lot like regret. "Is that what you think?"

"Am I wrong?"

Drew took a deep breath and appeared to choose her words carefully. "It was true, certainly in the beginning, but things changed. Things between us changed."

If Hannah didn't know better, she'd think Drew was saying she'd changed her mind, that maybe she wished she'd never left. The possibility sat heavy in her chest. She'd spent so much of the last few weeks trying to get over Drew. The idea of the whole situation being thrown back into disarray left her—what? That was the problem. She didn't even know. "I can't have this conversation with you right now."

A shadow passed across Drew's face, but she didn't argue. "Of course. I didn't mean to interrupt your work. I won't keep you."

A wave of guilt spread through her. "Let's talk later, maybe, when it can be just the two of us."

Drew nodded. "Sure."

"I'll have everything you requested delivered to the restaurant first thing in the morning."

"That would be great. Thanks."

Drew started to leave, making Hannah feel like even more of a heel. "I do appreciate it, you know, what you're doing. I'm sorry if I seemed ungrateful."

Drew sighed and it sounded like resignation. "I'm glad to be a part of it. I hope you believe that."

She left then, leaving Hannah standing alone in the middle of the bustling farm stand. Someone brushed past her with a pumpkin, jarring her back to the moment. A line had formed at the register, so she hustled over to help weigh produce and total purchases. Drew's words echoed in her mind—things between us changed.

Hannah tried to shake it off. She did not have time to obsess about Drew right now. She had a business to run, and to save. The next few days could very well make or break the future of Three Willows Farm. Even with all the help she was getting, she needed to be on her game if she expected it to go well.

Things didn't slow at the farm stand until sunset. Between the abundant apple crop and the unseasonably warm week, it seemed as though all of Tompkins County had made their way through the orchard. McIntosh picked out early and people were going to town on Empire and Paula Red. She couldn't press cider fast enough and the doughnut machine hardly slowed. It felt like every other person made a comment about the gala, too. That felt good, knowing that so many of the attendees were customers, people who cared about the farm.

After closing down for the night, she sat down with Clare to go over the design for the gift certificates. Clare presented her with three options to choose from—one elegant, one quirky, and one kind of classic. Hannah gravitated to the classic look, but based on the vibe of the website and social media, she had a feeling she was supposed to pick the quirky. Hannah pointed to it. "We should go with that one, right? It goes better with everything else you've designed."

Clare grinned. "Consistency of brand. Exactly."

Hannah angled her head. "So why did you even show me the others?"

She shrugged. "I wanted you to feel like you had a choice."

"And what if I'd chosen one of the others?"

Clare shrugged again, this time with a slight wince. "I would have gently nudged you to the right one."

Hannah rolled her eyes, but chuckled. "Spoken like a true marketer."

"That is the point."

She resisted Clare's poking that she come home with her for dinner. She had enough on her mind already. Drew showing up like some butch in shining armor threatened the thin thread that held her in a calm, rational state of mind. What right did she have, showing up like some kind of savior? It was humiliating, insulting. It was sweet. Of course, she couldn't admit that because it would mean letting go of just how mad she was at Drew for leaving in the first place.

She got home and showered, then ate a piece of cold lasagna standing at the sink. She half watched a movie before going to bed, lying awake and thinking about Drew. Where was she staying even? How long would she be in town? And how in the world was Hannah supposed to be gracious and appreciative when being anywhere close to Drew made her heart ache?

Chapter Thirty-Two

Drew looked around the dining room. If the restaurant glowed on opening night, tonight it sparkled. The regular tables had been moved out to make extra space. Hi-tops with stools lined the perimeter. Under Clare and Kristen's direction, Nick had managed to suspend a zigzag of twinkle lights from the ceiling. Between that and the mini red carpet photo area they'd set up, it felt more like a fancy gala than dinner at a farm-to-table bistro.

The change in setup had allowed them to sell two hundred tickets instead of eighty. Even without the auction Nick's wife had dreamed up, they'd be able to give Hannah a check for twenty thousand dollars, enough for her to at least make a down payment on the land. The party hadn't even started and already it was a success.

If only she could say the same about things with Hannah. It had been her idea to keep her involvement secret until the last minute because she'd guessed Hannah wouldn't take it well. But to have it play out just as she'd imagined left a hollow feeling in her chest. Maybe after the initial shock wore off, things would be better. Maybe when Hannah realized she was back to stay, or would be in the near future.

She shook her head. There'd be plenty of time to worry about the train wreck of her personal life. Tonight she wanted everything to be perfect. The stakes were too high for it to be anything else.

"Why do you look like you might throw up? Is it something in the kitchen or the girl?"

She hadn't heard Javier approach. Not only had he snagged her two hot chefs for the event, he'd come himself. He'd also donated a thousand dollars, an especially generous gesture since she'd given her resignation less than a month into working for him. "The girl. The kitchen couldn't be better, thanks to you."

He offered his signature shrug and a flick of the wrist. "What can I say? I'm a hopeless romantic."

"Let's just hope the girl feels the same way." Even if the gala wasn't a play to get Hannah back, she hoped it helped her cause rather than hurt it.

"I've got a good feeling." He winked at her. "And I'm usually right about this sort of thing."

Javier went off to talk with Nick about the artists whose work hung in the restaurant. He'd gotten it in his head to redecorate one of his dining rooms with a more idyllic feel. Drew turned to go back to the kitchen, then froze.

Hannah stood less than twenty feet from her, looking absolutely stunning. Her hair fell in soft waves around her shoulders and the deep green of her dress suited her coloring perfectly. She'd put on makeup—more than Drew had ever seen her wear, but still minimal by most standards. The result made her look at once glamorous and wholesome. Drew opened her mouth to say something, but no words came out.

"Hi." Hannah's smile seemed uncertain. It tore at Drew's heart.

"Hi."

Hannah laced her fingers together. "I wanted to apologize for my behavior earlier. I wasn't expecting to see you and I reacted badly."

A little of the tightness in her chest eased. "You don't need to apologize. I'm sorry I didn't tell you myself. I was afraid if you knew I was involved from the beginning, you'd nix the whole plan."

Hannah chuckled softly. "I guess you know me pretty well."

There were a thousand things she wanted to say. Several of them included throwing herself at Hannah's feet. She'd yet to settle on one when Clare and Kristen bounded through the dining room holding hands. They stopped short. "Sorry," Clare said.

"Yeah." Kristen angled her head toward the bar. "We'll be over there."

"It's okay." As much as she wanted to talk to Hannah, as much as she didn't want to let Hannah out of her sight, the doors would be opening any minute. "I should get back to the kitchen."

"Yeah. Big night." Hannah offered a slightly more confident smile. "We'll talk later?"

"That would be great."

Hannah watched Drew disappear into the kitchen. She couldn't decide if that had gone well or made things worse. She'd have to wait to find out. She had more pressing matters.

Nick and Javier appeared, along with Leda. Leda gave her arm a squeeze. "Ready?"

She took a steadying breath that did little to steady her. "As ready as I'll ever be."

Nick offered her a reassuring smile. "Let's do this."

Twenty minutes later, she was certain she'd shaken more than a hundred hands and exchanged almost as many hugs. She recognized many of the faces from the farm, which warmed her heart. A few were strangers, perhaps fans of Drew or the other chefs visiting from the city. Baker and her girlfriend came, which was very sweet. Jenn was solo but chatted up a group of people in no time.

She turned to greet the next person in the makeshift receiving line and found herself face-to-face with her father. She'd known her parents and brothers bought tickets, but seeing him—in a tie, even—was a shock to her system. She hugged him, then her mother. "Thank you for coming. It means so much to me."

He nodded briskly. "It's clear you've built something people care about. Of course I'd be here."

"Thanks, Dad."

As if sensing she was on the verge of tears, her mother gave her hand a quick squeeze. "And we're excited to try all the fancy chef food."

Her dad grunted at that. Hannah laughed. "I think you'll be pleasantly surprised."

By eight, the majority of guests had arrived. Waiters snaked through the crowd with no fewer than a dozen small bites. Several stations had been set up as well, serving everything from lamb skewers to fig and goat cheese turnovers.

Hannah sampled a few things, too wired to eat much but wanting to be able to thank and compliment the chefs. She could tell immediately which items were Drew's. They were complex without being fussy, and to her at least, the most delicious.

At eight thirty, she moved to where Nick had set up the portable microphone. Nick was already there, waiting for her with an encouraging smile. She gave him a nod and he flipped it on. "Good evening."

He thanked everyone for coming, talked about his vision for Fig and how integral Three Willows had been to making that vision a reality. He told a story about bringing his kids to the farm to pick apples, how they spent the whole afternoon having a picnic and running around and just being a family. For the second time that night, her eyes pricked with the threat of tears. When he finished, the room filled with applause. Then he handed her the mic.

She looked out at the sea of faces. Never in her life had so many eyes been trained on her. Combined with the emotions coursing through her, it was enough to make her dizzy. She scanned the crowd, looking for a friendly face where she could focus her attention. Immediately, as though Drew wore a homing beacon, Hannah's gaze connected with hers.

It should have confused her, overwhelmed her even more. But in that moment, the crowds melted away and a sense of calm settled in her. Drew smiled and Hannah knew in that instant everything would be fine. She opened her mouth, trusting the right words would come. "I wish I'd thought to prepare something, because my heart is so full and there is no way I'll be able to express just how much all of this means to me."

Drew's smile grew and she offered a nod of encouragement. Hannah took a deep breath and continued. "When I started Three Willows Farm close to seven years ago, I wanted to grow good food and give people a place where they could be a part of that. I had no idea that I'd wind up with a huge extended family, all caring about the same thing. It's been so much fun and so much hard work, all rolled into one. Tonight, seeing how deep that support goes, is more than I could have even dreamed. I'm humbled and I'm grateful. Thank you."

Maybe not the most eloquent speech, but the entire room broke into applause. As much as she'd managed to keep it together throughout the evening, her resolve evaporated and the tears came. Maybe not the gross, sniffly kind, but not a single graceful tear either. Nick stepped forward and thanked everyone again for coming. He reminded people to collect their u-pick vouchers before leaving and said he hoped to see everyone at the restaurant, and the farm, soon.

Conversations resumed and people began milling around. Hannah found herself pulled into at least a dozen more hugs. In spite of herself, she scanned the room for Drew. Hannah didn't see her, though. She'd probably gone back to the kitchen. Or maybe she'd left already to spend time with her friends visiting from the city.

By the time the restaurant had emptied, she was exhausted. She had never considered herself an introvert, but apparently she did have a limit to how much interacting she could handle in one day. But she wasn't done yet. She still needed to talk to Drew. It couldn't wait any longer.

She walked into the kitchen and found Drew talking quietly to Poppy. It was like the night of the soft launch, Drew's first night as head chef. But so very much had changed. The restaurant had established itself as a destination in the Finger Lakes. Drew had left and come back. Hannah had come close to losing the farm, only to have it saved by an overwhelming show of love and support from her community. From Drew.

Oh, and there was the matter of losing her heart. As much as the last few months had turned her life on its head, none of it held a candle to realizing she'd fallen in love with Drew. Well, falling in love with her, breaking up with her, and now. What now?

Before she could answer that question for herself, Drew turned. The smile Drew offered was again hesitant. So different from all the confidence of that first night, or all the other nights since.

As if sensing the magnitude of the moment, Poppy stepped back, then vanished. Hannah took a deep breath. "Hey."

Drew's eyes never left hers. "Hey."

"I don't know what to say." It might have been a less-than-ideal response to the night, but it was the truth.

Drew shook her head. "You don't have to say anything."

She fidgeted with the pair of bracelets on her wrist, willing herself to be brave. "I can start with thank you, at least. I'm so completely humbled by all this."

"You'd have done just as much for anyone else."

Hannah frowned. Was that true? Nick, sure. Some of the other farmers, even. But would she have done it for Drew?

"I need you to know, though, I didn't do it to get you back. I believe in what you're doing. I wanted to be part of making sure you keep doing it."

She couldn't explain why, but Drew's words did more to Hannah than thinking it was some grand romantic gesture. "I know."

"Don't get me wrong. I still want you back. I want it so badly I can taste it. But I can't have you feel like you owe me something or that I have some kind of upper hand. We can't build a foundation on that." Drew's eyes flashed with conviction.

If Hannah hadn't already been in love, she would have gone tumbling. "Taking you back has nothing to do with tonight."

"Good, because—wait. Did you say taking me back?"

"I did. Although I'm not sure I'm crazy about that phrase."

Drew raised a brow. "No?"

She didn't like being humbled, but when she was wrong, she owned it. And now was the time to own it. "I mean, the idea that you did something wrong and being together would be because I took you back."

"I left." Regret shadowed her face.

"You did." Hannah had a flashback to the emptiness of those first few days after Drew had gone. "But it was your dream. And I kind of drove you away."

Drew grinned, so much more like herself. "You did drive me away."

"In my defense, it had as much to do with your family as anything else. I couldn't bear the idea of making you choose."

"I can appreciate that now. I'm sorry I couldn't before."

Hannah shook her head. "Don't apologize. We did what we thought was best."

"How could such good intentions go so terribly wrong?"

She chuckled. "Well, the road to hell is paved with them, right?"

"So I hear." Drew looked away, then met Hannah's eyes again. "Can we go back to the part where you're taking me back? Or getting back together? Or whatever we're calling it?"

Hannah took a deep breath. She could do this. "I've missed you, Drew. I've missed you more than I thought it possible to miss a person. I'm crazy, stupid in love with you and I desperately hope you feel the same way about me."

"I'm crazy, stupid in love with you, too." Drew smiled slowly. Not an elated sort of smile, the kind that came with the giddy happiness of being all caught up in someone. It was a calmer, sturdy sort of smile that Hannah could count on, day after day, year after year. "I want to be with you more than anything."

Hannah resisted the urge to launch into Drew's arms and pretend their happily ever after was sealed. "But I don't want to be the reason you give up your dream job, your home, all that."

Drew shook her head. "I already quit."

"You did?"

"To be fair, Javier had decided I was miserable and encouraged me to. My family, too."

In all her thinking and dreaming about Drew, she'd not imagined Drew miserable. Interesting. "I'm sorry I made you miserable."

Drew shrugged. "Turns out, I'm not only in love with you."

That didn't sound right. "What?"

"I'm in love with this place and the people and the quirky little life I built over the last few months. I want you, but I want it all. I need you to understand that my being here isn't a sacrifice."

Oh. Just like with the fund-raiser, it meant so much more to hear Drew say that. It gave her this buoyant feeling—hope that things might actually work out after all. "You really mean that?"

"I do."

It was more than she'd even dared to dream. "I'm really glad."

Drew lifted a finger. "One question."

"What's that?" Drew wasn't about to propose, was she? That might be too much.

"May I please kiss you senseless now? I'm not sure I can take it much longer."

"I'll do you one better." She threaded her arms around Drew's neck and kissed her, pouring every drop of longing she'd stored up over all the hours, the days and nights that dragged into weeks, since she'd kissed her last.

She heard the door from the dining room swing open. "Oh, thank God," Nick said, and then the door swung again.

Drew smiled against her mouth, but she didn't stop kissing her. When the door swung again and was followed by giggling, Hannah pulled away. Kristen and Clare peeked around, phones in hand.

Clare said, "We're capturing this moment for posterity. You can thank us later."

Drew turned but kept one arm around Hannah. "I'll go ahead and thank you now, as long as you text me the picture."

She'd not been annoyed, but Drew's comment completely lightened the mood. "Ditto, kid. And no social media, please."

Clare shrugged. "I'll just save it for the wedding."

The girls disappeared, leaving Drew and Hannah alone in the kitchen. She turned to Drew. "Where are you staying?"

"I'm back at my old place, much to my landlord's amusement."

"Ah."

"But I'd really love to come home with you, if that's what you're asking."

Her farm was safe. Drew was back and, by all accounts, truly wanted to be. And they were together. For as low as the last few weeks had been, everything in her life had righted itself. She refused to pick which part made her happier. Fortunately, no one was asking her to. She smiled at Drew, letting the happiness permeate her like a hot bath after a long day. "Yes, please."

Chapter Thirty-three

The down payment satisfied the bank and, a week after the gala at the restaurant, Hannah put in a purchase offer on the land. The owners had received an offer on the house from an aspiring hobby farmer who only wanted ten acres to play with, so she got the fifty she already used and another twenty for little more than the original asking price. What had threatened the very existence of her farm had become an opportunity to grow it. In the span of a few weeks, she'd gone from nightmares about closing to daydreams of putting in blueberry bushes and cherry trees. It made her time on the tractor much more fun. Apricots, maybe, in addition to cherries.

Hannah looked over from her perch atop Bertie and caught Drew waving at her from behind the barn. She'd gone back to the city for a couple of weeks to help Javier transition and had only returned the night before. The memory of how they'd spent that night warmed her from the inside, despite the chill of the October morning.

She returned the greeting and steered the tractor that way. Once she was closer, she cut the engine and hopped down. Even though they'd parted ways only a couple of hours before, she didn't think twice about pulling Drew in for a slow, sensuous kiss. "I didn't expect to see you here today."

Drew was scheduled for her first day back at Fig, but now that Three Willows' offerings were mostly apples and hardy winter vegetables, there was no need for produce pickups every other day. Drew shrugged. "Uh, cider doughnuts?"

Hannah rolled her eyes, but laughed. "Of course. Silly me. Did you get some yet?"

"Clare swatted my hand and told me they weren't ready yet. I think she was mad at me for walking in on her and Kristen making out."

Hannah closed her eyes for a moment. "We discussed no making out on the clock."

"To be fair, she was making doughnuts, too. And there weren't any customers yet."

She smiled. "I'm not really mad. I love that she's young and in love and unafraid to show it."

"And I love what a good older sister you are. Makes me wish I had some siblings."

"Yeah, but you haven't met my brothers yet."

Drew cringed. "Does it bother you that I'll be working on Thanksgiving?"

"Oh, God, no. It's actually a relief."

Drew raised a brow.

She'd brought Drew home for dinner a couple of times. Despite her anxiety, Drew handled it all so well. If anything, she managed Hannah's father better than she did. "Not that I don't want you to meet my brothers. They're not all that bad. And my dad seems to love you. It's just, all together, they can be a lot."

Drew laughed. "You're adorable. Thank you for being understanding, but trust me when I say, when the time comes, I can handle it."

"Right, right. I know. Maybe Christmas."

"Maybe. And maybe you'll come to the city with me for a few days after New Year's? Nick's decided to close the restaurant for the first two weeks of January."

Hannah envisioned another trip to the city, but also day after day with Drew, hunkered in from the snow and with nowhere to be. "Absolutely. Especially if we can also have a few days of doing absolutely nothing."

Drew kissed her. "Deal."

"Did you really just come for doughnuts?"

"I was hoping to make out with you, but I just learned the boss frowns on that."

She gave Drew a look of mock exasperation. "Did I not just kiss you?"

"Well." Drew dragged out the word, like she wasn't quite ready to concede the point. "There wasn't any tongue. And I didn't touch your boobs at all."

Hannah bit her lip, but a snicker still managed to escape. "What am I going to do with you?"

"Help me pick out pumpkins for my porch?"

That sounded like way more fun than turning over what remained of the tomato field. "I suppose I could do that."

Drew took her hand and they headed over to the pumpkin patch. It was one of Hannah's favorite parts of the farm, mostly because it needed virtually no tending after being planted in the spring. Well, that and the fact that it never failed to make her feel like she'd landed in the middle of *It's the Great Pumpkin, Charlie Brown.*

"Wow." Drew looked around. Hundreds of pumpkins covered the ground. Complete with vines. She thought she'd seen enough of the farm that nothing would surprise her. She'd been wrong.

"I know, right?"

"It's almost like a cartoon."

Hannah laughed. "I was literally thinking the same thing."

"How am I supposed to pick?"

Hannah gave her hand a squeeze. "First, you decide on size, then whether you want one that's traditionally attractive or wonky."

"Wonky?"

Hannah pointed to a pumpkin that resembled a basketball. "Attractive." Then she pointed to one more elongated, almost pear-shaped. "Wonky."

Less than a year ago, Drew had never set foot on a farm. And now she couldn't imagine anywhere she'd rather be. "Why do I feel like this is a test of my character?"

Hannah didn't crack a smile. "Oh, it totally is."

She was kidding, of course, but Drew took the proposition seriously. "I'm fond of physical beauty." She trailed a hand down Hannah's back and over her rear end. "But it's all about the personality."

Hannah laughed again. "Well said."

Drew selected four pumpkins. Hannah told her she needed an odd number, that it looked better that way. "Thank God you're here. I could have made a rookie pumpkin mistake. All two of my neighbors would have been horrified."

She settled on five. The more the merrier, right? They loaded them into one of the old wagons left in the field just for pumpkin transport and Hannah walked with her to her car. Drew put them in her trunk. "So, you'll come back to my place after work, yeah?" Hannah asked.

"I'm going to come to your place every night until you tell me I can't."

"I'm going to hold you to that."

"Good." Drew took a deep breath, still a bit in awe of just how happy she was. "I love you, you know."

"I love you back." Hannah grabbed the front of Drew's jacket and pulled her close. Drew sank into the kiss and allowed herself to think about what a lifetime of kisses might look like.

"Hey, no making out on the clock."

Drew didn't have to look in the direction of the voice to know it was Clare. It was only fair, really, that she would interrupt them now. She stopped kissing Hannah but didn't let her go. "Do you have doughnuts for me? I don't want to hear a word from you if you don't have doughnuts."

Clare lifted a small paper bag and gave it a shake. "Hot and fresh, just for you."

Drew walked the short distance to where Clare stood and took the bag. "You're a goddess. Thank you. Make out on the clock as much as you want."

"You really did come for the doughnuts, didn't you?" Hannah was shaking her head.

Drew shrugged. "A multipurpose visit."

Hannah rolled her eyes but laughed at the same time. "Go to work. I'll see you tonight."

Drew gave her a quick kiss on the cheek. "Yes, dear."

Drew headed into town. She was early shift today and the first one at the restaurant. She'd negotiated with Nick to promote Poppy from sous chef to chef de cuisine. Not only did the promotion lessen the chances she'd leave any time soon, but it allowed Drew to share more of the kitchen management duties with her. The result was two full days off every week and a couple of nights that didn't require her to stay through close.

Had someone told her a year ago she'd be looking for less oversight in her kitchen, she'd have called them crazy. About as crazy as the idea she'd choose living in the country, choose a small restaurant rather than one with an international reputation. She had always hated being wrong. Like so many things in her life, that had changed. Sometimes, being wrong was exactly what was required to make everything right.

Chapter Thirty-four

Hannah sighed. Best Christmas morning ever. She burrowed deeper under the covers and closer to Drew. "Do we have to?"

Drew kissed the top of her head. "I think we do."

"Yeah." She gave Drew a squeeze. "I know, but I had to ask. I don't ever want to leave this bed."

"Man, you get lazy in the winter."

"Hey." Hannah poked Drew in the stomach. "Can I help it if you feel like perfection?"

Drew shifted, pushing Hannah onto her back and rolling on top of her. She used the advantage to tickle Hannah's ribs. "Perfection, huh?"

Hannah squealed and squirmed. She'd never considered herself an overly serious person, but Drew brought out a playfulness in her that still caught her by surprise. She pushed at Drew's hands but without much force. "Okay, okay. You win."

Drew wrapped her fingers around Hannah's wrists and pinned her hands over her head. She leaned in and kissed Hannah firmly. "Oh, I know I win. And to show what a gracious winner I am, I'll make you a huge breakfast before we have to go to your parents' house."

Hannah winced. This was the first big holiday they'd be doing the family thing. She wasn't nervous, really, but she wasn't sure she was looking forward to it. Not because of Drew. She always had mixed feelings about big family gatherings.

She looked at Drew, felt that familiar swell of love, and pretended to weigh her options. "Deal. I'll let Daisy out and put on the coffee."

Drew kissed her again before getting out of bed. Even with a plan in place, she couldn't resist the sigh of disappointment at the broken contact. She might argue the label of lazy, but one thing was for certain. She was pretty hooked on waking up with Drew. The fact of it didn't bother her nearly as much as she thought it might. Which was a good thing considering the gift she'd picked out for Drew. And the ask that went with it.

She pulled on pajamas and padded downstairs. She opened the back door for Daisy, then headed to the kitchen to start the coffee. Drew was already preheating the oven and pulling things from the fridge. Now that the farm was closed for the season, they had a lot more mornings like this. Every time, it gave Hannah such a feeling of contentment. "Do we get to open presents, too?"

"Yes. The cinnamon rolls need to bake and cool some before we can eat. Let me get them in the oven and I'm all yours."

She so loved the sound of that.

Twenty minutes later, they sat on the sofa with steaming mugs of coffee and the aroma of cinnamon wafting through the house. Daisy stretched out on the floor next to the wood stove. Drew took a long sip from her mug and looked at Hannah excitedly. "Stockings first?"

Stockings hadn't been a big deal in Hannah's family. Mostly socks and ChapStick and some candy. Drew had schooled her on this and she was proud of her first attempt at stuffing. "Sure."

Drew snagged them from their hooks and they dove in. Any illusions Hannah had about winning stockings was quickly dispelled. She'd done decently enough, but Drew had managed to stuff hers with the small, the silly, and the utterly delightful. Socks, yes, but socks with tractors on them. Her favorite fancy hand cream. Salted caramel truffles from a store they visited on their trip to New York City.

They tore into the gifts under the tree next. Drew was ecstatic for the set of pans Hannah picked out with Nick's help. Hannah adored the high-end work boots she'd been eying for close to a year. Not that she was looking for a sign, but being able to pick out just the right gifts for each other made Hannah feel like they were on to something. "Your last present from me is upstairs."

"Oh, really?" Drew's tone was beyond suggestive.

Hannah feigned exasperation. "In the guest room."

"Are we role playing? I could be into that."

"Stop it." Hannah swatted at her, but without conviction. Honestly, she was kind of nervous about how Drew might react. Too late to change her mind now. She grabbed Drew's hand. "Come on."

"Coming." They climbed the stairs and Hannah opened the guest room door. She gestured for Drew to go in first.

Drew swallowed the bubble of apprehension. She let go of

Hannah's hand and stepped into the room. In the middle, right on top of the rug next to the bed, sat a dresser. Well, technically a chest of drawers. One that looked just like the one in Hannah's room. Only this one had a big green bow on top. "I love it."

Hannah chuckled. "You look so confused right now."

"Um, not confused. I mean, I don't have much furniture up here." Drew didn't dislike it. It was just the last thing she'd expect Hannah to give her.

"So, here's the thing."

Oh, good. There was an explanation. Drew knew she was missing something.

"It's just like mine. I got it at the same place."

"It's very nice. And I'm not just saying that because half my clothes live in plastic storage totes."

"Well, I was thinking it would be nice to have a set that matches. If you decided you wanted to keep it here."

"Here?"

Hannah offered her shrug and a smile. "Leave it here and fill it with your stuff."

Realization dawned. "Hannah, are you asking me to move in with you?"

Hannah bit her lip, nodded. "I am. It's okay if you feel like it's too soon. You could use a decent piece of furniture either way. But you've been spending all your time here anyway." She shrugged again. "And I like that."

"Hannah. I..." There weren't too many things in Drew's life that had left her speechless.

"Or you can just leave it here with some stuff in it. That would be okay."

Drew shook her head. Her fumbling for words was giving Hannah the absolutely wrong impression. She closed the distance between them, wrapped her arms around Hannah's waist. "I would love to move in with you. That's the best present."

"Really?"

Seeing Hannah unsure did funny things to Drew. It made her feel protective and possessive and something else. Something she didn't have a word for. "I am so crazy in love with you. You know that, right?"

The uncertainty vanished from Hannah's eyes. "I do know it. And I feel the same way."

Drew took a deep breath. "Can I confess something?"

Hannah tipped her head to the side. "Of course."

"I've been thinking about moving in together. I just couldn't figure out how to broach it."

"Yeah?"

"Since your house is the most logical, it seemed presumptuous of me."

Hannah chuckled. "Guess it's a good thing I'm not afraid to make the first move."

Drew nodded, her heart impossibly full. "I guess it is."

"You know, we really could just skip my parents' house." Hannah gave her a playful look. "Stay in all day, argue over who gets which side of the closet."

Drew scratched her temple. "Do you anticipate arguing over the closet?"

"No."

"What if we go to your parents' house, do the family thing, then swing by my place on the way home for some of my things?"

Hannah pouted. "All right."

Drew pulled Hannah into her arms and kissed her again. "You know it's going to be okay, right? I promise I'll be on my best behavior."

"It's not your behavior I'm worried about." Hannah took a deep breath. "I know it will be fine. If anything, you make more sense to my father than I do."

Drew laughed. Hannah's father did seem to like her. It had surprised her at first. From everything Hannah had told her, she expected him to have a problem with his daughter bringing home not only a woman but a biracial one at that. Yet somehow, they'd clicked. Whether it was her job or how close she was to her family, or the fact that she'd lost her own father—she'd never know. But she wasn't about to argue with it. "He gets me is all."

Hannah's expression softened. "You get him. And you manage to walk the line between respect and deference perfectly. I never quite managed that."

"And Clare is bringing Kristen, right? We definitely have to be there in solidarity." They'd been officially dating for a couple of months, and even though both families were supportive, it was still a big and scary thing for a teenager.

"I wasn't seriously suggesting we bail." Hannah shrugged. "Mostly."

"I know. And if you really didn't want to go, we wouldn't."

"You're the best, you know that?"

"I am." Drew nodded, her tone serious. "And I'm going to drag you to visit my family for the better half of a week, so you'll have plenty of time to repay me."

Hannah grinned. "For the record, I'm really looking forward to that."

"Good. My mother and Grann are beside themselves that I'm bringing you home."

"I'm excited to see them again."

Drew was, too. Like, over-the-moon excited. It was amazing the difference a few months could make. "Good. Now, let's go gorge ourselves on cinnamon rolls before we have to get ready."

"They're out of the oven, right?"

"Yes, and ready for icing."

"So it wouldn't be a tragedy for them to sit on the counter just a bit longer."

Drew had an inkling where this conversation was going, so she played along. "They should stay warm for quite a bit, actually."

"I thought maybe we could make a detour to our room. Specifically our bed." Hannah put the emphasis on "our" in a way that made Drew's heart melt.

"Oh, there's definitely time for that."

Hannah took her hand and led her down the hall. Just as she had in the guest room, Drew paused in the doorway. There was no confusion this time. No hesitation, either. She simply wanted to take a moment to savor the reality of what she and Hannah had just agreed to.

"You're not having second thoughts, are you?"

She was being dragged to bed by the woman she loved and was going to spend the day with that woman and her family. After, they'd come home—to their home—and probably make love again. "Not a single one."

Drew stepped the rest of the way into the room. Into Hannah's arms. And into the life they were going to build together. There wasn't a place in the world she'd rather be.

About the Author

Aurora Rey is a college dean by day and an award-winning lesbian romance author the rest of the time, except when she's cooking, baking, riding the tractor, or pining for goats. She grew up in a small town in south Louisiana, daydreaming about New England. She keeps a special place in her heart for the South, especially the food and the ways women are raised to be strong, even if they're taught not to show it. After a brief dalliance with biochemistry, she completed both a B.A. and an M.A. in English.

She is the author of the Cape End Romance series and several standalone contemporary lesbian romance novels and novellas. She has been a finalist for the Lambda Literary and Golden Crown Literary Society awards, but loves reader feedback the most. She lives in Ithaca, New York, with her dogs and whatever wildlife has taken up residence in the pond.

Books Available From Bold Strokes Books

Dangerous Curves by Larkin Rose. When love waits at the finish line, dangerous curves are a risk worth taking. (978-1-63555-353-6)

Love to the Rescue by Radclyffe. Can two people who share a past really be strangers? (978-1-62639-973-0)

Love's Portrait by Anna Larner. When museum curator Molly Goode and benefactor Georgina Wright uncover a portrait's secret, public and private truths are exposed, and their deepening love hangs in the balance. (978-1-63555-057-3)

Model Behavior by MJ Williamz. Can one woman's instability shatter a new couple's dreams of happiness? (978-1-63555-379-6)

Pretending in Paradise by M. Ullrich. When travelwisdom.com assigns PR specialist Caroline Beckett and travel blogger Emma Morgan to cover a hot new couples retreat, they're forced to fake a relationship to secure a reservation. (978-1-63555-399-4)

Recipe for Love by Aurora Rey. Hannah Little doesn't have much use for fancy chefs or fancy restaurants, but when New York City chef Drew Davis comes to town, their attraction just might be a recipe for love. (978-1-63555-367-3)

The House by Eden Darry. After a vicious assault, Sadie, Fin, and their family retreat to a house they think is the perfect place to start over, until they realize not all is as it seems. (978-1-63555-395-6)

Uninvited by Jane C. Esther. When Aerin McLeary's body becomes host for an alien intent on invading Earth, she must work with researcher Olivia Ando to uncover the truth and save humankind. (978-1-63555-282-9)

Comrade Cowgirl by Yolanda Wallace. When cattle rancher Laramie Bowman accepts a lucrative job offer far from home, will her heart end up getting lost in translation? (978-1-63555-375-8)

Double Vision by Ellie Hart. When her cell phone rings, Giselle Cutler answers it—and finds herself speaking to a dead woman. (978-1-63555-385-7)

Inheritors of Chaos by Barbara Ann Wright. As factions splinter and reunite, will anyone survive the final showdown between gods and mortals on an alien world? (978-1-63555-294-2)

Love on Lavender Lane by Karis Walsh. Accompanied by the buzz of honeybees and the scent of lavender, Paige and Kassidy must find a way to compromise on their approach to business if they want to save Lavender Lane Farm—and find a way to make room for love along the way. (978-1-63555-286-7)

Spinning Tales by Brey Willows. When the fairy tale begins to unravel and villains are on the loose, will Maggie and Kody be able to spin a new tale? (978-1-63555-314-7)

The Do-Over by Georgia Beers. Bella Hunt has made a good life for herself and put the past behind her. But when the bane of her high school existence shows up for Bella's class on conflict resolution, the last thing they expect is to fall in love. (978-1-63555-393-2)

What Happens When by Samantha Boyette. For Molly Kennan, senior year is already an epic disaster, and falling for mysterious waitress Zia is about to make life a whole lot worse. (978-1-63555-408-3)

Wooing the Farmer by Jenny Frame. When fiercely independent modern socialite Penelope Huntingdon-Stewart and traditional country farmer Sam McQuade meet, trusting their hearts is harder than it looks. (978-1-63555-381-9)

Shut Up and Kiss Me by Julie Cannon. What better way to spend two weeks of hell in paradise than in the company of a hot, sexy woman? (978-1-163555-343-7)

Emily's Art and Soul by Joy Argento. When Emily meets Andi Marino she thinks she's found a new best friend, but Emily doesn't know that Andi is fast falling in love with her. Caught up in exploring her sexuality, will Emily see the only woman she needs is right in front of her? (978-1-163555-355-0)

Spencer's Cove by Missouri Vaun. When Foster Owen and Abigail Spencer meet, they uncover a story of lives adrift, loves lost, and true love found. (978-1-163555-171-6)

Unexpected Lightning by Cass Sellars. Lightning strikes once more when Sydney and Parker fight a dangerous stranger who threatens the peace they both desperately want. (978-1-163555-276-8)

Without Pretense by TJ Thomas. After living for decades hiding from the truth, can Ava learn to trust Bianca with her secrets and her heart? (978-1-163555-173-0)

Escape to Pleasure: Lesbian Travel Erotica, edited by Sandy Lowe and Victoria Villaseñor. Join these award-winning authors as they explore the sensual side of erotic lesbian travel. (978-1-163555-339-0)

Ordinary is Perfect by D. Jackson Leigh. Atlanta marketing superstar Autumn Swan's life derails when she inherits a country home, a child, and a very interesting neighbor. (978-1-163555-280-5)

Royal Court by Jenny Frame. When royal dresser Holly Weaver's passionate personality begins to melt Royal Marine Captain Quincy's icy heart, will Holly be ready for what she exposes beneath? (978-1-163555-290-4)

Strings Attached by Holly Stratimore. Rock star Nikki Razer always gets what she wants, but when she falls for Drew McNally, a music teacher who won't date celebrities, can she convince Drew she's worth the risk? (978-1-163555-347-5)

The Ashford Place by Jean Copeland. When Isabelle Ashford inherits an old house in small-town Connecticut, family secrets, a shocking discovery, and an unexpected romance complicate her plan for a fast profit and a temporary stay. (978-1-163555-316-1)

Treason by Gun Brooke. Zoem Malderyn's existence is a deadly threat to everyone on Gemocon, and Commander Neenja KahSandra must find a way to save the woman she loves from having to make the ultimate sacrifice. (978-1-163555-244-7)

A Wish Upon a Star by Jeannie Levig. Erica Cooper has learned to depend on only herself, but when her new neighbor, Leslie Raymond, befriends Erica's special needs daughter, the walls protecting Erica's heart threaten to crumble. (978-1-163555-274-4)

Answering the Call by Ali Vali. Detective Sept Savoie returns to the streets of New Orleans, as do the dead bodies from ritualistic killings, and she does everything in her power to bring their killers to justice while trying to keep her partner, Keegan Blanchard, safe. (978-1-163555-050-4)

Friends Without Benefits by Dena Blake. When Dex Putman gets the woman she thought she always wanted, she soon wonders if it's really love after all. (978-1-163555-349-9)

Invalid Evidence by Stevie Mikayne. Private Investigator Jil Kidd is called away to investigate a possible killer whale, just when her partner Jess needs her most. (978-1-163555-307-9)

Pursuit of Happiness by Carsen Taite. When attorney Stevie Palmer's client reveals a scandal that could derail Senator Meredith Mitchell's presidential bid, their chance at love may be collateral damage. (978-1-163555-044-3)

Seascape by Karis Walsh. Marine biologist Tess Hansen returns to Washington's isolated northern coast, where she struggles to adjust to small-town living while courting an endowment from Brittany James for her orca research center. (978-1-163555-079-5)

Second In Command by VK Powell. Jazz Perry's life is disrupted and her career jeopardized when she becomes personally involved with the case of an abandoned child and the child's competent but strict social worker, Emory Blake. (978-1-163555-185-3)

Taking Chances by Erin McKenzie. When Valerie Cruz and Paige Wellington clash over what's in the best interest of the children in Valerie's care, the children may be the ones who teach them it's worth taking chances for love. (978-1-163555-209-6)

BOLDSTROKESBOOKS.COM

Looking for your next great read?

Visit BOLDSTROKESBOOKS.COM
to browse our entire catalog of paperbacks, ebooks,
and audiobooks.

Want the first word on what's new?
Visit our website for event info,
author interviews, and blogs.

Subscribe to our free newsletter for sneak peeks,
new releases, plus first notice of promos
and daily bargains.

SIGN UP AT
BOLDSTROKESBOOKS.COM/signup

Bold Strokes Books
Quality and Diversity in LGBTQ Literature

Bold Strokes Books is an award-winning publisher
committed to quality and diversity in LGBTQ fiction.